Farewell to a Stranger

For a long moment, he gazed at her little face, framed in the window of the coach. "Goodby, sweet Caroline . . . and thank you," he said.

"It has been a thrilling adventure," she said softly, and the moonlight gleamed in her eyes.

She held out her hand to him. But he bent his head to her parted lips. Unable to move or protest, she could only yield to the sudden strength of his embrace . . . then the coach was off, speeding her into the night. Back to safety she would go, back to respectability, back to a world without the one man she had come to love . . .

A DUEL
OF HEARTS

Barbara Cartland

Pyramid Books • New York

A DUEL OF HEARTS

A PYRAMID BOOK

Pyramid edition published February 1970
  Sixth printing, August 1972

ISBN 0-515-02651-4

Printed in the United States of America

Pyramid Books are published by Pyramid Communications, Inc.
Its trademarks, consisting of the word "Pyramid" and the
portrayal of a pyramid, are registered in the
United States Patent Office.

Pyramid Communications, Inc.,
919 Third Avenue, New York, N.Y. 10022

1

'What is the hour?' Caroline asked, not taking her eyes from the road ahead of them.

Sir Montagu pulled his gold watch from his waistcoat pocket, but it was difficult for him to see the hands. They were moving fast and, although the moon was rising, trees cast dark shadows over the narrow roadway so that it was a few seconds before he was able to reply:

'It wants but three minutes to nine-thirty. We have done well!'

'I hope you are not over optimistic, sir,' Caroline answered, 'for methinks this by-lane of yours, although unfrequented, has taken us longer than if we had kept to the highway.'

'I swear it is shorter,' Sir Montagu replied. 'I have travelled it often enough and I suspect Lady Rohan will be bemused at having the other road to herself.'

Caroline laughed.

'If we do reach your sister's house before they arrive, I shall ache to see their faces when they perceive us a-waiting them. Do you really think, Sir Montagu, they are watching the road behind them and wondering why we are not in sight?'

'I imagine that is precisely what they are doing,' Sir Montagu smiled, 'unless they think we are ahead of them.'

'Which—pray Heaven—we are!' Caroline cried fervently. 'How much further have we to go?'

She whipped up the horses as she spoke and the light phaeton sprang forward at an even greater speed.

'Not more than four miles, I should think,' Sir Montagu replied. 'We join the main highway about a mile from here.'

'. . . In front of Lady Rohan's greys,' Caroline added, her voice gay and excited.

She saw that they were approaching a turn in the road and reined in the horses slightly. Although they had been going for over an hour and a half, the chestnuts were by no means tired and Caroline, with a little thrill of pleasure, realised that Sir Montagu had not boasted when he averred they were the finest bred pair of high-steppers in London.

The phaeton swung round the corner and the moonlight revealed two or three cottages clustered round a village green. Facing the stocks and duck-pond was a small gabled inn, its signpost swinging creakily in the wind, its windows bright with light. But Caroline noticed only that the road widened and was straight for the next quarter of a mile. She lifted her whip, but as she did so the small groom at the back of the phaeton raised his voice.

' 'Cuse, m'lady, but I suspicions there's somethink powerful wrong with th' off wheel.'

'Something wrong?' Caroline asked in consternation. 'I feel nothing.'

' 'Tis rattling like a bone-box, m'lady, and I reckons us ought to 'ave a look at 'un.'

'Lud, if it isn't enough to try the patience of a saint,' Caroline exclaimed, reining in the horses and pulling up opposite the small inn. 'Hurry, boy, hurry,' she added impatiently. 'I swear you are but imagining disaster.'

The groom scrambled down. Sir Montagu, after leaning over the side of the phaeton, also descended. He spoke to the groom in a low voice and they both peered at the wheel.

'Surely there is nothing amiss?' Caroline asked after a moment, her voice anxious.

'I am afraid the boy is right,' Sir Montagu replied. 'There is a pestilential crack in the axle. I believe it would be definitely dangerous for us to continue.'

'This is beyond everything,' Caroline cried.

'Well, maybe it isn't as bad as might be feared,' Sir Montagu said soothingly. 'Suppose, Caroline, you wait in the inn while I enquire if there is anyone in the yard who can repair the axle.'

The groom ran to the horses' heads while Caroline descended.

'Was there ever such ill-fortune?' she asked Sir Montagu angrily. 'Here we are well up to time and only a few miles to go when this occurs.'

'Mayhap it will only take a few minutes,' he suggested consolingly. 'Come inside, Caroline. It is not too ill a place. I have rested here before and a glass of wine will serve us well. My throat is dry with dust.'

'Very well, if it please you,' Caroline said. 'But instruct them to attend to the wheel with all possible haste.'

Sir Montagu turned to the groom.

'Now hurry, lad, find the ostler and bring me tidings as to what can be done.'

'Aye, sir,' the boy replied, as Sir Montagu, sweeping off his hat with a gesture, opened the door of the inn to allow Caroline to enter.

It was a small place, low-ceilinged and oak-beamed, with an atmosphere of cleanliness and cheer, and the parlour had a log fire burning brightly in the big fireplace. There was only one occupant sitting before it, his feet outstretched to the flames, a glass of wine at his elbow. He glanced up casually as the door opened. When he saw who stood in the doorway, he sat up abruptly, his eyebrows raised in astonishment.

He was a young man, Caroline noted, dressed in the height of fashion, his well padded olive-green coat trimmed with sparkling buttons. His dark hair was arranged in the latest windswept style and he would have been good-looking save that his thick eyebrows nearly met across the bridge of his nose in what appeared to be a perpetual frown, and his full mouth turned down at the corners as if he viewed life with a constant sneer.

'If you will seat yourself by the fire,' Sir Montagu was saying to Caroline as they entered the room, 'I will order a bottle of wine.' He raised his voice, 'Hi, landlord.'

The young man in the green coat sprang to his feet.

'Reversby!' he exclaimed. 'What are you doing here?'

It was obvious both by the tone of his voice and by the expression on his face that he was none too pleased to see Sir Montagu. The latter turned slowly and paused before he replied in his most suave tones:

'I collect no reason why I should answer that question? You have not bought the place, have you?'

Caroline felt uncomfortable, for it was obvious that the two men had no liking for one another, then she suddenly remembered her own position and that she did not wish to be recognised. She turned her head away, hoping that the size of her fashionable bonnet would cast a shadow over her face, and she was thankful to hear a woman's voice ask:

'Would her ladyship like to step upstairs?'

'Indeed I would,' Caroline answered, and she moved quickly from the parlour into the outer hall where a pleasant-faced, middle-aged woman curtsied to her and, lifting high the candle she held in her hand, led the way upstairs.

'This way, your ladyship. Mind the top step if you please. 'Tis not the same height as the others and is often a trap for the unwary.'

They reached the landing in safety and the woman opened a door.

'I hope your ladyship will find this room comfortable. It is our best and seldom in use; but when we received Sir Montagu's message this morning, we set to and gave it a right good clean. The bed has been aired too, your ladyship, and hot bricks have been in it the whole day. You will find it comfortable enough, I swear to that, for only last Michaelmas I filled it afresh with the finest goose feathers.'

The landlady pulled back the covers ready to display to Caroline the comforts of the big feather bed which bulged high under the oak four-poster, but Caroline was standing very still, her eyes wide and dark.

'Did I hear you say you had a message from Sir Montagu this morning?' she asked.

'Indeed I did, m'lady. A groom arrived just before noon. He told us that Sir Montagu would be staying the night here, and very honoured we were to hear of it, for Sir Montagu is an old and valued customer, to be sure. And when the groom added that Sir Montagu would be accompanied by his lady, we were fair excited, for though Sir Montagu has been coming here at various times these past two years and more, 'twas the first we had heard that he was wed. Oh, he's a fine gentleman, m'lady, and though maybe 'tis a little late, may I offer your ladyship our most humble felicitations.'

'Thank you . . . thank you,' Caroline said slowly, and in such a strange tone that the landlady glanced at her sharply.

'But 'tis tired you are, m'lady, and here I am chattering away when I should be getting your supper ready. It's hoping I am that it will gain your ladyship's approval, though maybe 'tis not so fine as what you are used to, but there, we can but do our best, and if your ladyship will ring when you're ready, I will come back and escort you downstairs.'

'Thank you,' Caroline said again.

The door shut behind the landlady and Caroline was alone. She stood very still for several seconds and then gave a sudden shiver before she raised both her hands to her cheeks.

Now she was in a mess, in a tangle such as she had never dreamed or imagined. As the full significance of the landlady's words crept over her, she felt herself shiver again. So Sir Montagu had meant to stay here, had arranged it all, and the trouble over the wheel was but a bit of play-acting between him and his groom. Fool that she had been to be tricked so easily. And yet had she not been more of a fool to be inveigled in the first place into taking part in this wild race, if indeed it had been a race?

Bewildered and frightened, Caroline began to think back over all that had happened in the past twenty-four hours and to blame not only Sir Montagu but herself too. Yes, she was at fault from the very beginning.

She had known Sir Montagu Reversby was an outsider. She had been warned about him often enough, and yet it was those very warnings which had obstinately made her accept his company. How crazy she had been! How wilful, how perverse! And it had brought her to this.

The Countess of Bullingham, Caroline's godmother, was presenting her this season because her mother was not well enough to leave the country and endure the exhausting formalities of launching a *débutante*. There was not, however, room in Lady Bullingham's town residence for Caroline to stay with all her retinue of attendants, so her father's magnificent mansion—Vulcan House, in Grosvenor Square —had been opened, and Caroline resided there with a cousin, the Honourable Mrs. Edgmont, as chaperon.

But this did not prevent Lady Bullingham from keeping a strict surveillance over her charge, and little escaped her ladyship's eagle eye.

'I detest that man Reversby, Caroline,' she had said as they drove home from a ball at Devonshire House. 'I should give him the cold shoulder if I were you.'

Caroline laughed.

'He is very persistent, Ma'am. He offered for me for the third time this evening.'

'Offered for you?' Lady Bullingham's voice was shrill. 'How dare he? What impertinence! As if you—the toast of the season and the greatest heiress of the year—would look at him.'

'His very impertinence amuses me,' Caroline answered. 'He is not easily cast away.'

'He will never enter the portals of my house,' her

9

ladyship replied. 'Offered for you indeed! I cannot imagine what your father would say.'

Caroline laughed. She could well imagine the chilly indifference with which her father would sweep Sir Montagu from his path, but at the same time it was an undeniable fact that she met him everywhere. He seemed in some way or another to obtain the entrée to most houses, and the way he asserted impertinently that he intended to marry her made her laugh even while she did not take him seriously.

She might have heeded her godmother's warning more readily had not Lady Bullingham with a singular lack of tact incited Lord Glosford also to warn Caroline against Sir Montagu. Caroline considered the Earl of Glosford a bore. She was well aware that her godmother wished her to marry him for, as the future Duke of Melchester, he was a notable catch from the matrimonial point of view.

Caroline, however, cordially disliked Lord Glosford's ladi-da and effeminate ways, and as she had no more intention of taking his offer seriously than she had Sir Montagu's, it was irritating to be lectured by him.

'The fellow's a trifle smoky, you know,' he said languidly, 'in fact, he's not up to scratch, Caroline. I should give him the go-by.'

'Thank you, my lord,' Caroline remarked, 'but I consider myself a better judge of human nature than your lordship is of horseflesh.'

This was a palpable thrust because Society had been chuckling for weeks over the tale of how Lord Glosford had paid five hundred guineas for a horse which had been found after a few days to have been doped for the sale.

It was perhaps Lord Glosford's ill-advised words and her godmother's continual nagging which had made Caroline accept so readily Sir Montagu's suggestion of a secret race. He had spoken about it to her at a ball and then made an assignation for them to meet the following day in the park.

Mrs. Edgmont could do nothing when, during a stroll in Rotten Row, Sir Montagu walked beside Caroline and spoke in such a low voice that she was unable to overhear the conversation.

'Rohan has vowed that his wife is the best whip in the country, and that he will match his greys against my chestnuts driven by any female I like to suggest,' Sir Montagu said. 'The race is to my sister's house near Sevenoaks, and the wager is one thousand guineas.'

'And you propose that I drive your chestnuts?' Caroline asked.

Her eyes were sparkling. She knew Sir Montagu's chestnuts. They were incomparable, and it was difficult, too, not to wish to beat Lady Rohan, who was often insufferable when she boasted of her feats with the ribbons.

'I know of no one else who could defeat her ladyship,' Sir Montagu said softly.

Caroline hesitated. She knew she ought to refuse, she knew that a race on which large sums were wagered was not the sort of sport in which any well-bred girl should indulge, let alone Lady Caroline Faye, only daughter of the Marquis and Marchioness of Vulcan . . . and yet the temptation was so great.

'I suggest,' Sir Montagu went on in his soft silky voice, 'that no one shall know whom I nominate as my whip until the race is run. One phaeton shall start at Hyde Park Corner and the other from White's Club. There will be starters at both places and only when the race is won shall we reveal the identity of the winner.'

'But how shall we keep it a secret?' Caroline asked. 'Mrs. Edgmont will question me if I wish to leave the house after we have dined.'

'You can leave a note saying that you have made arrangements to meet some friends and will be in the company of Lady Rohan. You will be home earlier than if you had been to a ball, and if your chaperon learns the truth she will be too proud of you to chatter overmuch.'

Mrs. Edgmont would be too horrified not to wish to keep it quiet, Caroline thought, but she felt the excitement was worth any risk—even her godmother's anger. It would be a thrill such as she had never known before to race against the tried and famous Lady Rohan, who was spoken of always as a nonpareil with a whip.

There might be trouble later, but Caroline had never lacked courage. She raised her firm little chin.

'I will do it,' she told the gratified Sir Montagu, 'but it must be a dead secret until the race is over.'

'I swear it,' he replied.

She could be sure now that he had kept his word. Of course there had been no race, no bet, no competing phaeton driven by Lady Rohan. It had just been a trick to get her into his power and, for all she knew, he might not even have a sister living near Sevenoaks. All she could be certain of was that it seemed inevitable that she must stay

11

here tonight as Sir Montagu's wife, and the price of his silence would be the announcement of their engagement.

Caroline shivered again as she thought of it. There was something oily and unpleasant about Sir Montagu. She had always known him for a commoner, even though it had amused her to flaunt him in the face of her other admirers who were all much younger, and who often found it difficult to compete with his wit and insolent effrontery.

Caroline looked around the bedroom, at the big four-poster bed, at the fire burning in the small fireplace, at the vase of flowers standing on the dressing-table with its frilled muslin petticoat.

Sir Montagu had chosen a pretty setting for his treachery. The mere thought of his thick, smiling lips, his dark eyes and his rather large hands filled her with a terrified repulsion. She had got to escape, she had got to get away from here. But how? How?

If she made a scene, if she called for the landlady and insisted on being sent back to London in a post-chaise, it would still cause a scandal. Besides, there was always the chance that they would not heed her, they might even think that it was just the shyness and the fright of a bride. It would be easy for Sir Montagu to over-rule her protests, to constitute himself her jailer as well as the legal lord and master they believed him to be.

Caroline looked wildly round her once again and then she crossed to the window. She threw wide the diamond-paned casement. The moon was giving more light than when she had entered the inn. It flooded the small garden which lay behind the house and beyond it she saw the darkness of trees. A wood! Caroline stared towards it and then looked down. Below the window was a drop of perhaps five or six feet on to a flat piece of roof which might cover a small larder or scullery. At the side of this, dimly outlined in the shadows, Caroline could see a water butt.

She stood staring down at it and made up her mind. She crossed the bedroom to the door and bolted it; then, hurrying to the casement, she swung herself on to the window-sill. Her dress of French velvet, with its rucked hem and full sleeves gathered and slashed with satin, was somewhat difficult to manipulate, but Caroline was used to climbing.

Indeed this was by no means the first occasion on which she had climbed out a bedroom window. Time and time again as a child she had been punished by her governesses and by her parents for climbing out of her bedroom at home, and playing truant in the park or going down to the beach when she should have been asleep.

Very carefully Caroline lowered herself out of the window until there was only a drop of a foot or so, then she finally let go of the sill. She landed with a thump on the flat roof and held her breath for a moment afraid that someone below might have heard her. But nothing happened. Everything was quiet save for a very distant burr of voices and laughter which might be coming from the tap-room.

Caroline peered down. It still seemed a long way to the ground, but there was the water butt and she realised that she must set her foot on the edge of it, holding on to the wall meanwhile. The only real danger was that she might fall into the butt itself; but Caroline was sure-footed besides being able to balance herself cleverly, and with the exception of a scratched finger, a large tear in her skirt where it caught on a nail, and a great deal of dust and dirt on her hands she reached the ground without mishap.

She paused for a moment, then peeped in at the window nearest to her. As she had guessed, the flat roof was over a scullery. It was in darkness, but the door was open and beyond it she could see the big kitchen of the inn. The landlady was bustling around and there were several other people there as well. There were two young women with round, red cheeks under their mop caps and a man with a bald head and wearing an apron, who looked as if he might be a potman. They were laughing and talking together and even though the window was closed, there was a savoury odour of roast meat.

Caroline did not wait to see more. She picked up her skirts and ran swiftly across the garden into the darkness of the trees on the other side. The wood was not thick and, as it was still early in the year, the undergrowth was not high. There was a small path running between the trees and Caroline followed this. She had no idea where it might lead her, but her one idea was to escape as far as possible from the inn. She hurried on, deciding as she went that the main road to Sevenoaks must lie in this direction and that, if she could reach it, she would doubtless find a coaching house where she might procure a post-chaise which would carry her back to London. Once or twice she stumbled over briars which lay across her path; they caught, too, in her skirt and Caroline had several times to stop and disentangle them from the velvet, which was not improved by this rough contact with nature.

She had walked for some minutes when she heard voices. She stopped quickly. 'Were they already in pursuit of her,' she wondered. She had imagined it would be some little time before they ascertained that she was not in her room; and as the bolt that she had placed across the door was a heavy one, it would require quite considerable strength to break it down.

Then she realised that the voices she heard were ahead of her and not behind as might be expected if someone was coming from the direction of the inn. She listened. Suddenly a cry of pain, of horror or indeed of agony, rang through the wood. It was just one cry, and then there was silence.

Caroline's heart seemed to stop for a full second, and then beat again so fiercely that it almost leapt from her body. She pressed herself close against a tree truck, holding on to it tightly with both her hands. The cry seemed to echo in her ears, but it was not repeated; instead she heard the sound of someone crashing through the undergrowth, moving swiftly almost as if running.

For one terrified moment she thought the person was heading in her direction. She pressed herself even closer to the tree, hoping wildly that she would not be seen. But the footsteps turned before they reached her. She heard them passing, she even saw someone moving through the shadows. She believed it to be a man, but the moonlight was deceptive and she was too frightened really to be certain of anything save that the footsteps were receding further and further away.

She listened to them, hardly daring to breathe, until she could hear them no more, and then there was silence—that strange, pregnant silence which follows a sudden noise. The wood seemed unnaturally quiet. Before there had been rustlings, the movement of small animals in the undergrowth, the flutter of a disturbed bird; now there was only silence, a silence which in itself was a fiercesome thing.

At last Caroline drew a deep breath. She moved from against the tree, aware for the first time how tightly she had clung to it. There were marks on her hands where she had pressed them against the bark. She brushed them against each other and brushed away some leaves and dust from the front of her dress. Then she went on.

The little path she had followed still wandered ahead of her and eventually came to a clearing. The moonlight was bright, the trees were cut back to form a circle and on the far side of it Caroline could see the walls of a cottage. Studying it carefully, she perceived that the cottage was nothing more than a shell. Its thatched roof had fallen in, the doorway was dark and empty, and the bricks were crumbling away.

There was nothing to be frightened of, Caroline told herself severely; but she was well aware that her breath was coming quickly and that her heart had never ceased pounding against her breast since that strange cry had echoed through the wood. Going forward a few more paces she stopped, and an exclamation of horror burst from her parted lips. There on the ground in the centre of the clearing was the body of a man.

He was lying crumpled up on the ground, one leg pinned under him, his arms outstretched, his hands wide open as if in utter defencelessness, and his head thrown back so that from where Caroline stood she could only see the sharp line of his jaw. Horror-stricken she stood there, seeing as if in a nightmare the moonlight shining on the buckles of his shoes, on the buttons of his black coat, and on a burnished knife-hilt where it stood out from the front of his neck. Below it a dark stream stained the purity of his frilled shirt.

For a moment Caroline's wits seemed to leave her, and she could only stand and stare, not asking herself whether she should go forward or go back, but paralysed with the horror of those white, empty hands motionless on the rough grass. And then, as she looked and kept on looking, she heard someone coming.

The movement had come from the other side of the wood—firmly, purposefully, someone was approaching. There was a crackling of dry sticks, the rustle as if a man thrust his way impatiently through the branches of the trees.

At last, just as the footsteps seemed to reach the clearing itself, Caroline moved. She was for turning and running away, following the path down which she had come even though it led her back to the inn; but her knees felt too weak to carry her, and a sudden overwhelming faintness made her go no further than the trunk of a great oak tree against which she leant.

'I must get away,' she told herself, and yet she could not move.

It was a frailty for which she despised herself but in all her sheltered life she had never seen a dead man before, and his death cry was still echoing in her ears.

She leant against the oak and saw a man step into the clearing. He was tall and wearing a high beaver hat, his blue coat and buckskin breeches were exquisitely cut, and even in that bemused moment Caroline guessed that he was a gentleman of importance by the way he held his head and the commanding way with which he pushed his way through the bushes and into the clearing.

He walked on and saw the man lying on the ground.

'By God! What is this?'

He spoke aloud and his voice seemed to echo sharply amongst the trees.

It was that sound, the sound of a human voice which made Caroline take hold of her failing consciousness.

'I must away,' she whispered through dry lips, and turned once again towards the path down which she had come.

The gentleman in the clearing must have seen her movement, for even as she took two steps from the shelter of the oak he looked towards her and whipped a pistol from his pocket.

'Stop!' he called. 'Who are you? Come here this instant!'

Caroline stopped. There was something in the stranger's voice which demanded obedience. Very slowly she came forward into the moonlight.

'A woman!' the gentleman exclaimed and put the pistol back in his pocket.

He swept off his hat.

'Your pardon, Madam. I was not expecting to find a lady lurking here and in such circumstances.'

His voice was steady and quite unperturbed and Caroline found it stiffened her pride, so although she was still frightened and her hands were trembling, she was able to drop him a curtsey.

The moonlight was full on his face. She found herself looking at the most handsome man she had ever seen in her life. The moonlight turned his hair to bronze, but his eyes, set wide apart beneath a broad forehead, were grey as steel and seemed strangely penetrating.

'Might I ask what you are doing here, Ma'am?' he en-

16

quired, as Caroline did not speak, 'and also if you have any knowledge of . . . this?'

He indicated with his hat the body on the ground. His voice was quiet and yet so authoritative that Caroline felt compelled to offer him some explanation of her presence.

'I was . . . walking through the wood, sir, when I heard voices . . . then suddenly there came a cry . . . a cry of terror or of pain . . . afterwards I heard someone moving quickly in that direction.'

She made a little gesture with her hand, and was conscious as she did so of the dirt on it.

The gentleman replaced his hat on his head and kneeling down, felt for the fallen man's heart.

'Is he . . . quite dead?' Caroline asked, and try as she would she could not prevent a tremble in her voice.

'Without any doubt! Whoever struck the blow struck to kill.'

He got up and stood looking down at the man's face.

'Strange,' he said, as if speaking to himself. 'Strange, very strange indeed, for I was to meet him here.'

'You know . . . the man, sir?'

'Yes, I know him. He is a lawyer called Isaac Rosenberg. A rascal it is true, but I would not have even rascals meet their death in such an unpleasant fashion.'

'And you came here to meet him, sir?' Caroline asked.

She did not know why she was so curious, but something made her want to know more about this stranger.

'Yes, at his invitation,' he said quietly, 'and that reminds me . . .'

He looked down at the dead man, dropped once again on one knee and put his hand into the lawyer's pocket.

'Ah, they are here!' he exclaimed, and there was satisfaction in his tone.

He drew out a packet of letters. Caroline could see there were perhaps half a dozen of them tied together with tape and sealed with a red seal. The gentleman slipped them into his own pocket, then he hesitated a moment and murmured as if under his breath:

'I wonder if they are all here?'

He felt in the dead man's other coat pocket which was empty, and then inserted his hand in the inside breast pocket. There was something there—a sheet of writing paper. He glanced at it and stood upright suddenly tense.

Caroline, looking up at him, thought once again that he

was, without exception, the most handsome man she had ever seen in her life; and yet there was something strange in his face. It was an expression she could not fathom for the moment; and then, as she watched, he crumpled the piece of writing paper in his hand and threw back his head with a sudden sharp laugh which had no humour in it.

'The devil take it, but someone has paid a wonderful attention to detail.'

'What is it, sir?' Caroline asked.

He looked at her as if he had almost forgotten her presence.

'It is a jest, Madam,' he replied, and his voice was sarcastic. 'A monstrous jest, I grant you, but one which will doubtless give pleasure, though not to me personally.'

'I do not understand,' Caroline said.

'Why should you?' he asked. 'But I will explain. This poor rogue here has been murdered for the express purpose of putting a rope round my neck. He was invited here to meet me. I was lured to this very spot. Here he is dead at my feet, and here am I all ready for justice to overtake me!'

'But sir,' Caroline exclaimed. 'You did not kill him, I can swear to that.'

'Why, so you can! That indeed makes the joke even more enjoyable. Who knows you are in these woods?'

'No one, sir! No one at all. I did not intend to be in them myself until but a short while back.'

The gentleman threw back his head and laughed again.

'The jest grows vastly more amusing,' he said, 'and what is more, the plot becomes further entangled. How angry the perpetrator of this elegant murder will be when he finds that you can swear to my innocence!'

'Oh, but, sir,' Caroline cried, suddenly alarmed, 'I don't wish to swear. . . . I mean, if it is a question of saving you from the gallows, but . . . but, sir, it was my intention that no one should know that I had been here . . . it will be terrible for me, I assure you, should it be revealed, especially in a Court of Justice, that I was here at this hour of night.'

The gentleman smiled.

'In which case, Madam, may I beg of you to disappear as quickly as possible, for if I am not mistaken very shortly someone will come and discover the corpse and, if they are fortunate, the murderer lurking by it. So run away, Madam, as fast as your little feet can carry you, otherwise you will be embroiled in this most unpleasant and very unsavoury crime.'

'But sir, I cannot do that,' Caroline exclaimed. 'Of course I cannot leave you when I know you to be innocent, but . . .'

'There is no but, Madam, you must go.'

'And you?'

'I shall await justice.'

'But why?' Caroline asked. 'Why must you be so stupid? If you are not here, they cannot prove that you murdered the man. It has to be proved, you know.'

The gentleman shrugged his shoulders.

'I do not cling to life so earnestly as all that, Madam; in fact, to put it briefly, life is of no particular interest to me at the moment. I would as soon die this way as any other.'

'Then you are either demented or foxed,' Caroline cried angrily. 'There are plenty of decent ways of dying, sir, but to die through treachery, to give in meekly to what you have declared yourself to be nothing but a plot must be surely the action of a coward or a craven. Come away, sir, while there is yet time, and if they have to find the murderer, let them hunt for him.'

Caroline spoke passionately. The man listened to her with a smile on his lips. Then he shrugged his broad shoulders.

'Madam, you have convinced me. I will do your bidding. May I at least escort you out of the wood, if it is your desire to leave it?'

He would have offered Caroline his arm, but at that moment she put up her hand warningly.

'Listen!'

They both stood very still. From the far side of the wood in the distance, in the direction in which Caroline had come, there were voices and the sound of people moving through the trees.

Caroline gave a little gasp.

'Quickly,' she whispered. 'They may be searching for you or . . . for me.'

The gentleman turned swiftly.

'This way then,' he said. 'My horse is not far away.'

He led the way across the clearing and entered the wood. Caroline followed him. It was not easy going, for the trees were thicker here and more than once the branches swung back to smack her across the face, while her skirt and the laces at her neck got caught in the brambles; but impatiently she dragged herself free, following the stranger as he forged ahead of her, conscious all the time of the raised voices and noisy movements behind them.

At last, after what seemed to Caroline an eternity of discomfort, the trees cleared and she saw standing tethered to one of them a horse.

'Here we are,' the gentleman said. 'Can you ride pillion?'

'Yes,' Caroline replied briefly.

He lifted her in his arms, swung her up on the horse's back, and sprang into the saddle. She put her arms round his waist. There was a sudden babble of noise, the sound of voices raised high.

'Do you hear that? They have found the body,' the gentleman said. He spurred his horse and they started off at a quick canter across the open field which lay beyond the wood.

2

They had travelled some distance and the wood was almost
out of sight before Caroline, breathless from the speed at
which they were moving and the difficulty of keeping her
balance, gasped out:

'Where are we going, sir?'

Her companion reined in his horse until it settled down
to a walk and replied:

'I live near here—at Brecon Castle, and, by the way, my
name is Brecon.'

'I seem to have heard of the Castle,' Caroline said reflec-
tively.

'Oh, I dare say you have. It is a curst beauty spot and
the people come in crowds to gape at its Norman towers.
Perhaps you have viewed it from the roadway.'

Caroline stiffened, and was just about to reply haughtily
that she was not in the habit of viewing castles from the
roadway or as one of a crowd when she remembered her
torn dress and dirty hands and realised that the stranger
had no idea of her station in life. With an effort she kept
back the words which trembled on her lips and said
meekly:

'I am sure I would recall your fine Castle, had I seen it.
Am I to understand that you, Sir, are Lord Brecon?'

'You are,' was the answer. 'And now I will give myself
the pleasure of showing you my Castle.'

'You intend to ride back to your own home, my lord?'
Caroline questioned.

'Yes! Why not?'

'But surely that would be a very unwise thing to do?
You told me but a few minutes back that the poor man in
the wood was murdered by someone who wished to fasten
the crime on you. If they suspect you, will they not repair
at once to Brecon Castle in search of your lordship and en-

quire where you have been this evening, especially during the hour in which the man recieved the blow which killed him?'

'By Jove!' Lord Brecon exclaimed, 'you are either as quick as any lawyer, Madam, or else an ardent reader of novels from the Circulating Library.'

Caroline laughed. It was only too true that her parents had reproached her not once but a dozen times because she enjoyed the more lurid type of romance.

'Nevertheless,' his lordship continued, 'there is something in what you say. What, then, do you suggest that we do?'

'Have you no trusty friends?' Caroline asked. 'I remember once that a farmer of good standing was brought for questioning to the magistrates because he was suspected of being involved with a smugglers' gang. A great many people thought him guilty, but he had three friends who swore he had spent the night in question playing cards with them. My father said later, "It is difficult enough to detect one man in a lie, but four avowing the same falsehood would be too much even for a judge and jury".'

'Your father spoke truly,' Lord Brecon said, and he turned the horse's head in another direction. 'I will be as wise as he and seek if not three loyal friends at least two.'

Again Caroline realised that he had misunderstood her, and it was with difficulty that she prevented herself from saying that her father was on the Bench when the farmer was questioned and not in the dock.

But perhaps such misunderstanding was all for the best, she told herself, for now that she knew the identity of Lord Brecon it was of the utmost importance that he should not know hers.

'I have remembered two friends who will be of service to me, but we have two miles to go in order to find them,' Lord Brecon said. 'Can you bear to continue our journey as we are or is the discomfort too great?'

'I shall be all right, thank you, my lord,' Caroline answered.

'Zounds, but my manners are most remiss, Madam,' Lord Brecon ejaculated suddenly, 'for I have not enquired as to your wishes. You must forgive me, but the events of the last half-hour have left me somewhat bemused.'

'I understand, my lord.'

'We ride now towards Sevenoaks. Is that direction to your liking?'

'I am pleased to say that it will suit me well,' Caroline said with dignity, thinking that when she got to Sevenoaks she would hire a post-chaise to take her back to London.

'Would it be an indiscreet question,' Lord Brecon asked, 'now that we are so well acquainted, to enquire your name?'

'Caroline . . .' Caroline began, and then stopped quickly.

Her thoughts had been engaged with the idea of returning to London and absentmindedly she had almost answered his question truthfully.

'Yes,' he prompted.

'. . . er . . . Fry,' Caroline finished, adding the first name which came to her mind.

'Your servant, Miss Fry, and now perhaps you will relieve my curiosity and tell me why you were walking through the woods at the very moment when Isaac Rosenberg was struck down by some treacherous hand.'

Caroline thought quickly. She had been concentrating so much on Lord Brecon's troubles that she had not had time to prepare a story for herself, but luckily once more the novels from the Circulating Library stood her in good stead, and slowly she began to propound a story which she hoped sounded plausible:

'I have had the most dastardly ill luck, my lord. I have been acting as companion to a lady of quality. I have not been in her service long, in fact only a few weeks, but long enough to be horrified and even disgusted by the lady's character and behaviour. She was extremely eccentric and much of this was due to her partiality for the brandy bottle. However, this evening instead of her feeling sleepy, as so often happens after she had dined, she insisted that we take a drive. She thought the night air would clear her head, so her coach was fetched and we drove for some miles during which she spent the entire time berating me for faults I have never had and for mistakes I have never made.

'I was patient with her, for indeed it was my duty to be humble; but after a time she grew bored even with the sound of her own voice, and asked me to pass her a hand-mirror, which I carried for her in my reticule. I passed it to her as she requested, but unfortunately the coach lurched just as the mirror was exchanged between us—and maybe, too, her hand was unsteady from the amount of brandy she had drunk—anyway, the mirror fell to the ground and was smashed.

23

'In a fury of anger she accused me of bringing her bad luck and vowed that from that very moment she could not bear to look upon my face again. She called the coach to a halt and set me down on the road. I pleaded with her, asking that at least she should take me back to her house where I might collect my clothes and leave on the morrow, but she would not listen. Flinging the wages she owed me in the dust at my feet, she commanded the coachman to drive on.'

'Monstrous!' Lord Brecon exclaimed. 'Entirely monstrous! Such women should not be allowed to exist.'

'I found myself on a narrow, unfrequented road,' Caroline went on, 'but had the idea that, if I went through the wood and struck across the field, I should reach the main highway to Sevenoaks.'

'So you would,' Lord Brecon answered, 'but it is a mile or so and you would have found it tiring walking.'

'And that, my lord, is how I came to be in the wood,' Caroline finished, delighted with her tale which she felt confident his lordship believed without question.

'So now, if I convey you to Sevenoaks, you think you can find a post-chaise or a stage-coach to carry you back to London?' Lord Brecon asked.

'That was my idea,' Caroline replied.

'Your home then is in London?'

His words awakened a sudden nausea in Caroline for her home. In that moment she had an overwhelming desire to be at Mandrake, to see her father and mother, to know herself safe and secure and under their protection again.

She wondered what stories Sir Montagu might tell when he returned to town. She foresaw explanations and excuses which would have to be made both to her godmother and to her chaperon, Mrs. Edgmont. It was all rather frightening; and swiftly Caroline, impetuous as ever, made up her mind. She would not go back to London; she would not risk encountering Sir Montagu, at least until she had had time to consider how to treat him. She would go to Mandrake; and what was more, she would tell her mother the truth of what had happened and beg her forgiveness. It was typical of Caroline that, when she had done wrong, she invariably owned up; and now it was with a deep sigh of relief that she visualised the end of her journey and her mother's unfailing understanding and sympathy.

'No, my lord,' she said aloud, 'my home is near Dover

24

and it is there I would fain go until I find another position.'

'Then we must contrive to get you to Dover,' Lord Brecon replied, 'and it seems to me that the sooner, the better. Are you game to go a little faster, for if we amble on at this rate, it will take us half the night to reach my friends?'

'Go as fast as you like, my lord,' Caroline said and tightened her hold around his waist.

Lord Brecon spurred the horse into a gallop, after which Caroline had thoughts for nothing but keeping her seat and holding her head low to prevent her bonnet from blowing away. It seemed to her that they travelled for quite a long time before Lord Brecon reined in his horse and exclaimed in tones of considerable satisfaction:

'There! This is where I thought they would be!'

Caroline looked up and saw in the field ahead of them flickering lights and the outline of low, curved roofs and tiny, thin chimneys which she could not for the moment recollect as belonging to any type of house she had ever seen before. Then, as she stared, understanding came to her. The field was filled with round-topped caravans and set amongst them a number of large wagons.

'Gipsies!' she exclaimed in surprise.

'No, not gipsies,' Lord Brecon contradicted her; 'a menagerie, and the owner of it is the loyal friend you would have me seek.'

'A menagerie!' Caroline exclaimed. 'How exciting! I have seen one at St. Bartholomew's Fair.'

'And that is where I imagine Grimbaldi will eventually end his tour,' his lordship replied.

By this time they had reached a gate into the field; but when they would have passed through it, a boy came out of the shadows and barred their way. Dark-skinned, with long lank hair hanging around his face, he looked suspiciously like a gipsy, and behind him appeared a woman with an equally dark countenance who held one child in her arms and had another holding on to her skirts.

'Hi ye,' the boy shouted, 'th' show's over for tonight. Ye can't come in here at this hour.'

'Our business is with Mr. Grimbaldi, boy,' Lord Brecon answered. 'Lead me to his caravan.'

'With the boss?' the boy questioned doubtfully, a trifle awed by the rider's air of authority. 'Ye are sure on it? He didn't say he were expecting visitors.'

'These are th' quality, son,' the woman said in a low voice, 'do as the gentleman bids.'

Lord Brecon threw a silver piece in the air. The boy caught it deftly.

'This way, sir,' he said, with a change of tone, and ran in front of the horse until he came to a big caravan set a little apart from the others, and painted crimson with silver carvings.

There was light from the uncurtained windows and a light, too, streaming from the open door above a flight of steps.

'Hi, boss,' the boy called. 'Here's a swell cove as says he 'as business with ye.'

Caroline, looking over the field, saw that there were over a dozen lighted caravans; the large wagons she had perceived were arranged in a circle and in front of many of them candles still flickered gutteringly. Childishly she wished she could have seen the animals, but most of the wagons were by now closed or covered for the night, and in the far corner of the field a fire had been lit round which there were grouped a number of people obviously the attendants or keepers.

As she stared around her, a man came out on to the top steps of the caravan. He was a big man, with broad shoulders and great muscled arms bulging under his crimson coat, and so tall that he had to bow his head to pass through the low doorway. He straightened himself and saw Lord Brecon.

'My lord!' he cried. 'This is indeed a welcome surprise.'

'May I come in, Adam?' Lord Brecon asked, dismounting and adding, 'I have brought a friend with me.'

The boy ran to hold the horse. Lord Brecon dismounted then held out his arms to Caroline. She bent forward, felt his hands grasp her waist, was conscious as he lifted her of his strength, the nearness of his face to hers, and that her heart quickened suddenly. Then her feet were on the ground and Lord Brecon slipped a hand under her elbow.

'Let me help you,' he said.

He guided her over the uneven ground to the steps of the caravan and she climbed them with the helping hand of the man at the top.

'May I bid you welcome, Madam, as a friend of his lordship's?' the man said.

'Thank you,' Caroline smiled.

26

'This is my old friend, Adam Grimbaldi, Miss Fry,' Lord Brecon said. 'His name is foreign, but his blood is English.'

'That's true enough, as your lordship knows, and my heart is English too. Oh, but 'tis good to be back in one's own country.'

'I thought you would think that despite the triumphs you enjoyed in France,' Lord Brecon said.

'Won't you be pleased to enter, Madam?' Mr. Grimbaldi said to Caroline, indicating the door into the caravan.

'Thank you,' Caroline said again, and bending her head so that the feathers on her bonnet should not be caught on the carved lintel, she moved inside.

When she raised her head again, she almost gasped with astonishment. There was a woman in the caravan, and a stranger person Caroline had never seen in the whole of her life. She had been reclining on a bunk at the far end, and now as Caroline entered she rose to her feet.

She was very small and attractive in a piquant, foreign manner, and she had long hair dyed the colour of guinea gold which hung in a great cloud to well below her knees. She was dressed in Turkish trousers made of some thin, gauzy material, and the upper part of her body was bare save for two large silver breast-plates set with precious stones. Caroline was so surprised at her appearance that for the moment she could only stare, forgetting her manners, until the woman said politely with a French accent:

'*Bon soir, Madame.* You have come, alas, too late to see ze animals!'

'I was afraid so . . .' Caroline began, but the woman was not listening to her. She was turning eagerly with a smiling mouth and sparkling eyes to welcome Lord Brecon who had just entered the caravan.

'M'lord,' she cried. 'I am so verry happy to see you. I thought you had forgotten Zara.'

She sped towards him as she spoke, both hands outstretched, and when he would have taken them and raised them to his lips, she raised her face, instead, and he kissed her. Caroline's astonished eyes were round.

'And how do you like England, Zara?' Lord Brecon asked.

He was looking fondly at this strange woman, Caroline noticed, and one hand was still held in hers.

'Ugh, but I detest it. It is cold, and ze audiences are slow to applaud. They are not warm like the French or noisy

27

like the Germans. They are silent, and who can know if they are pleased or . . . how you say? . . . disgusted?'

Grimbaldi laughed.

'I have told Zara we are an undemonstrative people,' he said. 'She will get used to us in time.'

'And your tigers? What do they think of us?' Lord Brecon asked.

'They think like me,' Zara said proudly. 'If there is not a great deal of . . . what you call . . . clapping, they think they are not a success . . . they sulk, they are sad . . . and they are verry difficult for me to handle.'

'Poor Zara!' Lord Brecon exclaimed, and then he looked towards Caroline.

'I must introduce you to Madame Zara, Miss Fry. She is the greatest and probably the only woman tamer of tigers in the world. She has had a phenomenal success on the Continent and now we are honoured to have her in England.'

'I hope I shall have the pleasure of seeing Madame Zara perform,' Caroline said politely.

'Won't you sit down, Miss Fry?' Mr. Grimbaldi asked, bringing her a chair.

'Thank you.'

Caroline accepted the chair and as she sank into it realised how tired she was.

'Miss Fry and I have had a fatiguing ride,' Lord Brecon said. 'Speaking for myself I am both hungry and thirsty. Can we avail ourselves of your hospitality, Adam?'

'But of course,' Mr. Grimbaldi answered, 'though I am afraid the fare is not that to which you are accustomed, my lord. Would eggs and bacon be too simple a dish?'

'I should welcome it,' Lord Brecon said. 'What about you, Miss Fry?'

'I cannot imagine anything I would rather eat,' Caroline said with a smile, 'for indeed, having dined at six o'clock I am exceeding hungry!'

'Then eggs and bacon it shall be, Adam, and if you have it—a bottle of wine?'

'There I have something I am not ashamed to offer you, my lord,' Adam Grimbaldi answered. 'Champagne which I have brought from France.'

As he spoke, he drew a bottle from a cupboard at the back of the caravan and set it on a small table.

Caroline looked around her and was amazed to see how compactly everything fitted in. There were cupboards and shelves, pictures and ornaments. The bunk bed was piled

high with cushions while the floor of the caravan was con-
cealed by a fine Persian rug.

'How cosy this is!' she exclaimed.

'My caravan is not so big as this one, but 'tis far, far
prettier,' Zara answered. 'But you are tired, Madame. Will
you not take off your bonnet and make yourself comfortable?'

'Yes, I would like to do that,' Caroline said, and raising
her arms, she undid the strings of her bonnet and drew it
from her head.

It was big and rather cumbersome as was the fashion at
the moment, and though she was aware that her hair must
be untidy, she was too tired to worry about her appearance. It was only as she threw her bonnet down on the
bunk and the light from the lantern which swung above
their heads glittered a little in her eyes that she looked
across the caravan to see the expression on Lord Brecon's
face and realised that he was seeing her face clearly for the
first time.

There was a look of surprise as well as of admiration in
his eyes, and after a second Caroline's eyes dropped, conscious that she was blushing a little under his scrutiny. She
had no idea how lovely she looked as she sat there with the
light shining on the red-gold of the tiny curls which framed
her white forehead.

Her face was a perfect oval, small and exquisitely set
upon a long, white neck. Her nose was very short and
straight and her mouth full and naturally red. There was
something so exquisite in the drawing of her face and the
grace of her body that, looking at Caroline for the first
time, people invariably found it hard to believe that she
was not just the illustration of some enchanting fairy-tale.

But her eyes were the loveliest thing about her. They
were very large and vivid with life, laughter and mischief.
Caroline's beauty was not a set, statuesque type, but something so pulsatingly alive that no one could be with her for
long without feeling both the tempo of their own mind and
body respond to her natural gaiety and enthusiasm for living.

Tired as she now was, she could not hide the eagerness
in her voice as she asked:

'Do tell me about your Menagerie. Have you many
animals?'

'A fair number, Ma'am,' Adam Grimbaldi answered,
'and I am especially proud of my lions. I have three and

the eldest one, Caesar, is as tame as a lap dog. I brought him up from a cub and he will allow me to do anything with him.'

Mr. Grimbaldi was obviously intensely proud of his menagerie, and he would have talked of it for hours to Caroline had not he been interrupted by the boy with the dark hair bringing in the eggs and bacon so that he must cease talking of his work and see to the entertainment of his guests. When they had eaten, and drunk a glass of champagne, Lord Brecon said:

'Now, Adam, I want to tell you why I am here. You must be curious, although with the greatest forbearance you have not asked me any questions.'

'I knew you would speak in your own good time, my lord. You wish, I think, for me to be of service to you. You have but to command.'

'Do you mean that, Adam, even though it means unpleasantness with the magistrates?'

Mr. Grimbaldi shrugged his shoulders.

'Magistrates are invariably unpleasant,' he said. ' 'Tis of little consequence.'

'In France we have a verry rude word and a verry rude name for them,' Zara said, 'but I will not offend the ears of ze young lady by repeating it here.'

Lord Brecon laughed.

'All right, Zara, I know it.'

'Then you agree with me?' she asked.

'I agree with you,' he answered.

She smiled and then her expression changed.

'M'lord, you have not killed a man in a duel? You are not wishing to flee ze country?'

Lord Brecon shook his head.

'No, Zara, it is not as easy as that. Perhaps I had better explain from the beginning. You had best close the door, Adam.'

Mr. Grimbaldi rose and closed the door of the caravan. Lord Brecon finished his glass of champagne and said:

'I returned to England about three months ago. As you both know, I have been abroad for nearly two years, travelling in France and Italy. I came back to find a warm welcome from my mother, and my friends appeared equally glad of my return. I was, however, informed shortly after my arrival that a distant cousin had died and I had been made the guardian of his daughter, Melissa—a girl of fifteen, who was shortly going to Paris to finish her education at one of the more famous Academies for Young Ladies.

'I made my ward's acquaintance and found her a pretty if somewhat brainless child. It was a shock to me when I learnt a week after she had left for the Continent that she had been having a clandestine love affair with a much older man and one with a distinctly unsavoury reputation. It was, I am convinced, quite an innocent flutter on the part of Melissa, but unfortunately she wrote to the gentleman in question several letters of a somewhat passionate nature. Through a lawyer of very doubtful antecedents this unutterable bounder requested me to pay him five thousand guineas for these letters, failing which he would use them to damage and defame irrevocably my ward's reputation.

'I went to see the lawyer, a man called Isaac Rosenberg, and informed him that his client would receive from me but one thousand guineas on the return of the letters and not one penny more. I also told him that, unless his offer was accepted within three days, I guaranteed to horsewhip his client the length and breadth of St. James's Street and have his name posted in every club as a blackmailer.'

'And what did he reply to that? Adam Grimbaldi asked.

'I had a reply yesterday morning,' Lord Brecon went on. 'It was a letter which somewhat surprised me. It was signed by Rosenberg and said that he particularly wished to see me on a matter which he was certain would give me extreme satisfaction. For reasons which he could not enumerate he would like me to meet him this evening at the ruined cottage behind *The Dog and Duck* in Sevenoaks Lane. I was rather surprised at this because frankly, though the ruined cottage is well-known as a local meeting place for lovers and also for those who wish to engage in a duel, it was not a place I should have thought would be known to a London lawyer. However, I was prepared to keep the appointment, and I repaired to the cottage at the time appointed, only to find Rosenberg murdered with a knife stuck deep into his neck.'

'The Lord take us!' Adam Grimbaldi ejaculated.

'But who had done it?' Zara asked.

'That I have no idea,' Lord Brecon answered. 'When I reached him, he had not been dead long. The body was warm and Miss Fry, who was in the wood at the time, heard him cry out.'

'You see ze man murdered?' Zara asked, turning to Caroline.

'No, I only heard his cry and heard someone leave the wood.'

'He had not been robbed,' Lord Brecon went on. 'The letters from my ward were in his pocket. I took them; and if I had not been suspicious that there might be others on his person, I should not have searched further, but I did so and in the inside of his coat I found this.'

As Lord Brecon spoke he drew a sheet of paper from his pocket and Caroline saw that it was the one which he had taken from the dead man. He held it out now.

'Do you see?' he asked. 'It bears my name.'

'What does it say?' Zara asked.

'It is a letter purporting to have been written by me. It invites Rosenberg to meet me at the ruined cottage behind *The Dog and Duck* in Sevenoaks Lane on Wednesday next, and it tells him to bring the letters because I am ready to agree to the conditions of his client.'

'And you never wrote it?' Mr. Grimbaldi asked.

'Never in my life,' Lord Brecon answered. 'Nor had I any intention of ever agreeing to his client's blackmailing tricks. For all I know Rosenberg's letter to me was also a forgery. Only one thing is obvious—that the poor wretch came to the trysting place because of a false letter which would make me responsible for his presence there, and was murdered by someone who meant to pin the crime on me.'

'Yes, that is indeed to be deduced,' Adam Grimbaldi agreed, nodding his big head. 'Could it have been the shabby cove to whom the letters were written?'

'I think not,' Lord Brecon replied. 'If he wanted the five thousand guineas, he would not have wished Rosenberg murdered and the letters taken from him. By my death he would gain nothing. No, it would have been to his advantage to have kept me alive.'

'Then who else could it be?' Zara asked.

'I do not know,' Lord Brecon answered. 'Presumably there must be people who wish to be rid of me, but I really am not prepared to name them.'

'And how can we help you in this?' Adam Grimbaldi asked.

'Haven't you guessed, Adam?' Lord Brecon enquired. 'Then your brain isn't as quick as Miss Fry's, for it was her idea that I should find two or more good friends who would swear that I had been in their company this past hour or two. It would not do for me, you see, to admit that I had been to the ruined cottage, for until the murderer of

Rosenberg is found I am the person most likely to be the gainer by his demise.'

'Zounds, but of course,' Grimbaldi exclaimed. 'Bacon-brained I am not to see it before! Well, my lord, as far as I'm concerned, and I know I can speak for Zara, you've been here with us the whole evening. You watched the show, you came back to this caravan and we sat talking and drinking until it was time for you to go home. Not only Zara, but my men—and their women—will swear to your presence.'

Lord Brecon smiled.

'Thank you, Adam. I knew that I could rely on you.'

He put out his hand and the other man grasped it. Zara made a wide gesture with her arms which threw back from her white shoulders the heavy, cascading cloak of hair.

'But that is such a trifle to ask of us! I was expecting to do more, so verry much more for you, m'lord, and now I am sadly disappointed.'

'You were ever generous, Zara,' Lord Brecon said, and taking one of her gesticulating little hands, he raised it to his lips.

Caroline gave a sigh.

'So everything is settled,' she said; 'and now, my lord, perhaps it would be wise for me to make some arrangement to continue my journey.'

'But of course, Miss Fry. I have been selfish enough as it is, concerning myself only with my own affairs and not with yours. Adam, is it possible to obtain a post-chaise?'

'But of course,' Mr. Grimbaldi replied. 'I will send the boy to the nearest inn. Where do you wish to go, Madam?'

'I wish eventually to reach Dover,' Caroline answered. 'But if one could take me from here to Maidstone, I could perhaps . . .'

'We will find one to take you the whole way,' Lord Brecon interrupted; and then, as Caroline would have disputed this with him, he said: 'Please permit me to arrange this. It is my pleasure to do so. The chaise, on my instructions, shall take you home.'

With a little smile Caroline realised that he thought she was considering the cost, and so she ceased to argue with him and thanked him gratefully.

Adam Grimbaldi called the boy and sent him off to the inn, then opened another bottle of champagne. By now Caroline was sleepy and yet she found herself vividly aware of Lord Brecon. She wondered, as she watched him,

33

what it was about his face which was so different from other men.

He was exceedingly good-looking, it was true, but it was more than that. There was something reserved and strange about his eyes, something which seemed to suggest that he held himself in check. Even his laughter was not always spontaneous, and his smile, charming though it was, had often a sadness or cynicism about it.

'He hides a secret, I am sure,' Caroline told herself; but she could not by any logic justify her instinct in the matter.

Although it was so late, Caroline felt that she could not leave the menagerie without seeing some of the animals. When the boy had returned to say that post-chaise would be with them in half an hour, she begged that she might see the lions, the tigers, and the kangaroo, which was a very new purchase of Adam Grimbaldi's and of which he was inordinately proud.

They went from wagon to wagon. Most of the animals were asleep. They blinked in the light of the lanterns while the more savage of them growled at being disturbed.

'You must come and see us when we get to St. Bartholomew's Fair,' Adam Grimbaldi said as they finished their tour of inspection.

'I would not miss it for a thousand guineas,' Caroline cried.

'If all else fails, Miss Fry, you might ask Adam to find you employment with his Menagerie,' Lord Brecon suggested.

'The idea tempts me extremely, my lord,' Caroline replied, 'but I have a suspicion that my father and mother would not approve.'

'No, perhaps not,' Lord Brecon laughed, 'but your lady of quality sounds more ferocious than a dozen wild animals.'

'As indeed she was,' Caroline replied.

The boy came running to say that the post-chaise was outside. Caroline thanked Mr. Grimbaldi for his hospitality and said good-bye to Madame Zara. Lord Brecon escorted her to the post-chaise. He had a short conversation with the groom and Caroline heard the clink of guineas. Then he came to Caroline's side, and taking up a rug with which the post-chaise was provided, he tucked it carefully round her knees.

'Do you think you are safe to travel this long distance

alone?' he asked. 'I wonder if it would be wiser for me to accompany you.'

'Oh no, my lord,' Caroline said quickly. 'There is no need for that. I shall be perfectly safe, and I shall be at Dover soon after breakfast. I have nothing of value on me to attract the attention of highwaymen and to tell the truth I shall sleep.'

'Then a good journey to you, Miss Fry, and may I thank you for all you have done for me?'

'It was nothing,' Caroline answered.

Lord Brecon was speaking to her through the window of the chaise so that she could not see his face very clearly, but her own was lit by the moonlight and her eyes, raised to his, were shining.

'It has been a very thrilling adventure,' she added softly.

'We will not meet again,' Lord Brecon said; and then as he looked down into her face, he added: 'Good-bye, sweet Caroline . . . and thank you.'

She held out her hand to him; but when he took it, he bent his head not to her fingers but to her parted lips. Before Caroline was aware of his intention, before she could move or protest, he had kissed her full on the mouth. As he drew back from the door of the chaise, the groom whipped up the horses and Caroline was carried swiftly on her way.

For a moment her thoughts were too chaotic for her to feel anything but astonishment, and then anger replaced her surprise.

'How dare he?' she said aloud. 'How dare he?'

No man had ever touched her mouth before, and Caroline lifted the tips of her fingers to it, wondering to feel the warmth of her lips.

'How dare he?' she repeated.

So that was what it was like to be kissed! She felt again the strength and yet the softness of his mouth on hers, was conscious of the strange, startled throbbing of her heart and the fire which seemed to rise in the base of her throat and choke the very breath from her body. That was a kiss!

Caroline smiled to herself in the darkness. Oh well, it was no use being angry; it was perhaps a fitting finish to an exciting adventure.

She put her head back against the coach; but, tired though she was, sleep did not come to her. Why, she wondered, had Lord Brecon said they would not meet again?

Was it because he thought that his path and that of a paid companion were unlikely to become entangled with so much difference in their social status? Or was it for another and less simple reason?

She found herself visualising him very clearly. How good-looking he was, how strangely different from all the other men she had ever known! He was older, of course. She guessed him to be about twenty-six or twenty-seven, but even so there was more personality in his little finger than in the whole of Lord Glosford's long, languid body.

Brecon! It was an attractive name, but Caroline wondered what his intimates called him.

She fell asleep about half an hour before they reached the first posting inn, and then awoke with a start because she had been dreaming. While the horses were being changed, she went into the inn to wash her hands, and beholding her reflection in a mirror was horrified at her appearance.

No wonder Lord Brecon had easily believed her story of being a paid companion. Her once impressive dress of rich velvet was stained, dusty and torn beyond repair. The lace at her neck had become tattered where she had forced her way through the branches of the wood, and her hands were literally filthy from climbing from the window and touching the green bark of the trees.

It took Caroline some time to wash and tidy herself, but even so she delayed the post-chaise a few more minutes while she wrote a note to Mrs. Edgmont and asked that it should be sent to Vulcan House in Grosvenor Square by post. She received the landlady's assurance that it should go first thing in the morning. Caroline was not quite certain, however, that this would be done, for they were all tired in the inn and had been asleep when the groom of her post-chaise had awakened them. But the sight of a guinea, which luckily she had with her in her purse, was enough to redouble their assurance with a ring of sincerity which had been lacking before. When Caroline rejoined her chaise and started once again on her journey, she was sure that Cousin Debby would not be long without news of her movements.

The rest of the journey to Dover was uneventful. Caroline slept easily and peacefully, the sleep of a tired child. She was so glad to be on her way home, so sure of her welcome and her parents' ability to smooth away all her difficulties that even her twinges of conscience over her original acceptance of Sir Montagu's invitation did not keep her awake. Caroline had not yet learnt to worry.

Her life to date had been a very pleasant one. To begin with she had been born and brought up at Mandrake, one of the loveliest houses in the country and by far the most magnificent. The foundations of Mandrake had been laid by Sir Justin de Faye who had come to England with William of Normandy, and every succeeding generation of Fayes had built on to and enriched the house until the great roofs now covered a vast treasure store of incalculable value and interest. And as Mandrake had grown during the centuries, so had the family who owned it acquired wealth and honours, titles and distinctions.

No wonder the 15th Marquis of Vulcan was proud of his heritage, no wonder he loved every inch of Mandrake, from the ancient Norman Keep which still stood sentinel on the furthest point of the white cliffs, to the exquisite ballrooms and *salons* added but forty years ago by his mother to the design of Robert Adam.

The 14th Marchioness, Caroline's grandmother, had been banished from Court because of her insatiable passion for gaming. She had created a court of her own at Mandrake and reigned there supreme until she had been stoned to death by the smugglers whom she employed to sally forth from the secret caves below the house to procure for her illicit goods from France.

With her death, a raffish, extravagant and exotic era came to an end, and for Caroline Mandrake meant peace, a quiet beauty and an atmosphere of unbroken joy. Her father and mother had such an overwhelming love for each other that the whole place was enchanted, and everyone who lived at Mandrake with them seemed to reflect some of their radiant happiness.

But in Caroline's veins ran the proud, turbulent, courageous blood of the Fayes. Each of her features, every movement she made, every action she performed was as much the accumulation of centuries as were the grandeur and dignity of Mandrake itself. She had inherited the pride, the loyalty and the integrity of her ancestors, but also their deep passions, their determination and strong-willed obstinacy. Much of her grandmother's beauty was hers too —a beauty which was already a legend of the eighteenth century. Yet while that flawless perfection of line and grace was born again in Caroline, it was combined with something of her mother's loveliness. Serena, Marchioness of Vulcan's purity and sweetness of heart shone like a flame; no one who knew her could look into her clear, blue eyes and not be aware of her spiritual qualities.

In Caroline one could find that same purity and straightforward honesty, but her temperament and personality were like the waves she had watched from her nursery windows as she grew up, and their music had ever been a part of her thoughts and dreams. White-crested, dashing headlong against the steep cliffs, breaking the emerald and sapphire of the smooth water; wild, untrammelled and tempestuous; or gentle waves, moving rhythmically as a woman's soft breathing and sinking finally in soft surrender against the golden, sunlit sand.

Caroline's moods were as varied and as unexpected. Her mother would sigh over her, afraid of what the future would hold for a girl so breathtakingly beautiful and also so vividly and emotionally alive.

Loyalty and singleness of purpose were virtues Caroline had to a fault. Once, when she was but ten years old, a young groom who looked after her pony was taken to court on a poaching charge. Caroline learnt of it and without asking permission or even telling anyone of her intention she rode off full gallop to Dover. She stormed into the court, demanded of the magistrates that she should give evidence in the defence of her groom, and was so plausible and persuasive that the boy was released to return with her to Mandrake.

At home her absence had been noticed and her father was organising a search party when she returned. Lord Vulcan questioned Caroline somewhat severely, for both he and Lady Vulcan had been extremely frightened at their daughter's disappearance. But Caroline's explanation was very simple:

'He was my friend, Papa!'

'And supposing he had been found guilty and sent to prison?' Lord Vulcan asked.

'I would have gone with him,' Caroline replied, and added with unanswerable logic, 'You would then have had both him—and me—freed.'

Lady Vulcan worried over her daughter as she grew older, even while she could not help but be proud of her. Caroline was so exquisite both in body and mind that it seemed impossible to find a flaw anywhere. She might be impulsive, impetuous and at times mischievous, but no one had ever known her do an unkind action or an ungenerous one.

The servants adored her and she had more friends than it was possible to remember. When she appeared in London, it was not only her name and background of wealth and position which made her the most important *débutante* of her year, it was her loveliness, her friendliness and her exuberant, whole-hearted joyousness which made her a magnet to attract admirers of both sexes.

One thing only surprised her godmother. Caroline, after four months in Society, was as heart-whole as the day she first left Mandrake. As 'The Toast of the Town' and 'the Incomparable' she had offers in plenty, but she declined them all with a firmness which left her admirers with little hope that she was just coy or indecisive.

'I cannot suspicion who you imagine will make a better match,' Lady Bullingham said sarcastically after Caroline had refused Lord Glosford.

'I know someone who will,' Caroline answered, her lovely little face alight with amusement at her godmother's anger.

'Who then? For I vow I could read *Debrett* from cover to cover without enlightenment.'

'He may not be there,' Caroline smiled.

'Not in *Debrett!* Lord save us, girl! Do not tell me that you contemplate a *mésalliance*. 'Tis more than I can bear. Who is he? I demand an answer! Who is he?'

'Alas I do not know,' Caroline replied. 'For I have yet to meet a man I could love.'

Sometimes she had doubted if such a man really existed; yet when the morning sun woke her, streaming through the windows of the chaise, she knew that for the first time in her life a man's name trembled on her lips. She felt alight with happiness and, pulling down the window, took deep breaths of the fresh, salty air. In the distance she could see the first glint of the blue sea.

She gave the driver of the post-chaise instructions to drive to Mandrake and added that he was to take her, not to the front door, but into the stable yard. If he was surprised, he did not show it and he gave Caroline the impression that it was all a matter of indifference to him, and that he was only concerned with his own return to Sevenoaks. All the same she was anxious to keep her identity hidden from anyone who might inform Lord Brecon of her destination.

Accordingly, when she drove into the stable yard at Mandrake and her father's old groom came hurrying out to see who could be arriving, she jumped out of the chaise and drew him to one side.

'Reward the man well, Harry,' she said; 'give him breakfast and send him about his business. On no account tell him who I am. If he enquires, inform him I am an unimportant guest in the house, or one of the upper servants, it matters not.'

'Very good, m'lady,' Harry said, and then added with the familiarity of an old servant: 'Oi reckon yer ladyship has been up to one of yer pranks again.'

Caroline did not deign to answer this, but stepped with dignity towards the back door. On reaching it, however, she moved swiftly and with the obvious desire not to be seen along the long corridors until she reached some narrow stairs which led to the upper rooms.

She hurried up them and finally reached her own room without encountering anyone save an under-housemaid whom she sent in search of Maria. The latter, a young country girl who had looked after Caroline for the last two years, came hurrying to her in a few seconds' time.

'M'lady,' she exclaimed. 'But we were not expecting you. I thought you were in London. You could have knocked me down with a feather when I was told your ladyship was here in this very house. I thought I must be a-dreaming. Are you real, m'lady? For I assure you I am in so much of a dither that I am not certain whether 'tis your ladyship or a ghost.'

'No, it is I, Maria, and now help me out of these things.'

'Oh, m'lady, your gown. Whatever have you been doing to yourself?"

'Sh, Maria. Ask no questions, but throw it away before my mother sees it. It is beyond repair. Now give me one of my muslins and make my hair as tidy as possible.'

Half an hour later as the Marquis of Vulcan was coming out of the breakfast-room, he was surprised to see his daughter, bright-eyed, fresh, and exceedingly pretty in a crisp white muslin tied with blue ribbons, descending the grand staircase.

'Caroline!' he exclaimed. 'Where have you sprung from? I had no idea you were here.'

'Good morning, Papa,' Caroline said, dropping a curtsey and then holding her face up to be kissed. 'Say you are pleased to see me, for I vow I am enchanted to see you.'

Lord Vulcan put his arms round her and held her close. 'You should have sent us word,' he said. 'Why are you home? From all reports you were enjoying the giddy whirl of high Society.'

'I wanted to see Mama,' Caroline answered, 'and you too, of course, Papa dear.'

'As it happens I was just writing to you,' Lord Vulcan said. 'The letter would have gone to you this very day. I had news to impart.'

'News?' Caroline questioned.

'Yes,' Lord Vulcan replied. 'Come into the library, Caroline. I have something to tell you.'

He linked his arm through his daughter's and drew her into the big library which overlooked the sea. The room was brilliant with sunshine and Caroline sat herself on a cushioned window-seat. It had been a favourite place of hers as a child and as she sank down on the seat she gave a sigh of utter content.

'It is good to be home,' she murmured. 'What is your news, Papa?'

'It concerns your mother,' Lord Vulcan replied.

'Mama?' Caroline questioned quickly. 'She is not ill, is she?'

'No, not ill exactly, but she is not really well,' Lord Vulcan answered, his handsome face grave. 'You remember when she was laid up last winter with a tiresome cough which the doctors could not cure. Well, I had Sir Henry Halford, the King's physician, down from London last week, and he advised that your mother have a change of air, and indeed a change of environment. He is anxious for her to spend a month or so in Italy and then perhaps a little time by Lake Como. I am taking his advice, Caroline, and your mother and I leave next week for the Continent.'

'Oh, Papa!' Caroline exclaimed.

'I was afraid you would be rather surprised,' Lord Vulcan smiled.

'But if Mama is ill, I must go with her.'

Lord Vulcan shook his head.

'No, Caroline, though it was to be expected that you should suggest it. To begin with, Sir Henry desires that for the first part of the journey she shall have complete freedom from all anxiety; and secondly, to be honest with you, we are rather looking forward to going away alone together. Much as we love you, Caroline, and our two boys, you are none of you very restful people.'

'Well, really!' Caroline exclaimed, then she laughed. 'A second honeymoon, Papa, is that the idea? It is a little late in the day when you have a daughter of seventeen and two large sons at Eton.'

'We do not feel it is too late, nor that we are too old,' Lord Vulcan replied with dignity. 'In fact we are both eagerly looking forward to an elopment from our responsibilities. Besides, I have never been able to take your mother abroad until now. The war lasted so long and when first it was over, there always seemed to be children to interfere with our plans.'

Caroline made a little grimace.

'What a nuisance we must be to you.'

'On the contrary, you have been a great joy to us, but you have given us moments of apprehension. And that reminds me of something I want to ask of you, Caroline. I want you to promise not to upset your mother in any way.'

'Upset her? Why should I?'

'Because the one thing that disturbs her is the thought of leaving you behind. She has worried incessantly at not being able to go to London to entertain for you your first season. We feel sure that your godmother is doing it admirably and that Cousin Debby is a good chaperon; but at the same time your mother and I would have liked to be with you. That, as you know, has been impossible owing to her low state of health, and now I have had some difficulty in persuading her to take Sir Henry's advice. She was afraid to leave England because of you, Caroline. To tell the truth she is quite certain you will be up to mischief if we are not around to keep an eye on you.'

'Papa, that is monstrously unfair,' Caroline cried.

Lord Vulcan, with a twinkle in his eye, held up his hand.

'No, Caroline. If you think of it, you will admit you have caused us a great deal of anxiety these past years; and now that you are launched on the world, it is only to be expected that we should worry about you.'

'There is no need,' Caroline began haughtily, and then was silent.

'All I ask,' Lord Vulcan continued after a little pause as if he waited for Caroline to say something more, 'is that, if you are in any trouble before we leave, you either keep it to yourself or confide in me. Your mother is not to be worried. Is that understood?'

'Yes, Papa.'

'And now perhaps you would like to relate to me why you have come back so unexpectedly.'

Caroline hesitated. She looked out to sea and debated within herself whether she would tell her father or not. Then, as she pondered, she thought how enraged and angry he would be when he heard of the trick that Sir Montagu Reversby had played on her. Her father would be furious, she could be certain of that; in fact he might even consider it his duty to call out Sir Montagu or, if not to fight a duel on her behalf, to horsewhip him. Lord Vulcan would not hesitate to go to any extremity where his honour and the honour of his family were concerned.

He was proud and at times extremely autocratic if people went against what he considered the correct and decent code of chivalry. It would be amusing, Caroline thought, to see Sir Montagu cringing before her father, and yet all this would take time. If Lord Vulcan were to go to London, it would be unlikely that he and her mother could leave next week for the Continent. No, in this matter and on this occasion she must be both silent and unselfish.

With a little sigh she turned towards her father.

'I have nothing to tell you, Papa,' she said. 'I just had an overwhelming desire to see you and Mama. Perhaps it would be more honest to say that I was homesick and so . . . I came home.'

'Cousin Debby is with you?'

'No, Papa.'

Lord Vulcan frowned.

'You came alone?'

'Yes, Papa. I decided on the spur of the moment.'

'Now Caroline, you know that I do not allow you to travel about alone.'

His voice was angry, but before he could say more Caroline had sprung from the window-seat and put her arms round his neck.

'Pray do not be vexed with me,' she pleaded, her soft cheek against his. 'I know it was wrong of me to come, but I wanted to see you, and Cousin Debby, nice though she is, would have taken an age. There would have been days of packing and preparations before I got to Mandrake. As it

43

is, I left last night and I am here this morning. Forgive me, Papa, and we will not tell Mama for fear it would worry her.'

'Caroline, you are a sad romp,' Lord Vulcan sighed, but she knew by his tone that she had appeased him.

'It is no use your telling me that things are right,' he continued, 'for I know full well something is wrong. I can feel it in the air, but I will not force your confidence, my dear.'

'I will look after myself,' Caroline promised. 'Don't worry. You know, Papa, I'm beginning to find out that you are a bit of a humbug.'

Lord Vulcan raised his eyebrows.

'Humbug?' he asked.

'Yes,' Caroline replied firmly. 'You see, when I lived here at Mandrake, I thought you the best, the most handsome and the most exemplary man in all the world; but when I got to London I found out that once you had been an inveterate gamester, a dead shot, an incomparable whip and a fascinator of every lady, young or old, in the whole of the *beau-monde*. Now is that not the truth?'

Lord Vulcan laughed.

'Who has been telling you stories, Caroline?'

'A large number of people. If I do anything the least out of the ordinary, they shrug their shoulders and say, "What else can you expect from Justin's daughter?"'

'Caroline, you little devil, you are making it up,' Lord Vulcan protested, but he was laughing all the same.

'It is true, I swear it,' Caroline replied. 'Papa, you had a prodigious reputation.'

'I will not lie to you, Caroline,' Lord Vulcan said. 'I was not entirely blameless at one time, but that was before I met your mother.'

'And afterwards?' Caroline asked.

'I fell in love, my dear, and my whole life was changed. I have been a very happy man and a very fortunate one.'

Caroline was silent for a moment and then she said in a very small, quiet voice:

'How does one know when one is in love?'

Lord Vulcan stood up and looked down at her; then he put out his hand and taking her chin between his fingers, turned her little face up to his.

'Listen, Caroline,' he said, 'I will tell you when you know you are in love—when you feel that any sacrifice is worthwhile for another person, when you feel that no deed

44

of bravery is too great to perform, no risk too great to be taken on their behalf, when you would die for them, or better still—live to serve them. That, then, is love.'

Caroline's eyes met his fearlessly; and then, as he released her, she looked out to sea. The sun pouring through the windows glinted on her shining hair and a sudden smile transformed her whole face.

'So that is love,' she said softly; and turning, she ran from the room.

3

The Honourable Mrs. Edgmont read the letter she held in her hands a second time, then folded it and, dropping her lorgnette, went in search of Caroline. She found her playing the spinet in the ante-room to the silver drawing-room. When Caroline saw her cousin and chaperon enter the room, she jumped up and ran towards her.

'You have had a letter from my godmother? she said. 'I saw it when the post arrived. What does she say, Cousin Debby?'

'That is precisely what I have come to speak to you about, Caroline,' Mrs. Edgmont replied in a grave voice.

Caroline sighed.

'When you talk to me in that voice, Cousin Debby, I know there is something amiss. Tell me quickly.'

Mrs. Edgmont looked flustered. She was a small, grey-haired woman who, a quarter of a century earlier, had been married for only a few months before her elderly husband died of a complaint of the chest, and the brief period of her marriage had left so little mark on her that she invariably seemed the personification of a spinster.

She was quiet, precise and well versed in all that a lady should know of deportment and good manners. At the same time she had a sweetness of nature and a kindliness which made her young relations really fond of her. She was a distant cousin of the Marquis of Vulcan and therefore well born, and she had such an exemplary character that no one more suitable could have been found to act as chaperon to Caroline.

Besides, Mrs. Edgmont had been left in constrained circumstances and she was exceedingly glad of the emolument which the Marquis paid her, and which enabled her to live in comfortable circumstances once again. At the same time she was terrified that she might fall short of her duties. Caroline was so high-spirited, and indeed on occasions so mischievous, that Mrs. Edgmont went in hourly fear and trembling of what she would discover next.

Her hand shook now as she opened the Countess of Bullingham's letter.

'Your godmother,' she said to Caroline, 'is vexed, my dear.'

'About my leaving London?' Caroline asked.

'It was ill-bred, you know, to depart without explanation or farewell.'

'Yes, I know,' Caroline said, 'but I wrote her a long letter of apology explaining that when I heard that Papa and Mama were going abroad, I hurried off to them by postchaise without thought or preparation.'

'But that was not exactly the truth,' Mrs. Edgmont said reproachfully.

'Now, Cousin Debby, you know that was the one possible explanation which would mollify my godmother. If she is vexed, there must be something else besides my absence which is annoying her.'

'There is indeed, Caroline, yet I hardly understand of what she writes.'

'Oh, tell me what she says,' Caroline said impatiently.

Mrs. Edgmont fumbled with the sheets of writing paper which were scrawled over with untidy handwriting.

'She speaks of rumours,' she said at length, peering shortsightedly at the letter through her lorgnette.

'Rumours? What sort of rumours?' Caroline asked.

'She says, *"rumours ill-becoming a Young Lady and especially one in Caroline's Exalted Position".*'

'Go on,' Caroline said. 'What else does she say?'

'She speaks of *"Someone of whom I have warned Caroline repeatedly and whose Name should in No Way be connected with hers".* She adds that 'tis unfortunate that your father and mother are leaving for the Continent or she would have given herself the pleasure of calling on them to discuss the matter.'

Caroline uttered an impatient exclamation.

'That is just what I was afraid of, Cousin Debby,' she said, glancing over her shoulder as if she might be overheard. 'Well, thank goodness Papa and Mama go tomorrow and she won't have time to see them. Pray heaven she hasn't taken it into her head to write, for Mama would be upset and you collect Papa said that was on no account to happen.'

'Yes, yes, I know that, Caroline; but at the same time 'tis difficult for me to know what to do. If I behave correctly, I should, having received this letter, speak with your mother at once.'

'Now, Cousin Debby, dear Cousin Debby, you know you will do nothing of the sort. Mama is not to be worried . . . and if you speak to my father,' Caroline added, guessing that that solution had already occurred to Mrs. Edgmont, 'he will only be angry and you know as well as I do that Mama will guess what is wrong. He cannot keep anything from her. They are too devoted for either of them to hide a secret.'

'That is true enough, I must admit,' Mrs. Edgmont said. 'But oh, Caroline, what does your godmother mean?'

'I know not and I care less!' Caroline answered; 'anyway, cease to perturb yourself, Cousin Debby, for I'm not returning to London.'

'Not returning to London?' Mrs. Edgmont echoed in astonishment. 'But, Caroline, you cannot mean it; you, the Belle of the Season, with invitations to balls for months ahead? How can you possibly talk of not returning to London?'

'Well, I'm not, not at any rate for the moment,' Caroline answered. 'We will stay here, Cousin Debby, and then the rumours about me will die away. People will chatter for a day or two until something more exciting occurs and then they will forget about me.'

'But what are they chattering about?' asked the bewildered Mrs. Edgmont. 'Caroline, I think you should be frank with me. What happened that night when you left a note saying that you were in the company of Lady Rohan? Why did you not come back to Vulcan House and how did you find your way here—alone and unattended?'

'Never mind, Cousin Debby. It is a long story and I have no wish to bore you with it now. You have been very good about keeping everything from Mama's ears. Forget this silly letter from my godmother until they have left tomorrow and then you and I will decide on our plans for the future.'

'Caroline! Oh, Caroline, I fail to understand you,' Mrs. Edgmont cried. 'You must go back to London. What will Lady Bullingham say if you remain down here after your parents have gone, and what will happen to all your *beaux*? They will miss you sadly, Caroline, and worse still, they might even . . . forget you.'

'There is not one that I care a fig for,' Caroline retorted.

'That is very silly,' Mrs. Edgmont admonished. 'When I think of that charming young man, Lord . . .'

'If you mention Lord Glosford,' Caroline interrupted, 'I shall scream. You know quite well that my godmother and you only like him because he is a future duke. He is bird-witted and the most dead bore I have ever met. I vow that I cannot spend five minutes in his company without wishing to yawn. I don't care how good a match he may be, I will have none of him.'

'Now attend to me . . .' Mrs. Edgmont began, but Caroline was not listening. She had heard the sound of a coach and horses outside in the courtyard and ran to the windows to see who might be arriving.

A very splendid cavalcade met her eyes. There was a coach of blue and silver with coachman and postillions in a livery of blue and silver to match. Four horses, all perfectly matched greys, pulled the coach while there were outriders also on grey horses riding ahead. Caroline stared for a moment, then she gave a little cry of delight.

'It is my Lord Milborne,' she said. 'Oh, how delighted I am! He must have come to bid farewell to Papa and Mama.'

She turned from the window and ran across the room to the door.

'Now if *he* were to offer for me, Cousin Debby,' Caroline said, her eyes twinkling, 'I should accept him with alacrity.'

'But Caroline, he is far too old,' Mrs. Edgmont cried in a scandalised tone.

'Yes, but he is a man and not a nincompoop like your precious Glosford,' Caroline retorted, and had vanished before Mrs. Edgmont could think of a suitable rebuke.

She sped down the passage, into the hall and had run so swiftly through the front door and down the wide stone steps to meet the Earl of Milborne that she was beside him as he descended from his coach.

'Uncle Francis!' she cried and flung her arms round him.

'Well, Caroline,' Lord Milborne exclaimed. 'I didn't expect to find you here nor indeed to receive such a greeting. I had heard that you were a lady of fashion these days and that the bloods were dueling daily outside Vulcan House.'

'You are not to tease me, Uncle Francis,' Caroline said, holding on to his arm. 'As for the bloods, I have little use

49

for them, and I have never met one who was half as attractive as you, my lord.'

'Flatterer,' Lord Milborne said, but he looked down at Caroline with deep affection.

He was the Marquis's oldest friend and he had known Caroline since she was a baby. Although he was no blood relation, she had called him Uncle Francis since first she had begun to talk. Tall and distinguished, Lord Milborne at fifty-five was, in Caroline's estimation and indeed in many other women's, a most attractive man; but all attempts to bring him to the altar had failed and he lived alone in his big house and managed his vast estates single-handed, although there were invariably a dozen lovely women wishful of chasing the sadness from his eyes and eager for the chance of dispersing the air of loneliness and reserve which seemed so indivisibly a part of his personality.

Next to her own home Caroline thought Lord Milborne's the most perfect house in the world. The seat of the Earls of Milborne for four hundred years, Sale Park had been rebuilt in the reign of Queen Anne. The present mansion of mellow red brick ornamented with fine stonework was set among gardens of such surpassing beauty that their fame had spread from England to the Continent, and artists wrote from as far as Italy asking if they might visit Sale Park and view the grounds.

Caroline and her parents spent many happy weeks every year as guests of Lord Milborne, but even as a child Caroline was aware that sometimes her host and most beloved playmate seemed lost in a gentle melancholy, and always when the time came for them to return home she was conscious that they left behind a lonely figure despite the grandeur and beauty of his great possessions.

Now with Caroline chattering gaily Lord Milborne reached the hall before the Marquis, hearing the sound of their voices, came hurrying to meet them.

'Welcome to Mandrake, Francis,' he said. 'Come into the morning-room while I send for a glass of wine. Serena is upstairs, but she will be informed immediately of your arrival.'

Still hanging on to Lord Milborne's arm Caroline went with the two men into the lovely room looking over the rose garden.

'Is it really true you are leaving tomorrow?' Lord Milborne asked Lord Vulcan.

'Indeed it is, and greatly daring, we are crossing to Calais by the new steamer; you know a service has been started these past two months.'

'I believe they are very comfortable,' Lord Milborne replied, 'and if the weather is good they get there in under four hours. But will not my lady be frightened?'

'Serena says not,' Lord Vulcan replied, 'and after all we are not such old fogies that we dare not try anything new, although Caroline here will have us believe that we are thoroughly out of date.'

'I can well believe that,' Lord Milborne said, 'for I hear Caroline has set London by the ears. In the clubs they talk only of her beauty, and mothers with eligible daughters are ready to die with mortification.'

'Uncle Francis, now you are bamming,' Caroline protested, blushing.

'Well, if you need someone to fight a duel to defend your honour,' Lord Milborne said, 'I am still considered quite a decent shot—senile though I may be.'

'Let us have no talk of duels,' Lord Vulcan interjected quickly. 'Caroline has promised to be very good while we are away. But tell me about yourself, Francis. We were expecting you the day before yesterday.'

'And I would have been here,' Lord Milborne replied, 'had I not been held up by the most tiresome murder.'

Caroline stiffened suddenly.

'That is the penalty of being the Chief Justice,' Lord Vulcan said carelessly. 'Anyone we know?'

'Oh, no one of any consequence, I assure you,' Lord Milborne said. 'A lawyer called Rosenberg. He was murdered about four miles the other side of Sevenoaks, and I have had to spend two days interrogating witnesses—a name, needless to say, without meaning, for as usual no one had been helpful enough to view the crime being committed.'

'Did you find the murderer?' Lord Vulcan asked.

'No, but strangely enough they tried to implicate young Brecon. You remember his father, Justin? He was a tiresome, difficult man. I had a difference of opinion with him about twenty years ago over a mill. He was in the wrong, of course. The bruiser he was backing committed a foul quite early in the fight, but Brecon was a pig-headed, obstinate fellow so, because I was proved right, we never spoke to each other again, and he died the following year. I seem to recall some gossip in connection with his death, but I cannot at the moment collect what it was about.'

'And you say his son is accused of a murder?' Lord Vulcan asked.

'Well, not exactly accused,' Lord Milborne said. 'It was all very strange. This man Rosenberg was found stabbed and two men came forward to say that someone had told them that Rosenberg was meeting Lord Brecon that night. They either could not or would not say who had given them the information, but they were very insistent on it. Personally I think they had been bribed to bring in Brecon's name, but I could not prove it. Of course, Brecon had an excellent alibi.'

'Any reason who Rosen . . . whatever the man's name was . . . should want to meet Brecon?'

'Not as far as I could find out. He had no papers on him and the clerk from his office in Lincoln's Inn knew only that Rosenberg had had a letter that morning which seemed to please him, and he had left in the afternoon by post-chaise. He had not said where he was going, but merely intimated that he would return to the office the next morning.'

'Well, it doesn't sound a very interesting murder to me,' Lord Vulcan said. 'Ah, here is some refreshment,' he added as the door opened and a butler entered attended by two footmen carrying silver trays piled high with cold meats and game.

'Who found the body, Uncle Francis?' Caroline asked.

'Ah, Caroline, so you are interested in crime,' Lord Milborne said. 'I am not sure if one ought to talk about such things in front of young ladies; but strangely enough that was the most mysterious part of the whole episode. A gentleman found poor Rosenberg, a man by the name of Sir Montagu Reversby. I must say I had never heard of him before. He was an unpleasant sort of a fellow, suave and far too sure of himself to be genuine, if you can understand what I mean. He tried to get out of giving evidence, but I insisted on seeing him. Apparently he was in the wood that night with two grooms, searching for a lady.'

'A lady!' Lord Vulcan exclaimed. 'And what was she doing in the wood?'

'I have not the slightest idea,' Lord Milborne smiled. 'Now who she was. Anyway, they failed to find her, though apparently she was of some importance to

Reversby, for he had offered the grooms a guinea apiece for her capture.'

'But instead they found a corpse,' Caroline said, and gave a little laugh.

'It sounds comic, doesn't it?' Lord Milborne said, 'but I assure you there was more behind this. I think Reversby and his grooms were genuine enough; they didn't expect to find anything but a lady; but the other men were far more sinister. They stuck to their story that they had reason to believe that Lord Brecon had murdered this man and nothing I could say would shake them.'

'But Lord Brecon had an alibi?' Caroline said quickly.

'Yes, and a good one, though it was somewhat unusual,' Lord Milborne answered.

'Why unusual?' Lord Vulcan asked.

'He had, it appeared, spent the evening with the proprietor of a menagerie and a female who tames tigers,' Lord Milborne explained. 'In the morning he had not gone home but left for London as he wished to bid for a horse at Tattersall's. When he returned the following day and told me of his movements the menagerie people were fetched by my orders and proved to be excellent witnesses. Their story corroborated Brecon's in every particular. The rest of the enquiry was over so I had the advantage of hearing what the other witnesses had said while Brecon had not heard them. It would have been easy for him to make a slip had he been guilty.'

Caroline gave a little sigh of relief. If Lord Brecon had missed the enquiry he need not have heard that Sir Montagu was searching for a woman that night in the wood. She had not dreamt before that Sir Montagu might be implicated in the murder, and she felt quite shaken and faint at her narrow escape from the most terrible notoriety and scandal.

'Well, Francis, as Brecon had an alibi, why do the lies that were told about him perturb you?' Lord Vulcan asked.

'I am not surprised you ask that question,' Lord Milborne replied. 'I asked it of myself. Quite frankly, Justin, I took a liking to the boy. He is a very different type from his father; good-looking, well-set-up, looks you straight in the eye when you speak to him and has an air about him which is sadly lacking in some of the popinjays I see about nowadays. To be honest, he was a man after my own heart, and I could not help feeling there was something

53

behind this insistence on the part of the men—strangers they were, too—that he had murdered the lawyer.'

'Why, do you think he really did it?' Lord Vulcan asked.

'No, not by any means; but I think someone had paid the two men well to say so and rehearsed them thoroughly in the parts they had to play.'

'In other words,' Lord Vulcan said, sipping a glass of wine as he spoke, 'you think Brecon has a dangerous enemy?'

'I do,' Lord Milborne answered; 'and yet I have few grounds for such an assumption and could naturally only accept his statement that he had no suspicion whatsoever why anyone of his acquaintance should wish to murder Rosenberg and pin the crime on him.'

'He admitted to knowing the murdered man?'

'Yes, he told me that he had had dealings with the lawyer, but he thought him a most undesirable acquaintance and a rogue. He was quite open and frank about it and I saw no reason to doubt his word.'

'No, no, of course not,' Lord Vulcan said. 'So your verdict was "Murder by persons unknown"?'

'Exactly! If you want my opinion, it is a verdict which is given far too frequently these days. We are letting too many criminals slip through our fingers and giving them the opportunity to strike again another day.'

Caroline moved across to the window.

'Then you think, Uncle Francis,' she said quietly, 'that there is a likelihood that the murderer, whoever he may be, may try to implicate Lord Brecon on another occasion?'

'Yes, Caroline,' Lord Milborne said gravely. 'I am afraid that is what I do think. I am sorry if it be so, because I liked the lad.'

'And you have no suspicion,' Caroline asked, 'who this dangerous enemy might be?'

'Now, I didn't say that. I have suspicions, but they are by no means evidence and someone in my position has to be very careful when he opens his mouth.'

'And what is your suspicion, Uncle Francis?' Caroline asked.

'I have just told you, Caroline, I have to be very careful what I say,' Lord Milborne replied, cutting himself a slice of venison from the cold collation in front of him.

'Oh, Uncle Francis, but you must tell us,' Caroline insisted.

'I declare, Francis, you have got me intrigued,' Lord

Vulcan said. 'I hear quite enough of these cases as a Justice for Dover, but this one seems to have greater possibilities than the usual run of such sordid matter. Tell us whom you suspect, Francis. You are among friends here.'

'I have no secrets from you, Justin,' Lord Milborne said, 'but Caroline must promise me that she will not gossip. The chatter of women's tongues carries news far swifter than any mailcoach.'

'I promise you, Uncle Francis,' Caroline said quickly.

Lord Milborne smiled at her.

'Very well then,' he said. 'I will tell you what I know. In my position, as you can imagine, I hear a great number of things about a great number of people. It is my duty as Chief Justice of the County to pay attention to a certain amount of the stories I am told. Well, during this past year I have been hearing again and again of a young gentleman called Gervase Warlingham. His name has cropped up on several occasions when I have had reports of—shall we say?—unsavoury incidents occurring in the sporting world, such as a doped cock, a mill where one of the pugilists has been paid to let his opponent win—a definite disregard of the rules of racing—and always somewhere in the background when these things occurred has loomed the figure of Mr. Gervase Warlingham. This same young man has also, I hear, been playing the tables pretty high. He is Lord Brecon's first cousin and is, incidentally, heir presumptive to the title, although there is no reason why Brecon, who is young and healthy, should not marry and have a large family.'

'But if he should not be so fortunate, then Mr. Warlingham inherits,' Lord Vulcan said drily.

'Exactly,' Lord Milborne agreed.

'What does he look like?' Caroline asked.

'I am afraid I have not the pleasure of his acquaintance,' Lord Milborne replied, with a smile. 'I remember his father. He was a dark-countenanced fellow with a violent temper and a perpetual attack of gout which kept him in a state of unceasing fury, but I have not met his son. I shouldn't be surprised if he isn't as anxious to avoid me as I him.'

'You really think that it was he who murdered Mr. Rosenberg, and tried to get Lord Brecon arrested for it?' Caroline asked breathlessly.

'Now, Caroline, you mustn't put words into my mouth,'

Lord Milborne replied. 'All I have said is that I have my suspicions and further than that I will not commit myself.'

'Do not plague his lordship, Caroline,' Lord Vulcan said. 'I cannot think what has happened to your mother. Run upstairs and see if you can find her.'

Caroline did as she was bid; but when the Marchioness, who had been delayed by superintending the packing, had gone downstairs, Caroline went to her own bedroom and stood for a long time looking over the sea.

Lord Brecon was in danger. She had saved him once, for if he had not had an alibi that night, it would have been hard for him to prove that he had not had a hand in the murdering of Isaac Rosenberg; and worse still, had she not hurried him away from the clearing and Sir Montagu and the grooms had found him, they would have found also the false note and the letters which the lawyer had come to sell.

It would then have been well nigh impossible to prove his innocence, and Mr. Gervase Warlingham could have had high hopes of succeeding to the title and the family estates.

Should she warn Lord Brecon, she wondered, that there might be more attempts of the same sort in the future? Yet how could she write such a letter and how indeed could she explain such intimate knowledge of his affairs without revealing her own identity and betraying Lord Milborne's confidence? What a tangle it appeared to be!

Caroline sighed. Yet it was difficult to forget Lord Brecon's face. How handsome he was, how strong! As Lord Milborne had said, there was an air about him which made him appear different and outstanding from all other men. But what good would his strength be against treachery? Even the strongest man could be laid low by a vile intriguer who would stoop to the very lowest crime to gain his own ends.

'I must do something,' Caroline said to herself, but what it was to be she had no idea.

Yet her thoughts were continually of Lord Brecon. Every moment when she was not actively engaged with helping her father and mother or talking with Lord Milborne she found herself thinking of him and the danger in which he stood. More than once she played with the idea of confessing to Lord Milborne the part she had played on the night of the murder, but she realised that nothing would be gained by this. Lord Brecon's name was cleared and all she would do would be to reveal her own folly in trusting so obvious an outsider as Sir Montagu Reversby.

As she lay awake that night, restless as the waves she could hear beating below the cliffs, Caroline wished that she could tell someone of her difficulties and ask advice. She was honest enough to confess to herself that she was afraid of going back to London. She had no desire to meet Sir Montagu again; she was more anxious, too, than she was ready to admit to Mrs. Edgmont about the rumours that were being spread about her.

It was difficult to know what Sir Montagu would say. He was not likely to tell the whole truth, for it would make him look a fool to have got so far and then to have lost his prey just at the moment of capture. It would be to invite a gale of laughter at his expense. Yet at the same time he could harm her. Caroline was well aware of that, and to have driven alone with him after dinner was in itself an indiscretion which would draw upon her head the most violent censure of Society.

'I was a fool!' Caroline said aloud in the darkness, and yet she could not entirely regret what she had done.

Had she never gone to *The Dog and Duck* she would never have met Lord Brecon. It was impossible to think of him without remembering his kiss; and though she blushed in the darkness as she thought of it, it was painful to remember that he had kissed Zara, that strange, exotic tamer of tigers, as easily and with, it seemed to Caroline looking back, as much enthusiasm. With his looks and position and estates there must be dozens, if not hundreds of women in his life and it was bitter to recall that he said they would not meet again.

Caroline knew both jealousy and misery that night and there were dark lines under her eyes the following morning when she said good-bye to her father and mother before they drove off to Dover, but they attributed both that and her listlessness to her sadness at their departure.

'Try to be good, Caroline,' Lady Vulcan said, drawing her daughter aside from the hall into the morning-room. 'For I am troubled at leaving you, my dearest.'

'Do not fret, Mama,' Caroline said. 'Go away, enjoy yourself, and get really well. If you worry, the whole journey will be for nothing and Papa is looking forward to it so much.'

'I know he is,' Lady Vulcan said softly.

In her feather-trimmed bonnet she looked so young and

57

lovely that it was difficult to believe that she was the mother of a girl of seventeen. At thirty-six Serena Vulcan was in the height of her beauty. Her face always calm and lovely had become even more radiant with the happiness of the passing years. Caroline, regarding her perhaps for the first time as a woman rather than as her mother, could understand her father's overwhelming love and pride in his wife.

'Have a lovely time, Mama,' she said impulsively; 'you deserve it. And don't think of me at all. I shall come to no harm.'

'I wish I could be sure of that,' Lady Vulcan said anxiously. 'You are so sweet, Caroline, but so like your father.'

'And what is wrong with that?' Caroline asked, her eyes beginning to twinkle.

'What are good points in a man are not so admirable in a woman,' her mother answered. 'When your father wants something, his determination would overpower an army of opposition, and you are the same. Women should be soft and gentle and pliable—not brave, determined, courageous and daring.'

'Am I all those things?' Caroline asked.

'Yes, all of them,' Lady Vulcan sighed. 'I might add impetuous and impulsive as well.'

'Mama, you are being most unfair,' Caroline protested.

'Am I, darling? To make me happy you must promise me that while I am away you will try to be all woman. After all, there must be some of me in you somewhere.'

Caroline gave a little shout of laughter.

'Lud, Mama, you are wonderful! I will be demure and frail and I will try to fall in love with someone just as domineering as Papa.'

'You will be lucky if you find anyone half as splendid as your father,' Lady Vulcan said seriously; and then, as Caroline bent forward to kiss her, they heard Lord Vulcan's voice from the hall.

'Serena! Are you ready?'

'It is time to go,' Lady Vulcan said. 'Goodbye, darling, please remember all I have told you.'

'I will be really feminine, Mama,' Caroline dimpled, then stood on the top of the grey stone steps to wave good-bye as the big claret-coloured coach sped away down the drive.

Mrs. Edgmont, standing beside her, wiped her eyes.

'Oh, I do hope they are quite safe,' she said. 'I would not

venture in one of those smoky steamers for a hundred guineas.'

'Oh, I would love it,' Caroline exclaimed. 'You must be modish and move in the times, Cousin Debby. This is 1821, not the Middle Ages.' Then as if she thought her words had been too scornful she slipped her arm through the older woman's and added: 'Come and make plans. Let us repair to the breakfast-room. It is nice and cosy there and we will ring for some chocolate. I ate no breakfast, I was so distraught at the thought of Mama and Papa leaving us.'

'Indeed, I wish they had not gone,' Cousin Debby sighed.

Caroline rang for the chocolate and when it came, poured a cup for Mrs. Edgmont and one for herself. She took a sip and then almost dreamily, for she was deep in her own thoughts, asked:

'Have you ever heard of Lord Brecon?'

Mrs. Edgmont put down her cup with a little clatter.

'How strange that you should ask me that, Caroline. Why, only yesterday morning by the same post as I had the letter from your godmother I received one from Brecon Castle.'

'From Brecon Castle!' Caroline exclaimed, sitting bolt upright in her chair. 'Cousin Debby, whom do you know at Brecon Castle?'

'I was just about to tell you, dear. I have the letter somewhere in my reticule.'

She searched in her bag of blue velvet, taking so long in finding the envelope that Caroline could have cried out with impatience.

'Ah, here it is,' Mrs. Edgmont exclaimed at last. 'Now let me see. Yes, I was not mistaken. It is from Brecon Castle, Cuckhurst, Kent.'

'Cuckhurst!' Caroline exclaimed. 'Is that the name of the village?'

'It must be,' Mrs. Edgmont replied.

'That is strange, too . . .' Caroline began, and then checked herself. 'Go on, tell me about the letter and whom it is from.'

'It comes from a very old friend of mine,' Mrs. Edgmont replied; 'actually she is a connection of my husband's. A dear woman and of course, a gentlewoman by birth called Fanny Hall. She is older than I am, but no one offered for her, and when her father died she was left in very

59

straitened circumstances. She was a governess for some time and then a year ago she became companion, so she tells me, to the Dowager Lady Brecon.'

'What else does she say?' Caroline asked eagerly.

'She writes to me,' Mrs. Edgmont continued, 'because she has decided to give up the post. By great good fortune her brother, who went out to India with the East India Company, has come home with quite a considerable fortune. He wants dear Fanny to keep house for him; and so, after many years of working in other people's homes, she will have the happiness of tending one of her own.'

'Did she tell you anything about Brecon Castle and the people in it?' Caroline asked.

'Yes, she writes a great deal of the Dowager,' Mrs. Edgmont replied. 'She is devoted to her and very sorry to leave her; but she adds that there are other people in the house on whom she will be pleased to turn her back. She says: *"I will not tire you with details, my dearest Debby, it is sufficient to say that nowadays People obtain Positions of Trust and Responsibility which they abuse to the fullest extent—People who, because of their Behaviour, are not entitled to style themselves Ladies".*'

'Something or somebody has upset her,' Caroline said with a smile.

'Of course, dear Fanny is too discreet to mention any names,' Mrs. Edgmont said.

'Which makes the letter very dull,' Caroline commented.

'Oh, I don't think so, dear. Let me see if she says anything else. Yes, *"The servants come and go continually and who shall blame them under the Circumstances?"* '

'What circumstances?' Caroline asked.

'She does not relate them, dear,' Mrs. Edgmont replied, scanning the closely written pages.

'How truly maddening!' Caroline complained. 'Is there nothing else?'

'No, just that she is sorry to leave and wonders if I could find anyone to take her place,' Mrs. Edgmont replied.

'What is that?' Caroline asked quickly.

'She wants me to recommend a new companion for the Dowager,' Mrs. Edgmont answered. 'Now, let me think. Is there anyone I would consider suitable? It is a pity that that nice daughter of your father's attorney is not available. She was looking for a position of the same sort last year, I remember, but I believe she is perfectly satisfied where she is at the moment.'

Caroline got to her feet.

'Wait a minute, Cousin Debby,' she said. 'I have an idea. . . . Yes, a very good idea . . . in fact, I have the very person for you.'

'Indeed, Caroline, and who might that be?'

'Er . . . there . . . there was a girl at school with me. She was nice and I was very fond of her.'

'I thought you disliked everyone at Madame d'Alber's Academy,' Mrs. Edgmont said suspiciously. 'You were only there three months, Caroline, and you came home vowing that you would not set foot inside it again, declaring that everyone was unkind to you.'

'No, no, there were exceptions. I dare say I said that, but I was so frightened that Mama would insist that I should go back for a further term. I could not have borne it, Cousin Debby. Most of the girls were prim little hypocrites—I hated them! But there was one there, no two, of whom I was very fond, and this particular girl of whom I speak is the very person to be companion to the Dowager Lady Brecon.'

'Is she of good breeding, Caroline?'

'Oh, very good,' Caroline answered. 'I assure you that she comes of a most distinguished family. She is well-educated and of great sensibility. Please recommend her, Cousin Debby. I should be so glad if you would.'

'Well, of course, Caroline, if she is a friend of yours and in need of employment, I will do my best. Where is she living at the moment?'

Caroline took a deep breath.

'Now that is the strangest thing, Cousin Debby. There was another girl at school with me, who was in fact my only friend . . . with the exception of course of this girl of whom we are speaking . . . and Harriet, for that is my other friend's name, lived at Cuckhurst; I have only just recalled it, but her father was the Vicar of Cuckhurst and her fees at the school had been paid through the kindness of his patron. I never bothered to find out who the patron was, but now I am sure it must have been the Dowager Lady Brecon or even Lord Brecon himself.'

'But what has your friend to do with this other girl?' Mrs. Edgmont asked, bewildered.

'The girl I wish you to recommend is living at the moment with Harriet at Cuckhurst,' Caroline exclaimed triumphantly.

'I understand; at least I think I do,' Mrs. Edgmont said. 'It all seems somewhat of a tangle.'

'Not really, Cousin Debby. All I beg is that you will be vastly obliging and write at once to your friend Fanny saying that you are recommending a very suitable person for the position, while I will write to my friend and tell her of your kind recommendation.' Caroline paused and then added breathlessly, 'And yes, I know—I will drive over and stay the night with Harriet and then I can take your recommendation in person.'

'Really, Caroline, I cannot think such extreme measures are necessary,' Mrs. Edgmont said. 'I am sure the Vicar of Cuckhurst would be embarrassed by your visit and the letter can quite easily go by post.'

'But I would love to see Harriet again, I swear I would,' Caroline said. 'Pray do not put obstacles in my way, Cousin Debby. It is all settled and you will be doing a real kindness.'

'Well, I do not know what to think,' Mrs. Edgmont said. 'I wonder, Caroline, if I really ought to recommend someone I have not actually met. It is all very well for you to speak for the girl, but what does anybody else know of her—your mother for instance?'

'Oh, but Mama knows her,' Caroline said hastily. 'She knows her well and likes her very much.'

Mrs. Edgmont smiled.

'That, dear, is different. Why didn't you say so at the beginning?' Then she added: 'Perhaps it would be wise to write to your mother on the matter and ask her for a personal letter of recommendation.'

'Cousin Debby, how could we wait for that?' Caroline asked in dismay. 'Why, the position might be filled a thousand times over before Mama could reply.'

'Yes, yes, of course! Well, if you assure me that your mother knows this girl. Has she stayed here?'

'Yes, of course she has,' Caroline said, 'and both Mama and Papa are devoted to her, in fact they treat her like one of the family—she might be their own daughter. Now sit down and write to your dearest Fanny while I send a groom off to tell Harriet I am arriving on a visit.'

'Do you wish me to accompany you, dear?'

'Oh no,' Caroline replied. 'I will take Maria with me. They might not have room for more than one guest.'

'Well, it seems a long journey when the post could easily

take the letter' Mrs. Edgmont said. 'But if it gives you so much pleasure, Caroline dear, I dare say there is no harm in it.'

Caroline hurried towards the door.

'Write the letter now,' she pleaded. 'Please, Cousin Debby.'

'Yes, of course, at once,' Mrs. Edgmont said, feeling for her lorgnette. Then, as Caroline had almost shut the door after her, she gave a little cry. 'Caroline! Caroline!'

'What is it?'

'You have omitted to tell me the girl's name.'

'Oh, how silly of me,' Caroline said. 'It is Caroline Fry.'

'Why, she has the same name as you,' Mrs. Edgmont said.

'Yes, isn't it strange?' Caroline answered; 'but then I have always said that mine was a monstrously common name.'

Caroline sped upstairs to her own room where she penned a letter to Harriet Wantage. Then having stuck a wafer on the envelope, she carried the note with her own hands to the stable yard.

'What can Oi do for ye, m'lady?' old Harry asked.

'I want a groom to take this at once to Cuckhurst,' Caroline said. 'It is for the Vicarage; and tell him, Harry, that he is not to wait for an answer.'

'Them seem queer instructions to Oi, m'lady. 'Tis usual for a groom who has travelled all that distance to have his glass o' ale and put his horse in the stable for a rest.'

'I care little what is usual,' Caroline said. 'You are to tell the messenger, Harry, that he is to leave the letter and turn about forthwith. Here's half a guinea. Tell him from me that he can go to the nearest inn and get his ale, but he is not to wait at the Vicarage. Is that clear?'

'Very good, m'lady. Oi suppose this one o' them new-fangled ways o' be'aving as ye have learned up in London Town, but blessed if Oi can see the sense on it.'

Leaving the old groom grumbling to himself, Caroline went back to the house. Although he might argue with her, she knew her commands would be carried out and that now she ran no risk of receiving a refusal to the suggestions she had made in her letter to Harriet.

There was a rising sense of excitement within her. The night before she had lain awake worrying, trying to find a way to help Lord Brecon, and now miraculously things were happening. The plan she had in mind was a dangerous one, and yet she believed she could carry it through. Just for a moment she thought of her mother.

'But I am not doing anything wrong,' Caroline argued, 'I am helping someone. I am being kind and unselfish, and besides, in the position of companion I shall certainly not be able to be anything but subdued, well behaved and very, very womanly.'

She had reached her own room by this time and she made a grimace at her reflection in the mirror. She certainly did not look very like a companion. There was something very aristocratic about her lovely face, and something rather wild and untrammelled, too, in the way her red-gold curls danced around her forehead and over her tiny ears. Caroline seized a brush and tried to smooth them down, but they defied her, and after a moment she threw down the brush on the dressing-table and going across to the bedside, pulled the bell rope violently.

It was only a few seconds before she heard Maria's feet come running down the passage. She came quickly into the room.

'Lawks, m'lady, but I thought you were taken ill. The bell rang so violently as almost to startle me out of my skin.'

'Start packing, Maria,' Caroline said.

'Is your ladyship going away?' Maria asked.

'Yes, and I am taking you with me.'

'Oh, m'lady, how glad I am! I have been humiliated at your being maided in London by that stiff-necked old hag at Vulcan House. " 'Tis my place to attend to Lady Caroline," she told me. "I was here before she was born." "If you told me, 'twas before the house was built, I would believe you," I says, and she hated me from that moment, m'lady. 'Twas rude, I grant you, but I couldn't abide her taking you off my hands like that after you had chosen me as your very own maid.'

'Yes, yes, Maria,' Caroline said absently, 'but we are not going to London.'

'For how many nights shall I pack, m'lady?'

Caroline walked across to shut the door which was slightly ajar.

'Listen, Maria,' she said. 'Can you keep a secret?'

'You know I can, m'lady.'

'Will you do me a service then?'

Caroline's tones were grave.

Maria's eyes opened wide, her smiling, chattering mouth was still and solemn. She was silent for a moment and then in a voice quiet and strangely unlike her usual tone, she said:

'I would give my life for you, m'lady. You know that.'

'Thank you, Maria, I know I can trust you,' Caroline said. 'Well, we are going on a journey of vast import. It is to help someone—a man who is in grave danger.'

Maria clasped her hands together.

'Oh, m'lady, 'tis, then . . . a journey of love.'

For a moment Caroline looked startled. She stood very still and there was a sudden loveliness in her face and in the depths of her eyes which had never been there before.

'I believe you are right, Maria,' she said softly. 'It is a journey of love.'

4

Caroline bent forward and looked out of the window of the coach. It was travelling fast, for Lord Vulcan had his coaches specially built for speed and the new roads invented by Macadam made journeying both smooth and swift.

'We shall be there soon,' she said to Maria who was sitting beside her. 'The last milestone said *"Three miles to Cuckhurst"* and we must have done over half that distance by now.'

'Oh, m'lady, I am so frightened,' Maria quivered.

'Try not to be so chicken-hearted, Maria,' Caroline answered. 'It is quite simple, as I have told you. Immediately we arrive I am sending the coach on to Brecon Castle with two letters, one the recommendaton from Mrs. Edgmont, the other from myself asking for an interview. You can travel in the coach until it reaches the drive, then you must get out and walk. You go to the back door, enquire for the housekeeper and present the reference that I have given you. Do not forget that I signed it wth my mother's name, and you had better ask for the position of an under-housemaid.'

'Oh, m'lady, supposing they have a suspicion that the reference is forged?'

'Really, Maria, you are too nonsensical,' Caroline exclaimed. 'Who would imagine any such thing? You promised to help me, Maria, and this is the one way you can do it. You are likely to hear far more in the servants' hall than I am in the dining-room, and if I get the position of companion to Lady Brecon, you can put in a good word for me with the other servants; say that I am continually staying at Mandrake and that Lady Caroline Faye is devoted to me, for indeed I dote upon myself.'

Maria giggled for a moment, and then her face grew serious again.

'I don't know what to think of it all, m'lady, indeed I

66

don't, for 'tis heading for trouble you are, as sure as I'm sitting here.'

'Stop croaking, Maria, and remember that this is no prank—we go to save a man's life.'

'Well, I'll do my best, m'lady, because I promised you I would, but if you asks me——'

Caroline interrupted her with a cry.

'We are arriving, Maria! See, this must be Cuckhurst village. There is the church, and yes . . . that must be the Vicarage. Slip well into your corner, for I have no wish for you to be seen.'

'Oh, m'lady, m'lady——' Maria started, but at that moment the carriage door opened and a footman let down the steps.

Caroline stepped out. As soon as she reached the ground, she turned and spoke to the coachman on the box.

'Boddle!' she said in a low voice.

'Yes, m'lday.'

He touched his hat and bent down to hear what she was saying.

'You are to take the two letters I have given you straight to Brecon Castle. You are not to rest there or here in the village. Is that understood? You are to start immediately on the return journey to Mandrake. If you need to put up the horses, do so in the next village or when you get to Maidstone.'

'Aye, m'lady, but——'

But Caroline did not wait to hear his protestations. She knew it was essential to her plan that the servants from Mandrake should not gossip in Cuckhurst. She turned and walked towards the Vicarage. It was a small, grey-gabled stone building set in an untidy, uncared for garden. As she passed up a narrow walk between flower beds, the front door suddenly opened and a girl stood there with a startled expression on her face. She stared at Caroline and then began to run down the path.

'Caroline!' she exclaimed. 'Caroline! But I was not expecting you. You wrote that a Miss Fry was arriving.'

Caroline put out her hand and drew the girl close to her.

'Listen, Harriet,' she said quickly, her voice hardly above a whisper. 'Is your father within?'

'Yes, Caroline, I believe so, but——'

'Then hear me! He is on no account to know who I am. *I* am Miss Fry. Do you understand, Harriet? I am Caroline Fry, who was at school with you.'

'But, Caroline, I fail to understand. What does——'

'I will explain everything to you later,' Caroline interrupted. 'Just remember for the moment that I am Caroline Fry, the girl you were expecting. Do you hear me?'

'Yes, Caroline, and I will do my best, but 'tis all bewildering. I . . . don't know what to think.'

'Then pray cease thinking,' Caroline answered. 'Do precisely as I tell you, Harriet. It is vastly important, I assure you, or I wouldn't ask you to utter a falsehood. But, please, make no mistake, it is of the greatest moment to me.'

'Then of course I will help you,' Harriet said, and smiling, Caroline bent to kiss her.

She was small in height with a sweet expression and trusting brown eyes, and she might have been pretty except that her hair was badly arranged and her dress of striped cambric was ill-fitted and outmoded.

Caroline remembered that at school Harriet had always been kindly and unselfish, eager to help other people and grateful for any small favours the richer and more distinguished pupils would condescend to show her. She hoped that Harriet would also be staunch and reliable, but as she looked down into her brown eyes wide with astonishment and at the vulnerability of her thin, rather pinched little face, Caroline was half afraid.

'Shall we go into the house, Harriet?' she asked, as her hostess, bemused and astonished over what she had heard, seemed to have forgotten her duties.

'Oh, but of course, be pleased to enter, Caroline,' Harriet said, a wave of colour sweeping up her face at the thought of her negligence.

They stepped through the stone porch into the hall of the Vicarage. It was oak panelled, the ceiling was dark with age and mildewy with damp, and everywhere there were signs of poverty. The rugs were threadbare, the chair by the empty fireplace was sadly in need of being upholstered and the other furniture was in no better condition.

Caroline pulled off her gloves and waited for Harriet to show her the drawing-room, but at that moment a door opened and the Vicar came into the hall. Elderly and red-faced, Adolphus Wantage was both a snob and a bully. He had never wished to be ordained to Holy Orders, but as the youngest son of a none too prosperous country squire it was the only career open to him.

He had but one real passion in life and that was hunting. The two horses which he kept in his stables were well fed and well groomed, however meagrely his household fared in consequence. He came into the hall at a leisurely pace, not putting himself out unduly to greet a guest whose position in life was such a lowly one as Miss Fry's; but when he saw Caroline, her beauty and her deportment instinctively made him bow a little deeper than he would have done under ordinary circumstances.

'I must bid you welcome, Miss Fry,' he said in a deep, rather hoarse voice which sounded as if he suffered from a perpetual cold in the head.

Caroline dropped him a curtsey.

'Thank you, sir. It is exceeding kind of you to offer me your hospitality.'

'Harriet tells me that you have come from Mandrake. Surely the coach is not returning forthwith. I have made arrangements to put them up in the stables for a few hours at least.'

'How exceeding kind of you, Reverend Sir,' Caroline replied, 'but by Lord Vulcan's orders they must be back to Mandrake as swiftly as possible.'

'A pity! A pity!' the Vicar exclaimed. 'I would not like his lordship to think we could not accommodate his coach and servants. You left his lordship well, I hope?'

'Very well,' Caroline answered, and realising by the glint in the Vicar's eye that he was interested in the doings of nobility, she added: 'Lady Caroline Faye sent her love to Harriet and her best respects to you, sir.'

'Indeed! Indeed!' the Vicar said. 'Harriet was at school with her I believe.'

'Yes, sir, and she often speaks of Harriet and swears she was the nicest girl in the whole Academy.'

Harriet blushed, but the Vicar looked at his daughter with distaste.

'Her grand friends pay little attention to her,' he said in a grumbling voice. 'Although it is not surprising when she is dull-witted and seldom makes the best of her appearance. Look at Miss Fry, Harriet! Why do you not furnish yourself with a driving dress and hat of such distinction? It is not impossible, surely, for Miss Fry, as we know, has her living to make, and so cannot be riotously extravagant.'

'Oh, sir, you flatter me,' she said, throwing the Vicar a languishing glance. 'It is but a simple little garment that I made myself. You must allow me to assist Harriet in the choice of her wardrobe. She always looked charming at school.'

'And well she might,' the Vicar replied, 'for the Dowager Lady Brecon paid both for Harriet's schooling and her gowns while she was being educated. Now things are different and Harriet has to economise, as we all have. But I must not bore you with these squalid details of our daily existence.'

'You would never do that, sir,' Caroline answered swiftly, 'but pray speak to me of the Dowager Lady Brecon, for I expect Harriet has told you that I am to apply for the post of companion to her ladyship.'

'You will find her, as might be expected, a true lady of quality,' the Vicar replied pompously, but Harriet interrupted quickly.

'Oh, Caroline, she is so sweet, so gentle, so gracious!'

'You have indeed reassured me,' Caroline said. 'I only pray that my application will be successful.'

'Indeed we must hope so,' the Vicar said; 'and if you do go into residence at Brecon Castle, perhaps you can contrive that Harriet is asked there more often than she has been this past year or so. Goodness knows what the stupid chit did to muff her welcome, but she hasn't been invited there half as frequently as I might expect.'

'Oh, Papa, must you tell Caroline things like that?' Harriet said, crimson with mortification.

The Vicar merely looked at her, snorted and turned towards his study.

'I will see you at dinner, Miss Fry,' he said, and Caroline in reply dropped him a little curtsey.

Upstairs, sitting in her bedroom overlooking the garden, she related to the wide-eyed Harriet the real reason for her visit. Caroline had considered carefully whether it was wise to take Harriet into her confidence, but she had decided that it was essential for her to have someone in the neighbourhood to assist her. There were letters for one thing. Mrs. Edgmont must have some address at which she could write to her, otherwise she would become suspicious; and if Harriet was to intercept the postman, as she planned, she must be given a reason for Caroline's disguise.

After thinking it over Caroline decided to tell Harriet everything of what had occurred, save the true reason why she was at *The Dog and Duck* on the night of the murder. It was easy to omit all mention of Sir Montagu and merely say that she had been forced to pull up at the inn owing to trouble with the wheel of her carriage.

Her explanation of her being in the wood was that she went in search of a lap dog which had got lost, and she told Harriet that she had hired a post-chaise to take her back to Mandrake because she was too frightened to return to the inn in case she should be involved in the investigations regarding the dead man.

As it happened, Harriet was not likely to notice any flaws or discrepancies in Caroline's tale. She sat listening with an expression of the utmost astonishment upon her face, her hands clasped together, her mouth a little open, and only when Caroline had finished and had explained the part that she wished Harriet to play in helping her, did her hostess take a deep breath and cry out:

'But, Caroline, 'tis the wildest, most intriguing romance I have ever heard. I can hardly believe 'tis true, and yet, if you say so, then I must believe it; but oh, how can you venture into Brecon Castle after all you have learned? Why, you may be murdered yourself.'

Caroline laughed.

'Nonsense, Harriet. No one has anything to gain from my death! Besides, what would you have me do? Stand aside, say nothing, and let a good man be hanged by such treacherous, dastardly means.'

'If he is a good man,' Harriet said enigmatically.

'What do you mean?' Caroline asked. 'Are you speaking of Lord Brecon?'

Harriet nodded.

'Tell me about him,' Caroline said. 'Tell me everything you know.'

' 'Tis little enough!' Harriet replied. 'I have known him, or course, since I was a child, but he is much older than I. He seemed a very nice boy. He always smiled at me and once, when he was coming back from hunting, he gave me a lift on his horse. His mother has always been kindness itself and because Mama was a very, very distant cousin of hers, she sent me, as you know, to Madame d'Alber's Academy.'

'Yes . . . Yes,' Caroline said. 'Go on.'

'Well, Lord Brecon—his intimates call him Vane—was at Eton when I was a little girl and afterwards he went up to Oxford. Everyone liked him around here although they only saw him in the holidays. Papa liked him too and used to say what charming manners he had, what a good seat he had on a horse and how well he went to hounds. They all hoped that, when he was old enough, he would take over the Mastership and then . . . well, then he altered.'

'Altered?' Caroline repeated. 'In what way?'

' 'Tis hard to explain.' Harriet answered. 'You see, I have not been asked to Brecon Castle very often since I left school; it angers Papa, but really there is no reason why they should invite me. I am too young to be friends with Lord Brecon—and besides he has many friends of his own who certainly have nothing in common with the local Vicar's daughter—and Lady Brecon is bedridden. She never leaves her bedchamber.'

'I had no idea of that,' Caroline exclaimed.

'Oh, did I not tell you?' Harriet said. 'I suppose it never occurred to me. She has been ailing for years. She never goes out or sees anyone. She just lies in her room with her books and her birds. They are the only things which interest her except her son. She adores him.'

'You were saying that he had altered,' Caroline reminded her. 'Continue, Harriet.'

'It is so difficult to put into words,' Harriet said, knitting her brows. 'Everyone talks about it in a sort of way, but there is nothing that they can actually say, if you understand what I mean. It began—this alteration—after he was twenty-five and took over the management of all his estates and wealth himself—there were trustees before that; I don't know who they were, but Papa could tell you.'

'That is immaterial,' Caroline muttered.

'At twenty-five Lord Brecon became his own master,' Harriet continued. 'From that moment—so they say—he seemed a changed person. He became wild and reckless. He was always risking his life in the most idiotic ways; for instance, they had a steeplechase blindfolded one night through the Park, along the river bank and across the Common, which is above five miles up the road. There are quarries there and it is very broken ground, and Papa says it is a miracle that no one was killed, although one rider broke his back and another his collarbone.'

'What else did he do?' Caroline enquired.

'Some of the things Father will not mention in front of me, but I hear that his friends changed,' Harriet said. 'All kinds of strange people were asked to the Castle who had never been there before. These were not only raffish Society from London, but men and women of other classes

72

too. I think Papa must have protested to Lord Brecon on one occasion when they had a rout at the Castle which lasted all through Saturday night and continued until after midday on Sunday when the villagers were going to Church. I don't know what happened, because Papa would never speak of it for he was so angry, but I believe Lord Brecon was very autocratic and told him to mind his own business. Anyway after that Papa has always been against him, saying that he will come to a bad end, that he will break his neck or end in prison.'

Caroline gave a little exclamation.

'The village gossip about him too,' Harriet continued, 'and being the Vicar's daughter I hear them. The old people shake their heads and seem worried. You know how, when they have lived on an estate all their lives, they consider themselves part of the family. They are always talking about Lord Brecon more or less under their breath. There is nothing exactly that one can get hold of, it is just a feeling that things are wrong and getting worse. Oh, Caroline, what a dolt you must think me, but I vow I cannot explain it better than that.'

Harriet threw out her hands with a little gesture of helplessness, and Caroline bent forward and kissed her.

'You explained it exceeding well,' she said, 'and it is indeed helpful.'

She rose from the bed on which she had been sitting and walked to the window.

'I have a feeling,' she said, 'that I shall be able to help Lord Brecon.'

'Oh, Caroline, I hope so,' Harriet said, 'but at the same time I am afraid because you are going to the Castle. It is a strange place and there are rumours about it too. There are supposed to be ghosts there, and none of the villagers will go anywhere near it after dark. They say they have heard wild, unearthly shrieks coming from the old towers.'

'I do not credit there are such things as ghosts,' Caroline said scornfully. 'Tell me, what was the last Lord Brecon like?'

'I have no idea,' Harriet replied. 'He died when I was quite tiny—sometimes I think there was a mystery about him too. People seem curiously reluctant to talk about him, and if I question Papa, he always changes the subject and talks about the Dowager Lady Brecon. She is, in truth, a lovely person, with nothing sinister or strange about her, but it just seems as if she is hardly living in this world.'

73

Caroline gave a little sigh of impatience.

'It sounds a sorry tangle to me,' she said, 'but at the same time I want above all things to stay at Brecon Castle. Oh, Harriet, suppose I fail to obtain the position.'

She looked across the room at the clock on the mantelpiece.

'It is four o'clock,' she said. 'One thing is certain and that is that Maria must have been accepted, otherwise she would have returned here as I instructed her.'

'If she has been fortunate, perhaps you will be fortunate too, dear Caroline,' Harriet said. 'It is a good omen. But oh, I am frightened for you. I wish you weren't set on this dangerous pretence.'

'No harm can come to me, whatever happens,' Caroline said. 'That is so long as we keep Cousin Debby from being suspicious. You must meet the postman every day, Harriet. It would be a catastrophe if your father saw letters addressed to me arriving here and found out who I really am.'

'Let us hope he will never do that,' Harriet cried in alarm, 'for although he would not be angry with you, he would half kill me for lying to him. Oh, Caroline, when you told him you had made your dress yourself, I nearly laughed out loud. It is so like a man not to recognise it as the most elegant and expensive gown which must ever have come from Bond Street.'

'Pray Heaven no one else guessed it either,' Caroline said. 'I told Maria to pack all the most dowdy and drab dresses I possess and I spent hours taking the feathers and ribbons out of my bonnets to make them look less modish, but even so I am afraid I don't look a depressed gentlewoman sadly in need of a salary.'

'Indeed you don't,' Harriet giggled, 'but after all you can always say that Lady Caroline Faye, who is so devoted to you, presented you with her cast-off gowns.'

Caroline clapped her hands.

'Bravo, Harriet, that is a brilliant idea. We shall make an intriguer of you yet; and what is more, I promise you one thing—when this subterfuge is at an end, I will buy you the most lovely gown that can be procured in the whole of London, and you can have any of my dresses that may please you.'

'Oh, Caroline, can I really?'

Harriet sighed in ecstasy, then added:

'But what is the use? I see no one here from one year's end to another. I housekeep and sew for Papa and everything I do for him seems to irritate him the more. He wanted a son, you see, Caroline, and he has no liking for a dutiful, but very dull daughter.'

'Poor Harriet, don't let it make you miserable,' Caroline said. 'We will find you a husband and then you shall forget all this drudgery.'

'Well, he will have to be blind in both eyes and doubtless so halt and decrepit that no one else will accept his offer,' Harriet said; and then, as Caroline would have argued with her, she sprang to her feet with a little cry.

'Look!' she said. 'Look who is coming down the road!'

Caroline turned hastily to the window.

'I can only see a groom,' she said in a voice of disappointment.

Somehow for one moment she had expected to see someone very different.

'It is a groom,' Harriet agreed, 'but look at his livery.'

'Purple with crimson facings,' Caroline said. 'Are those the Brecon colours?'

'They are indeed,' Harriet answered. 'The groom is callling here. See for yourself.'

The two girls watched while the man dismounted, tethered his horse and walked up the path to the front door, a letter in his hand. Harriet ran downstairs and was breathless when she reached the bedroom and held it out to Caroline.

' 'Tis for you,' she said.

Caroline looked down for a moment at the letter and then slowly because her fingers trembled, she opened the envelope. She read it quickly and flung her arms round Harriet.

'Her ladyship will see me,' she cried. 'She will see me tomorrow at three o'clock. Oh, Harriet, the first step has been taken. The curtain is rising on the most thrilling and exciting drama.'

Caroline was too excited to sleep much that night, and even if she had not been kept awake by her own thoughts, she might well have lacked sleep through worrying over Harriet.

It was obvious that the girl's home-life at the Vicarage was one of serfdom and misery. She had been right in saying that her father was irritated with her, for never at any moment was she free from his nagging and fault-finding.

Dinner had been a simple, but well-cooked meal which Caroline had enjoyed. She was seldom fussy about what she ate; but the Vicar, while eating everything set in front of him and swilling it down with several pints of claret, had complained the entire time about the cooking, the dishes selected and the way in which they were served.

'I must apologise, Miss Fry,' he said more than once, 'but you see before you a man who is sadly neglected. It was God's will that my poor wife should be taken from me; but I had hoped that my daughter, my only child, would try in some trifling way to take her place! But Harriet has no initiative, no sense, and is indeed but a poor housewife, and it will be my fate—for I see that no man with his wits about him is likely to offer for her—to have her permanently on my hands until my dying day.'

Caroline would have liked to throw her plate at him and tell him exactly what she thought of him, for his continual grumbling amounted almost to a persecution of Harriet; instead she could only cast her eyes down demurely and say that she hoped Harriet would improve as she grew older and that she would do her best to help her.

It was not easy for Caroline, who was used to expressing her opinion forcibly on every possible occasion, to hold herself in check, but she said what she thought in no uncertain terms when she and Harriet went up to bed.

'Does he always berate you in such a way?' she enquired angrily.

'Who, Papa?' Harriet asked. 'Oh, he is more polite since you are here. Most times he boxes my ears and once he threw a dish of stewed eels straight at me. It scalded my arms most terribly and I bore the marks for weeks.'

'He is a brute,' Caroline said. 'I will rescue you somehow, Harriet, but first of all I have got to rescue Lord Brecon.'

Harriet, who had tears in her eyes, gave a little unsteady laugh.

'Why, Caroline, you are only a female and yet you talk as if you had the determination and strength of ninety men rolled into one.'

'At times I believe I have,' Caroline answered. 'I feel like quoting my mother's funny old maid, Eudora. She always says things in such a solemn voice which makes them sound as if they were bits out of the Bible; but more than once I have heard her say, "If the cause is right, strength will be given you." That is what I believe now, Harriet.'

'And I hope your faith will be rewarded,' Harriet answered, 'especially where I am concerned.'

She bent to kiss Caroline and then the Vicar's voice boomed up the stairs, making them both jump.

'Harriet, where is my candle? How often have I to tell you that I want my candle left at the foot of the stairs? Come down and find it for me this instant, you cork-brained idiot.'

'I'm sorry, Papa . . . I'm coming . . . I am indeed sorry,' Harriet cried, and rushed from Caroline's room, shutting the door behind her.

Poor little Harriet! The sweetness in her face and in her eyes reminded Caroline of the wistful expression of the spaniels at home at Mandrake. She curled down in the bed, wishing for the moment that she was safe at home with the sound of the waves in her ears and the gentle peace and security of Mandrake sheltering her. Then she thought of the morrow and her heart beat a little faster as a feeling of excitement rose within her. Tomorrow she would see Lord Brecon again. Harriet had said he was called Vane. Caroline whispered the name to herself.

After breakfast the following morning, while Harriet had innumerable household duties to do, Caroline said she would take a walk. Harriet had told her that at the far end of the village she could see Brecon Castle from the road and she imagined that this must be where the crowds came who, Lord Brecon had told her, gaped at the Norman towers.

It was a sunny, warm morning and Caroline wore a straw bonnet trimmed with bunches of blue ribbon to match her white batiste frock which had a bodice of blue silk ornamented with white fringe. Then as she left the house she put up a sunshade, intending it to be less of a shelter from the sun than a protection against curious eyes.

There was not much likelihood of anyone recognising Lady Caroline Faye in this part of the world, she thought; but at the same time she was anxious to take no chances. It was always possible that a coach or phaeton passing along the road might contain some of her friends; but once she was established in Brecon Castle there would be little need for her to venture outside the grounds.

She walked down the village street, seeing only a few women cleaning out their cottages and an ancient man with a long white beard seated on a bench outside *The Pig and Whistle*. Caroline guessed that he was the oldest inhabitant, for every village seemed to have one, and wondered, if she got into conversation with him, whether he would tell her anything interesting about Brecon Castle and its inhabitants. She was almost tempted to try this, but decided it might draw local attention to herself, so she walked on demurely until, as Harriet had told her she would, she came to the great iron gates leading to the Castle.

They were very big and were flanked on either side by pillars which were surmounted by two huge armorial lions holding shields. Beyond the gates was a wall enclosing the park, but after Caroline had walked some way the wall ceased and was replaced by a hedge which ran beside a little stream. The hedge was low and another fifty yards brought Caroline to a place where she could see the Castle in all its majesty.

She was not surprised, as she looked at it, that the people came from a long distance to view such a sight. Two great Norman towers were silhouetted against the sky, and on one of them stood a flagpole, the flag, crimson and purple, fluttering out in the morning breeze.

The Castle was very large and it was plain to see that, while this side was of Norman architecture in keeping with the two towers, there were, half hidden by some trees, later additions built, it is true, of grey stone, but of a very different design. The trees made a background for the Castle itself, and it stood partially surrounded by a moat which widened out on the north side to a large lake. There were swans passing to and fro beneath an archway and to Caroline's surprise they were all black. It struck a note which was faintly ominous; indeed the whole building had a rather dark and overshadowed air.

Perhaps it was the ivy twining its way over the towers, perhaps the towers themselves, solid and defiant with their arrow-slits, giving an appearance of grim strength in their breadth and height. Perhaps it was the windows of the other parts of the Castle which had not yet caught the sunlight and appeared like dark, watchful eyes in the grey surrounding stone.

Whatever it was, the whole picture was illogically and inexplicably sinister, and unaccountably Caroline felt herself shiver. This was not a happy house, she was sure of that. It was magnificent and grand in a cold, autocratic manner, but it was without the soft mellowness of weather-beaten stone and the convivial warmth which seemed to emanate from other houses, as for instance, from Mandrake, her own home, and Sale Park, Lord Milborne's lovely residence.

She stood looking at the Castle for a long time and found herself thinking of Lord Brecon as she had last seen him—his eyes looking down into hers, his lips seeking her mouth. Once again she could feel that kiss searing itself into her consciousness so that she could never forget it, and could recall again and yet again the sudden leaping of her heart within her breast, the quick intake of her breath. . . .

With an effort Caroline returned to the present and her view of the Castle, and became aware that quite close to her, drawn up on the side of the stream which acted as a boundary to the park, was a caravan. She glanced at it casually, thinking it must belong to gipsies. But the caravan held her interest, being rather more ornate than those used by the ordinary gipsy tribes. It was carved and painted in scarlet and yellow, while its occupants, a woman, a boy and two other children, who were sitting round a fire, seemed surprisingly clean.

Caroline looked at them without much curiosity and after staring once again at the Castle was just about to retrace her steps towards the Vicarage when she heard a noise. She looked round and saw coming down the dusty highway a man with a large dog. It was the dog which attracted Caroline's attention, for it darted ferociously at a small fox-hound puppy which emerged from one of the cottages, and without warning bit it fiercely so that the puppy, yelping with pain, rushed back into the cottage from which it had come.

The aggressive dog was large and of a breed which Caroline did not recognise save that she thought it might be in part a mastiff. To her surpise the man with it seemed quite unperturbed by the dog's savagery; in fact he was laughing as he came marching on towards Caroline.

He was a strange sight, dressed in rusty, dingy black with an old-fashioned full-skirted coat which hung nearly to his knees and an outmoded three-cornered hat on his grey wig. The lace hanging over his large hands, which swung at his sides, was dirty and as he drew nearer, Caroline saw that his back was humped.

Feeling now that neither the man nor his dog were desirable acquaintances, Caroline stepped further on to the side of the road, holding up her sunshade to shield her face. But even as she did so, she saw that a little girl who had been sitting round the fire by the caravan was throwing a ball into the air and trying to catch it. She was quite a small child, not more than two or three years old, and the ball, missing the tiny hands reaching out for it, bounced from the ground into the centre of the road.

The child toddled happily after her toy, but even as she reached the roadway, the great dog saw her and with a snarl turned to treat the baby as it had treated the puppy.

There was no time to think, hardly time to act, for the child, intent on finding her ball, had no sense of oncoming danger. She reached for it just as the dog bared its fangs. Caroline heard the dog snarl, heard the cry of someone behind her; then with all her strength she brought her open sunshade down hard on the dog's head, separating him from the child who, astonished and frightened, toppled over in the dust and started to cry.

After that things happened with extreme rapidity. There was a moment's stupefaction on the part of the dog, then his teeth met in the silk and lace of Caroline's sunshade. A woman came rushing across the road and picked up the crying baby, while the hunchback turned to Caroline with almost as much ferociousness as was shown by his dog.

'What do you think you are doing?' he asked, and his voice was harsh and nasal.

'Hush ye, hush ye, my little love,' the woman cried. 'Th' nasty dog won't get ye now. Th' kind lady has saved ye.'

Caroline spoke slowly and with great dignity.

'Sir, you would keep a dog such as that under proper control. It is a danger to all peaceful citizens.'

The hunchback looked at her. He had a huge, bulbous nose and small slit eyes set too closely together.

'When I want advice, I will ask for it,' he replied.

'Do you not realise,' Caroline asked haughtily, 'that your dog might have bitten this poor child most severely, even as it bit that puppy?'

'Children, puppies and for that matter young women, Madam, keep out of my way and my dog's,' the man said coolly. 'Come, Brutus.'

He bent down and took his dog, who was still worrying Caroline's sunshade, by the collar. He dragged him a few feet down the road and then without looking back or doffing his hat walked on, the dog growling in his throat as he went.

Caroline went silent for a moment in sheer astonishment. Never in the whole of her sheltered life had she been spoken to in such a manner. The woman broke in on her thoughts with cries of gratitude.

'Oh, Lady, how can I thank ye! My poor baby. Hush ye, my love. Ye are safe, quite safe. That terrible beast. He would have half killed her. How can I thank ye, Lady? 'Tis impossible.'

'Then please don't try,' Caroline said.

She put out her hand and touched the little girl's cheek. It was soft and warm. The child, her eyes still full of frightened tears, smiled shyly.

'Pwetty lady,' she lisped.

'There was never a truer word,' the mother cried. 'Yes, she's a pretty lady, my love, and a brave 'un.'

'The only risk I incurred was to my sunshade,' Caroline said, and looked down somewhat ruefully at the great jagged tears where the dog's teeth had ripped the silk.

'Why, Mother,' a voice said behind her. ' 'Tis the gentry mort who visited us with his lordship but last week when us were at Sevenoaks.'

Caroline turned swiftly. She recognised the boy who stood there. It was the dark boy with the long, lank hair to whom Lord Brecon had first spoken when they arrived at the menagerie, the boy who had led them to Adam Grimbaldi's caravan and had later gone in search of a post-chaise to take her home to Mandrake.

'But of course I remember you,' she smiled. 'What are you doing here and where is the menagerie?'

'Oh, Lady, 'tis bad fortune we've had,' the woman answered. 'My husband was mauled by one o' Madame Zara's tigers. He was acleaning out its cage when the beast sprang at him. 'Twas terrible ill he was three days. Now th' leech says he will live, but his flesh will take time to knit and it may be a month or so afore we can join Mr. Grimbaldi at St. Bartholomew's Fair.'

'I am indeed sorry,' Caroline commiserated, 'and in the meantime you are camping here.'

'His lordship gave us permission,' the woman said proudly. ' 'Tis a splendid place and useful to have th' stream so close at hand. Gideon picks up an odd shilling in th' village and in th' fields, and Mr. Grimbaldi—Gawd bless him—won't let us starve.' She paused for breath and added with tears in her eyes: 'But if anything had happened to our little Zarina, I wouldn't have known what to do with myself. Named after Madame Zara she is, and the apple of her father's eye.'

'Well, I am glad I could save her,' Caroline said, 'but who is that horrid man with the dog?'

The boy Gideon looked down the road and his expression was fierce.

'The leery cove has but recently come to th' Village, Lady, and the people around here hate him for all they are afeared on him. All Oi can tell yer is that his name be Jason Faken.'

'He is a horrible fellow,' Caroline said. 'I wonder anyone lets him have a house in a nice peaceful village like this. You should tell Lord Brecon about him, for he cannot want his tenants and employees to be treated in such a manner either by the dog or his master.'

'There is indeed some talk o' speaking to his lordship,' the woman said after a moment, 'but 'tis a little awkward, seeing as how Jason Faken has close acquaintance with his lordship's own cousin, Mr. Gervase Warlingham.'

'Oh, has he?' Caroline ejaculated. 'That is very interesting.'

'They tell that he was brought here by Mr. Warlingham,' Gideon went on. 'Th' gentry swell has visited the old geeser twice this past week for Oi've seed him with me own daylights riding down the road to his house.'

Caroline nodded her head. This all seemed to fit in with her preconceived ideas of Jason Faken.

'Well, keep an eye on him,' she said at length, 'for I am sure his lordship would not want anything unpleasant to occur, whether he be a friend of his cousin's or no.'

'Indeed we will do that,' Gideon's mother said, 'and if there is any service I or my family can ever do for ye, Lady, we will do it. Ye have saved my child today, maybe in our humble way we shall one day be able to assist ye in return.'

Caroline smiled.

'Thank you,' she said. 'I may need your help. One never knows.'

She held out her hand to the woman, who bent and kissed her fingers.

'Gawd bless ye for th' fine lady ye are,' she said, and there were tears in her eyes.

Caroline turned and walked slowly back to the Vicarage. She had much to think about and when Harriet exclaimed over her ruined sunshade, she threw it down in a corner saying:

'It was worth it, well worth it.'

But she did not give the bewildered Harriet any explanation of what she meant, and she was strangely silent during luncheon, at which fortunately the Vicar was not present.

'Shall I accompany you to the Castle?' Harriet asked when Caroline went to her bedchamber to tidy herself, and to smooth down her curls to what she hoped was a becoming demureness.

'Thank you, Harriet, but I prefer to be alone,' Caroline answered. 'I want to think, I want to prepare myself so that I have an answer to every question. It will not be easy to act the part of a humble dependent!'

'Not for you, Caroline,' Harriet said with a laugh, 'for I have always thought you very autocratic in some ways.'

'Oh no,' Caroline protested, 'not autocratic.'

'Perhaps that is the wrong word,' Harriet said, 'but you have such presence, such personality, Caroline, that I can't help feeling that anyone would be quite demented who really believed you to be a dependent.'

Caroline looked at herself in the glass. Her eyes were sparkling, the vivid, fiery gold of her hair was in pleasing contrast to the pale fragility of her skin.

'Don't I look like a poor gentlewoman?' she asked.

'Not in the least,' Harriet replied.

Caroline sighed.

'Well, what do I look like?' she questioned.

Harriet hesitated for a moment then she laughed.

'You look, Caroline, like a Lady of Quality in search of adventure,' she said, and for once in her life Harriet Wantage had the last word.

5

A footman flung open the big nail-studded oak door of the Castle and Caroline entered.

'I have called to see her ladyship,' she said in her clear, commanding voice, and an old butler with a pontificial dignity came forward and bowed low.

'Certainly, Madam. What name shall I say?'

'Miss Caroline Fry,' Caroline replied, and then in surprise saw a strange expression cross the butler's face.

For a moment she did not understand what was wrong until he straightened himself, turned away with what could only be described as a disdainful air, and with a gesture of his fat hand motioned foward a flunkey, gorgeous in purple and crimson.

'Show Miss Fry upstairs,' he said sharply.

Caroline suddenly realised that as a mere applicant for a post in the household she was not entitled to the courtesy or attention which would have been hers had the servants known her real identity. She was not certain whether to be angry or amused by the butler's behaviour, but the footman gave her little time for thought.

'This way please, miss,' he said, assuming a jaunty air and looking her over in what seemed to Caroline an appraising and impertinent manner.

He preceded her up the Grand Staircase and Caroline had time to notice the carved and pillared grandeur of the Great Hall and at the same time to be oppressed by the darkness and gloom of its furnishings. The walls were panelled from floor to ceiling and hung with ancient weapons. Suits of armour were displayed at the foot of the stairs and stood at every turn—lifeless sentinels which somehow gave an eerie and unpleasant feeling that one was being watched.

As they reached the first floor, an elderly woman stepped out from the shadows. She had big bones and a

84

gaunt, ugly face which was not unpleasant despite an expression of wary reserve. She wore a silk apron and Caroline judged her to be someone of importance in the domestic household.

'Her ladyship will see Miss Fry,' she said to the footman.

'Sorry, Miss Dorcas,' he answered, 'but Mrs. Miller gave orders that she was to interview the young lady first.'

The maid gave a sniff which Caroline gathered implied both distaste and impatience.

'Her ladyship is waiting,' she said icily, 'and I am here to take Miss Fry along to her.'

Ignoring Caroline, the two servants faced each other angrily.

'Now see here, Miss Dorcas,' the footman said, forgetting himself so far as to set his arms akimbo on his hips. 'You knows as surely as I does that Mrs. Miller gives the orders in this 'ere household. She says to me, she says: "When the young woman comes bring her straight to me, James," and who am I to argue? 'Tis more than me bread and butter's worth.'

'Her ladyship's companion has nothing to do with Mrs. Miller,' Dorcas snapped back.

'That's gammon and you knows it,' the footman said; 'and as far as I'm concerned, I wishes to keep this 'ere job, so into Mrs. Miller she goes, see!'

He walked across the landing and opened a door almost directly opposite where Caroline and Dorcas were standing. He swung it wide as if to usher in Caroline with ceremony; but even as he opened his mouth to speak her name, the words died on his lips, for it was obvious to all three people standing on the landing that Mrs. Miller was not ready to receive anyone.

She was reclining in a comfortable chair in front of the fireplace with her feet on an embroidered stool, her head lolling sideways against a satin cushion. Her mouth was slightly open, her eyes tightly closed, and even as they stood there staring at her she emitted an audible and most unladylike snore.

Caroline had time to note that Mrs. Miller was not unattractive. Her dark hair under a turban of striped gauze was arranged in fashionable curls and her dress, cut very *décolleté*, made no attempt to conceal the charms of her ample bosom. Caroline also perceived the nearly empty decanter of port standing on a small table and guessed, as she intercepted the look which passed between Dorcas and the footman, that it was no unusual occurrence for Mrs. Miller to be discovered at such a disadvantage.

The footman shut the door quietly.

'Your trick, Miss Dorcas,' he grinned, 'but I shall get it when her Majesty awakes if she hears we have seed her like this.'

'I'm not one for telling tales, James,' Dorcas said severely.

The footman smiled, but his bright eyes were on Caroline.

'Good luck, miss,' he said to her. 'Keep your mummer shut.'

Caroline smiled back at him. She felt she really had no alternative; then she followed Dorcas along the passage.

'Take no notice of that cheeky boy,' Dorcas said, 'for 'tis not his fault that things are as they are in this house.'

'Who is Mrs. Miller?' Caroline asked as they reached the end of the long corridor.

'You will find out soon enough,' Dorcas snapped, '. . . if you stay here.'

There was something in her tone which told Caroline that it would not be wise to venture any more questions, and she followed the maid in silence down yet another passage before they stopped in front of a pair of double mahogany doors. Dorcas knocked and a soft voice bade them enter.

Dorcas opened the door. For a moment Caroline was dazzled. The room was light and lovely after the ill-lit passages and the heavy gloom of the Hall and the Grand Staircase. The sun was streaming through two long windows and everywhere there were flowers—big bowls of hot-house blooms whose perfume filled the air. While Caroline was conscious of the fragrance of the flowers, she was also aware of the sound of twittering voices, the rustle of wings, the sudden little squawks and tweet of song birds. Then by the window she perceived two large cages and in them at least a dozen beautiful little green and blue budgerigars swinging on their perches or fluttering against the thin silver bars which kept them imprisoned.

Caroline was so interested in what she saw that it was a moment or two before she became aware that, lying in the far corner of the room in a bed half enclosed in an alcove and draped with pale pink curtains, was the woman she had come to see. She moved towards the bed and was surprised to see that the Dowager Lady Brecon was so young.

She had expected somebody very old, somebody wrinkled and white-haired; but the woman lying in bed had a sweet, unlined face and her fair hair was only touched with grey at the temples.

'Miss Fry to see you, m'lady,' Dorcas said, and pulling forward a hard chair, set it by the bedside.

'Oh, not that chair, Dorcas,' Lady Brecon said softly. 'It is uncomfortable, as well you know. Bring the little padded one. That is better. Will you not sit down, Miss Fry?'

She spoke to Caroline who, remembering her manners, swept her a deep curtsey and said quietly:

'It is very kind of you to see me, Ma'am.'

'It was kind of you to write to me,' Lady Brecon answered. 'Miss Hall unfortunately left yesterday or she would have been here to greet you. She gave me the letter she had received from Mrs. Edgmont and at the same time I received a letter from you, Miss Fry, saying that you were staying at the Vicarage. You know Miss Wantage?'

'Harriet and I were at school together, Ma'am,' Caroline answered.

'Oh, indeed. And you were friends?'

'Yes, great friends,' Caroline answered. 'I am very fond of Harriet.'

'A sweet child,' Lady Brecon said. 'And that reminds me, I have not seen her for some time. It is most remiss, but the days seem to slip by. I read, watch my birds and forget the world outside. It is wrong of me.'

'Oh no, Ma'am, not if you are happy.'

'Happy?' Lady Brecon repeated the word as if it were a question. 'It is many years since I have known happiness, but shall I say I am not discontented? I have chosen this way of life.'

'But, Ma'am, surely it is very dull for you,' Caroline said. 'You are not yet old and there are so many things that you might find of interest to do, to see, to hear.'

Lady Brecon laughed.

'Would you tempt me from my chosen path? Most companions prefer someone who is bedridden, who will not harry them from place to place and find fault. But I was forgetting, you are very young. Perhaps you will find it too quiet here.'

'Oh no, Ma'am. I want beyond all things to stay at Brecon Castle—that is if your ladyship will have me.'

'Mrs. Edgmont speaks very highly of you,' Lady Brecon said, 'but to tell the truth I am not very interested in references. I shall like to look at your pretty face, for I like pretty things. That is why this room is full of flowers and I love my birds. Do you not think they are pretty?'

'They are lovely, Ma'am,' Caroline exclaimed. 'My mother had a pair once and . . .'

There was suddenly a sharp knock on the door. Dorcas, who was standing at the far end of the room, started towards it, but before she could get there, the door opened and Mrs. Miller came into the room.

She moved with great impatience, her dress rustling around her feet, the tasselled scarf she wore over her shoulders swinging with the haste of her movements. She was, Caroline noticed, exceedingly good-looking, and taller and more commanding than she had seemed when she was asleep in her chair. Her eyes, now that they were open, were as dark as sloes and seemed to flash with an expression of her feelings which Caroline judged quite rightly was one of anger.

'You must excuse me, Ma'am,' Mrs. Miller said in a sharp, high-pitched tone to Lady Brecon, 'but this young person has forced her way here against my express wishes. I left word with one of the footmen that she was to be brought to me before you, Ma'am, were bothered with her, but my orders have been disregarded in a manner that I will not easily forget.'

'There is no question of my being bothered,' Lady Brecon said quietly. 'I wished to see Miss Fry and Dorcas brought her to me.'

'That is not the point,' Mrs. Miller said. 'I engage the servants for this household, Ma'am. Miss Fry should have come to me first.'

Lady Brecon sighed.

'I hardly think my companion, Mrs. Miller, ranks as a servant. However, I do not feel well enough to argue. I have engaged Miss Fry and she will take up her duties straight away.'

'But Ma'am . . .' Mrs. Miller began angrily.

Lady Brecon closed her eyes.

'My smelling salts, Dorcas,' she said in weak tones.

Dorcas came bustling forward, almost elbowing Mrs. Miller out of her way in her efforts to get to her ladyship. Mrs. Miller gave Caroline a look which, translated into deeds, would have struck her to the ground, then she turned on her heel and swept from the room.

Caroline, who had risen to her feet, stood by the bed,

uncertain and a little afraid. What would happen now? she wondered. But to her surprise, as soon as the door was closed, Dorcas put the stopper back in the smelling salts bottle and said:

'She has gone, m'lady.'

'That is indeed a relief,' Lady Brecon said in perfectly steady tones, and looking at Caroline she smiled. 'Sit down, child. You may think this a strange household. It is; and when you have been here a little while, you will understand why I prefer to remain in my own room; not that there is not reason enough for it, for I have never been strong enough to move about much since my last child was born.'

Caroline was just going to ask if she had any other children besides Lord Brecon, but to her surprise she caught Dorcas' eye. Dorcas was standing so that Lady Brecon could not see her from the bed and as Caroline opened her mouth, she shook her head warningly and put her finger to her lips.

'I detest disturbances,' Lady Brecon went on. 'I ask only to be allowed to live in this room in peace alone with my thoughts. But do not remain standing. Take off your bonnet, Miss Fry, and I would like you to read to me. There is a book of poetry there which I have found intensely soothing.'

Caroline laid her bonnet down on a chair, took up the book from a table beside the bed, and turning over the pages, came to one of her favourite poems. She knew she read well, for her governess had been most insistent that her elocution should be good. When she had finished the poem, Lady Brecon said quietly:

'That was charming! Read me another, my dear.'

Caroline was half-way through another poem when there came another knock at the door. Dorcas went to it, spoke to someone outside, then came across the room with a grim expression on her face.

'His lordship's compliments, and will Miss Fry descend to the Library.'

Caroline felt her heart give a sudden leap. So she was to see Lord Brecon. What would he say to her? She closed the book he held in her hand and looked at Lady Brecon.

' 'Tis certain she has made mischief,' Dorcas said in her deep voice.

There was no need to ask who 'she' was. All three women knew to whom Dorcas referred.

'Will you go down to my son?' Lady Brecon said to

Caroline. 'Please tell him that I have engaged you as my companion. I would like you to start immediately at a salary of twenty pounds a year. Dorcas will see that your trunk is fetched from the Vicarage. It is all settled.'

She closed her eyes for a moment as if the effort of making any decision was almost too much for her; and then, as Caroline curtsied, she opened her eyes again and added:

'I somehow feel you will not be bullied, child. Poor Miss Hall was sorely afraid, but you are different.'

'I hope so,' Caroline said softly, 'and thank you, Ma'am. I shall be very pleased to stay here as your companion.'

The footman was waiting outside the door to escort her downstairs. It was not James, but another white-faced youth who looked scared and made no effort to speak, so Caroline followed him in silence.

She longed to find out where Maria was, but she thought it wiser to say nothing for the moment, at least until she knew who in this household was likely to be friendly, and who not. The first thing to discover was what exactly Mrs. Miller's position was and how strongly she counted when it came to a battle of wills.

The footman opened the library door. It was another dark room filled with books and curtained in heavy, be-tasselled damask which seemed to exclude any sunlight which might have dared to invade the pervading gloom.

But Caroline had no eyes for the room. Standing on the hearth was Lord Brecon, and he was just as she remembered him except perhaps that, if it were possible, he was even better looking.

He was exquisitely dressed and yet she could not help but notice that his clothes could never make him seem a dandy. He was too strong, too broad in the shoulder, and even his hands, while they were white and well-kept, were forceful as if on occasion he would not be afraid to use them. He was standing now frowning, as he listened to Mrs. Miller who stood beside him, her red lips speaking spitefully, her dark eyes narrowed a little.

As Caroline entered, she turned towards the door and remarked:

'Ah, here is the person I wish you to dismiss, m'lord.'

Caroline came slowly into the room. She held her head high, her heart was beating fast and she had no idea how ethereal and exquisite she appeared against the dark background.

She said nothing, only moved forward slowly with her big eyes fixed on Lord Brecon's face. He stared at her for an astonished moment, then the frown vanished from between his eyes and he sprang toward her, both hands outstretched.

'Then it is my Miss Fry!' he exclaimed. 'I thought that there could not be two ladies of the same name, and yet it was hard to credit that you might be here in my own home. It is wonderful, and I am indeed glad to welcome you.'

It was difficult to take her eyes from Lord Brecon's pleased face, and yet Caroline had to look at Mrs. Miller.

'Then you know this . . . this person,' she spluttered.

'Indeed we know each other well, do we not, Miss Fry?' Lord Brecon asked. 'In fact, Miss Fry has been of the utmost service to me on one occasion, but that I think it would be wise to keep as a secret between ourselves. What say you, Miss Fry?'

'As you please, m'lord,' Caroline answered, but her eyes were sparkling as she looked up into his, and there was a dimple at the corner of her mouth.

'And now you must tell me why you are here,' he said, drawing her across the room and handing her with some ceremony into a comfortable arm-chair. Then he turned to Mrs. Miller who was still standing there, her white teeth biting furiously at her lower lip.

'We need not trouble you any more, I think,' he said politely. 'I am sure that my mother will wish Miss Fry to stay with her, and you can leave all the arrangements in my hands. Thank you, Mrs. Miller.'

He had dismissed her from the room and the woman knew it. She tossed her head in a haughty manner and dropped a small and very disrespectful curtsey.

'I hope in all sincerity that you are doing the right thing, m'lord,' she said, and swept from the room so quickly that Lord Brecon was unable to reach the door before she had opened it herself and passed through. He made sure it was shut and then turned round to look at Caroline.

'I have been thinking about you,' he said, 'and now you appear as if by magic. I am almost persuaded you are a wraith and may vanish as quickly as you have come. Are you really here?'

'Yes, I am here,' Caroline answered softly.

'Why?'

As he asked the question, he drew nearer, and then stood waiting for her answer, his eyes on her face.

'Because I wished to see you, my lord,' Caroline answered truthfully; then even as she said the words she realised the construction he might put on them and felt the blood come swiftly into her cheeks in a crimson flood. She dropped her eyes, adding hastily: 'I mean that I have something of the utmost import to impart to your lordship, something I was afraid to write.'

Lord Brecon was silent for a moment, then he asked:

'From your tone I gather it concerns what happened the other night. You have doubtless heard the verdict, "murder by persons unknown".'

'Yes, I have heard that,' Caroline said, 'and also that your lordship's alibi was successful.'

'Perfectly,' Lord Brecon said. 'Adam and Zara were unshakable though the Chief Justice questioned them closely. We all three saw him the day after the formal enquiry, for I deemed it wise not to appear in Court when the others were being questioned. It was just a chance, though a remote one, that someone might have seen me in the neighbourhood. But all was well. And now speak to me of the matter which you mentioned just now.'

Caroline got to her feet.

'Listen, my lord,' she said, her voice very earnest and serious, her hands clasped together in unconscious appeal. 'I have learned—and please, you must not ask me how I have learned it—that your life is in danger from someone who envies and indeed covets your position in life.'

'Indeed! Go on.'

Caroline faltered for a moment.

'It is more difficult to tell you than I thought, for after all I am but a stranger to you, an acquaintance of a few hours' standing.'

'On the contrary, I do not think that time matters particularly when it comes to a question of experience,' Lord Brecon said. 'We experienced many things together, things which with other people might have taken a lifetime, but which for us were packed into a few hours. If that does not make us friends . . . what will?'

'That is true,' Caroline said; 'in which case, my lord, will you forgive me if I seem to be impertinent, if I appear to presume on our . . . our friendship?'

In answer Lord Brecon bent down and took her hand in his.

'Whatever you said to me, Miss Fry,' he said, 'I should think it neither impertinent nor presumptuous.'

There was something in the warm clasp of his fingers and the tone of his voice which made Caroline blush again. Resolutely, however, she thrust her own feelings on one side and went on:

'Then, if I may speak freely, my lord, I have learned that this person, a close relation of yours and one who would benefit by your death, might easily be a great danger to your lordship.'

Lord Brecon released Caroline's hand and walked across to the window.

'You are speaking, of course, of my cousin, Gervase Warlingham. I will not pretend to you that I have not at times suspected him myself of being jealous of me. He is always short of money, always badgering me to pay his debts, and he shows but scant gratitude when I do; but at the same time I cannot conceive that he would connive at my death."

'You are fond of him, my lord?' Caroline asked.

Lord Brecon shrugged his shoulders.

'Not particularly. We have seen little of each other. Gervase went to Harrow and then his father bought him a commission in the Guards. Our paths have not crossed to any great extent.'

'And yet now you see him frequently?' Caroline persisted.

'By no means,' Lord Brecon replied. 'I had not set eyes on Gervase these past two years until I returned home last February. He came here to welcome me on my return, stayed a few weeks, and I have encountered him once or twice since then at White's Club. That is all.'

'He has not called on you this past week?' Caroline asked.

'No! Why do you ask me that?'

But Caroline did not reply. She was remembering what Gideon had told her. So Mr. Gervase Warlingham had been in Cuckhurst, had seen Jason Faken, and yet he had not visited the Castle. It was strange, and yet she wished to be sure of her facts before she said more. All that she had were suspicions; and besides, Gideon was only a circus boy, he might have been mistaken. She did not wish Lord Brecon to think that she gossiped of his affairs with the circus folk.

Lord Brecon turned from the window and walked across the room to her again.

'It is kind of you to tell me this, Miss Fry, but methinks you are entirely wrong in your suspicions of Gervase. When you meet him, you will like him, for he is a handsome fellow and has, I believe, many friends. He may be open-handed with his money—or my money if it comes to that—but I swear he is no murderer. No, Miss Fry, you are misinformed, and though I thank you for your interest in me, I must beg of you to believe me when I say that the ties of blood are stronger than covetousness, and Gervase is my first cousin.'

'Pray heaven you are right, my lord,' Caroline said. 'But will you promise to be careful?'

'Careful of what?' Lord Brecon asked. 'Losing my life? My dear Miss Fry, as I told you the first time we met, life is of little consequence to me. I would as fain lose it as retain it.'

As he spoke, it seemed to Caroline that a bitter expression shadowed his face and that there was a strange darkness in his eyes. He spoke heavily, as a man might who is under sentence of death, who has lost hope and for whom there was no future. It was a strange impression she received and yet it was unmistakable. For a moment she could only stare at him, knowing that he was looking inwardly at some hideous secret which she could not share, and speaking truthfully and without exaggeration.

She had a sudden premonition of danger. She felt and knew that all she had half sensed or guessed intuitively was but a fraction of the ghastly truth. It was as if something indefinably evil threatened Lord Brecon, creeping inexorably nearer and nearer while she was powerless to save him.

Caroline's horror must have shown on her face, for of a sudden Lord Brecon smiled and the darkness vanished from his eyes.

'But I must not trouble you,' he said. 'Yes, Miss Fry, I will be careful, if it pleases you.'

He spoke lightly and she knew that his promise was but to soothe her and he had no intention of keeping it. Daringly she put out her hand and laid it on his arm.

'Could you not tell me the truth?' she pleaded.

He looked down into her eyes and knew quite well what she meant. For one moment he seemed to stand there spellbound and hesitant, seemingly about to surrender the citadel of his thoughts, for his steel-grey eyes lightened and she had a glimpse of the light-hearted man he might have been—a glimpse of happiness and laughter and of something else which made her shy. Then the mask dropped once more and he gave a little humourless laugh, oddly reminiscent of the one he had given in the woods the night they met.

'Gad, Miss Fry, would you hound me?' he asked. 'I have nothing to tell, alas. You asked me to promise you that I would be careful and I have given you my word.'

Caroline turned her head aside. It was hopeless, she knew. The truth evaded her and there was nothing she could do about it.

'Then, my lord, if you will excuse me,' she said. 'I will return to your Lady Mother.'

She did not look at him and there was disappointment in her voice. She had moved only a step or two towards the door before he was at her side again and had taken her hand in his.

'You will stay, Miss Fry?' he said. 'You won't leave the Castle? I want you to stay.'

Still Caroline did not look at him, then he added:

'But, by God, I ought to ask you to go.'

The words seemed to burst from Lord Brecon's lips, his fingers tightened on hers, and she felt emotion vibrating through him so that she raised her eyes in wonderment to his face. Her eyes met his and then she was very still. Something magnetic passed between them so that Caroline quivered and felt her breath quicken. The whole world seemed to recede and there were only the two of them standing there. They were alone, man and woman facing each other across eternity.

A coal fell in the grate, shattering the spell which bound them. Caroline's eyes dropped and because of a shyness such as she had never known before she turned and without another word went from the room.

She heard the library door close behind her, a defiant little bang as she ran down the passage, across the hall and up the stairs.

She did not look around her; she had only one idea and that was to find herself back in the sanctuary of Lady Brecon's sunlit room. But even as she sped along the corridor, Dorcas appeared at the far end of it.

'Her ladyship is asleep, Miss Fry. I will show you to your bedchamber and inform you when she wakes.'

She stalked along the passage and Caroline followed her, her thoughts and feelings too chaotic and tumultuous for her to think of anything at the moment save Lord Brecon's face as it had been but a moment ago in the Library.

'Here is your room, Miss Fry. 'Tis near her ladyship's should she require you.'

Dorcas opened the door of a small slip of a bedroom. It was cheerless and rather chill as if it had not been used for some time, but Caroline saw only one thing in it—Maria, standing demurely by the dressing-table.

Dorcas gave Maria a sharp glance.

'Help Miss Fry with all she needs until her luggage arrives. After that assist her to unpack.'

'Yes, Miss Dorcas.'

Maria bobbed a little curtsey and then as the door shut she stared at Caroline while a broad smile transformed her plump face. Caroline held a warning finger to her lips.

'Wait a moment,' she whispered.

She crept towards the door, listened and breathed a sigh of relief.

' 'Tis all right,' Maria said. 'You are safe with her, m'lady. She is a decent sort is Miss Dorcas, harsh though she seems. It's more than I can say of anyone else in the household.'

'Oh, Maria,' Caroline exclaimed. 'I am so pleased to see you. Tell me what you have discovered.'

'A good deal, m'lady; so much in fact that I hardly knows where to begin. Oh, never have I seen such a household, all at sixes and sevens it is. 'Tis an eye-opener for me, I can assure you, m'lady, after living at Mandrake, to see the squabbling and wrangling in a house like this and the waste that goes on. Why, your ladyship would never believe it.'

'Yes, yes, I want to hear everything,' Caroline said, 'but first tell me, who is Mrs. Miller?'

'You may well ask that, m'lady,' Maria answered. ' 'Tis what I asked myself, for 'twas Mrs. Miller who engaged me. I saw the housekeeper first, a poor limp creature she is, too, frightened to death of that Mrs. Miller. But as luck would have it two housemaids had left this very week; one discharged for impertinence and the other one walked out because she could not stand Mrs. Miller's domineering ways.'

'But who is she?' Caroline asked again.

'Well, as far as I can ascertain,' Maria said, 'she is a connection by marriage of his lordship's aunt, Lady Augusta Warlingham.'

'Does Lady Augusta live here too?' Caroline asked.

'Indeed she does, and a stranger lady you never saw. 'Tis hard put I am not to laugh when I have to attend her in her bedchamber.'

'Yes, but go on about Mrs. Miller,' Caroline interrupted, knowing how easily Maria could be side-tracked from the main point of a story.

'It appears,' Maria went on, 'that Lady Augusta fair dotes on her nephew, Mr. Gervase Warlingham, the gentleman that your ladyship asked me to enquire about.'

'Yes, and what has he got to do with it?'

'Mrs. Miller's husband served with Mr. Warlingham in the Army and was killed, so I understand, at the Battle of Waterloo, and Mrs. Miller, being left with only a tiny pension, gets Mr. Warlingham to introduce her here when his lordship was away on the Continent. Lady Augusta was in charge then, but she doesn't care for housekeeping and so she gives Mrs. Miller full authority over the household; and when his lordship comes back she's in the saddle right enough, giving herself the airs and graces of the Quality.'

'I see,' Caroline said. 'So she is a friend of Mr. Gervase Warlingham's?'

'More than a friend, some say,' Maria answered, and added hastily, 'not that I should be repeating such vulgar gossip to your ladyship and you must forgive me for mentioning it. Oh, m'lady, you are too young to be mixed up with all this sort of thing, and what would your father and her ladyship say to such a sorry coil? Let's go home, your ladyship, let's get away from here. 'Tis wrong I was to agree to such play-acting, and I have a feeling that worse might happen.'

'What do you mean?' Caroline said. 'Worse might happen?'

'I am sure I don't know, your ladyship,' Maria replied miserably. ' 'Tis just a feeling I have in my bones, like a goose walking over my grave, and I can't explain it. I only know that I want to get back to Mandrake and take your ladyship with me.'

'Then you are going to be disappointed, Maria,' Caroline said, 'for I intend to stay here. I intend to get to the bottom of all the mysteries there are in this house.'

As she spoke she raised her chin and there was an expression on her face and a ring in her voice which her father would have recognised as being characteristic of the Fighting Fayes all down the centuries. Maria continued to argue but she knew she fought a losing battle, and finally she indulged in a fit of the sullens, muttering darkly that she could smell trouble in the very air she breathed.

By dinner time Caroline's trunks had come and Maria had unpacked and dressed her in a gown of pale blue figured gauze tastefully draped over a petticoat of blue sarsnet which was embroidered with silver spangles. It was an elaborate dress for someone in the lowly position of companion; but Caroline fortified with Harriet's idea that she was wearing Lady Caroline Faye's cast-off clothes, wished to look beautiful rather than demure, fashionable rather than humble.

She was not unduly perturbed by the expression on Mrs. Miller's face as she walked into the drawing-room where they were to assemble before dinner was served. Mrs. Miller was also modishly attired, but her dress of yellow and saffron stripes was of cheap material and she relied more on exhibiting the charms of her white shoulders and full bosom than on the cut or hang of her gown.

Looking at her and at her painted lips and ornately arranged hair, Caroline was certain that Mrs. Miller was not the respectable widow she appeared to be. She had seen women like her often enough in London and heard her godmother's frankly expressed opinion of them. Lady Brecon, lying an invalid in her own bedroom, might not realise it, but Mrs. Miller, Caroline was sure, was not the type of person to manage a distinguished house or even to be a guest in one.

As Caroline entered the drawing-room Mrs. Miller was speaking with an older woman whose appearance was so fantastic that Caroline concluded immediately that she must be the Lady Augusta Warlingham. She wore a wig of bright scarlet hair, frizzed and curled in an elaborate manner and ornamented with a bunch of crimson feathers held in place by a huge emerald and diamond brooch which matched the necklace of priceless emeralds round her yellow neck. She was very old, but her thin, wrinkled face was heavily rouged, the powder clogged in her wrinkles, while her old, short-sighted eyes were outlined with mascara. She pointed a claw-like hand at Caroline and cackled:

'So this is the girl, is it? Come here, child, and let me look at you.'

Caroline did as she was told, dropping a curtsey and standing before the old woman, waiting for permission to move.

Lady Augusta looked at her, raised a quizzing-glass, then laughed, a hoarse, chuckling laugh which somehow made Caroline like her, despite her extraordinary appearance.

'You are a pretty chit,' she said. 'Far too pretty, I am sure, for your comfort or for any other woman's. I am not surprised that Hester wants to be rid of you. Is that what pricks you, Hester, my dear?' she asked of Mrs. Miller. 'Too pretty, too pretty by far, and Gervase will be the first to notice it, eh?'

Caroline was amused to see that Mrs. Miller looked cross and uncomfortable.

'I was concerned only with Lady Brecon's comfort,' she said stiffly, but Lady Augusta laughed again.

'Stuff and nonsense, you are concerned only with your own feelings in the matter, as you always have been. Yes, she is pretty, too pretty for you to stomach, Hester. I should get rid of her—if you can.'

She chuckled again and at that moment Lord Brecon entered the room and the butler announced that dinner was served.

Lord Brecon always looked smart, but in Caroline's eyes he was resplendent in evening dress. His coat of royal blue satin was ornamented with sapphire buttons, and the snowy folds of his cravat were arranged with meticulous care in the very latest mode. He offered Lady Augusta his arm and they went slowly in to dinner, followed by Mrs. Miller and Caroline.

'We are a very small party tonight,' Lady Augusta remarked.

'My friends arrive tomorrow,' Lord Brecon answered. 'Twenty odd of them, so you won't complain then, Aunt Augusta.'

'Complain? Am I complaining now? It is a change not to be deafened by the chatter of raffish fools who can talk of naught but gaming and racing.'

'Well, you will hear them again tomorrow,' Lord Brecon said, and suddenly there seemed to Caroline to be a tremendous weariness in his voice as if he were bored to distraction at the thought of the morrow.

He looked at Caroline and then looked away, but she

was so acutely conscious of him that she could not eat, and thought that every spoonful she put into her mouth must choke her. She had never felt like this in her whole life before. Always she had felt assured, certain of her feelings and her actions, but now she felt as if her whole being had come alive. She was tingling with a strange warmth and excitement which quivered within her, and yet at the same time she shivered because she was half afraid.

'What is wrong with me?' she questioned, and knew only that dinner seemed at the same time interminably long and ridiculously short; long, because the courses seemed to draw out one after another, dishes too innumerable to remember; and short, because Lord Brecon was there and she wanted to listen to his voice as it came from between his lips, to watch him when he was not looking at her, to drop her eyes when he was.

When dinner was over and the ladies withdrew to the drawing-room, Mrs. Miller said to Caroline:

'I wish to speak to you, Miss Fry.'

Lady Augusta was moving ahead of them towards the drawing-room and Mrs. Miller opened the door of another room. Caroline followed her into a small breakfast-room. She noticed that the hearth was full of unswept ashes and although it was dark, the curtains were not yet drawn.

'A bad housekeeper,' Caroline thought and waited in attentive silence until Mrs. Miller should speak.

'I wish to say, Miss Fry,' Mrs. Miller began, 'that there is no need for you to dazzle us at night in a creation such as you are wearing at the moment. 'Tis unsuitable for someone in your position, and presumptuous for you to take advantage of Lady Brecon's absence to flaunt yourself before the other occupants of the Castle. I am in charge here, as you know, and unless you can find yourself suitable garments such as should be worn by someone in your humble station in life, then I shall make arrangements for the maids to bring you a tray in your room. In many houses a companion does not enjoy the privilege of eating with her employers, but Lady Brecon has—with what is in my mind, mistaken magnanimity—allowed it here. But if you wish for the company of your betters, it must be conditional upon your correct appearance. Is that clear?'

Mrs. Miller's bullying tone would have frightened anyone so young as Caroline had she really been anxious to retain her position, but Caroline had no real reason to be frightened of this vulgar woman.

She looked her in the face and said:

'I am sorry if my gowns displease you, Ma'am, but they are provided for me by Lady Caroline Faye who is reputed to have the best of taste. They are unfortunately all I possess. However, I will speak to her ladyship in the morning or if you prefer it tonight, and ask if my salary can be extended to buy the type of drab uniform which suits your pleasure.'

Mrs. Miller gasped for a moment, then found her voice.

'How dare you speak to me in that tone!' she said. 'If you think you can flaunt me in this household you are much mistaken.'

'Indeed!' Caroline retorted. 'I had the idea I was engaged by Lady Brecon and that my appointment was confirmed by her son—his lordship. Do I really need your approval, Ma'am?'

Mrs. Miller went quite white with rage. She spluttered and took a step towards Caroline as if she intended to slap her in the face. But Caroline's level gaze and unconsicous air of dignity made her change her mind. Instead, she stalked towards the door. As she reached it, she turned.

'You will be sorry for this,' she said in furious tones, 'sorry when you find yourself put out in the road without a reference and without a chance of further employment. When I am mistress here, you will change your tune, my dear Miss Fry, and that will be before you are very much older.'

She went out and slammed the door after her. Caroline gave a little laugh, then stood considering Mrs. Miller's words.

'So she intends to be mistress of this house,' she thought. 'Can she really have set her cap at Lord Brecon?'

It was possible, but not probable for Caroline was sure in her heart of one thing—Lord Brecon was not interested in Mrs. Miller.

6

Caroline opened her eyes and stretched out her arms.

'Lud, but this is an uncomfortable bed,' she said to Maria who was drawing back the curtains.

' 'Tis not the only thing that is uncomfortable in this house,' Maria answered. 'Oh, m'lady, I never thought I would live to see such a set of servants. Why, the head housemaid even had the impudence to tell me that there was no reason why I should trouble to bring you a cup of chocolate in the morning. "Miss Fry is only a companion," she says, "and is not entitled to extra attentions." Extra attention indeed! I nearly boxed her ears for her. But 'tis from Mrs. Miller they take their orders.'

Caroline sat up in bed.

'For goodness' sake, Maria, don't parade your partiality for me too obviously or they may guess that I am not what I seem.'

'If they weren't all cork-brained, they would guess it anyway,' Maria retorted, 'for no one could look less like a poor dependent than your ladyship.'

'Well, they must indeed be as you say,' Caroline replied, 'for everyone has accepted me as such, including Lady Brecon and . . . his lordship.'

Her voice quivered a little on the last words. She had been slightly piqued that Lord Brecon had not for a moment questioned her story of being a companion. It was understandable when he had first seen her dusty and dishevelled from lurking in a wood at odd hours; but now although it would have been dangerous, Caroline would have been gratified if he had seemed just the slightest degree suspicious or even surprised that she should be in need of employment.

She wondered what her father and mother would think

if they knew that their only daughter, whom they held to be the equal of any great lady in the land, not only had chosen so lowly a post, but had been accepted in it without question.

'Put me out one of my prettiest gowns, Maria,' Caroline commanded suddenly in a mood of defiance.

Maria, however, was more cautious and chose not one of Caroline's more elaborate dresses, but a simple muslin trimmed only with ribbons.

'Breakfast is downstairs, m'lady,' she said, 'but I credit you will be alone, for Mrs. Miller has asked for hers in her bedchamber, and his lordship is already out riding.'

'That reminds me, Maria,' Caroline said, getting out of bed and looking like some exquisite Greek goddess as she stood for a moment at the window, her body silhouetted through the transparency of her night-robe.

'Reminds you of what, m'lady?' Maria enquired when Caroline did not finish the sentence but was silent as she looked out over the green park as if searching for a glimpse of someone on horseback.

'What was I speaking about?' Caroline asked with a start. 'Oh yes, of course, I want you to find out who will be in the house-party which arrives today. I expect the housekeeper will have a list so that she can prepare the bedrooms. You must try to see it, Maria, and commit it to memory in case there is one amongst his lordship's guests who will recognise me.'

'Oh, m'lady, what a dreadful danger! I had not thought on it before,' Maria exclaimed in alarm.

'Why be scared until we discover if there is a reason for it?' Caroline asked and began to dress.

She found that her duties that morning were not very arduous. Lady Brecon slept late and Dorcas saw to all her needs until eleven o'clock. Miss Fry was then requested to read her ladyship the leading articles in the *Morning Post* and was given two letters to write, after which she was told that her time was her own until the Dowager awoke from her after-luncheon nap.

Delighted to be free, Caroline hurried down to the Vicarage, where she saw Harriet and enquired if there were any letters. There was one from Mrs. Edgmont, and Caroline despatched one she had written saying that she was very comfortable and happy at Cuckhurst and intended to stay at the Vicarage for at least several more days.

Her business done, Caroline walked slowly back towards the Castle. Although the building itself was sombre, the park and the gardens surrounding it were lovely and a great avenue of oaks boarded the drive. Where they ended there was a wrought-iron gate leading into the more formal gardens and Caroline, going through this, presently found herself on a broad grass walk at the end of which was a small Grecian Temple beside a water-lily pond.

She moved towards it, humming a little tune, for the warm sunshine made her feel light-hearted and happy. When she reached the Temple she saw that it was overhung with honeysuckle and rambler roses, and approached by three grey stone steps. She picked a spray of honeysuckle, smelt its sweet fragrance, and seating herself on the step took off her bonnet before she leant back against the cool marble of a rounded pillar.

It was very quiet and peaceful, swallows dived towards the lily pond, a peacock emerged from the shrubs, spread his tail in conscious vanity and strutted away across the lawns. There was the music of bird voices and the soft rhythmic buzzing of the bees moving among the flowers.

Caroline found herself dreaming a little so that it startled her considerably to hear someone say:

'You seem vastly serious, Miss Fry.'

She looked up and saw Lord Brecon standing beside her. He swept his hat from his head and she saw that he wore highly polished riding boots and carried a whip in his hand.

'Oh, my lord, what a start you gave me,' Caroline exclaimed.

'I am sorry if I intruded on your thoughts. I have been riding round my estate and thought it was time that I inspected the gardens. Perhaps it is as well that I did, for it appears to me that there is a great deal which needs doing and those gardeners of mine have been monstrously lazy these past months.'

'While you have been fault-finding, I, on the contrary, have been admiring your lordship's garden,' Caroline said.

'Have you indeed?' Lord Brecon said. 'May I sit down and hear what you have to say about it?'

'Of course,' Caroline answered, extending her hand with a little gesture of invitation towards the stone steps. Even as she did so, she wondered whether as a companion she should not have risen to her feet at Lord Brecon's appearance and dropped him a curtsey. However, it was too late now, and as if to make up for her ill manners she smiled at him very enticingly as he lowered himself on to the step beside her.

He took off his hat and threw it on the grass, then leaning back against another pillar turned half sideways to look at her. There was something embarrassing in his close scrutiny and after a moment Caroline turned her head away towards the lily pond. It seemed to her that the silence between them was dangerous and yet she could think of no words with which to break it.

'You are a strange girl, Caroline,' Lord Brecon said at last.

'Strange?' Caroline repeated, raising his eyebrows a little.

'Very strange,' Lord Brecon answered. 'I have known many women, but there are none with whom I can compare you.'

'Ought I to be pleased at that or apologetic?' Caroline parried.

Lord Brecon threw back his head and laughed.

'Jove, but you are quick,' he said. 'I remember how amazed I was the first few minutes of our acquaintance when you seemed to grasp the whole situation far better than I.'

'You are pleased to flatter me, my lord.'

Caroline's words were demure.

'Is that the sort of flattery you like?' Lord Brecon asked. 'Or shall I tell you that you are exceeding lovely—for it is the truth?'

Caroline felt the colour fly to her cheeks.

'It is kind of you to think so, my lord.'

'Unfortunately so many people must have told you the same thing.'

'Unfortunately?' Caroline queried.

'For me! I would like to have been the first.'

Caroline's eyes were on the spray of honeysuckle which lay on her lap. She picked it up, her fingers playing with it as if it were of considerable importance.

'So very lovely,' Lord Brecon sighed.

'The honeysuckle?' Caroline asked.

'Of course,' he replied gravely.

She looked at him then and laughed.

'You make me blush, my lord.'

'It is adorable! Do you know how long your lashes are when they lie against your cheek?'

105

'You would not expect me to answer that question, my lord?'

'In that case will you answer me another?' Lord Brecon asked.

'If I can,' Caroline replied, aware that the tone of his voice had changed.

'I want you to tell me,' Lord Brecon said softly, 'exactly why you came here to my home.'

'But I have already done so,' Caroline replied. 'I heard through Miss Hall, who was previously companion to your Lady Mother, that the position was vacant. Miss Hall wrote very glowingly of your mother's kindness to her and I was not afraid that I should encounter another ferocious and untrustworthy lady of quality.'

'Yes, yes, I know that,' Lord Brecon said a little impatiently; 'but was that the only reason why you came to Brecon Castle?'

'There was another reason, my lord,' Caroline said, 'of which I have also spoken. I wished to warn you.'

'Yes, and you have done that,' Lord Brecon said, 'I was thinking of it half the night. It was brave of you, Miss Fry, to be so interested in a stranger to whom you have once by chance afforded a service.'

'I was glad to be of assistance, my lord,' Caroline said.

Both their words were formal and yet so much underlay them. Caroline could almost feel Lord Brecon's insistence as he tried to draw some revelation from her lips, although what it was she was not entirely certain. Yet there was such an undercurrent of feeling between them that words mattered but little, while their eyes met one another's and their breath came quickly, and each was aware of some leaping flame within themselves which by the very magnetism in the air they knew was echoed in the other. Quite suddenly Caroline took fright. She felt shy, fearful, and yet a little exultant, all at the same moment. She sprang to her feet, moving the cool shadows of the little Temple out into the golden sunshine.

'I think, my lord,' she said a little incoherently, 'that it must be nearly the hour when your Lady Mother will awake and need me. I must return to the house.'

Lord Brecon did not move. He looked at Caroline and said very quietly: 'So you would run away from me?'

Caroline's chin went up as if she had been insulted.

'I never run away, my lord, but sometimes it is prudent not to court danger.'

'So you think I am dangerous?'

'I did not say so, my lord.'

Caroline was laughing a little now. She stood facing him, incredibly lovely as the sun made a burnished halo of her curls and the wind blew the softness of her gown so that it revealed the lovely outline of breast and hip.

Lord Brecon sprang to his feet.

'No, you are right. It is not I who am dangerous, but you.'

He walked over to her, standing so near that he almost touched her. He stood looking down into her face and when he spoke again his voice was hoarse. 'Who are you? Where have you come from? Why are you here?'

There was something fierce in the question, and yet Caroline knew that she need not answer. It was not her pedigree that he was wishing to hear from her lips, but other words, more intimate ones, words that were spoken just as surely as if her lips had broken the silence that lay between them.

For a moment Caroline could neither move nor speak. Lord Brecon seemed to hold her to him as closely as if he had put his arms around her; and then, just as she felt that she must cry out and break the enchantment of the moment, a voice interrupted them.

'And what do you two people find so engrossing?' it asked.

They both turned swiftly, startled out of the ordinary because for a moment they had been living in a world of their own into which no stranger could enter.

Lady Augusta stood there, her red wig covered by a huge bonnet festooned in feathers, her claw-like, be-ringed hand resting on a be-tasselled walking-stick. She looked a creature of fantasy, the white paint and vivid patches of rouge on her face seeming grotesque in the revealing light.

'Good afternoon, my lady,' Caroline echoed, feeling unexpectedly guilty as she dropped a curtsey.

'You are surprised to see me,' Lady Augusta asked, 'and none too pleased, eh? Well, who shall blame you? Youth will turn to youth the whole world o'er.'

'I found Miss Fry admiring the gardens,' Lord Brecon explained somewhat severely.

'And so you stopped to admire her, eh?' Lady Augusta said with a chuckle. 'Quite right, my boy; I should have expected the same when I was young and gay. They say the wenches are more prudish these days than we were—but I don't believe it. Females change their gowns with the fashion, but their feelings and their bodies under the frills and furbelows are still the same, I assure you.'

It seemed to Caroline that the old lady leered up at her nephew, and there was something insidious and rather nasty in the croaking old voice. She suddenly felt besmirched.

'If your ladyship will excuse me,' she said quietly, 'I would return to the house. Lady Brecon may be requiring my services.'

'I will excuse you right enough,' Lady Augusta answered, 'and so will lordship, although I'll be bound that he will be sorry to see you go. Take warning from me, Miss Fry, and beware of all households where your employer is a bachelor. They are dangerous to pretty girls like yourself, for while they love with great *éclat*, it is seldom serious.'

'Aunt Augusta!' Lord Brecon protested angrily, while Caroline, crimson with mortification, turned and ran swiftly towards the house.

Lord Brecon watched her go, then tightened his lips, his grey eyes dark with temper. As he stooped to take up his hat and riding whip, Lady Augusta stretched out her hand towards him.

'Give me your arm, Vane, and pray do not glare at me in such a haughty manner. I am no longer afraid of their passions. It was sensible of me to warn the chit. She is pretty enough, I am not saying she isn't, and if I am any judge of my own sex, her heart beats fervently every time she catches sight of your handsome visage. But what good can it do her? She is but a companion, Vane, and you have your position to remember.'

'I am not likely to forget that, Aunt Augusta,' Lord Brecon said bitterly.

'No, of course not, but women take such things to heart. Now be a sensible boy or you will regret it.'

Lord Brecon said nothing for a moment. Arm in arm they moved very slowly down the smooth, grassy walk. Ahead of them stood the Castle, its great stone towers seeming somehow to refute the sunshine and remain sombre and unlit even on such a brilliant day.

Lord Brecon looked at it and the expression on his face was inscrutable. Only as they reached the door which led into the Castle from the garden did he speak again.

'As you have said, my dear Aunt,' he remarked quietly, 'I will be—sensible.'

In the sanctuary of her bedroom Caroline stood looking at her reflection in the mirror. Her cheeks were flushed, but her mouth pouted a little and her eyes were mutinous at the thought of Lady Augusta's insinuations. But her heart still beat quickly at the emotions which Lord Brecon had aroused within her. She had never known herself to feel so strange.

Slowly she raised her hands and put them against her burning cheeks, then she sat down suddenly on the stool in front of the dressing-table and hid her face in her hands. What was happening to her? Never before had she felt like this; never had she been so strung up, so thrilled, so excited that a turmoil of emotions seemed to succeed one another in an almost endless procession. Her whole being strained towards some goal of which she was dimly aware and was yet too shy at the moment to give it a name.

She sat for a long time with her face hidden, forgetful of everything save of steel-grey eyes looking into hers, of a firm mouth which spoke words that had a far deeper meaning, of a face which seemed to lie ever before her eyes, causing her to foget all that had ever happened to her in the past, to exclude any anticipation of what might happen in the future. She could be aware only of that face and of the present.

Caroline's reverie was interrupted by Maria who came into the room carrying some laces and handkerchiefs which she had been pressing.

'Oh, I beg your pardon, m'lady,' she exclaimed. 'I had no idea you would be in.'

'I have just come back from the Vicarage,' Caroline said with a somewhat elastic regard for the truth. 'I called to see if there were any letters for me. There was one from Mrs. Edgmont, and she says there is no news worth recording and that all is well at Mandrake.'

Maria sighed. 'It seems an age, m'lady, since we left. How soon shall we return?'

'I know not, Maria, and would not venture to guess. We have not yet done what we came to do.'

'To save his lordship?' Maria questioned. 'At times I cannot help thinking, m'lady, that you are mistaken.'

'You have heard naught of Mr. Gervase Warlingham?' Caroline asked.

'Nothing helpful, your ladyship; but I will relate that during our middday meal I sat next one of the other housemaids. She is a stupid girl, but she has been in the house these past five years. "Is Mr. Warlingham pleasant," I asks her, "for I have heard he is a handsome gentleman?" She giggled. "There's one in the Castle as thinks so," she says. "And who might that be?" I questioned; but she would not tell me. Just giggled and said that it was more than her place was worth to go telling tales. "Besides," she added, "you will find out soon enough when he comes to stay." "And when might that be?" I enquired, but she shrugged her shoulders. "It might be today, might be tomorrow or the day after," she answers. "Mr. Gervase comes and goes when he pleases; and why not, seeing as how it will all be his one day?" "There is no certainty on that," I retorted, "for his lordship is as finely set up a man as ever I have seen. If he has a son—and there is no reason to think he should not have a dozen—then where would your precious Mr. Gervase be?" But she only giggles at me, and I could get no more out of her.'

Caroline got to her feet and moved slowly across the room.

'It is strange, Maria, that she should have spoken like that.'

Suddenly she stood still. She remembered Mrs. Miller's words the night before—'When I am mistress here.'

Yes, gradually the pieces were beginning to fit into one another like the pieces of a puzzle. Mr. Gervase Warlingham and Mrs. Miller. There was no doubt that Lord Brecon was in danger, grave danger, and at least she knew from which direction it would come.

While she was thinking, Maria slipped from the room to fetch a gown which she had told Caroline she had left hanging in the housemaid's room. A moment later, while Caroline was still deep in thought, she came running down the passage and slipped into the room, closing the door behind her.

'Quick, m'lady,' she said, drawing something from the spacious pocket in her apron.

'What is it?' Caroline asked.

'A list of the guests was lying on the table,' she said, 'and there was no one there. Glance at it quickly, m'lady, and then I must return it. If I am found to have taken it, I might easily be dismissed.'

Caroline took the list from Maria. It was written out in

untidy, flamboyant handwriting, which she guessed instinctively to be Mrs. Miller's, and against the guests' names were written the bedrooms they were to occupy. The majority of the visitors were to be gentlemen, Caroline noticed; and then as she glanced at each name, her anxiety lightened.

No, there was not one of them with whom she was likely to have come in contact during her season in London. Most of them bore strange names which gave her the impression that they were not of the *beau-monde*. There was indeed only one who bore a name which was even vaguely familiar and that was the Honourable Thomas Stratton. But she was almost sure that she had never met him.

'I have read it,' she said at length and handed the list back to the agitated Maria. 'We are safe. It contains no one of our acquaintance.'

Maria for once did not wait to gossip. Caroline heard her running down the corridor, then glancing at the clock she saw that it was nearly half past three. She tidied her hair and went to the Dowager's room.

Lady Brecon greeted Caroline with a smile and holding out a book of poems, she asked her to read them aloud. Caroline acquiesced and the afternoon passed pleasantly. They were conversing over a cup of tea when there was a knock at the door and Dorcas announced that Lord Brecon was outside.

'Ask him to come in,' Lady Brecon said, and as Caroline rose, she added: 'Pray stay; my dear. Vane usually comes to see me at this time, but unless he has anything private to impart to me, there is no need for you to retire.'

'Thank you, Ma'am,' Caroline said.

She bent her head as Lord Brecon entered, but she was aware that his eyes rested on her, and despite her utmost resolution the colour rose in her cheeks.

'Vane, darling, how well you are looking,' Lady Brecon said as her son drew near to her bed and bent down to kiss her.

'I have been riding,' he answered. 'It is lovely out today. I wish you would let me arrange to have you carried into the garden.'

Lady Brecon shook her head.

'I am happy enough here, dear boy. If I once allowed myself to leave this room, I might be involved in the turbulent difficulties of your great household, and I should dislike that above all things.'

111

'I know you would, and I will not plague you. Am I too late for a cup of tea, Miss Fry?'

'No, of course not, my lord,' Caroline replied in a low voice, conscious that she could not raise her eyes to look at him and that her hands trembled as they moved among the silver tea things.

'Miss Fry has been reading to me,' Lady Brecon said. 'She has a charming voice and we have both confessed to an admiration for the poems of that abominably improper Lord Byron.'

Lord Brecon laughed.

'Oh, George writes well enough—if only he would stick to writing! I saw him when I was in Italy.'

'And how was he?' Lady Brecon asked.

'Very handsome; and I am told the women find his haggard pallor irresistible. But then who knows what women will admire? What do you say, Miss Fry?'

Caroline knew that he was being deliberately provoking, but for the very life of her at that moment she could not find an adequate retort.

She murmured something inaudible and rose to carry a plate of sandwiches to the Dowager's bedside.

'Thank you, dear, but I will eat no more,' Lady Brecon answered. 'Miss Fry looks after me beautifully, Vane. I am so glad that dear Fanny Hall recommended her to come to me.'

'We are indeed fortunate,' Lord Brecon said with a smile, 'although I am afraid that Hester Miller will not agree with us.'

Lady Brecon sighed.

'Do not tell me of it, Vane dear. I have no wish to hear. But I suspicion we made rather a mistake in giving Mrs. Miller so much authority while you were away.'

'Well, we can always ask her politely to find another post,' Lord Brecon said.

He was looking at Caroline, and his tone was absent and careless as if he were not concentrating on what he was saying.

'There might be unpleasantness about that, Vane, since your Aunt was so insistent on her appointment. No, I am afraid the only solution will be to dismiss her when you marry.'

Lady Brecon spoke lightly, but her words had a strange effect on her son. Lord Brecon's hands tightened over the arms of his chair until the knuckles stood out very white. For a moment he sat looking into space with so much tension in his expression that Caroline felt that at any moment words would burst explosively from his lips; but the seconds ticked by and he did not speak and the Dowager, who was sipping her tea, did not notice that anything was amiss. Only Caroline waited, watchful and breathless, until Lady Brecon held out her cup to her with a little smile.

'Thank you, dear. Will you put it down for me?'

Caroline did as she was asked and when she turned again to Lord Brecon, he was sitting back in his chair relaxed. She had the impression that his face had not entirely regained its composure, but he did not glance in her direction. Instead he rose to his feet a little stiffly as if the action were somewhat of an effort.

'I must go now, Mother,' he said, 'my guests should be arriving.'

'That will be nice for you, dear,' Lady Brecon said. 'Come and say good-night to me if you can, but if you are detained I shall understand.'

Lord Brecon went towards the door. As he reached it, his mother asked:

'Do you wish Miss Fry to join you at dinner, Vane? Or have you too many women in your party already?'

'No, of course, we shall be pleased to see Miss Fry,' Lord Brecon replied.

He spoke, it seemed to Caroline, with a deliberate indifference and there was something so cold in the tone of his voice that she felt almost as if he had slapped her. He went from the room and the door closed behind him.

She longed beyond anything to know what had happened. Why had the mere mention of marriage perturbed and upset him so intensely? Was that the secret she had always suspected him of hiding? Had he a wife hidden away somewhere? What else could cause such a convulsion of feelings? She could not understand him, but there was little time to ponder over his behaviour for she had to pay attention to the Dowager who was speaking to her.

'It is so delightful to have my son back again. I think I told you, Miss Fry, that he has been abroad for nearly two years. I missed him terribly, but soon after his twenty-fifth birthday he seemed ill, or at least not in his rightful health. No one seemed to know what was wrong with him and of course he refused to go to a physician. You know how self-conscious men are when it concerns their ailments, but finally I persuaded him to take a trip abroad. It is good for all young men to see the world.'

'What happened after his twenty-fifth birthday to upset him?' Caroline enquired.

'I do not collect there was anything specific that upset him,' Lady Brecon replied vaguely. 'He just seemed generally run down, mopey and ailing, which was so unlike Vane, for he was always high-spirited and happy. He was a beautiful baby and a charming little boy.' She looked at Caroline and smiled. 'I expect you will laugh at me for being an adoring mother, but he is all I have and so I am afraid he is my dearest and, indeed, my only interest in life.'

'I understand, Ma'am,' Caroline said softly.

'How sympathetic you are, Miss Fry,' Lady Brecon smiled. 'But one day, when you have a son, you will feel the same. Like me you would do anything in the world to give your child happiness.'

There was silence for a moment and then, as Caroline did not speak, Lady Brecon said almost wistfully:

'You would think Vane would be happy, wouldn't you? Owner of this fine Castle and its vast estates and with a considerable fortune?'

'His lordship should be happy,' Caroline prevaricated. 'As you say, Ma'am, he has so much.'

'Yes, so much,' the Dowager repeated but she sighed. 'So much.'

Dorcas came into the room and took up the tea-tray. She looked sharply towards the bed and Caroline had the impression that she half-sensed that Lady Brecon had been talking intimately.

'You are tired, m'lady,' Dorcas said. 'I think Miss Fry should leave you now and that your ladyship should have a nap before dinner. It will do you good.'

'Very well, Dorcas,' Lady Brecon agreed and smiled at Caroline. 'Come and see me, dear, before you go down to dinner, and wear a pretty gown. Youth passes so quickly—make the best of it.'

'I try to do that, Ma'am,' Caroline replied. 'And I will wear one of my prettiest gowns to please you.'

In her own room she was at least free to think, yet puzzle as she might, Lord Brecon's behaviour at tea could not be explained. A dozen possibilities presented themselves, but Caroline discarded them one by one. The idea that

114

Lord Brecon had made a secret and disastrous marriage early in life and could not escape from the consequences of his mistake was one that she resolutely refused to countenance. Yet her mind returned to it again and again and as she dressed, her brows were wrinkled with thought and perplexity.

She would have worn one of her more elaborate ball gowns had not Maria protested that it would arouse suspicions, if not in the household, at least among the guests. To please her Caroline chose in the end a more simple dress of embroidered tulle which had a bunch of pink roses on the bodice and an embroidered scarf to match.

It was a pretty dress and became her well, and it was with a consciousness of her own beauty that she entered the drawing-room where the guests assembled before dinner. Despite her close scrutiny of the list Caroline was still a little apprehensive and she glanced searchingly at Lord Brecon's visitors as she entered, but she was relieved to find that not only had she never seen one of them before, but it was extremely unlikely that they would have moved in any society favoured by her godmother.

The gentlemen were mostly older than Lord Brecon and it was obvious from a certain coarseness both in their appearance and behaviour that they were not of the *bon ton*. Also it seemed from their conversation that they took little interest in anything save gaming in one form or another. They spoke of mills, races and cock-fights as if with them they were an everyday occurrence. Caroline was not surprised to see that the candles were lit in the card room and the tables set out ready for an evening's gambling.

The women were not particularly interesting. Several were flirtatious widows, and two or three of them had come with their husbands. Another, Mrs. Clarence Piggott-Rowe, was a middle-aged woman of almost masculine appearance but with a clear wit and, as Caroline learned later, a reputation for being the most dashing rider to hounds in three counties.

A prodigious amount of food and drink was consumed at dinner, but Caroline ate little. She found herself quite amused by the gentleman on her left. He was the Honourable Thomas Stratton whose name had seemed familiar.

Mr. Stratton was dressed in the extreme of fashion. His shoulders were padded to an extravagant width, the points of his collar were so high as to make it impossible for him

115

to turn his head, his waistcoat was striped and his coat of superfine cloth was of a startling shade of peacock-blue, ornamented with buttons of rubies and diamonds. He spoke with the bored drawl of a dandy; but Caroline, noticing that his eyes were often amused, guessed this was a deliberate pose and that he was really as *blasé* as he wished to appear.

Having regarded Caroline languidly through his quizzing glass, Mr. Stratton made little effort at conversation until his lordship's excellent wines began to take effect. Then he talked and the story of his life was somewhat unusual.

'I am the sixth son of an impoverished peer,' he told Caroline. 'I had resigned myself to enter the Church or sail for the Colonies, when my uncle, a devilish difficult fellow, who had quarrelled with all my brothers, died and left me a fortune. The Lord knows he would have quarrelled with me too if I hadn't kept out of his way. I am now in the happy position of being rich, and the unhappy one of not knowing what to do with myself. I have been brought up to be humble, self-effacing and thankful for the small mercies that life could offer me. And small enough they were, I can assure you! I am at the moment wealthy enough to indulge in any fancy which might take me, but unfortunately my fancies have been blunted by ill-usage. Now that I can afford to accept invitations and to give them, parties have lost their savour. There is no such anti-climax as when the unattainable becomes attainable. To tell the truth I am *blasé* of society before I have begun to enjoy it. Blister it, 'tis a monstrous position and though I ask every soul I meet, no one can suggest a cure.'

Caroline laughed.

'Have you sampled the delights of London, sir?'

'But indeed I have! I have spent over a year there, but the boredom of it nearly kills me. When I was poor, I had to make myself into an entertaining companion so that I paid for my supper; but among the rich no one attempts to be entertaining. They are just rich and devilish dull!'

'Oh, sir, I vow you are peculiarly critical,' Caroline said.

'Take the young females in Society,' Mr. Stratton went on, sipping his replenished glass and warming to his point. 'I declare the way they languish and ogle a man is enough to make one cry from sheer ennui! To be fashionable I have, to be sure, declared myself the slave of the latest beauty and avowed that unless she will have me I shall be

116

cast into utter despondency. There is no doubt that she is an incomparable, but what is one among so many?'

'And who is this unique lady?' Caroline asked, and Lord Brecon, who surprisingly had been listening to the conversation, although he was three places away, leaned forward to ask:

'Yes, Thomas, who is this lady who has at last captured your ice-bound heart? For I vow I thought you would never fall a victim to the fair sex?'

'Other women could not be mentioned in the same breath as the incomparable,' Mr. Stratton answered. 'I will give you her name and toast her at the same time. To the Beauty of all Beauties—the Lady Caroline Faye.'

He raised his glass, while Caroline felt the colour drain from her face as she stared at him.

'Lady Caroline Faye,' Lord Brecon repeated slowly. 'I think I have heard of her.'

'Damme, of course you have heard of her,' Mr. Stratton ejaculated. 'The very question in your voice, Brecon, shows what a yokel you are. Why, her ladyship is the talk of the town.'

'That is true enough,' remarked Mrs. Piggott-Rowe, who was sitting on Lord Brecon's right, 'and in more ways than one.'

'What, Ma'am, do you infer?' Mr. Stratton asked haughtily.

'Oh, I won't spoil your romance, Tommy, me dear,' she answered, 'for like Vance here I am delighted to hear that you have lost your heart at last. I swear I was ready to bet you had been born without that necessary organ. But there are ugly rumours circulating about your Lady Caroline and another. And who should that be but our old enemy Montagu Reversby!'

'Good God! That damned fellow!' Mr. Stratton said thumping the table. 'If ever there was a vulgar piece of goods, 'tis he! If I heard him so much as mention Lady Caroline's name in my presence, I will blow a hole through him, the devil I will.'

'Now don't make a fool of yourself, Thomas,' Lord Brecon said. 'You know you never were a hand with the pistols.'

'Lady Caroline and Montagu Reversby,' Mr. Stratton ejaculated in a strangled voice. ' 'Tis a lie whatever they may be saying.'

'Now, now, Tommy,' Mrs. Piggott-Rowe said soothingly. 'It is no use making a cake of yourself. These Society wenches are all the same, and being as mad as fire gets you nowhere.'

'It'll get Reversby into the next world before he is much older, if he's not careful,' Mr. Stratton muttered.

Lord Brecon's attention was distracted by the lady seated on his left and Caroline, relieved that he had withdrawn from the conversation, asked Mr. Stratton quietly but in a voice that shook a little with surprise and fright:

'What is Lady Caroline like?'

Mr. Stratton took a long drink and when he set down his glass, Caroline saw that he was slightly foxed. He looked at her, however, with eyes that were strangely honest and unsophisticated.

'I will tell you the solemn truth,' he whispered slowly, 'because I like you and because—by Jupiter—you are the prettiest girl I have seen for a very long time. Damme, I will let the cat out of the bag. I have never met her.'

Caroline laughed.

'Then why do you pretend to admire her so vastly?'

'Because the fellows are always roasting me for not dancing attendance on some simpering wench. Blister it, the creatures had no use for me when I was poor, so I am damned if they are going to catch hold of my purse-strings now I am rich.'

Caroline laughed, but she had a certain sympathy for Mr. Stratton. She knew how persistent the matchmaking Mamas could be when there was a matrimonial catch in sight, and how cleverly they could out-jockey and snub out of existence a man who was not eligible from a financial point of view, however charming he might be otherwise.

She was, however, too shaken and alarmed by what had taken place at dinner to be able to concentrate exclusively on Mr. Stratton's troubles. It had been for her a moment of horror when she heard her name toasted, and she had thought that at any moment her identity was about to be revealed.

When the ladies withdrew to the drawing-room, she sat talking for a little while and then went upstairs to see if the Dowager had need of her. Lady Brecon was already settled for the night, but as she was often wakeful, there was a pile of books by the bedside.

'If you cannot sleep, Ma'am, would you like me to read to you?' Caroline asked.

'No, thank you, my dear,' Lady Brecon replied; 'I shall read a little to myself, then I shall doze, then I shall read again. Dorcas comes in several times during the night to replenish the candles. Like myself she is a bad sleeper and does not mind attending to my wants. You go to bed and sleep soundly—you need sleep when you are young.'

'But is there nothing I can do for you?' Caroline insisted.

'Yes, there is,' Lady Brecon exclaimed. 'I have just thought of it. Dorcas tells me that the housekeeper has not fetched a packet of bird-seeds which we left ready for the budgerigars in my son's library. I am afraid this means that she has not fed them today. She is a careless woman and I must get Mrs. Miller to speak to her on the morrow. If you would be so kind, dear Miss Fry, to take the packet and give the birds a little of the seed I would indeed be grateful. I cannot bear it that the poor sweets should go hungry.'

'Nor I, Ma'am,' Caroline answered. 'Where is the seed?'

'It is on the console table by the window,' Lady Brecon answered. 'Will you fill their china dish and at the same time see if they have any water. There are two pairs in the cage—they were my most prized and beautiful birds, but I wanted to give my son a present on his homecoming and there was nothing I valued more.'

'I am sure he understood that,' Caroline said softly. 'Pray do not worry, Ma'am, I will see that the birds do not go hungry.'

She took the packet of seed and slipped downstairs. The drawing-room door was open, and from it and the card room she heard sounds of laughter and both male and female voices intermingled. The gentlemen had already joined the ladies.

The Library did not open off the Great Hall, but was reached by a passage, being slightly apart from the *salons* on the ground floor. Caroline had learned from Maria that it was Lord Brecon's own sanctum and was not used by visitors, so she opened the door without hesitation and, as she had anticipated the room was empty. A fire glowed in the big fireplace and the tapers in the sconces on either side of the mantel-shelf had been lit, but this was not enough to illuminate the entire room. In the far corners it was dark and shadowy, and Caroline felt it was all rather eerie as she moved towards the bird-cage which stood beside the shrouded windows.

The birds were asleep on their perches. She found they had no seed left and very little water. They twittered a little at her approach and were not afraid. She looked at their pretty little blue bodies and wondered if they felt lonely and neglected down here after the warmth and brightness of Lady Brecon's bedroom.

'Poor little things,' she said aloud. 'You are exiled from home, aren't you?'

She filled their china dish, then put the packet of seed on the table where nobody could fail to see it in the morning, and decided that she herself would give them fresh water and make sure they were not forgotten in future. She was stroking the tiny birds with the tip of her finger when she heard the door open.

It was closed again decisively, and turning slowly, she saw Lord Brecon walk across to the fireplace. His head was bent and she had the instananeous impression that he was despondent and depressed. He walked to the hearth to stand looking down into the fire, the candle-light turning his hair to gold.

For a moment or two Caroline watched him. His face was hidden but she felt she knew that his eyes would be heavy, his thoughts concerned with the dark secret which seemed to overshadow him. Suddenly she had an insane desire to walk across to him, to put her arms around him, to draw his head to her breast and comfort him.

He was unhappy, and as surely as if he had told her so, she knew that his mysterious secret was weighing down upon him, crushing his youth from him, destroying what should have been a heritage of happiness. She ached for him, her whole heart went out to him in that moment as if he had been her son—a little boy in trouble.

She must have made a slight sound or perhaps a sixth sense told Lord Brecon he was not alone, for he turned sharply. For a moment he looked at Caroline in astonishment and then, as she walked slowly towards him her eyes on his, an expression of gentle tenderness on her face, he took two quick strides towards her.

'Caroline!' he said and his voice was hoarse. 'Caroline, I was thinking of you.'

His words seemed to shatter the last barrier which had stood between them. Caroline forgot everything save the fact that Lord Brecon was looking at her, needing her as much as she needed him. There was no time to think, no time to remember anything save that intense and over-whelming need one for the other.

They were past words, past explanations. There was only one possible expression for the tempest of their feelings. Before Caroline knew how it happened, before she was aware of any movement on her part, Lord Brecon's arms were round her. She felt herself crushed against him, felt a sudden flame of ecstasy and joy consume her, and then his lips were on hers and they were clinging together, the world forgotten.

7

How long they stood there Caroline had no idea for she was lost in a rapture beyond anything she had ever known or imagined. The wonder of knowing that Lord Brecon's arms were round her and the ecstasy of feeling his mouth on hers swept her away in a flood-tide of joy so that she was conscious only of him and the magnetic closeness of him.

After a time the insistent pressure of his lips awoke an answering fire within her so that she no longer lay passive beneath his passion. In a rising crescendo of emotion it seemed to her then that humanity could not know such a thrilling of the senses and not break beneath the strain. At last Lord Brecon raised his head and looked down at her.

'Caroline! Caroline!' he murmured, his voice caught in his throat.

For a long, long moment he looked at the perfect beauty of her face raised to his, at the half shy, half exultant softness of her eyes awakened for the first time to a knowledge of passion, and at the sweet trembling of her parted lips. The flush on her cheeks deepened beneath his scrutiny.

'You are so lovely,' he said at length, 'so perfect. I never believed it was possible to find such beauty in any woman.'

With a little inarticulate murmur Caroline hid her face against his shoulder.

'Are you shy, my love?' he asked. 'I thought that night when I first kissed you and saw the startled surprise in your eyes that I was perhaps the first man who had dared to touch your lips. Is that so?'

Caroline raised her face and looked at him.

'You know the answer.'

'Yes, I do,' he replied, 'for you are adorably innocent and transparently pure. Oh, Caroline, I love you so.'

'And I . . . love you, Vane.'

Her voice was low, hardly above a whisper, yet there was somehow a ring in it as if her love rose triumphant over her shyness. Lord Brecon took her chin between his hands and turned her face once more upwards towards his.

'My darling, my little love,' he said, and then his lips were on hers once again and they forgot all else.

It seemed as if a century passed before at length, Caroline, trembling from the violence of her own feelings, tried to draw herself away.

'You must . . . return to your guests . . . my lord,' she said, but her voice broke on the words and her eyes were held by his so that she caught her breath and quivered again in a sudden wave of ecstasy.

Lord Brecon drew her fiercely to him.

'I love you,' he said defiantly. 'Do you hear me? I love you.'

'Must you look angry when you say it?' Caroline asked, daring to tease him because of the sheer, exultant happiness which seemed to envelop her in a golden haze and sing within her heart a paean of thankfulness.

'Do I look angry?'

He asked the question indifferently; then suddenly he gave a groan, and taking his arms from Caroline so unexpectedly that she almost fell, he turned and walked away towards the hearth. He stood with his back to her, looking down into the fire and as she stared at his back in astonished perplexity, he said roughly:

'This is madness!'

'Vane, what ails you?' Caroline asked.

Lord Brecon turned and she saw that his face was very pale.

'Caroline,' he said, 'you must believe me when I tell you that I did not mean this to happen. It is true that I have loved you from the first moment when I saw your face fully in the light of a lantern in Adam Grimbaldi's caravan, but I thought that you had gone from my life forever. I knew that I should never forget you. As you drove away in the moonlight, I told myself "there goes the only woman I shall ever love".'

'I am glad,' Caroline said a little breathlessly, 'that you knew then.'

She moved towards him, but with a gesture of his hand he stopped her.

'Don't come any nearer,' he said. 'What I have to say

123

must be said. If you are close, it will be impossible, for if my arms are round you I shall again forget everything but you, Caroline.'

'And why not?' Caroline asked, her lips smiling at him even though she was half afraid because of the seriousness of his tone and the unexpected darkness of his eyes.

'That is what I have to tell you, God help me,' Lord Brecon said. 'I should have sent you away, Caroline, the moment you came here. Mrs. Miller was right, though she did not know it, when she asked me to dismiss you. I should have bid you go with all speed, have refused to look on your lovely, enticing face, have shut my ears to the sound of your voice, have quelled the unceasing ache within me to touch you, to feel your lips again.'

Resolutely Caroline moved nearer to him, put out her hand and laid it on his arm.

'Vane,' she said quietly. 'What are you trying to say to me?'

'Must I put it clearer?' he asked, almost angrily. 'I am telling you to go, Caroline . . . to leave me, to forget my very existence.'

'But why?' Caroline asked. 'Why?'

'That is what I cannot tell you,' he replied. 'Don't ask me that question, Caroline, for I cannot give you the answer.'

'But I do not understand,' Caroline cried. 'We love each other.'

'Yes, we love each other.'

He put his hand over hers as it lay on his arm and she felt the hard strength of his fingers. She looked up to find his eyes blazing with a passion which seemed almost to scorch her.

'We love each other,' he repeated. 'I love you, Caroline, love you with all my heart and strength—but I cannot marry you.'

Caroline went very pale. She felt the warm blood drain away from her, felt for one agonising moment as if she would faint. Desperately her eyes searched Lord Brecon's face and then at last in a very small voice which quivered she asked:

'Is it because of the difference of our stations, my lord?'

Lord Brecon made a convulsive movement. For a moment Caroline was afraid that he would strike her. But instead his hands reached out and gripped her shoulders,

124

holding her so fiercely and with such violence that she gave an involuntary cry of pain.

'How dare you say such a thing to me? How dare you ask me such a question. What has your position to do with a love such as we have for each other? Would you insult me by expecting such trivialities to matter when it concerns a passion such as mine? No, Caroline,' he added more quietly, 'no, of course not.'

'Then, if that is not the reason, why may we not be . . . wed?'

Her voice softened on the word and even as she spoke it she knew that for her it held the heaven of her dreams—to be Vane's wife, to surrender herself utterly to him, to be his completely and absolutely in the fullest sense of the word.

Lord Brecon took his hands from her shoulders and put them up to his eyes.

'I cannot tell you,' he said, and his voice was raw. 'Don't torture me, Caroline. Go away and leave me. Forget me if you can, but go quickly while I am strong enough to let you go.'

Caroline was still for a moment; then she drew herself up to her full height.

'And if I will not?' she asked clearly.

Lord Brecon stared at her.

'What do you mean?' he asked.

'I asked you a question,' Caroline said, and now all the strength and pride of the Fighting Fayes was present in her upturned chin. 'I asked you what would happen if I refuse to leave you; and indeed why should I go? I love you. I believe that you are in danger. I came here for the set purpose of warning you of that danger; and now that I know that you love me even as I love you, why should I go?'

Lord Brecon looked at her and his face softened.

'Oh, Caroline, my beloved,' he said. 'Was there any woman like you? But, my darling, it is useless. Our love is doomed. There is nothing we can do about it.'

'Please tell me why,' Caroline begged, 'only tell me! How indeed can I fight for you if I do not know what enemy I am fighting?'

'Alas, that I cannot tell you,' Lord Brecon said. 'It is not my secret. If it were mine alone, then I could speak; yet what good would it do for you to know, save that I should have the agony of seeing you turn from me in loathing and disgust?'

'If that were true,' Caroline said, 'then my love would indeed be a weak thing and unworthy of the word. I would love you, Vane, whatever you had done, whatever crime you might have committed, whatever secret, however sinister and fearful, lay hidden in your past. It is you I love, not your secret, and it matters naught to me what it may be.'

'My beautiful Caroline,' Lord Brecon answered unsteadily. 'If I should kneel to kiss the very ground on which you have trodden, it could not express the very smallest part of my reverence for you. No one could be as fine and as wonderful as you. But, my darling, it is hopeless! You have got to go, to leave this house, for I swear I cannot bear to see you day after day and not make you mine.'

Caroline took a deep breath.

'Answer me one question my lord,' she said, 'answer it truthfully and as if upon your oath. Would it be possible for you, in the eyes of the Law and in the eyes of the Church, to make me your wife?'

'It would be possible,' Lord Brecon replied hesitatingly. 'There is no impediment of that sort, but . . .'

'That is all I wish to know,' Caroline interrupted, and added triumphantly. 'Then I shall stay here in this Castle until you ask me to marry you.'

'Caroline, would you see me crazed?' Lord Brecon asked. 'I would give my right arm if I could beg you to be my wife, but it is not possible, for, as I have told you, our love is doomed. Go, Caroline, go away while you are yet young enough to forget that we have ever met. Your life lies before you; you have youth and beauty, and if you need money I will give you all that you need and more, but go, in God's name, go!'

There was so much suffering and pain in Lord Brecon's voice that instinctively Caroline moved a little closer to him as if to comfort him.

'Let me help you,' she said pleadingly. 'Trust me, please trust me, for between us we will find a way out of this sorry tangle.'

'There is no way out,' Lord Brecon said dully, 'no possible escape, Caroline. If there had been, I would have found it long ago.'

He looked at her then straightened himself.

'I know what you are thinking,' he said accusingly, 'you are thinking that I am a coward such as you called me once before; but for once, Caroline, you are wrong. I am

126

doing the bravest thing I have ever done in my life in sending you away. I am doing the decent thing, too, though it is hard for you to believe it.'

Caroline suddenly felt as if she could argue no more with him. There was something so positive in his assurance, so frightening in his determination that unexpectedly she felt the tears coming to her eyes and a closing in her throat so that she was prevented from speaking.

She turned towards the door. For a moment her own fighting qualities were extinguished. She was only a woman who had offered herself to a man and been refused. She walked very slowly across the soft carpet, her head a little bent, her fingers knitted together in a fierce effort to prevent her tears. She did not look back; she had only one idea—to find some privacy where she might gain control over herself and her own weakness. Even as a child Caroline had been ashamed when she must cry, and now she wanted to hide both her tears and her humility from the man who had caused them.

She had reached the door when Lord Brecon's voice made her pause. He stood quite still on the hearth watching her go, keeping such a tight hold on himself that his hands were clenched, his jaw set as a man who fights against overwhelming odds. But now a cry burst from his lips.

'Caroline!' he called, and then he strode across the room towards her. 'How can I let you leave me in such a manner?' he cried. 'Oh, my sweet love, I worship you!'

He swept her into his arms, holding her so closely against his breast that she could hardly breathe. For a long moment he just held her there, and as her eyes, misty with tears, looked up into his and her lips trembled, she was conscious of his rising desire for her and of a passion which swept over him like a tempest.

'I love you! God, how I love you!'

His voice was hoarse and once again he was kissing her, kissing her wildly, fiercely, possessively. His kiss seemed to draw her very soul from between her lips, then she felt his mouth on her eyes, on the hollows at the base of her neck and on the little blue veins above her breasts.

For a moment Caroline was too exhausted emotionally either to reciprocate his passion or to repulse it; she could only lie submissive beneath the hunger of his kisses, weak beneath a strength such as she had never deemed possible in any man.

127

'You are mine,' she heard him cry, 'mine. I defy fate to take you from me.'

He lifted her off her feet. She lay against his chest, helpless as a baby, and she saw he was transformed, his face alight with triumph and exaltation. At that moment he seemed like a god—a god who has attained his most cherished desire. She felt an inexpressible joy; then as if a light had been blown out she saw his expression alter.

Still carrying her, he opened the door of the Library and before she could be certain what he was about Caroline found herself set down on her feet and left without support. The door closed behind her. She heard the key turn in the lock and she was alone in the dimly lit passage.

For a moment she leant against the wall, too weak to move, too shattered to make any sense from the chaos in which her thoughts, feelings and passions were entangled. Then slowly, very slowly and unsteadily like someone recovering from a very long illness she began to walk down the passage towards the hall.

She heard great bursts of laughter and the sound of noisy voices coming from the drawing-room and the card-room. A footman passed her with a heavily laden tray, but she did not even see him. She moved like a sleep-walker up the broad staircase and along the corridors which led to her room. Only when she reached her own room and had thrown herself face downwards on the bed, her face buried in the pillow, did she find an expression for her feelings.

'Vane! Vane!' she cried, 'I love you! I love you,' and the tears streamed unchecked from her eyes.

It was thus Maria found her the following morning, for she had slept from utter exhaustion after a storm of weeping which had seemed a greater agony than anything she had ever known.

'M'lady,' Maria exclaimed in horror, 'you haven't been to bed. Why are you still in your evening gown? Are you ill, m'lady? Why did you not ring for me?'

'No, I am not ill,' Caroline answered, 'at least I think not. My head aches, and . . . Oh, Maria, I am so unhappy.'

The words came out with a rush before she could prevent them, and Maria looked at her both in astonishment and in horror.

'Unhappy, m'lady? Then 'tis leaving this moment we are for Mandrake. We will not stay in any place that makes you unhappy, not to save His Majesty himself from being

128

murdered. We will go home, m'lady, and then everything will be all right.'

'But it won't,' Caroline said miserably, standing up so that Maria could unfasten the creased and crumpled evening gown.

'You are cold, m'lady,' Maria said accusingly as Caroline gave a little shiver. ' 'Tis not surprised I am, seeing how you slept this past night. Warm the weather may be, but not warm enough for that. Now put on this wrap, m'lady, and get into bed. Sip your chocolate while 'tis hot and I will start packing right away.'

'No, do not do that, Maria,' Caroline said wearily, 'but, if you remember, we came for a special reason and that reason still exists.'

Maria sighed.

'I declare, m'lady, I don't know what to do. If I did my duty as I sees it, I should take you home whatever you may say to the contrary, but I've never been able to gainsay your ladyship, and that you well know.'

'Then do not try to do it now,' Caroline said.

She finished her chocolate and lay back against the pillows.

'Have I time for a sleep, Maria?'

'Indeed you have, m'lady. Miss Dorcas has just informed me that her ladyship will not be requiring your services until noon, having passed an ill night herself. Go to sleep, m'lady, and if you'll put the bell when you awake, I'll bring you some breakfast.'

'Thank you, Maria,' Caroline said. 'I feel unaccountably drowsy; but before you go, tell me, is there any news?'

'Only one thing,' Maria said. 'Mr. Gervase Warlingham comes tonight. I heard Mrs. Miller with my own ears inform the housekeeper of the fact; and what's more, she instructed that he be given the bedchamber next to her own.'

'Tonight!'

Caroline was wide awake now.

'Yes, m'lady, for tonight there is to be a big party, guests are invited from the county and there will be over fifty to dine. 'Tis Mrs. Miller who has invited them in his lordship's name, for I understand she aches to give parties and play the hostess, especially if Mr. Warlingham is there to watch her do it.'

'I understand,' Caroline said, and gave a sigh of relief. At last she was to meet Mr. Gervase Warlingham.

'I would not leave for Mandrake now, Maria, not if you gave me a thousand guineas,' she murmured.

'You go to sleep, m'lady,' Maria said. 'Perhaps you will think otherwise when you awake.'

'There is not a hope of that,' Caroline replied; and as Maria pulled the curtains, she turned her face to the wall and dropped into a dreamless slumber.

With the elasticity of youth there was little trace on her face of her stormy, unhappy night when she woke. Gone was the despair she had known during the night; she could only remember that Vane loved her and she loved him. What did secrets, however sinister, matter when the rapture of their love could sweep them into a Paradise where all else was forgotten? Vane's determination not to marry her was, she thought, equalled by her determination that he should do so; and as her heart quickened its beat at the thought of belonging to him, it was easy to believe that time would prove her the victor.

Caroline was smiling when she visited Lady Brecon later in the morning. The fears and terrors, the utter misery she had experienced alone in the darkness seemed exaggerated and unreal now that the sun was shining and the Dowager's little budgerigars were chirping happily in their cages. Caroline was certain that there was a way to solve the puzzle, she was sure that eventually she would save the man she loved both from danger and from the despondency of the secret he guarded so carefully.

'It is a glorious day, Miss Fry,' Lady Brecon said.

'Yes, Ma'am,' Caroline agreed.

'Too nice for you to stay indoors,' Lady Brecon said. 'I am going to have a sleep this afternoon, child, so I suggest you go into the gardens or visit Harriet at the Vicarage. That reminds me, I believe my son is entertaining this evening. Dorcas tells me that preparations are going on in the household. It would be a kind action to ask little Harriet Wantage to come for dinner, and she will keep you company.'

'Harriet would be delighted, I am sure, Ma'am,' Caroline said.

'Well, go and invite her,' Lady Brecon commanded, 'and Dorcas will inform Mrs. Miller that it is at my invitation.'

Caroline smiled at this, for she knew quite well that Lady Brecon was sparing her an unpleasant moment with Mrs. Miller who would doubtless make trouble at an extra guest whom she had not included in her own list.

'Her ladyship is sweet,' Caroline thought as she returned to her own room, 'but pitiably weak. Personally I could not bear to let a woman such as Mrs. Miller rule my household.'

But she was beginning to suspect that Lady Brecon had a definite object in excluding herself from the world. She might have been a nun, so divorced was she from any interest outside her own room. Dorcas sometimes related scraps of gossip to her, but Caroline was sure that Lady Brecon listened more for Dorcas' sake than because of her own curiosity. It was a strange behaviour for the châtelaine of a great Castle and even stranger on the part of a mother, especially one as devoted as Lady Brecon was to her son; and yet doubtless, Caroline thought, she had a good reason for her refusal to battle with the trials and difficulties of ordinary, everyday life.

Caroline went to her wardrobe to search for a suitable dress for Harriet to wear that evening. She found one, a gown of pink sarsnet trimmed with bunches of moss roses and forget-me-nots which, as it happened, had never suited her, for her hair was too brilliant for such a colour; but she knew it would be an admirable frame for Harriet's dark brown hair and trusting brown eyes.

She was just about to ring for Maria and tell her to pack the gown into a parcel when she glanced out of the window and saw an elegant figure strolling across the lawns towards the stone gazebo which stood at the far end of the formal garden. It was Mr. Stratton, and as Caroline watched him she remembered their conversation of the night before.

He had been amusing about his present circumstances, and yet a real bitterness lay beneath his jesting. He did in truth find that his fortune had deprived him of much of his belief in human nature when it thrust him unexpectedly into high Society. Underneath his dandified posturing he still held to the simple standards and unaffected virtues he had known in his days of poverty. And Caroline could understand his almost childlike yearnings to be loved for himself alone. She sighed for him, because she found an echo of such an aspiration in her own heart. Even now there was a tiny lingering doubt whether Lord Brecon might not change his mind about marriage when eventually he learnt her real station in life. And although she told herself firmly that she was being unfair and disloyal to the man she loved and that he was too fine a person, too strong a character to

131

be swayed by such superficialities, the poisoned thought recurred.

Impatient and angry with herself, Caroline concentrated her attention on Mr. Stratton. And as she watched him seat himself in the gazebo, she gave a little exclamation. She had an idea! She ran across the room and tugged at the bellrope.

When Maria came hurrying in response to her summons, Caroline said to her:

'Pack up that pink dress, Maria, and also that striped cambric with the fichu. Do you remember it? It was a dress I wore in a masque when I had to appear as a simple village maid. I told you to pack it in case it proved useful.'

'Yes, indeed, m'lady,' Maria answered. 'It is here and I have laid it in the bottom drawer of the chest. But why should your ladyship require it now?'

'Because I have a plan,' Caroline said. 'Take it, put it with the evening gown, and hurry as quickly as you can to the Vicarage. Speak with Miss Wantage alone; tell her I have sent you; dress her in the striped cambric, arrange her hair as modishly as you can, Maria, and tell her to expect me within the next twenty minutes. When she sees me, she is not to mention that I have sent her the gowns, make that quite clear.'

'Oh dear, m'lady,' Maria moaned, 'what new scheme is afoot? I declare my head whirls with your ladyship's plottings.'

'Cease chattering, Maria, there is no time,' Caroline commanded. 'Hurry to Miss Wantage and tell her exactly what I have told you. I am saving someone else, but this time not from death but from a lonely spinsterhood.'

Caroline, smiling at Maria's gaping mouth, went downstairs and out into the garden. She strolled across the lawns, obviously deeply engrossed in the flowers. Mr. Stratton rose as she approached the gazebo. Caroline, who was looking very attractive in a chip-straw bonnet trimmed with bunches of lilies-of-the-valley and leaf-green ribbons, gave a pretended start.

'Lud, sir, but you surprised me. I was not expecting to find anyone lurking in this secluded spot.'

'I sought it for that very reason,' Mr. Stratton answered, and then he added hastily: 'Do not misunderstand me, Miss Fry. I value your presence here, it is the rest of the party from whom I would escape. Blister it, a more noisy, uncouth collection it has seldom been my misfortune to encounter. Brecon must be crazed to invite such company.'

'Oh, Mr. Stratton, then you are not enjoying yourself?'

'I never seem to do that these days,' he replied gloomily.

Caroline seated herself beneath the gazebo.

'It is obvious, sir, that you have too great sensibility for the society in which you move. It is not of course for me, a poor dependent, to criticise, but I did not think his lordship's guests last night were greatly distinguished for their brains.'

Mr. Stratton laughed.

'You put it most genteelly, Miss Fry; but I agree with you, they are a bacon-brained crowd. Those of them who weren't too foxed gamed until the dawn, and when I left them just now they were sitting down to the tables again. Try as I may, I cannot bring myself to pay a serious attention to gaming.'

'And why should you, sir?' Caroline asked. 'But now I must leave you to your reading. I envy you the enjoyment of that book I see beneath your arm.'

She rose to her feet.

'Must you leave me, Miss Fry?' Mr. Stratton asked.

'Alas, I must,' Caroline sighed, 'though I assure you, sir, I would far prefer to linger in such congenial company. But I have to carry a message for her ladyship to the Vicarage and I vow I am scared to death to take it.'

'Scared?' Mr. Stratton asked. 'May I enquire why?'

'It is the Vicar, sir,' Caroline said, lowering her head as if in embarrassment, her voice very low. 'He is indeed a most unpleasant gentleman.'

'Makes himself unpleasant to you, does he?' Mr. Stratton said grimly. 'Well, we'll soon settle that, for I will accompany you on your errand, Miss Fry, if you will permit me.'

Caroline clasped her hands together.

'Oh, sir, would you really? It is too much to ask of you when you would rest here in comfort.'

'I am delighted to be of service, Miss Fry. Tell me more of this Vicar.'

'I find the Reverend gentleman very unprepossessing,' Caroline said demurely, casting down her eyes. 'But that is not all. He is exceeding unkind to my poor friend, his daughter, Miss Harriet Wantage. She was at school with me and a more charming, gentle soul one would find it hard to meet anywhere. I will tell you in the strictest confidence, sir, that her father is monstrously cruel to her.'

'Cruel? What then does he do?' Mr. Stratton asked curiously.

As they walked across the green lawns and on to the long drive which led to the village, Caroline regaled him with a tale of the Vicar's cruelties which lasted nearly the whole way to the Vicarage. If she drew somewhat freely upon her imagination, she told her conscience that it was not without justification, for Harriet's pale, frightened little face haunted her.

They reached the Vicarage and Caroline had a quick glimpse of Maria peeping out of an upstairs window before she opened the gate into the untidy and ill-kept garden.

'Pray heaven the Vicar is not at home, sir,' she said, 'for perhaps he will be angered with me for bringing a distinguished visitor such as yourself to the Vicarage without invitation.'

'If he is angry he had better not show it in my presence,' Mr. Stratton said with unexpected vigour, his languid air seemingly forgotten for the moment.

The front door was opened before they rang the bell and Harriet held out her arms in welcome to Caroline. It was Harriet, but a very changed person indeed, as Caroline saw with satisfaction. As she had anticipated, the simple but well-made gown with its fresh white fichu was vastly becoming and Maria had arranged Harriet's hair in the latest mode so that a dozen tiny curls framed her thin face giving it an unexpectedly piquant expression. Harriet's eyes were always her best feature, and they were wide now with excitement.

Caroline introduced Mr. Stratton and Harriet led them into the cheerless, threadbare sitting-room.

'I have an invitation for you, Harriet,' Caroline said. 'Her ladyship hopes that you will come to dinner at the Castle this evening. A number of people from the County have been invited and she feels you would enjoy the party.'

'Oh, Caroline, how exciting,' Harriet exclaimed; then her face dropped. 'But perhaps Papa will not let me accept.'

'I will try to persuade him,' Caroline said. 'Where is he?'

'He is in his study,' Harriet said. 'He is writing his sermon for Sunday. It always makes him exceeding ill-tempered.'

'You wait here,' Caroline said. 'I will tell him of the invitation.'

'Dare you do so?' Harriet asked breathlessly. 'I vow I could not ask him myself. I am sadly in disgrace today for the goose we had for luncheon was over-cooked. Papa was half an hour late, but he swore that was no excuse. Oh, Caroline, there was such a to-do, and he threatened to flog me if dinner was not more to his liking. Do not anger him more . . . perhaps it would be wiser to make my apologies to her ladyship and not trouble Papa.'

'Leave him to me,' Caroline said.

'Oh, Caroline, how brave you are!' Harriet cried, and turning to Mr. Stratton she asked, 'Is she not, sir?'

'Mr. Stratton won't think so,' Caroline smiled, 'for I assure you, Harriet, that he is never afraid of anything except being bored.'

'I'm sure he isn't,' Harriet said in simple flattery and Mr. Stratton smiled at her with a most un-*blasé* spontaneity.

Caroline left them alone in the sitting-room and went across the hall to the study. She knocked and found the Vicar not, as might be expected, sitting at his desk; but stretched out comfortably in a big leather armchair, a glass of wine at his elbow. He got up slowly when he saw Caroline in the doorway and she swept him a deep curtsey. Tactfully and making full use of the most fulsome flattery which, as she anticipated, he absorbed with the greatest of ease, Caroline informed him of Lady Brecon's invitation and received his reply that Harriet was a fortunate brat to be asked anywhere, seeing how dumb she was.

'All the same, I have a very good mind to punish the little idiot by making her stay at home this evening,' he ruminated. 'She's plagued me today beyond endurance.'

'Oh, sir, you could never be so cruel,' Caroline expostulated, and added archly: 'Why, I declare, you are but bamming, for I perceive a twinkle in the corner of your eye.'

The Vicar capitulated.

'Very well then, tell the chit she can go, tho' the lord knows what she will wear, for she looks like a ragbag at all times.'

'I took the liberty, sir, of bringing her a dress of my own,' Caroline said quickly. 'It belonged to Lady Caroline Faye and I know her ladyship would be only too delighted for Harriet to wear it this evening.'

'If the girl were not so daft, she would make herself a decent gown,' the Vicar grumbled; 'but settle it amongst yourselves.'

'Thank you, sir, you are indeed generous,' Caroline said, then she hesitated and added in a tone of nervous fluster: 'I think . . . I ought to mention, sir, that . . . that a gentleman accompanied me here.'

She hesitated, cast down her eyes, then raised them again and twisted her fingers together with every appearance of helpless agitation.

'I know I ought not to have brought him, sir . . . but I could not help myself. He was very insistent, and though he has had these few moments alone with Harriet, I feel sure it will have done her no harm.'

'Harm!' the Vicar growled. 'What do you mean by harm?'

'Oh, nothing, sir, nothing,' Caroline fluttered. 'To be fair, he speaks most pleasantly and I know little of him save that he is a sixth son and his father impoverished. . . .'

'I want no paupers and hangers-on in my Vicarage,' the Vicar said sharply. 'They bode no good to anyone—he has no business to force his way in.'

'Oh, sir, I fear it was my fault,' Caroline wilted.

'I can well believe that you could not prevent him pushing himself forward, Miss Fry. It would be difficult for someone in your position to say nay to one of his lordship's guests, but here I am my own master. Where is this penniless jackanapes?'

The Vicar picked up his glass of wine, swilled it down his throat, wiped his mouth and strode red-faced and pompous, into the drawing-room.

Harriet and Mr. Stratton were laughing as he entered, and Caroline, following behind the Vicar, had time to note that Harriet was looking amazingly pretty with flushed cheeks and shining eyes.

'Harriet,' the Vicar boomed in a voice of thunder, 'the fire in my study is half out, and there is no wood and no coal available. Find one of the maids and have it attended to immediately. How often have I told you to see that my fire is kept replenished? I might as well talk to a deaf-mute for all the response I get.'

Like an animal who has been constantly ill-treated Harriet cringed before her father.

'Yes, Papa . . . of course, Papa . . . I'm sorry, Papa . . .' she said and crept hastily from the room.

'As for you, sir,' the Vicar said furiously, glaring at the surprised Mr. Stratton, 'I would bid you good-day. Neither I nor my daughter have the time nor the inclination for visitors of your sort.'

He turned abruptly on his heel, nodded coolly to Caroline and went back into his study, slamming the door behind him.

Caroline looked at Mr. Stratton.

'We had better go,' she whispered. 'It will only be the worse for Harriet if we linger.'

As they got outside the front door, Caroline saw that Mr. Stratton's mouth was tightened into an ominous straight line and his jaw was set determindedly. There was no sign of boredom about him now.

'The man is an inexpressible brute,' he said fiercely; 'and to think that unhappy child has to endure him day after day. Such cruelty should be prevented, Miss Fry.'

'It should indeed,' Caroline said sadly, 'but what can anyone do? As for Harriet, I am afraid there is no hope for her, for she has not the strength, poor sweet, to rebel; and if she did, I believe her father would in very truth half kill her. No, she will live under the yoke of his cruelty until she wastes away in a decline, for she has no possible chance of escape.'

'Do not despair, we will find one,' Mr. Stratton said firmly; and Caroline turned her head aside so that he should not see her smile.

8

When Caroline and Mr. Stratton entered the Castle, they found Lady Augusta and Lord Brecon standing in the great hall. They were talking together and Caroline had the impression that Lady Augusta was pleading with Lord Brecon, for her bony, be-ringed fingers were clutching at his arm and her painted lips wore an ingratiating smile.

Lord Brecon looked stern but aloof, and Caroline thought that his face lightened at her approach. He was about to greet her but before he could speak Lady Augusta cried out:

'And where have you two young people been? I saw you sneaking off together unchaperoned. Fie on you, Miss Fry, you will be getting a reputation if you do not take care.'

Caroline dropped Lady Augusta a curtsey.

'I was on an errand for her ladyship,' she said stiffly.

Lady Augusta laughed and the hoarse, cackling sound seemed to echo round the dark walls.

'Hoity-toity! I declare the chit is piqued by me. Do not deny it, Miss Fry; but you must forgive the wagging of an old woman's tongue! 'Tis the penalty you pay for being passing fair to look on. And there Mr. Stratton will agree with me, eh, sir?'

Mr. Stratton murmured his acquiescence in polite but slightly embarrassed tones.

'Ha-ha, you rogue,' Lady Augusta cackled. 'Me-thought you were immune from the wiles of my sex, but I perceive I was mistaken. You have deceived us most skilfully. Has he not, Vane?'

She turned to appeal to her nephew, and Caroline, glancing at Lord Brecon, was surprised at the sudden anger on his face. For a moment she wondered what could have upset him and then she understood. He was jealous! With a little smile she turned to Mr. Stratton.

'My grateful thanks for your company, sir. You have been vastly obliging.'

She curtsied to Lady Augusta, asked leave to withdraw, and without looking again at Lord Brecon moved gracefully up the Grand Staircase well aware that she had left a sudden silence behind her—a silence which she was not surprised to hear broken by yet another cackling laugh from Lady Augusta.

So Lord Brecon was jealous. She was too well versed in the jealousy of the *beaux* who had courted her in London not to recognise the symptoms. The fact that Lord Brecon was vulnerable on this point was peculiarly satisfying, for, Caroline argued to herself, it might break down his obstinate silence and undermine his determination that she should leave the Castle.

Caroline smiled when, on reaching her bedroom she removed her bonnet; for the moment her own problems seemed less formidable and she was well pleased with what she had accomplished so far on Harriet's behalf. It was obvious that Mr. Stratton already saw himself in the role of knight-errant, which was just what she had intended.

He was a nice young man, Caroline thought, though a trifle dull with his prosing and posturing. But Harriet would find him entrancing, and if he should offer for her it would be the most splendid thing that could possibly happen.

Caroline thought of Harriet and was optimistic enough to be sure that she would find happiness eventually; but inevitably she could not help comparing Harriet's chances with her own and the smile vanished from her lips. All the fears and anxieties of the night before came rushing over her once again now that she was alone with nothing else to occupy her thoughts. And although resolutely Caroline told herself that she would not be afraid, that somehow she would discover Lord Brecon's secret and save him both from himself and from the danger which beset him, she felt for the first time in her life weak and ineffectual.

As the clock on the mantelshelf struck four, Caroline went down the passage and knocked on the door of Lady Brecon's bedroom. Dorcas opened it.

'I was wondering if you had come back, Miss Fry,' she said in her gruff voice; but her eyes were kindly and Caroline had the impression that Dorcas not only approved of her, but liked her.

She was well aware that to get into Dorcas' bad books would make things very difficult for any companion to her ladyship. Dorcas had what amounted almost to an adoration of her mistress. Nothing was too much trouble, nothing was too small, nothing too great where it concerned Lady Brecon's well-being. Dorcas fussed over her as if she were a babe in arms and Caroline could see that Lady Brecon had grown used to relying absolutely on Dorcas not only in things that concerned her physical comfort, but in everything else which touched her narrow, isolated existence.

It was really Dorcas who decided who should visit Lady Brecon or who should be kept outside with excuses that her ladyship was not so well or that her ladyship was asleep. It was Dorcas, too, who brought her news of what was happening in the household, choosing only those items which she wished to pass on and deliberately keeping back others if she felt they might disturb or worry her mistress. Yes, Dorcas' power was absolute and Caroline could not help but be glad that she had, as Maria would have said, 'got on the right side of her.'

'Oh, here you are, Miss Fry,' Lady Brecon exclaimed with a smile as she approached the bedside. 'How is little Harriet, and will she be permitted to visit us tonight?'

'Yes, indeed, Ma'am, and she was thrilled at the invitation.'

'You managed to contrive a gown for her?'

'Yes, Ma'am, it was one of Lady Caroline Faye's and should prove vastly becoming to Harriet.'

'You are a kind girl, Miss Fry,' Lady Brecon said softly, and Caroline flushed suddenly, half ashamed to receive praise for something which she knew in her heart of hearts had cost her very little.

It was then the thought came to her that very soon it might be possible to end this subterfuge. She would tell Lord Brecon of her real identity and then his mother. Perhaps when he learnt the truth, he would realise how deep and strong was her love for him and be gratified that she had dared so much on his behalf. But before she gave away her secret, Caroline wanted to be certain there was some chance of learning his, and at least she would wait until after the visit of Mr. Gervase Warlingham, for she was extremely curious to see the man who had in reality been instrumental in bringing her hot-foot to the Castle after she had learnt of Lord Milborne's suspicions regarding him.

140

'You are looking very pensive, Miss Fry,' Lady Brecon said, interrupting her thoughts

'I'm sorry, Ma'am'

'Of what were you thinking, or is it a secret?'

'I was thinking of you, your son, and the people here in this Castle,' Caroline answered truthfully

Lady Brecon sighed.

'Are they so very ill-bred?

'Indeed, Ma'am, I did not suggest such a thing!' Caroline exclaimed.

'Yet, I feel instinctively that they are not desirable acquaintances for Vane. I wish I knew what I could do about it, but I can only pray for him and hope that time will bring him wisdom.'

'Then you think that he is unwise, Ma'am?' Caroline asked.

Lady Brecon smiled.

'I did not say so, Miss Fry. It is only that I feel at times that he is restless, at war within himself. He does not tell me so, doubtless because he has no wish to worry me—but a mother senses these things.'

'You have no idea of the reason for . . such restlessness?' Caroline asked.

Lady Brecon shook her head.

'Alas, he does not confide in me. When he was a little boy he told me everything; but now, although invariably he shows me a loving consideration, I have no knowledge of what lies within his heart.'

There was a moment's silence which was broken by Dorcas bringing in the tea-things.

Caroline felt her pulses quicken. Would Lord Brecon come to tea today? Or would he avoid her because of what passed between them last night?

She made the tea, measuring the spoonfuls carefully from the crested silver caddy, and as she was passing a cup to Lady Brecon there came a knock at the door. She knew instinctively who it was even before Dorcas crossed the room, before she saw her bob respectfully.

When his lordship entered and came to his mother's bedside, Caroline saw that there were dark lines under his eyes as if he had not slept the night before. She rose and made her curtsey before sitting down again at the table and pouring him out a cup of tea.

Lord Brecon spoke to his mother and it seemed to

Caroline as if he deliberately turned himself away from her so that he should not look at her more than was absolutely necessary. She felt her heart ache suddenly. Why must he torture himself so? Why must he make them both so utterly miserable, when by a few words, by a single sentence he could transform the world for both of them? Nothing could be too bad or too terrifying that it could not be faced together; nothing, Caroline thought in her simplicity, could be so horrifying that it could not be bridged or conquered by love.

'Will you pour me another cup of tea, Miss Fry?' Lady Brecon asked.

Caroline rose to take the cup. As she did so, Lord Brecon spoke with a sudden harshness in his voice.

'Miss Fry will have told you, Mother, that her father has been taken ill and that she must leave us.'

'Why no, she has not mentioned it to me,' Lady Brecon said in surprise. 'Is this true? I am indeed distressed.'

Caroline looked across the table and met Lord Brecon's eyes. It seemed to her that they were as hard as steel and that his jaw was set unusually square. She was surprised by Lord Brecon's sudden attack, yet her wits were quick enough to find an answer without much difficulty.

'I did not tell you, Ma'am,' she said quietly to Lady Brecon, 'because I did not wish to perturb you unnecessarily. As his lordship says, my father is ill; but it is only one of his annual attacks of gout and my mother assures me that there is no reason for me to return home.'

'I am indeed glad of that,' Lady Brecon said, 'for I should hate to lose you, Miss Fry. You will think me most impetuous, Vane,' she said, turning to her son, 'but in such a short time I have a real affection for Miss Fry. I like to look at her and she has the most charming reading voice I have ever heard. You must come and listen to her one afternoon when you have the time to spare.'

'That will indeed be enjoyable,' Lord Brecon said, and Caroline fancied there was a note of sarcasm in his tone.

He rose to his feet.

'I must leave you, Mother. I have much to occupy me before this evening's rout commences. Mrs. Miller, it appears, has invited half the County, but I am afraid they will find themselves sadly out of tune with the majority of my guests.'

'Oh, Vane, try not to quarrel with anyone,' Lady Brecon said pleadingly. 'I would like you to live on friendly terms with all your neighbours. They used to be so fond of you, but now it seems to me that many old acquaintances are strangely aloof and I sense, too, an air of disapproval.'

'Mother, how can you know that, lying here and seeing so few people?'

'They write to me, Vane, and perhaps, too, I am particularly sensitive where you are concerned. Promise me to try and make yourself pleasant.'

Lord Brecon hesitated as if he debated within himself, and then suddenly he capitulated.

'Very well, Mother, if it gives you satisfaction, I promise to make an effort. And that reminds me, we shall have one unexpected guest who will give a tone to the evening.'

'Who is that?' Lady Brecon enquired.

'I have but this moment received a letter from the Bishop of Barnet,' Lord Brecon replied, 'saying that his lordship is on his way to Canterbury and will give himself the pleasure of dining here tonight. He has no idea, of course, that we are entertaining.'

'Oh, Vane!' Lady Brecon exclaimed in dismay, 'in that case would it not be wise to ask his lordship to dine another night?'

'I can hardly do that as he is already *en route.* I can, of course, turn him from the door and send him to *The Pig and Whistle,* but I hardly think the dinner there would tempt his lordship's palate, for he is an acknowledged epicure.'

'No, no, if he has started, we can do nothing,' Lady Brecon said, 'but I would not like the Bishop to be shocked by anything he might find here.'

Lord Brecon laughed.

'You need not worry, Mother, for his lordship is much more anxious to please me than I him. I have twelve good livings under my patronage and I know full well that the reason for his visit is not a desire for my company but because his lordship wants me to appoint his nephew to the incumbency at Weston Cross. It is a goodly benefice and is in a fine hunting country. That is why Brecon Castle is a convenient resting place this evening for his lordship, for I am well aware that by the time dinner is over he will find it too late to proceed to Canterbury and will remain here the night.'

'I am afraid these intrigues are far beyond me,' Lady Brecon sighed.

'Which is a good thing, Mother. Would you care to see the Bishop, if he stays, which undoubtedly he will?'

Lady Brecon shook her head.

'I think not, Vane. I find strangers difficult to talk with, for I know so little of the outside world. No, convey to the Lord Bishop my most respectful greetings and express my deep regret that I am not well enough to entertain visitors.'

'I will give him your message, Mother,' Lord Brecon said, and then without glancing at Caroline, he went from the room.

She felt strangely depressed when later she went to her own bedchamber to change for dinner. She knew now that Lord Brecon was determined to be rid of her, and though he had been balked for the moment, she was certain he would eventually find a way to drive her from the Castle, however hard she might make it for him to do so without upsetting his mother or arousing her suspicions.

There was only one possible thing Caroline could do now and that was to reveal her real identity. She had wished perhaps in vanity that Lord Brecon should propose to her while he still believed her to be Caroline Fry; but if he were determined on driving Miss Fry from the Castle, then she must meet him on his own ground and tell him who she was.

Caroline began to imagine how this might simplify matters. She could then send for Cousin Debby and stay on in the Castle as a guest. It might be just as easy for her then to watch for Gervase Warlingham and to circumvent his plans as it would be to do so as Lady Brecon's companion. Yet the difficulty was to be certain that he was making plans, and if he was, that they would be speedily put into operation. She had in reality so little to go on. There were the murder of Rosenberg, Lord Milborne's suspicions and Mrs. Miller's careless words spoken in the heat of anger. But that was all, unless she counted her own instinctive premonition that Lord Brecon was overshadowed by a very real danger.

It was all very perplexing, yet Caroline found it impossible to be downcast for long. Somehow she would win through, somehow she would find a way to save Lord Brecon and bring him happiness.

'What will you wear tonight, m'lady?' Maria asked, standing at the wardrobe door.

Caroline hesitated. She had meant to wear a quiet, rather

modest robe, but now it seemed to her that her pretence and disguise was almost at an end. Very well then, she would be dashing. Maria had on her instructions packed two of her loveliest and most elaborate gowns. Caroline had thought then that when she finally revealed herself she would wish to be transformed from a demurely garbed dowd into the modish elegance of a lady of fashion.

This was the moment, and she would dazzle the assembled company with one of the splendid creations that she had worn in London. Perhaps later tonight she might find an opportunity to speak with Lord Brecon, to tell him the truth. To be sure of her appearance would give her the courage and self-confidence to face him.

'Bring me the white gown, Maria, the one I wore at Devonshire House,' Caroline commanded.

Maria turned round in astonishment.

'But m'lady, 'tis far too grand! Why, anyone who saw you in that would guess at once that you are not whom you pretend to be.'

'I care not,' Caroline said recklessly. 'This farce is almost at an end, anyway, Maria.'

'Thank the good lord for that,' Maria ejaculated, 'for 'tis sick and tired I am o' it, m'lady. There's never a moment that I'm not waiting with my heart in my mouth to hear that something terrible has occurred to your ladyship and wondering how I'll dare confess to them at Mandrake how we came to be here, play-acting in parts for which your ladyship is ill-suited.'

'Perhaps you are right, Maria,' Caroline said. 'Well, I'll wear my best dress. It will at least make Mrs. Miller arch her eyebrows.'

' 'Twill indeed,' Maria said; 'but wait, m'lady, until you see her gown for tonight. 'Twould be daring in Vauxhall Gardens, let alone in a gentleman's house.'

'Well, mine at least is respectable,' Caroline smiled; but when she looked at herself in the mirror, she was not certain that that was the right adjective to describe it.

The dress was of the purest white satin covered with tulle and ornamented with row upon row of tiny scalloped lace frills. The bodice, which revealed the full beauty of Caroline's neck and shoulders, was embroidered with flowers fashioned from thousands of little opalescent pearls and the puffed sleeves were of transparent and delicate lace. There were pearl ornaments to be worn in her hair, a bracelet of real pearls for each of her wrists.

145

'Oh, 'tis lovely, m'lady,' Maria exclaimed. 'but all the same I've always been scared of this gown.'

'Scared, Maria?' Caroline asked in surprise.

Maria nodded.

'I'm superstitious, m'lady, and I've always heard tell that pearls mean tears.'

'What moonshine!' Caroline said sharply. 'And I swear this gown should be lucky, Maria, for the only other time I wore it I was the belle of the evening and had as many *beaux* as there were pearls upon it.'

'Then I hope it brings you luck tonight, m'lady,' Maria said.

Caroline was certain it would as, carrying her head high, she went from the room and down the passage which led to the Grand Staircase.

She was a little late. Already the drawing-room seemed full of guests. Caroline noticed that the house party were talking in little groups, looking awkward and somewhat out of place amongst the country squires and their ladies, who might be dowdy but were of gentle birth and autocratic in their own way.

Looking round for a friendly face, Caroline saw Harriet standing in a corner and Mr. Stratton beside her. She moved towards them, noting with satisfaction that Harriet looked extremely pretty in the pink ball gown and also seemed strangely at ease in Mr. Stratton's company.

When Harriet perceived that Caroline was approaching them, she gave a little cry of unaffected delight.

'Oh, Caroline, is not this a thrill! I am indeed excited to be here. Papa made a terrible fuss at the last moment and I feared he would forbid me to come. He declared this gown was too *décolleté* for the proprieties, and it was only after he had placed an old scarf over my shoulders that he finally permitted me to leave the house.'

'And where is the scarf now?' Caroline asked with a smile.

Harriet blushed.

'It is upstairs with my cloak. I am entirely ashamed of my behaviour, but it was such an old and dilapidated scarf! It is very wrong of me, but Papa will never know, will he, that I am not wearing it?"

Her face paled at the thought and Caroline was quick to reassure her.

'How could he know? Do not be a fidget, Harriet. We will keep your secret, will we not, Mr. Stratton?'

'You must forget your father and his bullyings for tonight,' Mr. Stratton answered, looking down at Harriet with an almost proprietary air. 'Instead you must think only of those who like myself have every intention of contriving that you enjoy yourself to the full.'

'Oh, sir, you are too kind to me,' Harriet said, raising her big brown eyes, which seemed to have already an almost dog-like devotion in them.

Caroline looked round her and at that moment saw someone whose face was vaguely familiar on the other side of the room. Staring at her was a tall young man dressed in the height of fashion and holding a quizzing-glass in his right hand. He raised it and as he did so Caroline wondered where she had seen him before; she had a most vivid recollection of those dark, frowning eyes and the downturned, sneering mouth.

Suddenly she remembered. She felt as if an icy cold hand clutched at her heart and the room seemed to swim giddily round her. As if in a dream she saw Mrs. Miller detach herself from a group of newcomers and, moving across to the young man with the quizzing-glass, whisper something in his ear. He appeared to listen to Mrs. Miller, but he continued to stare at her, and she thought the sneer on his lips was even more pronounced.

Abruptly Caroline turned her back and after a moment she found her voice.

'Tell me,' she said to Mr. Stratton, 'who is the man standing by the window with the quizzing-glass in his hand?'

'Which one?' Mr. Stratton asked vaguely.

'He wears a coat of wine velvet,' Caroline answered.

'Oh, I see him now!' Mr. Stratton said brightly. 'Why, surely you collect who that is? 'Tis Vane's cousin—Gervase Warlingham.'

His words only confirmed what Caroline had expected him to say. Now she remembered only too clearly where she had seen that face before—the eyebrows almost meeting, the thin, rather pinched nose. She could see him rising to his feet as she entered the parlour of *The Dog and Duck*; she could hear his voice—astonished, yet even in its astonishment petulant and annoyed—ask, 'What are you doing here, Reversby?'

Yes, it was undoubtedly the same man. She realised now that she ought to have anticipated that the young man in the parlour of the inn might be Lord Brecon's cousin about whom she had been so curious. But somehow, stupidly it seemed to her now, she had missed the connection. She had indeed thought of the man in the green coat, but had dismissed him from her mind while going over the events of the night, because she had calculated that there would not have been time for him to leave the inn to meet and murder Rosenberg before she reached the ruined cottage.

Yet now that Caroline thought it over, there was no reason why he should not have done so. She had taken some minutes to mount the stairs with the landlady and listen to her chatter in the bedroom. It had taken time for her to consider what she should do, to lock the door, to escape through the window, climb down on to the flat roof and then on to the water butt. Sapskull that she was! Of course there would have been time for a man walking swiftly and by a more direct route to reach the ruined cottage, to do what he had come to do and depart.

But even if that were so, how could she prove it? Would anyone believe her if she declared that Gervase Warlingham was at *The Dog and Duck* on the night of the crime? It was obvious that in some way he had covered up his tracks. Lord Milborne had not known of his presence there.

No, Mr. Warlingham had been clever over that; nevertheless she remained as a witness, should she be believed, of the fact that he was there.

It was in a bemused state that Caroline went into dinner. She hardly heard what her partners said on either side of her, she hardly noticed the glittering splendour of the table, ornamented with golden dishes and candelabra, decorated with yellow orchids and long sprays of smilax.

It was an elegant meal with dishes that did credit to the culinary skill of the cooks who had prepared them. Roasts of venison, mutton, beef and veal were served with succulent and exotic sauces. Chickens, pigeons and geese were stuffed with truffles, oysters and rare spices. A boar's head, a whole sucking-pig, several hams, and a brawn as colourful as an oriental mosaic were eaten cold. A pyramid of syllabubs and jellies was brought to the table with the fourth course, which consisted of over a dozen dishes; and even from the famous gardens of Sale Park Caroline had seldom seen such a profusion of hot-house delicacies as were proffered for dessert.

Caroline ate little and kept trying to force herself to understand what was being said to her, to listen attentively and to make at least intelligible answers even if they were not intelligent ones; but all the time her brain was puzzling over Mr. Warlingham's appearance at the Inn, of his acquaintance with Sir Montagu and, what was for the moment of paramount importance, the question whether he had recognised her.

She remembered how she had turned her head away that night in the parlour so that her bonnet should cast a shadow over her face. Perhaps he had not known who she was. It was unlikely that, if he had left the moment she had gone upstairs, he would have returned after committing the crime. He would have got away from the place as swiftly as possible so that there should be no witnesses to his presence in the neighbourhood and he might therefore not have known of Sir Montagu's search for her through the woods. Why, Caroline puzzled, had no one come forward to say that he had been there? The fact that Sir Montagu had not mentioned it proved one of two things—either Sir Montagu was in league with Mr. Warlingham or else the dislike of him which he had shown, as Caroline had thought most obviously, during their encounter in the parlour was genuine and he had no interest in Mr. Warlingham's movements and hoped such indifference was mutual. If the latter explanation was correct, then from Sir Montague's point of view the less people implicated in the whole affair the better.

Yet thieves and rogues hung together, and Sir Montagu may have had a very sinister motive for not betraying Mr. Warlingham. Oh dear, what could she make of it all?

Caroline's head reeled as she tried to untangle the facts and set them one apart from the other clearly so that she make a picture of the whole. But it was well-nigh impossible and she only knew that she was vastly relieved when the long dinner came to an end and the ladies withdrew from the room, leaving the gentlemen to settle down to their port.

'Do not desert us too long, m'lord,' Mrs. Miller said archly to Lord Brecon, 'for there will be dancing in the long ballroom and we will be aching for our partners.'

Lord Brecon bowed stiffly and Mrs. Miller, throwing a flashing smile towards Mr. Warlingham, followed the ladies from the room.

Her dress, as Maria had said, was indeed outrageous. It was a bright serpent-green satin and cut so low that when its owner sat at table it was hard to see that she wore anything at all above the waist. There were crimson feathers in her befrizzed hair and by the way she asserted herself, making every effort to persuade the guests that she was indeed the rightful hostess of the evening, Caroline was certain that she was but rehearsing for the day when she would in truth reign as châtelaine of this great Castle.

The ladies talked and gossiped in the drawing-room for over two hours before there was the sound of the gentlemen coming somewhat noisily from the dining-room. Caroline, who had been sitting beside Harriet, was well aware that the girl was watching the door, waiting for the moment when Mr. Stratton would reappear, and when he did she seized the opportunity to leave Harriet and slip away, moving from the drawing-room into an ante-room.

It was a small room and seldom used, so that it had an air of stiff formality. But tonight flowers offset the massive furniture and the dark tapestries which draped the walls. The long windows were open on to the terrace and Caroline stood for a moment looking out into the garden. The paths near the house had been decorated with lights. They twinkled and fluttered in the night breeze and beyond them she could see the shimmering silver of the lake and the dark imperturbability of its surrounding trees.

But Caroline hardly noticed the tempting loveliness of the garden, nor for a moment did she hear the distant violins begin the dreamy enticement of a melodious waltz. She was concentrating so fiercely on her problems that it was with a start that she heard a voice behind her say:

'Good evening, Lady Caroline.'

She turned abruptly. Mr. Gervase Warlingham stood in the doorway which led from the drawing-room. His lips were smiling, but there was something in his eyes which made Caroline shiver as she turned to face him with what she hoped was the correct degree of surprise.

'I beg your pardon, sir?'

In answer he shut the door behind him and advanced further into the room.

'I said,' he repeated, ' "Good evening, Lady Caroline".'

'I heard you sir, but felt I must be mistaken. My name is indeed Caroline, but I am Miss Fry, companion to Lady Brecon.'

Mr. Warlingham laughed unpleasantly.

' 'Tis a joke I could hardly believe for the truth when first I saw your ladyship! So you are indeed masquerading as a companion to the Dowager. Damme, it is a jest which will set all the clubs of London a-laughing.'

'Indeed, sir, then their sense of humour must be sadly deranged, for I see nothing peculiarly amusing in my position.'

Mr. Warlingham leant against the mantelshelf and looked at Caroline, then he laughed again.

'You are a plucky gamester,' he said, 'but I think your ladyship knows that I hold an ace.'

'Indeed,' Caroline remarked coldly.

'In fact,' Mr. Warlingham went on, 'it should be easy for you and me to come to an arrangement. You hold one card which might be useful to you, my dear Lady Caroline, but I think I hold the rest of the pack.'

'I am afraid, sir,' Caroline said coldly, 'you speak in riddles which I do not understand and which, to put it plainly, I am not particularly interested in understanding. If you will excuse me, sir, I will withdraw.'

'On the contrary you would be wise, Lady Caroline, for your own sake to stay and hear me,' Mr. Warlingham said, and there was something in his tone which made Caroline pause even as she turned towards the door.

'Wise?' she questioned, raising her eyebrows.

'Very wise from your own point of view. Shall I speak frankly?'

'If it please you,' Caroline answered, 'but I declare I am not particularly concerned for, as I have already said, you speak in riddles.'

'Then we will dispense with them,' Mr. Warlingham said. 'I am not a fool, Lady Caroline, and I know quite well why you are here. You have fallen in love with my very worthy cousin. But why you should go to the trouble to enter his house in such a disguise I cannot conceive, though doubtless you have your reasons. They are, however, not of interest to me. But what is of moment is to learn how much you will pay for me to keep the knowledge of your indiscretion from my cousin's ears.'

'And to what indiscretion do you refer?' Caroline asked.

'Do you want me to put it into words?' Mr. Warlingham asked. 'Very well then, I will. I will put it with a vulgar bluntness so that you cannot for a moment pretend to misunderstand me. I want, Lady Caroline, two thousand guineas from you in return for my promise not to reveal to my cousin or, if it please you, to anyone else that it was you Montagu Reversby was searching for in the wood at Sevenoaks on the night that Rosenberg was murdered.'

'Two thousand guineas!' Caroline exclaimed, 'and where, Mr. Warlingham, do you imagine that Miss Fry could find such a sum?'

Mr. Warlingham stood very upright.

'Enough of this farce,' he said. 'You cannot pretend to me. I saw you that night even though you took pains to turn your face from me. Besides, all London is talking of Lady Caroline Faye's drive with the raffish Sir Montagu.'

'And if they are,' Caroline said sharply, 'it is you who have spread the rumours.'

'Maybe, and maybe not,' Mr. Warlingham replied. 'Reversby, I believe, denies them, but who heeds what he says? People like to believe in the indiscretions of famous young women, especially those who have been too successful for the peace of mind of their own sex. But that does not concern me. What I require, Lady Caroline, is two thousand guineas for my silence.'

'And if I refuse to give them to you?'

'You wouldn't dare.'

'I would dare anything,' Caroline said coldly. 'I am not afraid of you, Mr. Warlingham. What if I should relate to those who are interested the information that you were at *The Dog and Duck* on the night of the murder? What do you think would be said then, you who have everything to gain if your cousin should be most unfortunately convicted of murder?'

'You are not without brains,' Mr. Warlingham said, 'but you forget, dear Lady Caroline, that in giving me away you will also betray yourself. Besides, surely a young lady travelling under such circumstances unchaperoned and in the company of a notorious rake would not be so observant? She sees a man she has never met before, and after she has heard of a crime, imagines he might be a certain Mr. Warlingham; but I, of course, was many miles away that night. I was dining, as it happened, in Curzon Street. There are several friends who can swear to my having been with them the whole evening. No, Lady Caroline, I think the card you hold is a very small one . . . while mine are trumps.'

Caroline felt her breath coming a little quicker. There was something so suave, so slimy in the way Mr. Warlingham spoke and in the arguments that he used that she felt it hard to keep her air of indifference. She could feel her anger rising and knew that if she lost her temper she would but play into his hands; all the same she was aware that he had caught her in a trap, a trap from which it would be hard to extract herself. But if she was frightened, she must on no account let him know it.

'You are very plausible, sir,' she said, 'but at the same time I think you overestimate the importance of the information you hold against me. I will be truthful and say that I am staying here under an assumed name, but I have every intention of telling your cousin and Lady Brecon tonight who I am and why I have come here.'

'That's as may be,' Mr. Warlingham smiled, 'but do you really intend to tell the man you love that you went to an isolated inn alone with Montagu Reversby?'

'That is my business,' Caroline snapped, 'and may I point out, sir, that it is no concern of yours?'

'On the contrary, it is my concern exactly to the sum of two thousand guineas. Pay me, Lady Caroline, for I know you can well afford to do so, and I will be silent for ever.'

'Or until it suits your purpose,' Caroline said quickly. 'No, sir, I do not intend to be blackmailed by you.'

'Then if you refuse me,' Mr. Warlingham said angrily, 'I shall go at once to my cousin and denounce you. You are staying here under false pretences, you are an imposter. I shall tell him who you are and also that Montagu Reversby thought himself very sure of your affections that night you drove along with him from London to *The Dog and Duck*.'

Caroline put out her hand and laid it on the back of a chair, as she wondered wildly what it would be best to do. She wanted time in which to think, time in which to tell Lord Brecon in her own words the story of her escape that night. She could remember all too clearly the scorn in his voice, the anger with which he had spoken of Montagu Reversby. What would he say when he learned that she also had been deceived by him, not in the same way as poor, stupid Melissa, but nevertheless tricked into making a fool of herself.

'Make up your mind, Lady Caroline,' Mr. Warlingham said menacingly. 'Which is it to be? The two thousand guineas or do I tell Vane?'

'And what should you tell Vane?' questioned a voice, and Caroline turned with a cry of horrors as Lord Brecon walked in through the open window.

His face was very stern as he came in from the darkness

153

of the night and she wondered how long he had stood there, how much he had heard. Mr. Warlingham had shut the door, but they had both forgotten the open windows and the terrace outside. Caroline felt herself grow pale and instinctively she raised one of her hands and laid it against the throbbing of her heart.

Lord Brecon walked into the centre of the room. He faced Mr. Warlingham as he stood on the hearth and he was so near to Caroline that she could have put out her hand and touched him.

'Well, Gervase,' Lord Brecon said in level tones. 'What is it you are going to tell me?'

'Now that you are here, Vane,' Mr. Warlingham said, 'I remember that there is no reason after all to inform you of something which is actually a secret between La . . . Miss Fry and myself. You will forgive me if I leave you, for I recall that I am engaged for the next dance.'

He turned and walked quickly towards the further door of the room. Lord Brecon watched him go. As Mr. Warlingham reached the door, he turned back and it seemed as if he might say something; but changed his mind and left the room in silence.

Lord Brecon turned to Caroline.

'Perhaps you would like to explain,' he said.

His tone was as frigid and there was an expression in his eyes which frightened her.

Once again she held on to the chair beside her. She was very lovely in the soft light of the wax tapers, and another man might have forgotten everything save the mysteries in her eyes and the soft curves of her lips. The quick rise and fall of her breasts moved the lace which veiled them and her fingers suddenly fluttered like a bird which has been captured.

'How much did you hear?' she asked in a low voice.

'Enough!' Lord Brecon answered; 'enough to know that you have lied to me. Who are you?'

'I am Caroline Faye.'

'And why are you here?'

'I answered that question last night,' Caroline replied. 'Oh, Vane, I came because, as I told you then, I love you.'

'Love me?' he asked, and his voice was bitter. 'A strange sort of love. What were you doing that night in the wood?'

'You must have already heard what your cousin said,' Caroline answered. 'I was brought to *The Dog and Duck* by a trick. I was enticed there by a gentleman whom I admit now I should have known better than to trust. I was a fool to have realised before what sort of man he was, but I escaped from him and you found me. That is all!'

'And the man's name?'

Lord Brecon spoke in a tone which seemed to freeze the very air they breathed.

'You know it already,' Caroline said and went towards him. 'Vane, I was going to tell you everything in my own good time. I did not wish you to hear it like this.'

She put out her hand and would have touched Lord Brecon on the arm, but he gripped her wrist and his fingers dug deep into her flesh.

'Answer me,' he said. 'What was the man's name?'

'It was . . . Montagu . . . Reversby,' Caroline faltered. 'But, Vane——'

'That swine!' Lord Brecon interrupted. 'That curst outsider who has already besmirched Melissa with his foulness. And you associated yourself with him, went with him willingly at night to a place where you would be alone.'

'It is not true,' Caroline said swiftly. 'He told me that there was to be a——'

'Be quiet,' Lord Brecon said so savagely that for a moment Caroline was stunned into silence. 'You have told me enough lies. I trusted you, I believed in you, and God knows I could not help but love you . . . and all the time you were deceiving me, pretending to be a companion to my mother, worming your way into my house, setting your snares, making me believe in you so that I was prepared to sacrifice everything for you—yes, everything I held dear.'

'Oh, Vane,' Caroline said. twisting her wrist a little to try and free it from his grasp. 'Oh, Vane, do let me explain.'

'I want none of your explanations,' Lord Brecon said; 'I am thinking of what to do with you. Love! You prate to me of love and what do you know of it? Lady Caroline Faye, the spoilt darling of a London Season, anxious to add yet another scalp to her collection, eager to boast she had gained the heart of a dolt who was so foolish as to love her.'

'But, Vane, if you would only let me——'

'No, you shall not speak,' Lord Brecon said. 'Those lips have uttered too many devilish falsehoods; instead you shall listen to me, yes, to me. Hear then what I have to say.'

He wrenched Caroline's arm so that she twisted round to

confront him. She looked up into his face and was suddenly terribly afraid. His eyes were no longer cold and steely, instead they were burning pools of anger. She saw that he was possessed by a fury which made him blind and deaf to all save his own anger. Never in the whole of her life had she seen a man so enraged, and because it was Vane, because it was the man she loved, she could not think what to do but must stand there trembling, her whole body quivering beneath the tempest of his fury.

'You came here intent on deception,' he said slowly, each word a separate weapon with which to wound her. 'Your lips uttered a thousand lies, your tongue was twisted with perjury. You made me believe you loved me. Doubtless it was some of your friends in London who think it but a light thing to take a man's heart and torture it. You led me on to speak to you of my love, you duped me, enticed me into the trap you had prepared so skilfully. You laughed at the finest action of my life when, thinking only of you, I tried to drive you from this house. God knows I wanted you to stay, I wanted to make you mine, I wanted to accept all that you offered me so readily with your lips. But because I was decent, because I believed in you and your innocence, I tried to send you away. You would not go when you could. You defied me, you refused to heed my warning. Well now, by God, you shall stay.'

Caroline stared at him in bewilderment.

'You shall stay,' he repeated through clenched teeth. 'I will make sure of that. You shall learn, Lady Caroline Faye, that it is not always wise to trifle with a man's affections. Come with me!'

Still holding her by the wrist, he turned and walked towards the door of the drawing-room.

'Vane, Vane, where are we going?' Caroline cried, but he did not answer.

Moving beside him because he held her prisoner, Caroline was conscious of the painful pressure of his fingers and of a strength and purpose which was irresistible. There was no gainsaying him, no possibility of her doing anything but obey his wishes as he led her swiftly across the drawing-room.

There were a few people sitting round on the sofas and they looked up in surprise; but Lord Brecon paid no heed to them and led the way, pulling Caroline after him, into the long ballroom where the majority of the guests were assembled. Some were waltzing, others were sitting round the walls watching the dancers while a footman offered them glasses of champagne and iced punch.

Breathless with bewilderment and from the speed at which he had brought her here and conscious of a sudden fear of him, Caroline could only gasp as Lord Brecon went up to the band and held up his hand for silence. The musicians ceased playing; the dancers brought to an abrupt stop, stared around them in astonishment.

'My Lords, Ladies and Gentlemen,' Lord Brecon said in a voice which echoed to the furthest corner of the room. 'I have an announcement to make. I have this evening—but a few moments ago—become engaged to be married. I have the honour to present to you my betrothed, the Lady Caroline Faye.'

There was a murmur of astonishment around the room, then a sudden hubbub of voices.

'Good luck to you, Brecon! Best of wishes!'

Everyone surged forward to offer their congratulations. Glasses were raised, and then above the general hubbub the loud voice of a red-faced hunting Squire cried:

'Here's long life to you both; tell us, Vane, me boy, when will the marriage take place?'

There was a sudden hush as if everyone watied for the answer.

Lord Brecon released his hold on Caroline's arm. He looked down at her and she was aware that the fire was still burning in his eyes, that his lips curved bitterly in the travesty of a smile.

'That is indeed a vastly important question,' he said, 'and I will answer it. I would wish you all to be present at my marriage. Lady Caroline and I will wed tonight. My Lord Bishop will, I know, grant us a special licence and perform the ceremony.'

There was a sudden gasp, then the hubbub and roar of voices broke out again.

Lord Brecon bent towards Caroline. She knew that he asked her a question; she could not hear what he said, but she saw the expression on his face and was aware that he taunted her. She lifted her chin and the lovely rounded column of her neck seemed in her pride to grow longer, so that her dignity was very apparent to all who watched her. In her heart she was frightened, but she fought against the

157

sudden stabbing of her fear and there was no trace of it on her face.

Without a tremor in her voice, and clearly so that her words were audible above the noise of the crowd, she said: 'Yes, I will marry you, my lord, here, this very night.'

It seemed to Caroline that everything became hazy and indistinct. There were faces all round her, faces which seemed to float dizzily in front of her eyes. There were voices exclaiming, questioning, praising, jesting; hands touched hers, lips brushed her fingers, persons pressed in upon her until she felt as if it was all part of a nightmare from which she could not awake.

Then at last she was conscious of one person individually. Someone portly and resplendent in purple, the great jewelled cross on his chest twinkling from the light of the chandelier over his head. It was the Bishop.

'What is this I hear of a betrothal?' he asked, and his voice boomed out resonant and challenging as if he spoke from a pulpit.

'May I present Lady Caroline Faye, my lord, who has honoured me with the promise of her hand in marriage?' Lord Brecon asked.

Caroline made a deep curtsey.

'Vulcan's daughter?' the Bishop questioned. 'Then let me indeed congratulate you, my dear boy. I have stayed at Mandrake—a magnificent place, one might almost say a palace. And the table set by the Marquis is a most treasured memory.'

'I must pay my respects to your father and mother, Lady Caroline,' the Bishop said affably, 'and tell them this betrothal has both my approval and my blessing.'

'Will you come with me into another room, my lord, where we can speak quietly?' Lord Brecon asked; and when the Bishop acquiesced, they moved slowly, the three of them, across the ballroom towards the door which led into the hall.

Just as they reached it, Mrs. Miller appeared. Caroline

thought that she must have been in the card-room and had only just heard the news, for there was an expression of astonishment on her face and the crimson feathers on her head were fluffed sideways as if she had been hurrying.

'They tell me, lord——' she started, but Lord Brecon interrupted her.

'You are the very person I wish to see, Mrs. Miller. Give instructions that the Chapel be opened immediately.'

'The Chapel?' Mrs. Miller's mouth dropped open for a minute and then she said quickly: 'But, m'lord, 'tis impossible. It has not been in use for years. Things are stored there and——'

Lord Brecon gave her one look which silenced the spate of words tumbling from her lips.

'I said immediately, Mrs. Miller,' he said, and they passed on, leaving her gasping after them.

As they reached the hall, Caroline felt a sudden faintness sweep over her.

'Will you excuse me, my lord?' she asked, 'for I would retire to my room.'

'As your ladyship wishes,' Lord Brecon replied with a courtesy which was curiously belied by the expression in his eyes. 'I will arrange that you are informed when my Lord Bishop is ready to perform the ceremony. I collect that will be about midnight.'

Caroline could only drop a curtsey and then move slowly away up the stairs, holding on to the banister. When she reached her bedchamber, the faintness passed; but she had been there only a few seconds before there was the sound of feet hurrying down the passage. Maria almost burst into the room.

'Oh, m'lady, I have but this instant heard the news. Is it a fact, m'lady, that you are indeed to wed his lordship this very night? I can barely credit my own ears.'

Caroline held up her hand.

'It is true, Maria, but I do not want to speak of it for the moment, I want to think.'

'Oh, m'lady, there is so little time. When one of the footmen came running out to the servants' hall shouting what he had heard, I was too dumbfounded to do ought but gape at him. The place is in regular turmoil. A wedding in the house. Why——'

'Oh, Maria, cease your prattle,' Caroline begged wearily.

'But, m'lady, what will they think on it at Mandrake?

160

What indeed will they say when they hear of your ladyship being wed at such an hour and in the house of a stranger? Oh, m'lady, think again. Wait until we have sent word to his lordship on the Continent, for I declare I would not dare to face his anger when he hears how this occurred behind his back, so to speak.'

Caroline was not listening to Maria. She was standing very still, her hands raised to her cheeks, her eyes far away. Then at last she turned and without a word went from the bed-chamber down the passage and to the door of Lady Brecon's bedroom.

It was already late and she was afraid that her ladyship might be asleep, but in response to a light knock she heard a low, sweet voice reply instantly and bid her enter. She went into the room.

It was in darkness save for the light of two candles by the bedside, and Lady Brecon was lying back against her pillows, a book lying open beneath her hand as if she had been reading.

'Forgive me for disturbing you, Ma'am,' Caroline said as she drew near to the bedside.

'What is it, child?' Lady Brecon enquired.

Caroline stood for a moment in silence. There was an expression on her face which caused Lady Brecon to ask:

'You are in trouble, Miss Fry? Can I not help you?'

'I have something to tell your ladyship,' Caroline answered in a very low voice, 'but it is hard to put into words.'

Lady Brecon put out her hand invitingly, and slowly but almost reluctantly Caroline gave hers into the older woman's sympathetic clasp.

'But how cold you are, my dear!' Lady Brecon exclaimed. 'And why are you trembling? Has somebody frightened you?'

'No, I am not afraid,' Caroline said quietly. 'It is only that I am a trifle overwrought. Your ladyship will understand why when I tell you that your son, his lordship, has but this moment announced to the assembled company downstairs that he and I are to be wed at midnight.'

'Wed!' Lady Brecon exclaimed.

'Yes, Ma'am,' Caroline answered, 'and that is not all. I must confess to your ladyship that I have deceived you. I am not Caroline Fry, but Caroline Faye, daughter of the Marquis and Marchioness of Vulcan. I came here and

161

solicited your kindness under false pretences. I can only ask your ladyship to forgive me and to believe that there was a very good reason for my deception.'

'And will you tell me that reason?' Lady Brecon asked quietly.

For one moment Caroline was tempted to pour out the whole story, to relate to Lady Brecon her fears and suspicions of foul play, of her premonition of danger and her conviction that Lord Brecon had enemies who would deprive him of his very life. Then, even as her lips parted to begin her tale, she remembered Lady Brecon's fragility and Dorcas' constant and unceasing care of her. She might be far less strong than she appeared and to learn that her only son was in grave danger might be shock enough to kill her.

Swiftly Caroline made up her mind to be discreet.

'I cannot, as I would wish, relate to you the whole story, Ma'am,' she said quietly. 'Will it suffice to tell you that I came here because I love your son? I have loved him since we first met.'

Lady Brecon's face softened.

'Then that, dear child, is all that matters. And Vane loves you?'

'I believe that he does,' Caroline replied.

'In which case I am happy,' Lady Brecon said, clasping Caroline's hand very tightly in hers. 'I have prayed for so long that Vane would find someone to love and that in return she would love him, not for his possessions or indeed for his looks, but for himself. I may be prejudiced, but in my opinion Vane is a very fine and a very lovable person. I have always desired that he should find a wife who would take care of him.'

Caroline raised her eyes wonderingly.

'Then you are not angry with me?' she asked.

'Not in the least. I liked you from the first moment that I saw your pretty face and in the very short time that you have been here I have grown to love you. I know of no one to whom I would rather trust my son's happiness.'

'Thank you, Ma'am.'

Caroline bent her head suddenly and kissed the hand that held hers.

'My dear,' Lady Brecon exclaimed, and there were tears in her eyes, 'kiss me properly.'

Caroline's lips touched the soft, delicate cheek; then as Lady Brecon relinquished her hand, she said:

'I am indeed deeply honoured, Ma'am, that you should trust me.'

'I am convinced that I can do so,' Lady Brecon said. 'I am not even questioning the reason for such haste. I will not even say that it seems to me unseemly, for you and Vane must follow the dictates of your own hearts. I shall but pray for you both.'

There was something in her sweet simplicity which brought a sudden sob to Caroline's throat.

'Oh, Ma'am, you are too kind. It is more than I deserve.'

'No, Caroline, don't say that, for if, as you have told me, you have done this because you love Vane, then indeed I understand. We are all capable of strange deeds and indeed great ones when they are done for someone whom we love truly and with all our hearts.'

Her words awakened an echo in Caroline's memory.

'Why, Ma'am, my father said much the same thing to me. He said any sacrifice is worth while, no risk is too great, if it is for someone we love.'

'Your father was right,' Lady Brecon said softly. 'No risk is too great.'

'Then I know I am doing what is right,' Caroline said. 'Thank you, Ma'am. And now I must leave you.'

'One moment.' Lady Brecon said. 'Will you pull the bell cord, my dear?'

Caroline did as she was told. She heard the faint sound of its tinkle in the next room. The communicating door between the bedrooms, opened almost instantly and Dorcas, fully dressed, came into the room. Lady Brecon glanced at her maid and saw the answer to her unspoken question on her face.

'So you have heard, Dorcas? Bring me the family veil for her ladyship and also my jewel case.'

Dorcas lit a taper from the glowing embers of the fire and held it to the candles on the mantelshelf. The warm golden light dispelled the shadows. From a big chest at the further end of the room she brought to the bed something packed carefully in white paper.

'This is the family veil, my dear,' Lady Brecon exclaimed. 'I would like you to wear it when you wed Vane, for I wore it myself, as have many generations of Brecon brides.'

'I would like to wear it,' Caroline said simply.

Again Dorcas crossed the room and this time she returned with a big square jewel case covered in blue leather and embossed with Lady Brecon's initials surmounted by a coronet. She placed it beside the bed and gave her ladyship the key.

'It is many years since I even saw my jewels, let alone wore them,' Lady Brecon said. 'These are my own. The family gems are kept in safety at a bank in London.'

She opened the case and Caroline saw rings, bracelets and brooches resting on velvet cushions in a glittering array. Lady Brecon lifted a tray and drew from the bottom of the case a tiara of diamonds. It was an exquisite piece, fashioned so that it would encircle the entire head. The stones were set with skilful craftsmanship in the shape of flowers and they glittered dazzlingly in the light of the candles, seeming almost to quiver into life as Lady Brecon gave the sparking crown into Caroline's hands.

'My wedding present to you, my sweet daughter-in-law to be,' she said.

'Oh, but, Ma'am, how can I take it?' Caroline asked.

'I desire you to have it,' Lady Brecon said firmly. 'It is my very own and the best that I have to give.'

'Then thank you, Ma'am, with all my heart,' Caroline said softly and she bent once again to kiss Lady Brecon on the cheek.

Picking up the lace veil, she said good-night and went towards the door. Dorcas opened it for her and to Caroline's surprise followed her out into the corridor. She obviously wished to say something which would not be overheard by Lady Brecon and Caroline waited for her to speak. Dorcas seemed more than usually gaunt and angular, but when she spoke her voice was softer, and not as harsh it it was ordinarily.

'I would like to wish your ladyship every happiness.'

'Thank you, Dorcas.'

'You will find it, m'lady, for you have a rare courage,' Dorcas said unexpectedly. 'Be not afraid, however strange some things may seem to your ladyship.'

The words seemed almost to be torn from her lips as if she spoke against an effort to keep silent.

'Thank you, Dorcas,' Caroline said gravely. 'I will try not to be afraid.'

'Yes, try, m'lady,' Dorcas said drily, 'for things are not always that which they appear to be.'

Caroline wanted to ask Dorcas what she meant by this enigmatic remark, but before she could ask the question the elderly woman had stepped back into Lady Brecon's bedroom and the door shut softly behind her.

Caroline went to her own room. Maria was waiting for her, still in a state of excited agitation.

'Oh, m'lady, 'tis all of a dither I am, for I was wondering where you had gone. What is it that your ladyship has in your hand?'

Caroline gave the veil and the tiara to Maria.

'Arrange these for me,' she said and seated herself at the dressing-table.

Maria opened out the veil. It was of the finest Brussels lace and as delicate as a spider's web.

'Oh, m'lady, 'tis beautiful!' Maria exclaimed and continued to talk while she draped the veil over Caroline's head and held it in place with the sparkling brilliance of the tiara.

Caroline did not listen to her. She was thinking of Lady Brecon's sweetness and Dorcas' unexpected words of encouragement. No, she would not be afraid!

Vane might be angry with her, but at least in his anger he had forgotten his previous determination to drive her from his life.

However hard it might prove to be, however horrible the revelations that lay ahead, Caroline told herself that anything was better than being separated from him. She was so sure of her love, so certain with an unshakable conviction that Vane was the right man for her and she the right woman for him that she could view Vane's secret, now that she would soon be in a position to share it with him, without much apprehension. She was confident beyond the possibility of any doubt that they had been meant for each other and that fate had sent them into each other's lives in such a strange manner for that very reason and ultimately, Caroline believed, things would work out better than if they had met in a conventional, carefree manner.

She had only to remember her indifference to the other men who had expressed their affection for her to ask herself whether she would have loved Vane so deeply and with such a consuming passion if they had been introduced at a ball and he had courted her with all the frills, elegance and unhurried courtesy of a conventional romance.

Such a course seemed somehow unthinkable in connection with Vane. No, their love was meant to be turbulent and violent. Perhaps it would feed on difficulties and, passing through them, be tempered so that pure and untarnished their affection for each other would last for all eternity.

Maria stood back to admire her handiwork.

'There, m'lady, I have finished. Never have I seen your ladyship look more beautiful!'

For the first time since she had sat down at the dressing-table Caroline looked at her reflection in the mirror. The soft, shadowy folds of the lace veil framed her face but did not entirely conceal the burnished glitter of her hair. The diamond tiara crowned her head. It gave her a regal look, seeming a fitting ornament to surmount the long elegance of her neck and to enhance the manner in which she proudly lifted her chin.

Yes, she was beautiful, but there was something more than beauty in the depths of her eyes, in the sudden trembling of her soft mouth. Here was the face of a girl who stands at the crossroads of life, reaching out towards womanhood, sensing the mysteries which lie ahead.

For a moment Caroline shut her eyes against the revelations she could read in her own face. It was almost too much to bear, this picture of herself half shrinking, half triumphant, a mixture of child and woman, suspended as it were between heaven and earth, yet with it all confident because the greatest of all emotions was stirring within her breast. She rose to her feet.

'What is the hour?'

Maria looked at the clock on the mantelshelf.

' 'Tis but a minute or two to midnight, m'lady,' she replied, and even as she spoke there came a loud knocking at the door.

Maria opened it. James was standing there, but as if he was conscious of the solemnity of the occasion his cheeky grin was missing and he did not even twinkle at her.

'His lordship's compliments, and he awaits her ladyship below.'

Maria shut the door and turned towards Caroline. There were tears in her eyes now and as she looked at her mistress they overflowed and ran down her cheeks.

'Oh, m'lady! M'lady!'

'Dry your tears, Maria,' Caroline said quietly, 'and go ahead of me to the Chapel, for I wish you to see me married. I will follow in one second.'

'Yes, m'lady,' Maria sobbed, 'but who will take you to

the altar? Oh, if only his lordship, the Marquis, was here! And what will he say at having missed the greatest day in your life?'

Caroline put her hand on Maria's shoulder.

'I would have liked above all things for Papa and Mama to be with me, but as they are not, Maria, wish me luck.'

'Oh, m'lady, I wish you all the happiness there is in the world. You know I do,' Maria sobbed, wiping her eyes on the corner of her apron.

'Then run along,' Caroline said, and obediently Maria went from the room, leaving her alone.

For a moment Caroline stood quite still in the centre of the room. Then she went down on her knees beside her bed. With her eyes closed and her hands clasped together she prayed the simple prayers that she had repeated every evening since she had been a child. She said them over very quietly, concentrating on them to the exclusion of all else, and when she had finished she felt suddenly at peace within herself and filled with a quiet strength which she knew would not fail her.

She opened the door of her bedchamber. Slowly she walked down the passage. It was very quiet save for the rustle of her dress and the soft movement made by the lace veil as it trailed behind her on the carpet. When she came to the top of the Grand Staircase, she looked below and saw that standing alone in the centre of the hall Lord Brecon was waiting for her.

As she came down the stairs, she was aware that he watched her, but as she drew near to him she saw that the expression on his face was inscrutable. It was indeed at that moment, it seemed to her, the face of a stranger. He gave her no greeting; there was no smile on his lips; and she knew, as he bowed and proffered his arm, that he was still angry.

In silence they moved through the hall and turned down the passage which led past the dining-room beyond which Caroline had never ventured. Now the candles were lit and the whole way was a blaze of light as far as she could see. There were flunkeys lining the walls. Soon she heard the distant murmur of voices, their tones lowered, it was true, but still the whispering, muttering, gossiping voices of people, and Caroline guessed that the guests were assembled and waiting for them in the Chapel.

She was not mistaken. Footmen flung open two high

double doors, there was a sudden burst of organ music, and Caroline saw that the whole company of Lord Brecon's guests were packed within the narrow stone edifice. Some were squashed into the oak pews, others lined the walls, many of the gentlemen leaning nonchalantly against the marble tombs and monuments, while the servants of the household peeped over the gallery, their mob-caps and powdered wigs white patches against the darkness of the heavily beamed roof. For a moment Caroline felt that she must shrink from the wave of curious faces turned to look at her. Her hand on Lord Brecon's arm trembled, yet she received no reassurance from him but felt herself drawn relentlessly forward.

The Chapel was a gloomy place despite the great gold candelabra each holding a dozen candles, which had been set one on either side of the altar. It was cold and chill and there was a smell of must and dust which made Caroline feel as if she could hardly breathe.

As Lord Brecon led her to the chancel where the Bishop and his private chaplain were waiting, Caroline looked up at the east window behind the altar and thought for a moment that it was draped with dirty curtains; then she saw that it was half hidden by cobwebs—cobwebs, dark and grey with age hanging like tattered lace from the beams of the roof, shrouding the stone arches and stained glass and ornamenting with beggar's rags the ancient reredos with its carved angels.

It was eerie and ghostlike, and when Caroline reached the altar steps and had her back to the assembled company, it seemed to her that she and Lord Brecon and the Bishop were a living picture menaced by the decay and dust to which all life must ultimately return.

Little details seemed to Caroline extraordinarily clear. The brightness of the silver cross as if someone had quickly rubbed away its tarnish, the purity of the lace-edged altar cloth, and in contrast the tarnished dimness of the embroidered frontal, its gold thread broken, its crimson surface pitted with tiny holes as if it had been eaten by moths. The floor of the chapel was dirty, but the two cushions placed for the bride and groom to kneel on were of spotless white satin.

The Bishop's voice boomed out. Once again a dreamlike spell seemed to descend on Caroline and hold her almost mesmerized so that she was able to watch what was happening with almost supernatural detachment. She could see herself standing pale, yet calm at Lord Brecon's side, hear her own voice clear and unhurried with the responses, watch her fingers, white and nerveless as if they were made of wax, pass from the Bishop's plump hand into the bridegroom's keeping.

Still in a dream she heard Lord Brecon say:

'I, Seymour Berkeley Frederick Alexander Treweeke, take thee, Caroline Justin, to be my wedded wife, to have and to hold from this day forward, for better for worse, for richer for poorer, in sickness and in health, to love and to cherish till death us do part, according to God's Holy Ordinance; and thereto I plight thee my troth.'

He spoke firmly and audibly but with a coldness which seemed to Caroline to be even more chilling than that of the Chapel itself. She knew that she shivered physically because of his tone, and yet it was not herself who shivered but some stranger—a woman who bore her name and spoke with her voice, but who had for the moment ceased to feel any emotion within a frozen breast.

Caroline held out her hand and Lord Brecon slipped the ring on the third finger of her left hand. It was not a wedding ring, she noticed, but a signet ring which he had taken from his little finger. On it was his crest engraved on an emerald. It was too big for her so that she must bend her finger to prevent it from falling off.

And now the service was ended, and bride and groom knelt to receive the Bishop's blessing. The organ, which had been playing quietly the whole time, burst into the Wedding March, and turning, Caroline and Lord Brecon faced their guests as they walked towards the door. Before they reached it, they were surrounded. Lord Brecon was being clapped on the back by the men, women Caroline had never seen before were kissing her on the cheek and speaking to her familiarly in flattering tones.

At last they were able to make their way back to the large ballroom. Here there was champagne to be consumed, healths to be drunk and so many expressions of good wishes to be answered that Caroline wondered when it would ever end. The musicians played, but no one wished to dance. The guests preferred to talk, a glass of wine in their hands, a jest upon their lips. It seemed to Caroline that hours went by until her lips were stiff with smiling. She was tired, with a tiredness which made her whole body ache.

She stood by Lord Brecon, but she might have been a

169

hundred miles away from him. Never once did he address her, never once did he even look in her direction. At last some of the more elderly people began to say good-night. Their carriages were called to the door and one by one they came up to express their good wishes all over again, to shake Lord Brecon's hand and kiss Caroline's fingers. Many guests, Caroline noticed, had returned to the card-room. Among them was Mrs. Miller. But Gervase Warlingham stood for a long time, leaning against the wall at the far end of the ballroom, watching the crowd round Lord Brecon and Caroline.

Caroline was well aware that he was there and more than once she found herself glancing involuntarily in his direction. She found it hard not to be conscious of him and she was almost physically sensitive to the venom he was pouring out in their direction. But when at last a large number of guests had gone, she saw that he too had disappeared.

There was a sudden lull. There was no one waiting for the moment to say good-night. Lord Brecon and Caroline stood alone in the ballroom save for the musicians still playing a melody and half a dozen gentlemen sitting at the far end of the room who, judging by their voices and laughter, were slightly the worse for drink.

Caroline looked up at Lord Brecon. It was the first time that she had looked directly at him or spoken to him since they were married. 'May I retire, my lord?'

She spoke formally and if he had turned his head he would have seen that there was pleading in her eyes, and that her lips asked him a very different question; but he barely glanced at her.

'If it please your ladyship.'

He bowed and offering her his arm led her formally to the foot of the Grand Staircase.

'The State Bedroom has been prepared for you,' he said. 'You will find your maid awaiting you there.'

Caroline hesitated. She would have spoken his name; she had already put out her hand as if she would lay it in his, but at that moment a party of guests burst from the card-room.

'Ah, there you are Brecon,' they called gaily. 'Come and drink a glass of wine with us.'

Lord Brecon turned towards them, and Caroline went quickly up the stairs. She knew where the State Bedroom was, though she had only peeped into it once on her way downstairs. There had been little to see for the shutters were closed and the furniture shrouded in dustsheets. Now the doors stood open and the candles were lit.

It was a vast room, its windows draped with curtains of hand-sewn tapestry, the great bed curtained in the same manner, while ostrich feather fronds surmounted the carved and gilt bedposts. The furniture was of gilt and marble and the walls were inset with panels of rose-tinted brocade.

But Caroline had little interest in her surroundings. All of a sudden she felt too utterly weary to bear even the weight of the diamond tiara, and as Maria hurried towards her she put up her hand to her forehead and swayed on her feet.

'You are tired, m'lady. 'Tis little wonder,' Maria cried, 'for it has been a vastly exciting evening both for your ladyship and for all of us. Come, let me undress you. You will feel better when you are free of that head-dress and your gown.'

Gently, as if she had been a child, Maria took off Caroline's pearl and lace gown, drew off her stockings and shoes and slipped over her head a night-robe of transparent softness. Then she brought her a pelisse of crêpe trimmed with lace.

'Sit by the fire, m'lady,' Maria suggested, 'and I will fetch you a cup of warm milk.'

'No, Maria, that is all for tonight. I only want to be alone,' Caroline said.

Maria smiled knowingly.

'Of course, m'lady, and I will not disturb you again, though you have but to pull the bell-rope should you have need of me. Shall I extinguish the candles, m'lady?'

'Yes please, Maria,' Caroline answered.

The candles were put out, the corners of the great room settled into shadow. But the fire was bright, the flames casting a glow on the ceiling and on Caroline as she sat in a low chair, her chin in her hand, her eyes looking deep into the flames.

How long she sat there she did not know. She was not really expecting anyone, feeling only that time waited and that the end, whatever it might be, was inevitable. It seemed to her that her past had been swept away from her and there was no promise as yet of the future.

171

The door opened. She did not turn her head, but she knew who had come into the room. Suddenly the feeling of detachment had gone completely. She was no longer tired. She came alive, she could feel the blood running quickly through her veins, her pulses pounding, a sudden excitement galavanzing her to life as if she had been dead and was resurrected. She heard his footsteps moving purposefully towards the centre of the room, and then there came his voice:

'Come here!'

The order was sharp, abrupt. Slowly Caroline turned her head and looked at him. He seemed silhouetted against the shadows, the firelight illuminating his face very clearly, flickering on the blue coat he had worn for their marriage, its diamond buttons twinkling like stars.

Caroline rose to her feet. She hesitated. There was half the length of the room between them.

'Come here!'

He spoke the order once again, and now she obeyed him. As she moved, she saw the wildness in his eyes and an expression on his face such as she had never seen before. She drew close until at last she stood before him, waiting, her robe falling about her feet, her hands holding the thin pelisse close across her bosom.

'I had not meant to come to you tonight,' Lord Brecon said harshly. 'I had intended to leave you alone, and yet I have come. I want to see if you can still look at me with innocent eyes, you who have lied and intrigued, you who have betrayed my love.'

'But, Vane . . . you must listen to me . . .' Caroline began; then before she could say more Lord Brecon put out his hand and laid it roughly over her mouth.

'I told you I have come but to see you, to look at the pretty bride I have gained—a bride who has already succumbed, it seems, to the charms of Sir Montagu Reversby.'

Caroline released her hold on her pelisse, put up her hands and tried to tear his fingers from her mouth.

'It is not true . . .' she managed to say, and then suddenly Lord Brecon's arms were round her and he was drawing her close.

'Are kisses the only thing that will stop you talking?' he asked, and his voice was bitter and insulting.

Then she was crushed against him, his mouth was on hers, and he was kissing her—kissing her wildly with hard,

172

brutal kisses which hurt and bruised her lips. It was a moment of agony; it seemed to her that his kisses must bruise her very spirit, for she knew them for what they were—the cruel and lustful expression of a mere bodily hunger.

They hurt her, they bruised her skin and the pain of them seemed to strike into the very depths of her soul, and paralyse her very will so that she could not struggle but, broken and breathless, must endure his onslaught without protest. She wanted to cry, out, to beg him not to strip from her the last illusion of his love; but her voice was gone. She was helpless and the savagery of his embrace was almost unendurable. She was near to fainting when she heard him say:

'Is that how Reversby kissed you? Like this? and this?'

His lips were on hers again, and then she felt them cruelly hard against her neck. His fingers gripped her shoulder; then with a sharp movement he tore aside her night-robe, and his lips caressed the little hollow between her breasts.

He gave a sudden cry which was half a groan—a cry both of triumph and of pain.

'God, but you are beautiful!' he exclaimed, and his voice was low and hoarse with passion. 'Why should I care what has happened to you in the past? You are mine now . . . mine . . . my wife.'

He swept her off her feet, lifting her high in his arms. The firelight revealed his face, distorted, diabolical, and it seemed to her that it was the face of a man who has suffered beyond endurance, and become a devil.

Then, as she cried out in a fear such as she had never known before, he carried her across the room towards the shadowy darkness of the great bed.

'Vane! Vane!' she cried. 'Do not frighten me. I love you. Oh, Vane, spare me!'

Her voice was hardly audible as it came between her bruised lips, and yet he must have heard her, for he paused, looking down at her as she lay in his arms, her head flung back, her torn night-robe revealing her nakedness, her pelisse trailing from her on to the floor.

'Please, Vane. Please!' Caroline whispered again, and now she was sobbing like a child who has been frightened.

The expression on his face altered and she knew that he had heard her.

With a sudden movement, so unexpected that she

screamed in sheer physical terror, Lord Brecon threw Caroline from him and on to the bed. She fell helplessly against the softness of the pillows. Then with a sound too inarticulate for her to interpret he turned from her and left the room.

10

When Maria called her in the morning, Caroline was sitting at the bureau writing. As Maria set down a cup of chocolate beside her, Caroline said:

'Take this letter and arrange to have a groom carry it immediately to Mandrake. I would not have Mrs. Edgmont learn of my marriage from other sources before I inform her of it myself.'

Maria gulped.

'Oh, m'lady,' she said, and Caroline looking up in surprise, saw that there were tears in her eyes.

'Why, Maria,' she asked, 'what has upset you?'

' 'Tis not that I'm upset for myself, m'lady,' Maria replied, 'but for you . . . for your ladyship.'

'Why?' Caroline asked. 'What has occurred?'

' 'Tis only something I've heard this very instant,' Maria answered, wiping her eyes.

'Well, tell me,' Caroline commanded.

' 'Twas his lordship's valet who told me,' Maria said.

Caroline's face which was already pale seemed to be suddenly drained of all colour.

'Has anything happened to his lordship?'

'Oh no, m'lady, nothing serious,' Maria cried out, 'but it was such a shock to learn that his lordship has just returned from riding. The valet told me that his horse was ordered late last night and he must have been riding ever since. They say in the stables that the poor animal was so tired that they had almost to carry it to its stall. Oh, m'lady, methought that you were so happy.'

Caroline rose to her feet and walked slowly from the desk towards the window. After a moment she said in a cold, distant tone very unlike her usual friendliness:

'That is enough, Maria. Take the letter as I have commanded you. I will ring the bell when I need you again.'

Ordinarily Maria would have expostulated at such an abrupt dismissal, but there was something about Caroline this morning which forbad any argument. Still wiping her eyes, Maria went from the room and Caroline was alone again.

Her eyes were heavy for want of sleep, for she had been awake all night staring into the darkness. She shivered now and seemed not to feel the glitter of the sun's rays as they shone on the casement and bathed the garden below.

She stood looking out for a long time. It almost seemed as if she had been turned to stone, for she made no movement and her breath came so softly that it barely ruffled the laces at her breast. She was conscious only of feeling cold, for the agony of mind through which she had passed in the night had left her drained of all emotion, depleted of everything save a sense of utter impotency. It was as if her thoughts themselves were paralysed, and as she stood there she wondered if she would ever be capable of feeling anything again.

There came a knock at the door, but Caroline did not answer it. Someone knocked again and then, when there was still no reply, went away.

With the same sense of detachment Caroline sat in her room all the morning. It was long after midday when Maria returned without having been summoned.

'Oh, m'lady, let me bring you something to eat,' she pleaded.

'If it please you,' Caroline said indifferently.

'You will make yourself ill, m'lady. Let me dress you, and if you take a turn in the gardens, 'twill perhaps bring back the colour to your cheeks.'

'No, I will stay here,' Caroline replied.

Maria left her and returned shortly with a tray laden with tempting dishes; but when she saw the food, Caroline felt a nausea come over her and she pushed the tray away, the delicacies untouched.

'Oh, please, m'lady, try to eat a mouthful,' Maria begged her; but Caroline shook her head.

'I am not hungry, Maria,' she said in a voice utterly without feeling.

Maria picked up the tray and set it on one side.

'There is a much-a-do downstairs,' she said conversationally, as if she hoped to tempt Caroline into taking an interest. 'The guests are all leaving.'

176

'Why?' Caroline enquired, without any spark of interest in her voice.

' 'Twould have been without decency for them to linger, m'lady, with you and his lordship wed. By tonight I understand there will be only Mr. Warlingham left and of course Lady Augusta and Mrs. Miller.'

'So Mr. Warlingham is remaining,' Caroline said, a faint inflection of interest creeping into her tone.

Maria nodded.

'Yes, m'lady, and I hear that the gentleman is in a fearful temper. Carried to bed he was last night by the footman, for he imbibed, so they say, until he fell under the card table.'

Caroline sat pensive. Maria sighed. It seemed nothing would arouse her mistress today.

She took up the tray and opened the bedroom door. There was obviously someone outside for Caroline heard voices; then Maria came hurrying back to the room.

'A message from his lordship, m'lady,' she said. 'He begs to inform your ladyship that the last of his guests will have departed by three of the clock and he will then await your ladyship in the Library.'

Caroline stared at Maria as if she were not quite certain she had heard the message aright, then swiftly a transformation seemed to take place. The colour came back into her cheeks, a light shone in her eyes; gone was her languor and the cold indifference of the morning.

'Three o'clock, did you say?' she asked, and her lips curved over the words as if they were very precious. 'Then I have time for a bath, Maria; and bring me back that tray. I am hungry.'

The grandfather clock in the hall was striking pretentiously as Caroline came down the Grand Staircase from her room. The Castle was strangely quiet after the noise and bustle of the day before and it seemed to Caroline more gloomy than ever. Without the lighted tapers which dispersed much of the darkness of the hall the oak panelling with its suits of armour created the usual atmosphere of ponderous mystery. Caroline thought that she had never noticed before how a sudden chill seemed to rise from the marble floor and it occurred to her that in the winter the whole Castle must be a place of bitter cold.

She went down the passage towards the Library. The door was closed. She hesitated for a moment before she

177

turned the handle. Her heart was beating fast and yet she was not really afraid. She was prepared to believe now that the events of last night had been but a nightmare. Perhaps she had exaggerated them, perhaps they had been but a fig-ment of the imagination. It was Vane she was going to see, Vane whom she loved and who she knew deep in her heart loved her . . . Vane who was her husband.

For a moment she looked down as if in confirmation at the emerald signet ring encircling the third finger of her left hand. Vane's ring, the ring which was a symbol of—come what may—the fact that he was hers and she was his. Caroline took a deep breath and raised the ring to her lips; then lifting her head high, she turned the handle of the Library door.

Lord Brecon was standing with his back to the fireplace, facing the door. Caroline had a moment's impression that he had been impatiently waiting for her coming, yet his face did not lighten at her approach and her heart sank to see that his eyes were brooding and there was a frown on his forehead.

'Your servant, Caroline,' he said briefly.

She dropped him a little curtsey from the doorway.

'Good-day, Vane,' she said in a voice that was far calm-er than her feelings. 'I understand that our guests have left.'

'*Our* guests?' he queried, then added quickly: 'Yes, of course, our guests. They have gone.'

She moved across the room until she stood beside him and raised her eyes to his. They were soft with desire, but he did not look at her, did not speak, and at length she prompted softly:

'You sent for me, Vane; you wanted to see me?'

'Yes,' he said. 'Come! I have something to show you.'

He turned and walked towards the door, holding it open for her to precede him. Wondering a little, she obeyed. When she reached the passage, she looked up at him ques-tioningly.

'This way,' he said sharply and turned not towards the hall but down the passage they had taken the night before when they walked to the Chapel. For a moment Caroline thought that it was to the Chapel Lord Brecon was leading her. Why she had no idea; and for a moment the wild thought came to her that perhaps he wished to revoke the vows they had made before the altar. But they went on

178

past the Chapel doors, down the passage, which grew narrower and darker.

They walked for some way until they came to a heavy door; it had huge iron hinges and was studded with iron nails. To Caroline's surprise it was locked, but Lord Brecon drew a key from his pocket. He opened the door and they passed through it, after which he locked it again behind him.

Some steps led down to a stone-paved hall on the other side of which was a winding stairway. Caroline looked around her and realised that she was in one of the towers. There was no mistaking the heavy Norman architecture, the slender arrow-slits through which little light could penetrate.

'Forgive me if I precede you,' Lord Brecon said, and walking into the hall he crossed it and went down yet another passage which ended with another locked door.

The whole place was chill and damp and, as far as Caroline could see, was unused. But when Lord Brecon opened the further door she had a surprise.

They stood looking into an almost identical stone hall, but this one was furnished. There were mats over the flags, oak chests were arranged round the walls and a fire was lit in a big stone fireplace. Again Lord Brecon preceded her, and crossing the hall, started to climb the stairs. As he did so, an old man, white-haired and in an ancient livery, which seemed to be too big for him unless he had shrunk, came hurrying through a doorway.

'Ah, m'lord! I was awondering who it could be,' he exclaimed.

'It is all right, Miggs,' Lord Brecon said. 'I will find my own way upstairs.'

'I hope I sees your lordship well,' the old man remarked, anxious, Caroline guessed, to hold Lord Brecon in conversation.

'Well enough,' Lord Brecon replied, 'and how is Mrs. Miggs?'

'Poorly, poorly, m'lord, though she'll be gratified to know that your lordship enquired for her. 'Tis her chest, m'lord. She doesn't seem to throw off her cough, though that ain't no surprise, for the moat makes these lower rooms terrible damp. As I've informed your lordship often enough, we shall be having the water right into the place one of these fine days.'

179

'Yes, yes, you have told me that before,' Lord Brecon said impatiently, and proceeded to climb the stairs, leaving the old man grumbling beneath his breath.

The stairs were narrow and twisting. They were carpeted, but Caroline could see that they were of rough hewn stone like the staircase in the other tower. They ended abruptly on a narrow landing which was faced by one door. Lord Brecon knocked on it and a voice bade them enter.

Lord Brecon opened the door. For a moment Caroline was too surprised to notice anything save the sunshine. It was streaming through two large windows which had been built into the south side of the tower. Then as she blinked her eyes, a little dazzled after the darkness of the passages and stairway, she saw that a woman had risen from where she had been sitting beside a fireplace protected with a nursery guard.

She was a pleasant-faced, elderly woman, wearing a grey dress, a mob-cap and the frilled apron of a child's nurse. She curtsied to Lord Brecon.

'Good-afternoon, your lordship. This is indeed an unexpected pleasure.'

'How are you, Nanny?' Lord Brecon asked; and then turning his head as if he looked for something or somebody, he added: 'And how is Cassy?'

'Not so well today,' Nanny said in a low tone; then raising her voice she called: 'Come along, Miss Cassy dear, don't be shy. Here are visitors to see you.'

She was looking towards the window-seat, Caroline noticed, and following her gaze, she saw that someone was hiding behind one of the heavy pink curtains which draped the window. The curtain quivered, and very slowly someone emerged. It was with difficulty that Caroline prevented herself from uttering a scream; it was indeed only her breeding and up-bringing which gave her the self-control to bite back the sound even as it reached her lips.

Coming from the curtains was a creature more monstrous than anything she had ever beheld. It was the height of a child, being only a few feet tall, but its head was huge and distorted, with a great bulging forehead from which the hair hung lankly over flattened and deformed ears. Its body reached almost to the ground, its legs were like two sticks, and its arms, although also thin and spidery, ended in large white hands with fat and stumpy
180

fingers. It had thick lips to its big mouth, and its eyes were small and unexpectedly bright.

It was all the more frightening because the creature was dressed neatly and even prettily in girl's clothes. Its dress of white muslin trimmed with pink ribbons seemed somehow to make a travesty of the fantastic body, and the pink bow tidying the coarse hair would have been ludicrous had it not been pitiable. The girl—if girl it was—lumbered across the room, her hands hanging at her sides, her fingers outstretched.

'Hullo, Cassy,' Lord Brecon said to her. 'Do you remember me?'

Cassy stared at him, before saying in a high, whining voice:

'Cassy wants the dicky-bird.'

'Now, Miss Cassy,' Nanny said sharply, 'that's enough of that. I have told you before you are not to talk about it. 'Tis very naughty.'

'Cassy wants to squeeze the dicky-bird,' the child repeated. 'Cassy wants to squeeze it 'til the blood comes . . . 'til the blood runs over Cassy's fingers . . . Nice dicky-bird! Cassy wants to feel its warm blood drip, drip, drip!'

'That's very naughty,' Nanny scolded. 'Now go and find your dolly, dearie, and forget about the dicky-bird. Do as I tell you, at once.'

Obediently Cassy turned towards a cupboard in the far corner of the room. The doors were open and Caroline could see that it was full of toys of all sorts and descriptions. Cassy went to it, pulled out a doll by its skirt and held it head downwards towards the ground.

'Cassy wants the dicky-bird,' she repeated in a fierce undertone. 'Cassy wants to feel its blood drip . . . drip.'

She looked towards her nurse as she spoke, and there was an expression of such evil cunning in the tiny eyes that once again Caroline almost cried out. Then a stream of saliva ran from the open mouth down the fat chin and the high voice continued defiantly:

'Cassy wants the dicky-bird.'

' 'Tis no use, m'lord,' Nanny said. 'She is in one of her moods today. She has been as quiet as anything the past week, but a bird settled on the window-sill this morning and it set her off. She's all right, as your lordship knows, if she never sees anything alive; but if she does, she gets like this and we shall have one of her bad turns, I'm afraid.'

181

'Yes, I expect so,' Lord Brecon said heavily. 'You have a draught if she gets violent?'

'Oh yes, m'lord, but I don't like to give it to her unless she is really bad. Sometimes she is as sweet as sweet; it was only the bird that set her off this morning.'

The nurse glanced towards Cassy as she spoke and Caroline saw that there was real affection on her face. Cassy suddenly threw down the doll she had been holding and came shuffling across the room. She went towards Caroline, and now her fingers were bent as if she would claw at her.

'Where's Cassy's dicky-bird?' she said fiercely. 'Have you got the dicky-bird? Give it to Cassy, give it to Cassy!'

Instinctively Caroline recoiled, but Nanny was between her and Cassy, a protective barrier.

'Come along, Miss Cassy,' she said quietly. 'I have got something nice to show you.'

She took the idiot's hand firmly in hers and spoke over her shoulder to Lord Brecon.

'You'd better go, m'lord. I don't like your lordship to see her like this, nor the lady who is with you.'

Lord Brecon opened the nursery door, and pale and shaken, Caroline slipped from the room. Even as the door closed behind them, they heard Cassy cry again:

'Cassy wants the dicky-bird. Cassy wants to feel its blood drip . . . drip.'

In silence Caroline went down the stairs. When they reached the hall, Lord Brecon opened the door at the foot of the stairway.

'Shall we talk in here?' he asked.

The room into which he showed her was almost identical with the nursery above it, save that the windows only began above eye level. It was comfortably arranged but had the air of not being used. Caroline looked round her and then her eyes returned to the windows.

'They are built specially high so that no one from outside can look in,' Lord Brecon said, as if he guessed her thoughts.

'I understand,' Caroline said in a low voice.

The old man came hurrying through the door.

'Shall I light the fire, m'lord? You will find it powerful cold in here. The room is seldom in use.'

'Yes, light the fire,' Lord Brecon commanded.

Caroline sat in silence while the old man kindled the flame, talking all the while.

182

'I wish I'd a-known you were a-comin, m'lord. We would have turned this room out. 'Tis seldom you pay a visit these days. Nurse was remarking only the night before last how it was since we'd seen your lordship. But there, you have much to occupy you, one can be sure of that, and when your lordship does come we should not grumble, for we have much to be thankful for.'

'You get your food all right?' Lord Brecon said.

'Oh yes, m'lord. My wife's own niece is giving us a hand now. She's a sensible girl and not a word would she say to anyone. She brings us our provisions from the village, and of course we get game from the keepers and vegetables from the garden as we always have done.'

'That's all right then,' Lord Brecon said. 'I will let you know when I am leaving, Miggs.'

"Thank you, m'lord. I'll be a-waiting in the hall, m'lord.'

The old man shuffled from the room and closed the door behind him. Lord Brecon stood with his back to the crackling fire, looking down at Caroline's bent head as she sat in the chair.

'Now that you know my secret I hope you are satisfied,' he said in a bitter voice. 'Now perhaps you will understand why I commanded you to leave the Castle, why I tried to save you from the consequences of your own impetuosity.'

Caroline raised her face, and it was white and drawn.

'Who . . . who is she?' she asked, and her voice trembled on the words.

'Cassy is my sister,' Lord Brecon replied. 'You would hardly credit it, but she will be four-and-twenty this year. Born a monstrosity, she developed gradually the murderous tendencies that you have just heard. It is impossible for her to see anything living but she desires to kill it. The physicians suspected early in her life that she might be that way inclined and all animals were kept from her, but unfortunately the caretaker's cat got into the nursery one day when Cassy was about six years of age. She killed it and sat there bathed in its blood, enjoying a satanic orgy. Since then she has wanted to kill and to go on killing.'

Caroline put her hands to her face.

'It is unbearably horrible,' she whispered.

'But Cassy is not the only skeleton in the family cupboard,' Lord Brecon said, and now there was a terrible veneer of lightness overlying the bitterness of his words as if it gave him pleasure to torture both Caroline and himself.

'When I was twenty-five, my trustees handed me the management of my estates and also entrusted me with the secrets of the Castle. Cassy was the first of them. Until then I did not know of her existence; but worse than Cassy, or so it seemed to me, they told me the truth of my father's death.'

'Your father?' Caroline asked.

'Oh yes, he was mad too,' Lord Brecon replied. 'When he was a comparatively young man, there was some scandal while he was up at Oxford. A friend of his was found dead in extremely peculiar circumstances. Nothing could be proved and my revered parent was obviously more careful in the ensuing years. But when I was three years old, Cassy was born; and I am informed that when he saw her the sight of her seemed to rekindle in him the madness which had been dormant for years. My mother was desperately ill after Cassy's birth and the baby's deformities were kept from her. When she was well enough to bear the truth, she was told that her child was dead. Only Nanny and old Miggs and his wife were entrusted with the dread secret that she was alive. The Tower was prepared for her and she was shut away here in the hope, of course, that she would die quickly. But lunatics live far longer than sane folk and Cassy is in actual fact extremely healthy.

'But as I was saying, after her birth I am told my father became very peculiar. He began to take an almost fiendish delight in sport. He never seemed to have enough of shooting, hunting and cock-fighting. He also took to wandering about the grounds at night. A poacher was found dead in the wood and there was no doubt at all that he had been murdered. One of my trustees was an eminent physician. He had since died, but on my twenty-fifth birthday he told me how he gradually began to suspect my father, how he had invited himself to stay here, anxious if possible to save an old friend from himself. Then in a fit of temper, because his boots had been badly cleaned, my father killed his valet. It was a deliberate murder. He flogged the man with a hunting crop and then, when he was unconscious, stabbed him with a knife. It was the physician who found the dead man in my father's bedchamber and realising what must be the consequences to my father, he took upon himself to advocate what I well believe was the only honourable solution.'

'What was that?' Caroline asked.

'He persuaded my father to take his own life. He told me

184

that he loaded the pistol with his own hand and then, having told my father what he must do, withdrew from the room. When he related the story to me, he said that he had never welcomed anything in his life as he did the sound of that pistol shot. With my father dead it was easy to hush up the crime. Fortunately the valet was a foreigner whose relations were not likely to make enquiries or cause a fuss. My father was buried with great pomp and ceremony, and no one except the trustees knew the whole truth of his death although it was impossible to prevent a certain amount of local gossip. Every possible care was taken to keep it from my mother; and just as they had managed to hide from her the fact of Cassy's existence, so they managed to conceal the knowledge that her husband was a murderer. I did not know it either until two years ago, and since then I have wished over and over again that they had had more of a respect for my feelings and had kept silent. Now at last you can understand what the future holds for me, Caroline—madness and the knowledge that I shall go the same way as my father went. Soon I shall want to kill and go on killing until far less fortunate than him, the gallows will claim me.'

Caroline gave me a little cry.

'Oh no, Vane! No.'

'It is true,' he said grimly, 'and I am not afraid to face it. Now perhaps you will understand why I am not particularly interested in saving my life. The sooner I die the better, for I would rather die cleanly than with my hands stained with blood.'

'Vane! Vane! Don't say such things.'

There were tears running down Caroline's cheeks, but she paid no heed to them. Instead she got to her feet, and standing beside Lord Brecon laid her hand on his arm.

'There must be some way out of this,' she said. 'There must be something we can do.'

'Do?' he questioned. 'There is nothing save to wait patiently for the end.'

'I won't believe it, I won't,' Caroline stormed suddenly. 'It is cruel and unjust. If there is a merciful God, He . . .'

'Can you believe in a God who would permit such things as Cassy?' Lord Brecon enquired.

'Yes,' Caroline answered quickly, 'for Cassy does not know, does not feel. It is not for Cassy that I ask justice, but for you, Vane. You are young, you are not mad!'

'Not yet!'

There was something so grim in his answer that Caroline could for the moment only sob uncontrollably. If her tears moved him, he showed no sign of it.

'Come, your ladyship,' he said after a few seconds. 'This has been a morbid revelation, I admit, but it need not disturb you unnecessarily. You have nothing to fear and the gaieties of London Society will soon dispel such horrors from your mind. My London mansion is at your disposal. It shall be opened, and my purse fortunately is long enough for you to indulge in whatever whims occur to you.'

Caroline raised her face from her hands.

'How can you speak of such things?' she asked quickly and in utter scorn. 'Do you think that frivolities could make me forget all this . . . and you.'

Her voice softened on the last word, but Lord Brecon remained unmoved.

'Perhaps I can understand your feelings,' he said, 'for I find it difficult to forget Sir Montagu Reversby.'

Caroline started as if he had struck her.

'How can you dare to speak of that man . . . now at this moment?' she asked. 'Once and for all, Vane, I insist on your hearing what occurred between him and me.'

Lord Brecon straightened his shoulders, and it seemed to Caroline as if he became immeasurably taller. His face was like marble as he said:

'I beg you to spare me, Caroline, for I am not interested.'

To Caroline's overwrought nerves this was almost the last straw. She stamped her foot.

'Very well then, if you prefer to believe defamations against me, which I could disperse in a few sentences, believe them. You say you are not interested, my lord; very well, I am not interested either.'

Lord Brecon bowed.

'For once we are in agreement,' he said. 'May I now escort your ladyship to more habitable parts of the Castle?'

He offered her his arm, but Caroline refused it with a disdainful glance. She was angry—angry with a fury which seemed to run through her veins like fire. The shock of what she had seen, the horror of Lord Brecon's revelations were all submerged for the moment in a feeling of intense rage because he would not hear her.

Then as they walked down the long passages, Lord

Brecon unlocking and re-locking the doors as they went, Caroline felt her anger ebbing from her and her love for him sweeping over her again in a warm flood. She loved him. What could it matter what his father had done or that the ghastly monstrosity which was his sister would for ever haunt her? What did it all matter beside the fact that Vane was Vane, the man she loved, the man for whom her whole being yearned. Nothing could quench such a love as hers, nothing could alter it.

And at last she could understand so many things. Now she understood why he had vowed for himself a life of celibacy, for he would not risk bringing into the world a creature such as Cassy. Now she understood why, in the full flood-tide of their revelation of their love one for another, he had made the supreme sacrifice of wanting to send her away from him, deliberately choosing loneliness and misery for himself that she might be saved from unhappiness. Only by her own persistence had she defied his determination, a determination which had been overcome by the blind jealousy that had been aroused in him when he learned of her association with Sir Montagu Reversby.

As they walked down the passage past the doors of the Chapel where they had been married the night before, Caroline suddenly knew something extremely surprising. It was that, strange though it might seem, she was grateful to Montagu Reversby. Yes, grateful, for had his very name not spurred Vane into wild, unconsidered action, she might at this moment have been driven from the Castle.

What she had learned was horrifying and unutterably ghastly. Vane's secret had indeed surpassed anything that she could have imagined even in her wildest fancies; and yet one simple fact remained, a fact unaltered, unchanged by everything which had occurred this afternoon. She loved him!

They reached the hall. They had not spoken since they left the sitting-room in the Tower, but it was easy to see where Lord Brecon's thoughts had been, for suddenly he pointed to the long line of oil paintings hung on the walls and said:

'These are my ancestors, from them I have inherited this Castle and—my blood.'

Caroline looked up at the pictured faces. They were mostly of men—men in Elizabethan ruffs, in splendid uniforms and in picturesque robes. They were all dark-haired, Caroline noted, and in one or two of the portraits there was an almost uncanny resemblance to Gervase Warlingham. As if her thoughts conjured him up, Caroline turned and saw him standing at the drawing-room door.

'Are you admiring our most illustrious family?' he asked Caroline with his usual sneer.

'I was just thinking, sir,' she replied, 'that in several of these pictures it is easy to trace a remarkable likeness to yourself.'

Mr. Warlingham laughed.

'Yes, the Warlingham characteristics are often strongly accentuated,' he said. 'Which reminds me, Vane, 'tis the exception for there to be a blond Warlingham. You must be a changling.'

'His lordship takes after his mother's side of the family,' a gruff voice said behind them.

Startled, Caroline turned her head to see Dorcas standing at the foot of the stairs. She looked severely uncompromising as usual.

'As you say, Dorcas,' Lord Brecon said, 'I take after my mother, but only where looks are concerned.'

Dorcas crossed the hall to Caroline's side.

'Her ladyship would be pleased to see your ladyship at your convenience.'

'Thank you, Dorcas. Inform her ladyship that I will be with her in a few moments.'

Dorcas curtsied and withdrew down the passage. She was hardly out of earshot when Mr. Warlingham said:

'Gad, how that woman hates me! And how she dotes on you, Vane! Did you notice that she sprang to your defence as if she were a tiger defending her young?'

'You must excuse Dorcas,' Lord Brecon replied, 'but she has been with my mother since before I was born and at times takes advantage of her position.'

'Oh, the familiarity of old retainers does not worry me,' Mr. Warlingham said airily, 'and pray do not let me interrupt your ladyship's inspection of your new possessions,' he added to Caroline, and she sensed the venom in his tones and the hatred in his eyes as he withdrew into the drawing-room.

Lord Brecon no longer looked at the pictures. Instead he stood stiffly in the centre of the hall and Caroline realised that he was waiting for her to withdraw. She looked up at him and suddenly longed to tell him that the horrors he had just revealed to her had not changed her feelings for him one iota—that perhaps her love had even deepened in pity and understanding. But his air of aloofness and the forbidding pride on his face made her suddenly shy, and the hall was not a convenient place for confidences. While she hesitated, he spoke.

'If there is anything your ladyship requires,' he said formally, 'you have but to ask for it. I am sending to London immediately to instruct my lawyer to open Brecon House in St. James's Square. It should be ready in a week's time if it would please your ladyship to travel there. Until then, if you have other plans in mind, perhaps you will inform me of them.'

Caroline forced herself to smile at him.

'I thank your lordship,' she said. 'A week will give me time to consider, time to think. Things have happened with remarkable speed these past few days and I must admit to being slightly bemused for the moment.'

'I understand,' he said.

'That is indeed gracious,' Caroline replied, 'and now I would visit your mother. We will meet at dinner, my lord?'

It was a question, and Lord Brecon answered it with a conventional bow.

'We will meet at dinner.'

Caroline turned away and went slowly up the stairs. She hoped he would watch her go, but he turned abruptly on his heel and she saw him walk away towards the library; then after a few seconds she heard the slam of a distant door.

11

Shock is a strange thing. With some people it acts on them instantaneously, so that they faint, cry or show other symptoms of an emotional nature; but with others, and perhaps these are the more exceptional, it often takes hours or even days before the effects of a shock are felt.

Caroline, walking along the corridor to Lady Brecon's room, felt only divorced from her immediate surroundings. She was so detached from reality that she could view herself and the events of the past twenty-four hours as if they were pictures of a vivid clearness but were not in actual fact an intrinsic part of herself. Only her love for Vane seemed a warm and living thing, and she clung to her realisation of this as if it were an anchor without which she would be adrift on a tempestuous sea of horror and fear.

Lady Brecon gave a little cry of delight at the sight of her.

'Come and kiss me, Caroline, my dear,' she said softly. 'I have wished above all things to see you today; but your abigail told Dorcas that you were remaining in your bed-chamber until after luncheon, so I could do naught but possess my soul in patience.'

Caroline bent and kissed her.

'I would have come to you at once, Ma'am,' she said, 'had I but known you desired it.'

Lady Brecon patted her hand fondly.

'I always desire to see you. Tell me now about your marriage, and Vane. How is my son?'

Caroline hesitated. She hated to lie to Lady Brecon and yet she knew that she must not disturb her with the truth.

'His lordship is well,' she replied at length, 'I have but just this instant left him.'

190

Despite the effort Caroline made to sound natural there was something in the tone of her voice which caused Lady Brecon to glance at her enquiringly. For a moment Caroline was afraid the Dowager would ask if anything were amiss; but with her usual habit of avoiding the unpleasant things of life she said nothing.

Because she was nervous, Caroline talked quickly.

'We were married in the Chapel,' she said. 'The Lord Bishop performed the ceremony and someone—I have no idea who—played the organ. I wish, Ma'am, that you could have been present on such an auspicious occasion.'

There was an uncomfortable silence. Caroline was aware that her glib sentences had not set Lady Brecon's mind at rest and she knew instinctively what her ladyship wished to hear. She desired to be told that her son was happy; she wanted to be sure that this marriage, undertaken so hastily and in such strange circumstances, had brought him the joy which, as his mother, Lady Brecon was well aware had long been missing from his life.

But try as she might, Caroline knew that she could not utter such falsehoods convincingly, so instead she said:

'I noticed during the service that Vane's formidable list of Christian names did not include the one by which he is always known.'

'No, for Vane is a pet name,' Lady Brecon answered. 'As you say, Caroline, the names he was given at his christening make a formidable array, so I chose to call him Vane because it was simple and because it was the name of someone whom I once loved very dearly—someone who died before Vane was born.'

'So that is the explanation,' Caroline said. 'I wondered.'

'Your surprise was to be expected,' Lady Brecon replied; 'for everyone addresses my son by the name I preferred for him.'

There was a pause while Caroline sought vainly for another topic of conversation, and then Lady Brecon said almost pleadingly:

'You do love him, Caroline?'

This was a question which Caroline could answer in all honesty.

'Yes, Ma'am, I love him with all my heart and soul.'

'I wanted to be sure of that,' Lady Brecon said happily. 'And now you will be able to look after him, Caroline, because often I have been afraid that there is a wildness about him. It is difficult to put into words and perhaps all young men are the same; but it is worse for those who have no father to guide them if they are wealthy and have a position in life. But all the same, it is of vast import to have such things, for poverty is hard, especially for a man of breeding.'

Lady Brecon seemed almost to be talking to herself, and Caroline sensed some deep anxiety behind her words.

'I give you my word that I will do everything in my power to make Vane happy,' she said, and rising to her feet she added: 'If your ladyship will excuse me, I would go and lie down. I feel strangely tired.'

'But of course, my dear,' Lady Brecon answered. 'Yester eve must have been a strain upon you. Let Dorcas escort you to your bedchamber and ring for your maid.'

'There is no need,' Caroline replied, but even as she spoke she suddenly felt too weak to argue, for now unexpectedly the shock of what she had seen and heard earlier in the afternoon was beginning to take effect.

By the time she reached her room she was shivering all over and her hands were as cold as ice. Maria was fetched and Caroline submitted without protest to being undressed and tucked into bed with a warm brick at her feet. The fire was blazing in the room but none the less she shivered and felt as if she would never be warm again. The chill seemed to have crept into her very bones and the physical discomfort of it swept away her detachment so that now she could see Cassy's cunning little eyes and hear her voice repeating itself over and over again. Caroline groaned and buried her face in the pillow.

'You are ill, m'lady,' Maria cried in consternation. 'Permit me to ask his lordship to send for his physician.'

'No, no, Maria,' Caroline expostulated. 'I know what is wrong with me and I assure you that a physician can give me no relief from my ills.'

Nevertheless it worried her that despite the blankets piled on the bed she continued to shiver until her teeth chattered as if she had a ague. She suggested to Maria that she should ask Dorcas if her ladyship had a bottle of laudanum.

'If I could sleep, Maria, I believe I would wake in perfect health. It is just that something has upset me and last night I did not close my eyes.'

Maria thought this a sensible suggestion, and having given Caroline a few drops of laudanum, she sat by the bedside until at length the shivering seemed to pass from her limbs and her eyelids dropped drowsily.

Caroline slept all through the night. At first in the deep, dreamless sleep of one who has been drugged; then, as the hours passed, the colour came back to her cheeks as she lay breathing easily and rhythmically as a child. it was only then that Maria tiptoed from the room and went to her own bed.

When Caroline awoke, the sun had been up for some hours. She stretched and sat up. For a moment she could hardly believe she had slept the whole night through; she felt fresh and invigorated and the memory of how she had crept to bed cold and shivering seemed now nothing more than a half forgotten fantasy. She got out of bed, went to the window and pulled aside the curtains.

The gardens below were golden with sunshine and Caroline blinked her eyes in its warm rays.

'I must get up,' she said aloud. 'What a lazy mistress the household will think they have in me.'

She rang the bell and Maria came hurrying into the room.

'Oh, m'lady, 'tis better you are looking this morning,' she exclaimed.

'Better?' Caroline smiled. 'I am well, Maria. Bring me my breakfast and a bath, for I would be about the house, not malingering here in my bedchamber.'

'I have been greatly perturbed about your ladyship,' Maria said as she bustled about the room. 'Why, when I put you to bed last night, your ladyship looked as if you had seen a ghost.'

'Perhaps I had,' Caroline sighed, and for a moment the horror of Vane's terrible secret overshadowed her.

But nothing could dim or dispel her courage this morning. She would see Vane, she told herself, she would talk with him and make him lower this barrier which he had erected between them, so that together they could try to find a way to dispel the terrors which barred their way to happiness.

'There must be some solution,' Caroline said aloud.

'What was that, m'lady?' Maria enquired.

'I was thinking my thoughts aloud,' Caroline answered. 'Maria, if you were confronted with something fearful, something which threatened your entire happiness, what would you do?'

Maria thought for a moment.

'I suppose if it was as bad as that, m'lady, I should pray.'

'And if prayer would not help you?'

'Then, m'lady, I suppose I should just have to make the best of it—whatever it was,' Maria said practically.

'I believe you are right,' Caroline said, 'and I shall try both your remedies, Maria.'

'Praying never hurt anyone as far as I can see,' Maria remarked, 'and if, as my mother always said, "God helps those as helps themselves," maybe prayer will show your ladyship a way in which you can help yourself.'

'Then I shall pray,' Caroline said, 'for I greatly need to be shown the way out of my difficulties.'

'And while your ladyship is praying I will fetch you some breakfast,' Maria said. 'Is there anything for which your ladyship has a fancy?'

'I am not over-particular,' Caroline replied, 'for I am exceeding hungry.'

'That is a good sign, m'lady.'

Maria smiled and hurried from the room.

Alone Caroline moved to the window again, but her thoughts were not on the view which lay beneath her. Maria was right, she thought. She must pray—pray for guidance so that she could do the right thing and help Vane in the right way.

She had a sudden longing for her father and mother. If only they were with her, if only she could put her problems to Lord Vulcan and hear his grave, sensible voice tell her what she must do. But they were far away and there was no one whose advice she could ask.

She was indeed dreading a letter from Cousin Debby. She expected to receive it today and it was only to be expected that Mrs. Edgmont would be both shocked and flustered at the step Caroline had taken in her parents' absence. And yet, Caroline asked herself, what else could she have done but marry Vane? It was true that he had proposed to her in a fit of ungovernable anger, but she was convinced that it was better to have married him like that than not at all. Even now Caroline did not regret the step she had taken. She would far rather be married to Vane with all his terrible secrets than not married at all, for she knew that, having known him, having felt his arms around her and his lips on hers, she could never care for any other man.

She had been meant for Vane from the very beginning

of their lives and he for her; and remembering how they had come together in such a curious manner, Caroline thought that the ways of God were indeed strange and mysterious and that somehow, even though it was not given for mortals to see it, there was a plan and a pattern underlying all things.

Caroline was praying, her face hidden in her hands, when Maria returned with the tray. There were eggs and ham, cold meats and a choice cut of salmon in the silver dishes. There was golden butter from the farm and honey from the Brecon bees, which were famous for their sweetness, and Maria had also brought a dish of red strawberries and a jug of cream with which to cover them.

'Thank you, Maria,' Caroline said as the tray was set down at her side.

'Miss Harriet Wantage is below, m'lady,' Maria said. 'She is anxious to see your ladyship and I said I would enquire if you would receive her.'

'Harriet! At this hour!' Caroline exclaimed.

' 'Tis nigh eleven of the clock.'

'How shameful!' Caroline smiled. 'Harriet will think I am an indolent London miss who never rises before noon. I must explain to her that my behaviour this morning is the exception and not the rule.'

'I cannot see that it matters, your ladyship, what Miss Wantage thinks,' Maria said disdainfully. 'After all, she is but the Vicar's daughter.'

Caroline laughed.

'Maria, you are a dreadful snob!'

'Yes, m'lady,' Maria agreed complaisantly, 'and now I will ask the footman to show Miss Wantage upstairs.'

Caroline was eating her strawberries when Harriet was announced. She rose and went across the room to greet her.

'Harriet, I am humiliated that you should discover me in *déshabille* at such an hour, but I was so exhausted last night that Maria drugged me with the laudanum bottle and I have only just awakened.'

'Forgive me for disturbing you,' Harriet said, 'but, Caroline, I had to see you, for I am in sore need of your help and advice.'

'Then sit down and tell me all about it,' Caroline said. 'Maria shall fetch you some fresh chocolate.'

'No, no, please do not trouble,' Harriet said; 'I require nothing. Indeed I think I will never eat again, for I am so excited, Caroline, and at the same time in such a twitter that I know not which way to turn.'

Caroline looked at Harriet with laughter in her eyes.

'Then dare I collect that you are in love, Harriet?'

A deep flush stained Harriet's thin cheeks.

'Oh, Caroline, is it so obvious?'

'Of course it is,' Caroline declared, 'for I vow I have never seen you look so pretty before.'

Harriet blushed even deeper.

'I never thought I would live to hear anyone call me pretty,' she said humbly. 'But, Caroline . . . he thinks so.'

'Meaning of course, Mr. Stratton,' Caroline hazarded.

Harriet nodded.

'And has he . . . has he offered for you, Harriet?' Caroline asked.

Harriet nodded again, obviously too overcome for words.

'But that is beyond all things wonderful!' Caroline exclaimed. 'La, Harriet, and of course you accepted him?'

In answer Harriet clasped her hands together.

'Indeed I know not what to say. I love him deeply and with the greatest respect, but . . . but he wishes me to elope with him and . . . oh, Caroline, how can I deceive Papa?'

Caroline gave a sigh and pushed her breakfast tray aside.

'Tell me everything from the very beginning,' she commanded.

Nothing loath, Harriet, who seemed to be almost bursting with excitement, began:

'It was the night of your wedding, Caroline. I cannot recall exactly how it happened, but I found myself walking in the garden with Mr. Stratton. He spoke to me of Papa and I explained to him as best I could without being disloyal that Papa had turned him from the house because he had learned that he was poor. "You must not blame my father too harshly, sir," I said, "for seeing that we ourselves live in most straitened circumstances, he has a great repugnance to poverty and dislikes above all things to be reminded of it." Mr. Stratton—Thomas he says I should call him now—asked, "And what do you feel about such things, Miss Wantage?" I answered him truthfully and said that, having been poor all my life, I had known little else but poverty and that we frail women were seldom afraid of what was familiar, however disagreeable it might be. Then he said, "If you fell in love with someone, Miss Wantage, and he was without wealth?" I replied with dignity, "If I fell in love with someone, Mr. Stratton, it would not matter a fig to me whether he was a king or a pauper. I would love him for himself and be proud to serve him even if he required of me that I should scrub his floors and cook his meals.' And then, Caroline . . . Oh, I can hardly tell you . . .'

Harriet paused breathlessly, her eyes shining.

'Go on,' Caroline prompted. 'It is the most intriguing story I have ever heard.'

'Well then,' Harriet continued, 'he turned to me, took my hand and said, "Miss Wantage, could you love me for myself alone?" and, Caroline, for a moment my heart seemed to stop beating and I thought I would swoon away at his feet.'

'But you didn't,' Caroline said with a little smile. 'What did you do?'

Harriet blushed again and said, dropping her eyes:

'I said . . . and, Caroline, was it very bold and unmaidenly of me? . . . I said, "But I do love you, sir, and it matters not if you are a pauper, for to me you will always be a king".'

'Bravo, Harriet,' Caroline exclaimed; 'and what happened after that?'

'I am afraid,' Harriet said in a very low voice, 'that I was so bemused by my own daring that I allowed him to kiss me. Oh, Caroline, I blush to think of it even now.'

'You have far more sense than I thought possible,' Caroline said. 'Go on, Harriet.'

'Well, after that I remembered Papa, and when Mr. Stratton . . . Thomas, I mean . . . suggested coming to the Vicarage to see him the very next day to ask for my hand, I begged him not to in a very frenzy of fear, for, Caroline, you know full well that Papa would have driven him away with a horsewhip. I told Thomas that and added that if Papa was really annoyed with me, he would send me away to his sister, my Aunt Roxana, at Ramsgate. She is as frightening as Papa himself and would make it utterly impossible for me to ever set eyes on Thomas again.'

'And what did Mr. Stratton say to that?' Caroline asked.

'He said that in these circumstances there was only one thing to be done, that we must run away to Gretna Green.'

'And you have agreed?' Caroline asked.

'That is why I have come to see you,' Harriet asnwered. 'Oh, Caroline, what shall I do? What shall I do?'

'There is no question on it,' Caroline replied. 'You must go with him, Harriet—to Gretna Green.'

'But, Papa, he will kill me if he catches me.'

'He won't catch you,' Caroline said reassuringly. 'I think you can safely leave that in Mr. Stratton's hands. All you have to do, Harriet, is to let him make the arrangements and to meet him at the time he asks.'

'He suggested nine o'clock this evening,' Harriet faltered, twisting her fingers together in an agony of indecision and helplessness. 'He sent me a note yesterday from Sevenoaks where he is staying and I vow it was the merest chance that it did not fall into Papa's hands. I nearly died with fright when a groom brought it to the house but two minutes before Papa returned from riding.'

'And in it Mr. Stratton suggested that you elope this evening?' Caroline said.

'Yes, he has told me to meet him outside the Castle gates,' Harriet said. 'It is a wise idea, I know, for if curious eyes see a post chaise waiting there, they will not credit for a moment that it is for someone from the Vicarage.'

'Mr. Stratton seems to have got everything well thought out,' Caroline said. 'He trusts you to be there and you cannot fail him. Why are you so worried?'

'But, Caroline, surely you understand. How can I run away with a strange gentleman of whom I know so little, and leave Papa and my home, and besides . . . Oh, Caroline, I have nothing to wear.'

There was such a *cri de coeur* in Harriet's voice over this last objection that Caroline could not help smiling. She rose to her feet and put her arms round the trembling girl.

'Now listen, Harriet,' she said, 'there is only one thing that matters and that if you are sure that you really and truly desire to wed with Mr. Stratton. Are you persuaded of that?'

' 'Tis the only thing of which I am beyond all hesitation positive,' Harriet answered, 'for, Caroline, he is indeed a most handsome, a most elegant gentleman and of the finest sensibility—and to think that he should love me . . . me of all people!'

'And you don't mind his being poor?' Caroline said. 'Has he related to you his exact circumstances or spoken of his family?'

'No, he has not spoken of such matters,' Harriet answered, 'and I know only what Papa has told me. I cannot imagine where he obtained such information, but it appears that he learnt that Thomas' family is impoverished. That was why he forbade me to speak with him again.'

Harriet paused, looked as if she might cry, and then went on with her story.

' "If you marry," Papa said to me, "though heaven knows 'tis unlikely enough that any man would be such a fool as to offer for you, I will take care that 'tis not some scallywag with pockets to let who will live on me." I am sure, Caroline, that Thomas would never consider such a degrading situation, but you know what Papa is like. And if he asks for my hand, Papa will enquire only as to the contents of his purse and my feelings will be his last consideration.'

'I am sure you are right there,' Caroline agreed. 'Very well then, Harriet, quite obviously there is nothing for it but to run away with your Mr. Stratton. To be honest, I think this is the greatest thrill he has known in years. He has found life a bore, Harriet, and, if I am not mistaken, to play the knight-errant to a maiden in distress and rescue her from a dragon—which of course is your papa—will be very much to his liking.'

'Then you think I should go?' Harriet faltered.

'Think?' Caroline enquired. 'I don't think, Harriet, I know you must. And now for your clothes. You cannot elope and not look attractive on such an auspicious occasion.'

'Mr. Stratton . . . I mean, Thomas . . . said that I was not to trouble to bring much with me. He promised to buy me all that I need once we were married; but, Caroline . . . I am sure he cannot afford such extravagances, and besides, I must wear something in which to travel.'

'Indeed you must,' Caroline said solemnly, 'and I will see to that, Harriet.'

'Oh but, Caroline, I did not mean to impose on you,' Harriet expostulated. 'I would not have you think that I came here for the very purpose of presuming on your generosity.'

'Fudge! As if I should think such a thing. You know I would like above all things to give you a gown for such a thrilling adventure; but I will not spoil Mr. Stratton's plans by giving you too many, for I guess that he wishes to dress you according to his fancy, and indeed I perceive that you are to be a very real interest to him and that you will disperse his *blasé* airs once and for all.'

'I have never seen him bored.' Harriet said quietly.

'No, my dear, and I hope you never will,' Caroline answered, 'for I predict that once you are wed you will settle down to a life of domestic bliss and Mr. Stratton will quickly forget how fatigued he was by high Society. And now for your clothes.'

Caroline rang the bell and when Maria answered it she was entrusted with Harriet's secret.

'You must speak of it to no one, Maria,' Caroline said; 'and now let us look in my wardrobe and find something suitable for Miss Wantage to travel in.'

'There is your pale blue merino, m'lady, with the embroidered bodice, and it has an elegant manteau in the same colour edged with swansdown.'

'The very thing!' Caroline exclaimed, 'and the bonnet which goes with it is entirely captivating. It will become you well, Harriet, and has the advantage of being warmer than most of my summer gowns. There is also a muff to match.'

'Alas, m'lady, I did not pack the muff,' Maria apologized.

'What a pity!' Caroline answered; then she added; 'But with any degree of luck it should be here by this evening. When I wrote to Mrs. Edgmont yesterday, I begged her to have my clothes despatched to me here as soon as possible. Now let me think. The groom would have reached Mandrake yester eve, and if the things were sent off before noon today they should arrive before dusk and Miss Wantage can take the muff with her. I have two other things I would like her to have—my green gauze with rose ribbons and the négligé of India muslin inset with thread lace.'

'Yes, m'lady,' Maria said.

' 'Tis over-generous of you, Caroline,' Harriet interrupted, 'but I dare not take so much. How indeed could I convey such luggage from the Vicarage to the trysting place? I can wear one dress and perhaps carry a night-robe in a small parcel, but that is all.'

'This is a problem!' Caroline said. 'But wait, I have an idea. Maria and I will arrange for your luggage to be hidden somewhere by the lodge gates. Is there anyone who can be trusted, Maria, to carry a box for you?'

Maria nodded her head and looked coy.

'There is James, m'lady. He has asked me to walk out with him and I am sure that anything I ask of him he would do and keep secret on it.'

'Then that is splendid,' Caroline said. 'James shall take the trunk—just a few things in it, Harriet, for I must not spoil your future husband's pleasure—and hide it by the lodge. Remember to pick it up before you start off on your journey.'

'Oh, Caroline, supposing I cannot find it,' Harriet faltered, 'and if Papa is following me or suspicious of where I am going, what shall I do then?'

Caroline sighed. She found it difficult to understand the hesitations and the apprehensions of the weaker members of her sex.

'I'll tell you what I will do, Harriet,' she said. 'I will meet you at the lodge gates myself. Maria will arrange with James to hide the trunk earlier in the evening. I will find it and wait until you arrive. You will not be afraid to look for me, will you, Harriet?'

'Oh no, indeed, Caroline, but why should you do this for me? 'Tis too much to ask. I would not think of troubling you.'

'It is no trouble, to be sure,' Caroline answered. 'I think perhaps I should be wise to be there in case you are too chicken-hearted at the last moment to embark on your great adventure. I will not let Mr. Stratton see me, and all you have to do, Harriet, is to flee from the Vicarage a trifle earlier. I will be at the gates at a quarter to nine o'clock and will expect you as soon after that as you can manage. Do not be any later in case Mr. Stratton in his impatience to be away with you is also early.'

'But, Caroline, how can I leave the Vicarage wearing a dress of yours?' Harriet asked.

'I had forgotten that,' Caroline exclaimed, 'although actually it would not matter your wearing a dress of mine save that it is a driving gown and your father might be suspicious. La! but I have an even better idea, Harriet. You must meet me at the gates, earlier still. You will change behind the trees and then be ready for Mr. Stratton when he comes. That will be safer, won't it, Maria?'

Maria nodded.

'Yes, indeed, m'lady, and I will come with your ladyship so as to help robe Miss Wantage and arrange her hair.'

'Nothing could be better,' Caroline exclaimed; 'now all is settled. I dare not invite you here, Harriet, for your father might consider it strangely unconventional for me to entertain so soon after my marriage, and besides, I think Mr.

Stratton relishes the idea of collecting you straight from the dragon's lair.'

Harriet giggled at this and then she was serious again.

'Oh dear! I am so afraid of Papa.'

'Mr. Stratton will protect you,' Caroline smiled, 'do not hesitate to tell him of your fears. And, Harriet, let me give you one word of advice. When you are married, if your father seems anxious to be friendly and to give his blessing to your marriage, don't be in too big a hurry to lose your dragon. He is your greatest asset, if you but knew it.'

Harriet wrinkled her brows in perplexity.

'But I fail to understand you, Caroline. Papa will never approve of my marriage. He would never give his permission for me to marry unless the gentleman who offered for me was wealthy or of noble birth, so indeed how should I ever find anyone to please him? Such distinctions are not for me.'

'You are far too modest, dear Harriet,' Caroline said, 'but remember what I have told you. I have my reasons for it.'

'I will remember, as you ask it of me,' Harriet promised.

'Now let us choose you a night-robe,' Caroline said; 'it must be of the most elegant transparency, and you will need a shift and——'

It was luncheon time before all the things necessary for Harriet's elopement had finally been decided upon; and when at length they were set aside for Maria to pack, Caroline said it was too late for her to bathe and dress and that she would have her luncheon brought to her room.

'Convey my apologies to his lordship,' she said to Maria, 'and say I hope that I may have the pleasure of speaking with him this afternoon.'

Maria went below with the message, but came back looking doleful.

'His lordship went out riding this morning and has not yet returned. Oh, m'lady, is there still something at variance between you?'

Caroline did not answer, but she was disappointed and discomforted. Why must Vane keep up this pretence of indifference? she asked herself. Why, indeed, would he not let her give him an explanation regarding Sir Montagu?

She sighed as she dressed, and decided that sooner or later she must force Vane to listen to her story. But it seemed as if he was determined to avoid her.

Caroline had tea alone with Lady Brecon in her room, and though she waited anxiously for Lord Brecon to appear as was his usual custom, he did not come.

After tea she wandered about the house, looking into the various rooms; and had she not been restless and depressed by his lordship's absence, she might have been amused at the difference in the servants' attitude. Whenever she encountered a flunkey, abigail, valet or page, they were almost embarrassingly subservient. After the indifferent and often disdainful air with which they had treated her when she was a dependent like themselves it was amusing to see how anxious they were to ingratiate themselves with her. As she went to her landing to change for dinner, Caroline had an idea.

Besides her personal problems where Vane was concerned and quite apart from the terrible secret they now shared, there was always in Caroline's mind an awareness that he was still threatened by his cousin Gervase. Their marriage had, she was certain, if anything, intensified the danger, and she could not forget the look on Mr. Warlingham's face as he stood watching them across the ballroom on the night they were married.

Sooner or later Caroline was certain that he would try once again to be rid of Vane; and it seemed to her that the sooner an incident occurred and, in being circumvented, revealed Gervase Warlingham in his true colours, the better it would be. What was frightening was the idea that with her mind otherwise preoccupied she might be lulled into a sense of false security. Gervase Warlingham's nefarious designs might prove themselves successful if he were lucky enough to take both Vane and herself unawares.

Caroline was sure that it was Mr. Warlingham from whom she had to save her husband. However oblivious Vane might be, she could sense danger in the very air of the Castle.

It was also obvious, Caroline considered, that Mrs. Miller was in Gervase Warlingham's confidence. They were acting in unison and she thought now that as Mrs. Miller was the more indiscreet and excitable of the two, it might be worth-while to inflame her further so that like all her sex she would find it hard to possess herself in patience and must act impetuously and on the spur of the moment.

It was but a vague plan, but nevertheless Caroline determined to act on it. She called Maria and sent her in search of the housekeeper. Mrs. Timmins came immediately, her dress of stiff black silk rustled as she walked, her hands were folded over the black apron which she wore as a symbol of her office.

'Good-evening, Mrs. Timmins,' Caroline said pleasantly, in the friendly tones which she had heard her mother use so often when speaking with the domestic staff.

Mrs. Timmins curtsied.

'Good-evening, m'lady.'

She stood waiting for orders. She was a sallow-complexioned woman of uncertain age, with frightened, short-sighted eyes and a nervous habit of licking her lips.

'How long have you been at the Castle, Mrs. Timmins?' Caroline enquired.

'Fifteen years come Michaelmas, m'lady, and I hope your ladyship will see your way to let me remain. If things weren't to your ladyship's liking when you first came, I hope you will not blame me. I was not to know who your ladyship was; and if the housemaids weren't as attentive as they should be, I can only beg your ladyship's pardon.'

'I am not blaming anyone, Mrs. Timmins,' Caroline said soothingly. 'I sent for you on a very different matter. I want the Chapel cleaned and set in order. It will not be any easy task, for it is a sorry picture of neglect, but the maids must begin on it tomorrow morning. Is that clear?'

'Indeed it is, m'lady, and it shall be as your ladyship wishes, although I'm afraid we shall have to ask the man-servants for their assistance in cleaning the ceiling.'

'I leave the arrangements in your hands, Mrs. Timmins,' Caroline answered, 'and now ask the chef to bring me the menu for dinner. There may be some slight change that I wish to make in it.'

'Very good, m'lady.'

Mrs. Timmins curtsied, but when she got to the door she hesitated.

'Forgive me mentioning it, m'lady, but Mrs. Miller has already approved the menu for dinner and has requested that the housemaids shall tomorrow——'

Caroline stood up.

'Let me make this quite clear, Mrs. Timmins. I am not interested in what arrangements Mrs. Miller has made or not made. My orders will be carried out as I have given them.'

Mrs. Timmins was completely overcome, and curtsied several times in her flurry.

'Yes, m'lady. Of course, m'lady. I will see that everything is as your ladyship desires.'

Caroline waited; and when the menu was brought to her, she crossed out the chine of mutton and ordered a fillet of veal with mushrooms and a high sauce. She also added roasted sweetbreads and hot lobster to the dishes listed in the second course.

The chef made no comment, but Caroline was not surprised to hear a knock on her door a few minutes later; and when she invited whoever was without to enter, Mrs. Miller came into the room.

The woman was in extreme good looks and Caroline thought that it was more than likely she was truly in love with Mr. Warlingham. She seemed more voluptuous than usual, her evening gown of scarlet silk net did little to conceal her ample charms, and her eyelids seemed heavy with the languor of love.

Caroline looked at her as if in surprise.

'Good-evening, Mrs. Miller; you wish to see me?'

'If you will be so kind as to spare me a few minutes,' Mrs. Miller said. 'I have no wish to trouble your ladyship, but I have just been informed you have given certain instructions to Mrs. Timmins and to the chef. Of course any order you give in the Castle shall be seen to immediately; but you will understand, my dear Lady Brecon, that it would be far easier if such orders could be given to me and I will pass them on to the staff.'

Caroline raised her eyebrows.

'Why should I do that?' she asked.

'Merely so as to facilitate that things are carried out speedily and that instructions do not overlap. You must see, Ma'am, that if you give orders and they countermand those I have already given——'

'Those you have given?' Caroline queried. 'But of course, Mrs. Miller, you cannot be so naïve as to imagine that you will continue to give orders here now? I am, as it happens, very conversant with housekeeping, and what is more, I intend to run my household in my own way. I do not propose to inconvenience you unduly, but it will of course simplify matters if you can find other employment as speedily as possible. I am sure Lady Augusta will graciously provide you with a reference.'

The expression on Mrs. Miller's face changed. Her lips tightened until they were only a thin line and her eyes narrowed until they were dark slits of anger. Twilight was falling, and Caroline, watching the woman opposite her change before her very eyes into something evil and malevolent, felt a sudden shiver of fear sweep over her. But she held her head high and her eyes met Mrs. Miller's unflinchingly.

'So you mean to be rid of me,' Mrs. Miller asked.

'But of course,' Caroline answered quietly. 'Did you expect anything else?'

For a moment Mrs. Miller seemed taken aback by Caroline's candour, and then her voice came hissingly between her lips.

'Your ladyship is making a big mistake. You will repent your decision.'

Caroline smiled. 'I think not, Mrs. Miller; and in truth I am somewhat particular as to the company I keep.'

Caroline meant to be insulting and she succeeded. Mrs. Miller quivered with the sheer violence of her feelings.

'You will be sorry for this,' she said, 'and so will your husband, if indeed he is your husband—as yet.'

Her mouth curved over the ugly sneer in the last words; then she turned and went from the room, closing the door very quietly and carefully behind her, which was more alarming than if she had slammed it.

It seemed to Caroline as if the room were dark because of the atmosphere the woman had left behind her. There was venom and a menace in her tone; and if Caroline had wished to stir up a rattlesnake's nest with a stick, she had succeeded. For a moment she was afraid, not for herself but for Vane; then even as the fear crept over her, something made her glance out of the window.

Instantly she sprang to her feet and ran to the casement. Coming across the park she could see a horse and rider. The horse was moving slowly as if tired, and the rider was slumped forward in the saddle, his head bent as if he too was utterly weary.

Caroline felt her heart beat at the very sight of Vane. She could sense that he was weary and despondent; yet she thought on an instant that she would rather have him thus than angry and arrogant, ready to battle with her once again over what she had done in the past.

She watched him until he was out of sight. When he had vanished, she gave a little sigh and then as swiftly turned it into a smile. She would meet him at dinner. All that mattered for the moment was that she would see him again, be close to him; and she knew in absolute certainty that whether he was angry or pleasant, disdainful or amused, she still loved him—loved him to the exclusion of all else.

12

Dinner was at seven o'clock. Caroline descended at a few minutes to the hour, wearing a gown of blue gauze sprinkled with stars which she felt was a singularly appropriate garment in which to pursue her plans for the evening.

As she had anticipated, her trunks had arrived from Mandrake late in the afternoon and the swansdown muff was included among the clothes Maria was packing for Harriet. The coach had also brought a long and hysterical letter from Mrs. Edgmont. Caroline had perused two or three of the closely written pages and then flung the letter aside with impatience.

She had expected Cousin Debby to be in a consternation at the thought of her marriage, but it seemed to Caroline at this moment that there were many other more important things to consider than the mere fact that a ceremony had taken place.

'I will read Mrs. Edgmont's effusion later,' she said to Maria, 'but I vow her reproaches merely depress me.'

' 'Tis not surprising the poor lady is reproachful,' Maria sniffed, but Caroline, sensing that Maria was about to start another of her grumbling lectures, did not reply.

As she came down the stairs, Caroline forced her feet to move slowly and with dignity when, had she followed her inclination, she would have run in her eagerness to see Vane again. However angry he might be with her, however wide the gulf between them, there was something entirely satisfactory in just being with him, in knowing that he was there, in watching his face and feeling the deepening of her own love for him at every encounter.

As she reached the hall, the butler, who had obviously been waiting for her, came forward and bowed:

'His lordship's compliments, m'lady, and he hopes that

your ladyship will accept his apologies for dinner. His lordship was riding until late and is fatigued.'

Caroline felt her spirits drop, and there was a very wistful expression in her eyes as she replied formally:

'Thank you; please convey my compliments to his lordship with the hope that he will enjoy a good night's rest.'

Dinner seemed to Caroline an unusually dreary meal. Mr. Warlingham, surprisingly enough, set himself to be pleasant. He asked her opinion on the new-fangled lighting called gas, which had been brought from Paris, and they discussed at some length the preparations being made for the Coronation of His Majesty the following month.

But nothing could entirely distract Caroline's attention from the empty chair which faced her at the far end of the table or indeed from the malignant looks cast in her direction by Mrs. Miller. The latter was all honey and sweetness when she turned her eyes languishingly in the direction of Mr. Warlingham, but she made no attempt to veil her hostility towards Caroline. Lady Augusta was, if possible, more malicious than usual, and though her chatter was amusing, Caroline had the impression that no one would escape the envenomed sting of her tongue.

During the whole meal, which seemed almost interminably drawn out, Caroline had the feeling of being alone and isolated among a formidable collection of enemies, and she missed Vane more than she believed it possible. Despite his despondency and despair there was some impregnable strength about him, and Caroline knew now that ever since she had come to the Castle she had, though previously she had not been aware of it, learned to rely on that strength and to feel in some curious manner secure within herself simply because he was there.

Now she felt as if waves of darkness reached out towards her. She could feel them clutching at her integrity, smothering her, drawing her down into their own diabolical depths of evil so that it was with a sigh not only of relief but of escape when finally the long meal drew to an end and the ladies left Mr. Warlingham alone with a decanter of port before him.

Caroline made her excuses to Lady Augusta and hurried up to her bedroom. Maria was waiting for her, holding in her hands a cloak of some soft, dark material.

'Where did you get that, Maria?' Caroline asked curiously.

'I saw it in one of the wardrobes along the corridor,' Maria answered. ' 'Twas hanging with some of his lordship's apparel and I but borrowed it for this evening. As your ladyship does not wish to be seen, it would be best to cover your gown.'

'How wise of you, Maria!'

She let the maid drape the cloak over her shoulders and found that it fastened with a big onyx and diamond clasp.

'I have an idea,' she said, regarding the cloak, 'that it is the kind of disguise worn by gentlemen on the Continent when they visit a festival.'

'Perhaps that is the reason for it being amongst his lordship's finery,' Maria answered. 'Well, no one will be requiring it this evening, m'lady, and 'tis just what you need.'

Caroline glanced at herself in the mirror.

'Indeed it is both useful and becoming,' she said with a little laugh.

The dark cloak, when it was thrown back a little, was in pleasing contrast to the sparkling brilliance of her gown. She raised the hood and covered her head, hiding the diamond stars which Maria had set amongst her curls. It gave her an air of mystery and there was something enticing in the pale oval of her face peeping from out of its dark frame.

Caroline turned from the mirror.

'Are you ready, Maria?'

'Yes, m'lady, and James took the trunk over half an hour ago.'

'Then we will start. Which is the best way for us to leave the house?'

'There is a side door, m'lady, which can be reached by a secondary staircase.'

'Then lead the way, Maria,' Caroline said, 'for I am prepared to trust myself entirely to you in this matter.'

Moving swiftly Maria led the way down the corridor and Caroline followed her. Fortunately there was no one about and they reached the side door by the secondary staircase without being seen.

Outside night had fallen, but it was not dark. The stars were beginning to twinkle in the sable of the sky and the moon was rising. It was a young moon and it seemed to hang pendent just above the tops of the highest trees.

Caroline and Maria walked quickly down the drive. As they neared the lodge gates, the church clock struck the half-hour.

'I told James to conceal the box in the bushes on the left-hand side,' Maria said. 'There are some rhododendrons there, m'lady, and they should make a welcome screen in case anyone sees us from the lodge.'

'I hope we can find it,' Caroline said. 'I had not realised until now how many bushes and shrubs there are just about here.'

'We will find it for sure, m'lady,' Maria said reassuringly, and then while Caroline waited on the grassy edge of the drive, started to push her way behind a high clump of rhododendrons.

' 'Tis here, m'lady,' she called, 'and there is a little clearing where it will be easy for Miss Wantage to change her dress.'

'She should be here by now,' Caroline said, looking towards the end of the drive where she could see the outline of the great gates and the heraldic lions silhouetted against the sky.

'Pray heaven the poor young lady's heart does not fail her at the last moment,' Maria sighed.

'What a terrible thought, Maria!' Caroline ejaculated, 'for I am convinced that Miss Wantage's whole life hinges on this moment. It may well be her only chance of escape from that unpleasant father of hers. If she misses it . . .'

'There is plenty of time, m'lady,' Maria said.

'I will not feel happy until I see her,' Caroline answered, moving a little nearer to the gates.

A moment later she gave a sigh of relief. Someone was running down the road, moving quickly, yet with an air of stealth and fear as if the devil himself were at her heels.

Caroline came out of the shadows.

'Oh, Caroline!' Harriet breathed, her breath coming quickly and unevenly between her lips.

'Ssh,' Caroline said warningly, 'let me open the gates before we speak. I have no wish for the lodge keeper to overhear us.'

'No, no, of course not,' Harriet answered, 'but oh, be quick, Caroline, for I am sore afraid.'

Caroline lifted the heavy latch and opened one of the gates just wide enough for Harriet to squeeze through it; then, taking her by the hand, she drew her behind the rhododendrons.

'Is all well?' she asked.

'Oh no, Caroline, by no means. I am sure Papa suspects.

He seemed so strange at dinner, restless and unlike himself, though maybe it was just my imagination.'

'If he had suspected you, he would have spoken of it,' Caroline said wisely. 'He did not hear you leave the house?'

'I told him I was just about to retire. Oh, Caroline, such shameful lies! I swear my conscience is heavy with them.'

'They are only white lies,' Caroline said soothingly, 'and even if they were not, Harriet, isn't it worth anything, even a heavy conscience, to know that soon, very soon, you will be a bride?'

Harriet put her hands quickly to her cheeks.

'It makes me blush to think on it. My heart is fluttering so violently that it feels as if it would burst from my very body. I am afraid, Caroline, afraid of what I am about to do.'

Harriet indeed was not underestimating her fears, for she was trembling all over and Caroline noticed when she took her hand that it was icy cold.

'Had I thought of it I would have brought a flask of brandy with me,' Caroline said, 'for I swear you need a ball of fire to give you courage, Harriet. But hurry, you cannot delay too long. Maria is waiting for you to change your gown.'

Harriet stood trembling.

'Oh, Caroline, I am not brave like you. Maybe it would be better for me to return home. I dare not risk Papa's anger by embarking on this mad adventure.'

'Fiddlesticks,' Caroline said sharply. 'Do not be so nonsensical, Harriet. Here you have a charming young man desirous of marrying you and you contemplate refusing his offer and returning to a life of slavery! Have you forgotten already what you felt when he kissed you? Have you forgotten what it means to have someone tell you that he loves you and that you mean everything in the world to him?'

'Oh, Caroline, Caroline, what am I to do?' Harriet wailed in an agony of indecision.

In answer Caroline put her hands on her shoulders and gave her a little shake.

'Pull yourself together, Harriet,' she said, 'I will tell you what to do and you must be guided by me, for I swear I have your interests at heart.

'You are so brave, Caroline,' Harriet said. 'If only I were like you!'

'You will look more like me when you remove that hideous gown,' Caroline said. 'Hurry, Harriet, we have none too much time.'

It was not easy to undress Harriet and dress her again in the darkness, but Caroline and Maria managed it, although Harriet herself was worse than useless, being half in tears and still so much of a tremble that her fingers were incapable of doing up a button or tying a ribbon.

But at length she was garbed in the pale blue gown, and Caroline set the bonnet trimmed with swansdown upon her hair and tied the ribbons under her chin.

'Now for the muff,' Caroline exclaimed, and as Maria presented it to Harriet she stepped back and gave a little cry of approval. A shaft of moonlight illuminated Harriet as she stood there, and made her look both elegant and distinguished despite the tears which continually gathered in her eyes and ran unchecked down her cheeks.

'You look entrancing,' Caroline exclaimed. 'No gentlemen could fail to wish to run away with you in that garb; but pray stop crying, for it is to a wedding you are going and not a funeral.'

Harriet gave a little gulpy laugh.

'Oh, Caroline, you are so droll but I am still sadly afraid.'

'What, of Mr. Stratton?' Caroline asked half scornfully. 'Then tell him so, for it will make him feel strong and responsible to have a weak little woman weeping on his manly chest.'

'He is more likely to cast me from him,' Harriet said miserably, 'for Papa says that nothing angers a gentleman more than a woman's tears.'

'Your Papa is nothing but a nincompoop,' Caroline said, 'and one day I hope I shall have the pleasure of telling him so. Now keep very still, Harriet, for Maria is going to wipe your face and put a touch of rouge on your cheeks.'

'Oh no, Caroline, 'tis immodest.'

'Rouge on your cheeks,' Caroline repeated firmly, 'and a rosy salve on your lips, so stop talking, Harriet.'

Maria had hardly finished her task, which was not an easy one, when there was a sudden clatter of horses' hoofs and the sound of a wheeled vehicle drawing up on the roadway.

' 'Tis he!' Harriet said. 'I cannot go . . . I cannot.'

'You are not going yet,' Caroline answered calmly. 'You

213

must keep the gentleman cooling his heels for several minutes at least.'

Harriet instantly looked alarmed.

'But suppose . . . Caroline . . . suppose he should not wait for me?'

'That would indeed be a pity,' Caroline answered drily, 'but methought you were undecided whether to accompany him or not?'

'Oh, I am,' Harriet said, 'but . . . Caroline, he is waiting!'

They could hear the jingle of harness, the sound of the horses pawing the ground impatiently. Then there was a hushed cough.

'I must go to him, I must,' Harriet whispered urgently. 'He will suspicion that I have changed my mind.'

'And you have not?' Caroline asked.

'No indeed, but what Papa will say I cannot imagine.'

'If you take my advice, you will get out of hearing of your Papa as quickly as possible,' Caroline said.

'And if he pursues us?' Harriet questioned suddenly in tones of the utmost horror.

'If he does, it will be up to Mr. Stratton to show his mettle. I think you can trust him, Harriet, and you should be across the border and married before your father catches up with you.'

'Oh I pray so, indeed I do,' Harriet cried, 'and now I must go. Thank you, dearest Caroline; I am for ever in your debt.'

'And what about your trunk?' Caroline asked.

'I will leave it,' Harriet said wildly.

'You will do nothing of the sort,' Caroline said. 'Maria, follow Miss Wantage and hand her trunk to Mr. Stratton.'

She reached out and put her hand on Harriet's arm.

'Listen, Harriet, if he asks who Maria is, say 'tis one of the Vicarage maids whom you can trust.'

'Yes, yes, I will do that,' Harriet said in a flutter; 'and now I really must go to him . . . supposing . . . just supposing . . . he felt he could wait no longer.'

She pushed her way through the bushes, hurried across the drive and squeezed her way through the open gate. Maria, picking up the trunk by its two handles, followed her sturdily, while Caroline, pulling the hood well over her face, peeped from the shadows, anxious to hear what happened.

One of the horses gave a sudden neigh as if it called out a greeting to Harriet, and then Caroline saw Mr. Stratton come to meet her. When she reached him, he put his arms round her and held her closely to him. She wilted against him, her head dropping for an instant to his shoulder.

'Thank God you are here,' Caroline heard Mr. Stratton say. 'I was curst afraid that something would prevent you from coming.'

'Oh, sir, it was not easy,' Harriet's voice faltered, 'and if we be going, let us go quickly, for my Father may discover that I am missing.'

'We will waste no time,' Mr. Stratton said in a firm voice.

It seemed that he suddenly perceived Maria, for as he led Harriet towards the coach he stopped and asked sharply:

'Who is this?'

But before Harriet could answer, Maria stepped forward.

' 'Tis Madam's trunk, sir, and you trust me with your secret for I will speak of it to no one. But oh, sir, begone swiftly, for I suspicion that the Reverend gentleman may give chase at any moment.'

'The devil he will!' Mr. Stratton said with a ring in his voice. 'Come, Harriet.'

It seemed to Caroline watching that he half lifted Harriet into the post-chaise. The trunk was set up beside the coachman, there was a crack of the whip, one of the horses reared up in excitement, and then they were off.

Maria came hurrying back through the gates and Caroline stepped out of the shadows to join her.

'That was splendid, Maria! You said exactly the right thing. Mr. Stratton will have no time for boredom if he is watching the road behind them all the way to Gretna Green.'

'And if the gentleman is not apprehensive enough,' Maria laughed, 'Miss Wantage's fears will keep him continually on the jump. Lawks, but 'tis sorry for her I am, m'lady, for she has not the courage of a mouse.'

'But she is so womanly,' Caroline said with a wicked little smile. 'Both you and my Mother should approve of a female who has all the tremors and vapourings of our sex.'

'That is all very well, m'lady, but there is such a thing as a happy mean,' Maria said sharply. 'Have you thought, m'lady, what his lordship, your father, will say when he learns what has occurred while he is abroad?'

Caroline gave a little laugh.

'Do not try to frighten me, Maria, or I shall start trembling and fluttering like Miss Wantage.'

Maria snorted and Caroline, moving beside her under the great oak trees, said:

'Don't fuss me, Maria; I have troubles enough upon my mind at the moment.'

'I know that, m'lady,' Maria said, her voice softening, 'and I am praying every moment of the day and night for your ladyship's happiness. If only there was something I could do!'

'Dear Maria. I know I can always rely on you,' Caroline said.

They had reached the end of the drive by now and Caroline saw the small gate which led into the gardens. She looked at the huge Castle lying ahead of them. For a moment she had the impression that it was like some monstrous beast crouching for a spring. She gave a little shudder.

'It is early, Maria, and a lovely night. I will go into the gardens. You return to the house.'

'Very good, m'lady,' Maria answered.

'I shall not be long,' Caroline promised, and turning aside, she opened the gate and let herself into the garden. She threw back the hood from her head and let the soft night breeze play among her curls. It was very quiet and still, yet there was the occasional rustle of wings, the coo of a startled wood pigeon, and the scuttling of small animals among the undergrowth.

Caroline was not frightened of the noises of the night. Ever since she had been a child she had loved the peacefulness of the world when most people were asleep. At Mandrake she had sometimes walked for hours in the darkness and from long experience found it easy to find her way even when there was no moon.

'I have cat's eyes, Mama,' she had told Lady Vulcan laughingly when her mother had said that she thought it was dangerous to go about at night without a light.

But Lady Vulcan's expostulations had no effect on Caroline. The night called her, she felt something within her respond to the thrill of the darkness, to the sense of adventure which changed the most familiar objects into strange, mysterious shapes.

Caroline turned along the grass walk which led to the little Temple. She felt a desire to go there again, to recapture those moments of her first day at the Castle, as she sat on the stone steps, when her reverie had been interrupted by Lord Brecon. How gay and light-hearted they had been during that brief encounter! Caroline could well remember the way their eyes had spoken words which never passed their lips, how the magnetism of Lord Brecon had aroused a strange fire within her which at the time she had not understood. She felt as if in the space of but a day or so she had grown immeasurably older. It was almost as if she had left her youth behind that day in the little Temple, her youth and also an innocence to which she could never return.

She gave a little sigh and, as she did so, stopped suddenly. She had heard a sound, the sound of voices. Someone was talking. Swiftly drawing to the side of the walk, Caroline pulled the dark hood over her hair again and gathered its folds so that her dress was hidden. She listened, then recognised the voice.

It was Gervase Warlingham who spoke, she was sure of it. There was no mistaking the harsh, metallic tone of his voice which seemed a fitting complement to his expression. Now someone else replied, but Caroline could not hear what was said.

Very carefully, keeping close against the bushes which bordered the grass walk, she drew nearer to the Temple. The bushes and trees gradually thinned until they stopped abruptly at the edge of the water-lily pond, beyond which stood the Temple. Now Caroline could see clearly, for the moonlight revealed the speakers.

She pressed herself against the trunk of a tree, being certain that the darkness of her cloak and the shadows from the leafy branches above her rendered her invisible, and saw standing in front of the Temple four people. One was Mrs. Miller. Her neck and bosom were very white in the moonlight, and the shadows played strange tricks with her expression so that her long nose and dark eyes were almost grotesquely witchlike. For a moment Caroline could not recognise two of the men who had their backs to her. Then with a start she remembered that she had seen that hunched figure with its shabby, full-skirted black coat before.

The hunchback turned his face sideways and she saw, as she suspected, that it was Jason Faken. Another man was a stranger with broad shoulders and from the look of his square head set on a thick neck and deformed ear Caroline guessed him to be a bruiser.

'That is agreed then,' she heard Gervase Warlingham say, and to Caroline's intense disappointment she realised that the conversation was at an end.

'Careful how you go to the stables, Jackson,' he added to the bruiser.

'I'll go by the fields, sir,' the man answered in a low voice.

He turned and disappeared into the shrubs which flanked the Temple. The hunchback watched him go; then he asked.

'You can trust him?'

'He dare not fail me,' Mr. Warlingham answered. 'I have information regarding him which would take him to the gallows any day, and he knows it.'

'Then I will bid you good-night, sir, and you, madam,' the hunchback said and, turning abruptly on his heel, he also disappeared behind the Temple.

Mr. Warlingham stood for a moment as if lost in thoughts. Mrs. Miller put out her arm and linked it through his.

' 'Tis well done, Gervase,' she said. 'We have no time to lose. If she should be with child, we will be undone.'

'That is true enough,' Mr. Warlingham said, 'but I dislike all schemes that are conceived too hastily.'

Mrs. Miller gave a little laugh.

'Better be too hasty than too late,' she said.

They were moving forward as they spoke and Caroline realised that they were going to pass her as they came down the grass walk towards the house. With an effort, because she was fascinated by the very danger of their nearness, she forced herself to turn her head aside and to press herself, if possible, even closer to the trunk of the tree.

She heard them move past her. They were so close that she could have put out her hand and touched Mrs. Miller's arm. And then she waited for several seconds, holding her breath.

Very slowly, very cautiously she turned her head. They were some way away now, but she could still see them clearly, still hear the soft tread of their feet, the sound of Mrs. Miller's skirt which dangled behind her, sliding silkily like a snake over the grass as she walked.

They were out of sight before Caroline felt it was safe to move. Now at last she told herself that she had something to go on. One thing was certain, she had been right in her

218

supposition that by spurring Mrs. Miller to anger she would speed up their plotting and force them into action. It was something to know that whatever they were planning to do they would do soon. It was better than waiting in fear and apprehension, not knowing when the blow might come. But how careful Vane must be, how completely they must both be on their guard!

Keeping to the shadows and not hurrying for fear she would overtake Mrs. Miller and Mr. Warlingham, Caroline made her way back to the Castle. She guessed that they would re-enter the drawing-room from the terrace, so she sought the side door which she and Maria had used earlier in the evening.

Once in the Castle she did not go up the stairs which led to the first floor. Instead she followed a passage which joined the main corridor so that she found herself walking past the dining-room and on towards the library. She was certain that she would find Lord Brecon there, and instead of knocking she opened the door boldly and went in.

He was sitting in front of the fireplace, his legs stretched out before him, a bottle of brandy at his elbow. Caroline noticed that he was still in his riding clothes. His boots were dusty and the expression on his face was of tiredness and depression.

He was staring into the fire as she entered and for the moment he did not turn his head. Caroline thought that he imagined she was but a servant come to tidy the room. After she had closed the door behind her, she stood for a moment looking at him, then she said softly:

'I would speak with you, Vane.'

The sound of her voice seemed to galvanise him. He turned his head swiftly and rose to his feet.

'Your pardon, Caroline,' he said. 'I was not expecting you.'

Caroline crossed the room to his side. She had forgotten that the hood was still pulled low over her head and now she flung it back with a gesture of impatience. Lord Brecon looked at her in surprise.

'Where have you been?' he asked.

'I have been assisting at an elopement,' Caroline answered. 'Harriet has this moment left for Gretna Green with Mr. Stratton.'

'For Gretna Green!' Lord Brecon ejaculated in astonishment.

'Yes, yes,' Caroline said impatiently. 'It is a charming

219

story, but I will tell you later. There is something of far greater import that I have to relate.'

Lord Brecon looked at her.

'Surely that is my cloak? he asked. 'I recognise the clasp, and I remember buying it to wear at a masque in Venice.'

'Doubtless for a clandestine visit to some fair charmer,' Caroline said, adding: 'Listen to me, Vane; this is not the moment for jesting. I was coming back from speeding Harriet on her way and walked through the gardens. I heard voices by the little Temple and I saw there your cousin Gervase, Mrs. Miller and a hunchback called Jason Faken.'

'Who is he?' Lord Brecon asked.

'You may well ask,' Caroline answered. 'He is a man who has come to live in the village and I have encountered him once before. He is an evil man and I should imagine that no one would employ him or seek his acquaintance unless they required evil done for them. There was another man with them besides, a man I did not recognise, but who spoke of returning to the stables. Vane, they were plotting.'

Lord Brecon looked at her with an air of supercilious amusement.

'Still believing in the dramatics, Caroline?'

'But they were, I promise you,' Caroline said earnestly; 'and as they passed me, Mrs. Miller said: "And if she should be with child, we shall be undone".'

'You think they referred to you?' Lord Brecon asked. 'They need not perturb themselves unduly.'

'Oh, Vane, do not be so stupid,' Caroline said. 'Can you not understand that you are in danger, grave danger, and that we must be prepared for it.'

'Prepared for what?' Lord Brecon asked.

Caroline stamped her foot.

'You are being deliberately obtuse, Vane, and you know it. Your cousin Gervase has committed one murder in the effort to put the noose around your neck. What is to stop him committing another?'

'Are you still inferring that Gervase Warlingham murdered Rosenberg?' Lord Brecon asked.

'Of course I am,' Caroline said. 'He was there that night at *The Dog and Duck*. I saw him as I entered the parlour, but of course I did not know then who he was. When I saw him here the other evening, I reasoned that there was time for him to leave the Inn, to go to the ruined cottage and commit the murder. It must have been him I heard moving away after that terrible cry which frightened me out of my wits.'

'Dear me, how interesting!' Lord Brecon said. 'What adventures you do have, to be sure, my dear Caroline. Who would have thought, when you set out on a romantic drive with such a charming companion as Sir Montagu Reversby, that you would end up beside a corpse? But you must tell me more about that evening, it must have been vastly entertaining.'

Caroline stamped her foot again.

'I vow there are times when you make me hate you, Vane,' she said. 'Can you not be serious about what is of real importance and forget a stupid triviality which is of little consequence?'

Lord Brecon's mouth curved.

'I have never looked upon Sir Montagu Reversby as a triviality.'

Caroline made a gesture of impatience.

'Oh, I am sick and tired of this talk of Sir Montagu,' she said. 'Once and for all, Vane, I am prepared to admit that I made a fool of myself in agreeing to his suggestion that I should race Lady Rohen to his sister's house at Sevenoaks. I doubt now if he has a sister or that Lady Rohan knew ought of the matter. I was tricked and duped, but like a dolt I believed him simply because I was vain enough to wish to make a show with the ribbons. When Sir Montagu forced us to stop at the Inn because he said there was a cracked axle, I learnt from the landlady that he had sent a messenger there earlier in the day and had booked a bedchamber for me as his wife!

'I was an idiot and I have paid for my idiocy, but I have thought since that, if it had not been for Sir Montagu's treachery, you might at this moment have been standing trial for your life.'

'I should, in fact, be extremely grateful to him,' Lord Brecon said sarcastically.

'I *am* grateful to him,' Caroline said softly, 'because if I had not driven with him that night, I should never have met you.'

Lord Brecon turned abruptly away as if he could not bear to look at her.

'I have been thinking things over,' he said and his voice was suddenly harsh. 'You have admitted, Caroline, to making a mistake, and I can also admit to having made one. When I married you the night before last, I was blind with

221

rage and anger because you had deceived me, because I believed that you were mocking at me, making a fool of my finer instincts. It was a crazy action, I see that now; but what we have done is not irrevocable, because to obtain a special licence from the Bishop I was forced to lie to him. I told him that I had your parents' consent to our marriage and he believed me. As you know, it is illegal to wed with a minor without the full consent of her parents or guardian. If you doubt my word, you can ask Thomas Stratton who is forced to. travel to Gretna Green to wed the lady of his choice. And so, Caroline, I propose to inform the Bishop that I was mistaken! Your parents have not given their consent to your marriage and therefore the ceremony can be declared null and void. You will be free—free to return to your old life.'

For a moment Caroline did not speak, the blood drained slowly away from her cheeks leaving her very pale, and then in a voice of repressed fury she said:

'How dare you insult me! Do you imagine for one minute that where I am concerned you can chop and change your mind as if I were a light o' love whom you could discard at pleasure? You married me with my full consent, and I would not under any circumstances consent to a dissolution of our marriage.'

Lord Brecon sighed wearily.

'Caroline, you are crazed! What can a marriage such as ours mean to you, now or ever? In this you must allow me to be the best judge. I shall ride over to the Bishop tomorrow.'

'And if you do,' Caroline said, 'I shall swear that I am your wife in fact as well as in name.'

Lord Brecon looked down at her.

'That would be untrue and unmaidenly,' he said sharply.

'It is better than being unmanly,' Caroline snapped back.

For a moment they stared at each other, their tempers rising.

'One day, Caroline,' Lord Brecon said, 'someone will give you the beating you full deserve.'

'And why not you yourself, my lord?' Caroline answered, throwing back her head.

Then suddenly, lifting her hand, she undid the glittering clasp which held the cloak round her shoulders. It slid from her shoulders to the floor revealing her in all the beauty of her sparkling dress, her shoulders and arms bare,

222

the white column of her throat held proudly as she faced Lord Brecon in her defiance.

He stood looking at her, but she was too furious to notice that some of the anger faded from his eyes.

'Beat me then,' she said in a low voice, 'or are you afraid . . . to touch me?'

Lord Brecon made no movement but it seemed to Caroline as if he towered above her.

'You are deliberately tempting me, Caroline. You will be sorry if you go much further, for you play with fire.'

'Indeed, my lord, I should not have suspected it,' Caroline said tauntingly.

He took one step towards her, then checked himself.

'I am warning you, Caroline,' he said, and now his teeth were clenched. 'If you tempt me further, I shall take you in my arms; and if I touch you, I shall bed with you, for there is a limit to any man's control.'

'And why not?' Caroline asked very softly, 'I am your wife.'

'Yes, you are my wife,' Lord Brecon said. 'I have not forgotten that; but have you remembered, Caroline, that the consequences of your being so in fact as well as in name, as you said just now, might result in your bringing into the world another Cassy? Have you forgotten that?'

The brutality of his question and of his voice broke Caroline's defiance. She gave a little cry and put her hands to her eyes.

'No, you have not forgotten Cassy, I see,' Lord Brecon said. 'She is not far away from us now, Caroline. She is here in this Castle. Would you not like to pay her a second visit and then tell me if you wish our marriage to continue, or whether you will not avail yourself of the freedom I offer you?'

Caroline did not reply. Her hands covered her eyes. For a moment she could only stand trembling, for Vane's words had conjured up too frighteningly the vision of Cassy, her fat fingers outstretched, her dribbling mouth whimpering for blood.

'There is no need to answer me,' Lord Brecon said. 'Your silence is answer enough. Go to bed, Caroline, and lock your door, for I intend to seek forgetfulness in the brandy bottle. Sometimes, under the influence of wine, men do strange things for which they are sorry when the morning comes. Go to bed, and may I wish your ladyship an undisturbed night?'

He bowed to her mockingly, and when Caroline did not move he threw himself down in the chair from which he had risen at her entrance and, taking up the decanter, filled the glass on the table by his side until it was full to the brim. Without looking at him, hardly conscious of where her feet carried her, Caroline turned and left him.

She went upstairs as he had commanded her. She knew that even her prayers had failed her now.

13

Caroline awoke with a start and remembered that she had not told Vane about Harriet. She must warn him, she thought, that Harriet had no idea of Mr. Stratton's real circumstances so that, if the Vicar questioned Vane about his friend, he should not say what an extremely advantageous marriage it was.

Caroline was convinced that it was essential at least until Harriet and Thomas Stratton were firmly established in their relationship to each other that the Vicar should continue to breathe the fire and smoke of vengeance.

'I must warn Vane,' Caroline said to herself and then remembered how she had left him the night before. Instantly she was angry with herself, for above all things Caroline despised weakness and she had indeed been weak when she had let Vane frighten and bully her into an indecisive frailty which was very foreign to her nature.

It was the reference to Cassy which had defeated her; yet now with the golden fingers of the morning creeping between the drawn curtains Caroline told herself that Cassy should not prove a battle-ground on which she would acknowledge defeat. If there were a thousand Cassys in existence, she would still love Vane and he would still love her. Let the future take care of itself! If later they must live in the shadow of fear with a ghostly horror of what might be continually in their minds, at least they might enjoy a fool's paradise for as long as they could.

Caroline pulled the bell-rope and got out of bed.

'I will not be frightened, I will not be intimidated,' she said aloud, 'for above all things I love Vane.' And the very reiteration of her love for him seemed to give her a new strength, a strength which would overcome all devils.

She remembered then that he had said that today he would visit the Bishop. She must prevent that at all costs. She must win him round to her way of thinking, for she was determined there should be no dissolution of their marriage even though that marriage so far had been only a duel of bitterness and conflict.

'You are early, m'lady,' Maria exclaimed from the door.

'Take a message to his lordship,' Caroline commanded. 'Inform him that I desire to see him on the most urgent matter before he goes riding this morning. Find out what time his lordship intends to step forth, and bring me my chocolate immediately.'

'Very good, m'lady,' Maria answered, and she hurried from window to window drawing the curtains.

The sunlight came flooding into the room. Caroline felt its golden warmth on her body. She raised her face to it, closing her eyes and imagining for the moment that it caressed her as Vane had done before he had become angry and incensed with her.

Engrossed in her thoughts, she did not realise that Maria had left the room and it was with a sense of surprise that she realised that she had returned, her errand accomplished.

'His lordship has received your message, m'lady, and will await your pleasure in the library. I understand the grooms have instructions to bring his horse to the door at half after nine.'

Caroline thought for a moment and then exclaimed:

'Maria, I have an idea. I will ride with his lordship. My habit came yesterday, did it not, in the trunks from Mandrake?'

'Yes, m'lady, 'tis here.'

'Very well, put it out for me,' Caroline instructed, 'but first send a message to the stable for a horse to be brought round for me at the same time as his lordship has ordered his.'

'Very good, m'lady,' Maria answered, and Caroline began to dress with a rising sense of excitement.

If Vane insisted on visiting the Bishop, she thought, then she would go with him. At least it would be a change to ride beside him over the countryside rather than to argue and bicker as they had done these past days in the gloomy atmosphere of the library.

How she hated that room, as indeed she hated the whole

Castle! It might be her future home, it might be against this background that she would have to create her happiness. But she knew that she detested the whole building. It was tainted, impregnated with gloom, misery and a sense of evil which was inescapable.

Never, she knew, would she be able to look at the towers without remembering whom they imprisoned; never would she be able to enter the Great Hall and see the long line of family portraits hung on its panelled walls without remembering that Vane's dark-eyed ancestors, looking down with a pictured benevolence, were in reality the cause of the monstrosity which was Cassy and were responsible for her murderous instincts.

No, she hated Brecon Castle though she loved its owner to the exclusion of all else. It was no use, Caroline thought, in a situation like this trying to argue what would be a sensible course of action, for even if she allowed Vane to dissolve their marriage, he would still be living in the world, still be overshadowed by his horrifying secret, still contemplating the misery and loneliness of a future isolated from all that could make a man's life happy.

Could she face the thought of that? She knew it was impossible. Not under any circumstances could she take up the threads of a separate existence, knowing that she must abandon Vane and leave him to his most unjust deserts. No, for good or evil, for better or worse, their lives were linked together. The vows that she had made at the marriage ceremony came to her mind. She repeated them to herself and knew that they were as sacred to her now as at the moment she had made them.

Cassy should not be allowed to interfere; Cassy should not render the Sacrament of Marriage null and void because of fear. Caroline recalled that last night Vane had given her a choice. She knew now, as she dressed, that her choice was made, her mind made up. This was the turning point. Now there would be no going back, no hesitating.

With a light in her eyes and a smile on her lips Caroline descended the stairs to the library. She was wearing a riding habit of pale green velvet trimmed with braid in a darker tone; the facings of her coat and cuffs were of shining satin and a long red feather curved from her high-crowned hat on to her shoulder. She looked lovely and she was aware of it, even before she saw the admiration in Vane's eyes as she entered the room.

He looked tired, but otherwise his looks were unimpaired by the way he had spent the night. He bowed to Caroline and waited for her to speak. Crossing the room, she stood close to him, raising her eyes, her lips curved in a smile.

'May I come with you this morning, Vane?'

His hesitation was too brief to be a reality.

'I would be honoured,' he said quietly. 'I have never seen you on a horse.'

'I hope you have something spirited to offer me,' Caroline said; 'my father's mounts are famous for their Arab strain.'

'That is a challenge which I must do my best to answer,' Lord Brecon said, and there was a faint smile at the corner of his lips.

'I have sent a message to the stables that I am riding this morning,' Caroline said. 'But it was on another matter that I wished to speak with you. It is about Harriet.'

'I remember you told me last night that she had eloped with Thomas Stratton,' Lord Brecon said. 'Do not tell me they have returned already?'

'No, of course not,' Caroline answered. 'It is only that the reason for their elopement was that the Vicar objected most forcibly to Mr. Stratton. This was perhaps in part my fault, for I informed him quite truthfully that Mr. Stratton was the sixth son of his father who is impoverished.'

Lord Brecon looked at her and then burst out laughing.

'Caroline, you are incorrigible. In other words, Thomas was interested in Harriet because she was forbidden fruit.'

'Exactly!' Caroline answered. 'I collect that things had been made too easy for him this past year; an eligible young man always has a following of hopeful spinsters.'

'But how does this concern me?' Lord Brecon asked.

'Well, I have the idea that, when the Vicar discovers that Harriet is missing, he will come post-haste here to discover if you have any knowledge of her whereabouts. Do not tell him of Mr. Stratton's real circumstances, for I believe that the longer he makes things difficult for the young people, the firmer will be the foundation on which they will build their future happiness.'

Lord Brecon laughed again.

'How many nefarious plots are evolving in that small head of yours?' he asked.

He spoke caressingly, but as Caroline glanced up at him quickly, he remembered what lay between them and stiffened. Caroline laid her hand on his arm.

'No, Vane, do not continue to be incensed with me,' she pleaded. 'Later I have many things to discuss with you, but it is too early for dramatics and heart-burnings. Let us go riding together and forget that we are anything but two carefree people who have met and . . . taken a liking for one another.'

Lord Brecon's face softened. He raised Caroline's hand to his lips.

'Shall we have one last day of pretence?' he asked. 'Let us pretend, then, that we have met, found happiness together, and that the future will be always fair.'

There was something in his voice and in the look in his eyes that made Caroline catch her breath and instinctively her fingers tightened on his.

'Yes, let us pretend just that, Vane. You do not intend to visit the Bishop today?'

Lord Brecon shook his head.

'No, tomorrow,' he answered. 'I have just read in the *Morning Post* that his lordship leaves Canterbury this morning and repairs to Knole as the guest of my Lord Sackville. Knole is but a few miles from here and so I will visit his lordship there. I read also that Lord Milborne, the Chief Justice, will be among the guests.'

'Uncle Francis!' Caroline exclaimed, deciding in that moment that nothing should prevent her accompanying Lord Brecon on the morrow.

But this was not the moment for arguments. Fate in the shape of the Bishop's movements had made it possible for Vane to offer her a truce. She was only too ready to accept any olive-branch however slender and to snatch at the chance of a delay, however short, in his plan to seek the dissolution of their marriage. She smiled at him, a sudden happiness illuminating her face.

'Let tomorrow take care of itself,' she said gaily; 'we have today, Vane—you and I.'

Once again he raised her hand to his lips; but he looked at her mouth so that she felt as if he kissed her. It was then that she vowed within herself that the day should not pass without her knowing again the thrill and the rapture of being close in his arms. The temptation to touch him was so strong that it was with an effort she turned towards the door.

'The sun is calling us, Vane, and the horses wait outside!'

Walking closely together, they came to the hall where

Bateson, the butler, was waiting with his lordship's hat and whip.

Lord Brecon took them and, moving to the front door, he stood for a moment at the top of the steps, looking down at the horses which were waiting for them. Both were fine animals, one a deep chestnut, the other so pale a grey that its coat was almost white. They were prancing restlessly, their grooms finding it hard to hold them.

'You have a good eye for horse-flesh, Vane,' Caroline said.

He smiled at her and there was an expression of pride on his face at her words.

'I rather flatter myself that my stable is exceptional,' he said; 'but I was not too confident after all I have heard of the Mandrake breed.'

As they spoke together, there was the sound of wheels and a smart yellow curricle drawn by a tandem of bays came spanking up the drive from the stables. A groom was driving and a small, sharp-faced tiger was perched behind. The tiger—a boy of about fourteen—jumped down and ran to hold the leading horse.

'For whom is this?' Caroline enquired.

'It belongs to Gervase, I believe,' Lord Brecon answered and turned his head towards Bateson who was lurking in the background.

'Is Mr. Warlingham going driving, Bateson?'

'Mr. Warlingham is leaving, m'lord.'

Lord Brecon raised his eyebrows.

'I had not heard of his decision to terminate his visit.'

'I suppose we must wait to say good-bye,' Caroline said, anxious that the dark presence of Mr. Warlingham should not dim this moment of happiness; yet already her thoughts were wondering at his sudden departure, seeking a reason for it.

Then quite clearly she found the answer. If, as she knew from last night, there was a crime to be committed or dirty work afoot, Mr. Warlingham would see to his alibi. It would not be policy for him to be in the Castle, although she doubted whether he would leave the neighbourhood.

She glanced quickly at the groom who was climbing down from the driving seat of the curricle. Yes, it was the man she had seen at the Temple last night. There was no mistaking that almost square head, thick neck and deformed ear; and now she saw that he must, as she had

230

suspected, have been a bruiser. The bridge of his nose was broken and there was a deep scar on his upper lip which gave his face a most unpleasant expression.

As he descended, the horses champed at their bits and the leader started to rear. Instantly the tiger raised his clenched fist and brought it down with extreme violence on the horse's nose. As Caroline gave a little gasp of astonishment, Lord Brecon ran down the steps and seized the boy by the collar.

'How dare you treat a horse in such a fashion?' he said angrily, and picking up the boy by the neck of his coat, he shook him as a terrier shakes a rat.

'That was a foul blow,' he continued; 'and if you were in my employ, I would dismiss you instantly.'

He shook him again and the boy with the white face screamed:

'I be sorry, Gov'nor, lemme go. I be sorry.'

In answer Lord Brecon released his hold so that the boy sprawled on the gravel.

'You had best get away from here,' he said angrily, 'for if I ever see you again ill-treating an animal in such a way, I will thrash you within an inch of your life. Do you understand?'

'Yus, sir, I be sorry, sir,' the boy whined, and jumping to his feet, edged away behind the curricle as if he were afraid that Lord Brecon would change his mind and thrash him there and then.

'What is happening?' a voice said beside Caroline, and she saw that Mr. Warlingham was standing in the doorway.

She did not answer his question, but wondered how much he had overheard. He descended to where Lord Brecon was soothing the frightened horse, patting and talking to it in a way it seemed to understand for instantly it became quieter.

'I must apologise, Vane, if my tiger is inexperienced,' Gervase Warlingham said.

'Inexperienced is hardly the word!' Lord Brecon said sharply. 'The boy has obviously no feeling for animals. You would do well to be rid of him, Gervase.'

Mr. Warlingham looked at the groom who was standing stiffly beside the curricle.

'See to it, Jackson,' he said briefly, and the man nodded.

'And now I must bid you farewell, Vane,' Mr.

Warlingham said. 'I have heard this morning that my presence is urgently required in London. It is hard to leave such a pleasant party, but I must tear myself away. Good-bye, Vane.'

He held out his hand and Lord Brecon shook it.

'Good-bye, Gervase. Come again when you feel like rusticating.'

'I shall look forward to availing myself of your invitation,' Mr. Warlingham replied, and turned to Caroline, who had come slowly down the steps while they were talking.

'Good-bye, my new and very charming cousin,' he said suavely. 'May I proffer a most sincere wish for your future happiness?'

There was something in his tone which made Caroline long to throw his wishes back in his face. Instead, she dropped him a curtsey and moved away without extending her hand.

'Good-bye, sir,' she said briefly.

Mr. Warlingham sprang into the driving seat and the grooms hurried to their places. With a flick of his whip the horses started off at a fine speed.

Caroline sighed as she watched the curricle out of sight. She was certain that they had by no means seen the last of Mr. Warlingham. Yet once again she had nothing on which to base such a suspicion.

The grey horse was brought forward; but when she waited for the groom to help her mount, Lord Brecon was before him and putting his hands on her waist, swung her up into the saddle.

'I have not forgotten how light you are,' he said softly.

She looked down into his face, forgetting everything save that she was in love and that she was speaking with a man who loved her.

As they rode away together over the green parkland, it seemed to Caroline that the day was enchanted. It was a feeling that was to deepen as the hours passed. Lord Brecon led her over the broad meadows of his estate on to the common where the land climbed high until beneath them lay a wondrous view of the country spread out in all its unspoilt loveliness.

They reined in their horses under the shadow of a clump of gaunt pine trees and there, as Caroline looked at the view, Lord Brecon looked at her.

'Is there anything lovelier than a lovely woman sitting on a fine horse?' he asked.

Caroline dimpled at him and asked softly:

'Can we rest awhile?'

'Why not?' he enquired and dismounting, tied his horse to a tree; then he lifted Caroline to the ground.

She spread her skirts over the soft carpet of fallen pine needles; the fragrance of them was in the air, and the only sounds were the buzzing of bees and the song of the birds.

Having tied Caroline's horse, Lord Brecon lowered himself beside her. He stretched himself out and reclining on one elbow, took off his hat.

'What are you thinking about?' he asked.

'You!' Caroline replied truthfully.

'And I think only of you,' he said. 'Caroline, I believe you are a witch, for you have cast a spell over me from which I can never escape.'

'I am glad of that,' Caroline said, 'for spells, if they be potent ones, invariably last a hundred years, or so I am told.'

'And what good would that be?' Lord Brecon asked. 'For I vow a hundred years with you, Caroline, would seem but as many swiftly speeding minutes and I should still be hungry for more.'

'Would you?' she whispered.

In answer he stood up and, reaching forward, took her hand in his. Gently he drew the glove from it, then turned it upwards and looked down at the network of lines crossing and re-crossing her palm.

'Shall I tell your fortune?' he asked.

'I am eager to hear it,' Caroline answered, 'but what payment will you require?'

In answer Lord Brecon pressed his lips lingeringly and passionately in the centre of her palm.

'Just this,' he said, 'unless your ladyship is generous enough to offer me more.'

Caroline felt the thrill of his touch run through her veins. For a moment she was very still and then she asked:

'How many women have you loved before you met me, Vane?'

He looked up into her eyes and laughed.

"That is a very feminine question, Caroline.'

'Would you rather I was not feminine?'

233

'On the contrary, I adore you as you are. It is seldom that I catch you out in a moment of weakness. Shall I answer you truthfully or would you prefer me to tell you a fairy story?'

'I would like the truth, Vane.'

Caroline leaned back a little, resting herself against the tree; and when the brim of her hat proved uncomfortable, she pulled it from her head and patted her curls into place. Then with a sigh of utter contentment she lay back again and said dreamily:

'Answer my question, Vane, for I am all impatience to hear it.'

He moved himself a little nearer to her.

'Very well,' he said. 'I will tell you the truth. I have known many women in my time, women of all types and nationalities; but until I saw you, Caroline, I had no understanding of what love could mean. Always, when I grew to know a woman intimately, I became bored, a trifle impatient perhaps with her stupidity, with the way she exploited her charms so very obviously, with her lack of brain and perhaps above all her lack of character. I believed in my stupidity that all women were the same, and that satiety must invariably follow familiarity. To desire was but, I thought, to be an-hungered, and when one was fed . . . one forgot the very sensations that had been aroused.'

Vane gave a little laugh which was half apologetic.

'Faith, how pompous I sound! But then, Caroline, I fell in love. How inadequate those four words are to express an experience such as ours. For is there not between us something else, something deeper and more significant which cannot possibly be explained in words?'

'And those other women?' Caroline began, but Lord Brecon bent towards her and suddenly his lips were very close to hers.

'Must we talk of them, darling?' he asked. 'They are only ghosts, poor, weak, trifling little ghosts which I find strangely hard to remember at this moment when you are close to me and I can feel your breath on my cheek—when I know that I have but to put out my hand to feel the beating of your heart.'

With a quickening of her senses Caroline drew a deep breath, and then he said:

'Look at me, Caroline.'

She looked into his eyes and knew then, as she had never known before, how completely he loved her. If he was caught in a spell of enchantment, then so was she, and a hundred years or a hundred centuries would make no difference—they could never escape. For a long, long moment they looked at each other; and then gently, with a tenderness that he had never shown before, Lord Brecon took her into his arms.

For a long time they sat there, close to each other, caught into a rapture more poignant, more beautiful, than anything they had ever known; and when at last Caroline moved to hide her face against his neck, he knew that she was near to tears.

Thereafter an hour passed and yet another. Sometimes they talked, sometimes they were silent, but all the time they were happy as neither of them had ever known happiness. Caroline trembled and quivered beneath Vane's embrace, but it was without that element of fear which he had aroused in her at other times. Now his tenderness made her understand, as his words and arguments had never done, the sheer selflessness of his devotion to her. Now she understood why even his passion and his utter need of her had been subdued to his finer instincts, to his belief, as to what was right and best for her.

'Oh, Vane,' she said at last with a little sob, 'if this can not go on for ever, then I would wish to die now here in your arms and would welcome such a death with joy.'

In answer he held her a little closer, but said quietly:

'We agreed not to talk of the future. Come, my love, you must be hungry. I will take you to an inn I know not far from here where we can find a meal of sorts, for I feel you would rather not return to the Castle and let others encroach upon our golden day.'

'No, pray do not let us go back,' Caroline cried.

The inn was a small one and they were the only guests; but honoured and delighted by their visit, the landlord brought forth his best, and luncheon, though simple, was an enjoyable meal.

When it was over, they rode again, and Lord Brecon, knowing the country, took Caroline by unfrequented ways to a long grass drive on which they could gallop, to a quiet wood through which they could wander, to a little stream where they let their horses drink while they sat talking on the bank which was golden with kingcups.

At last the sun began to sink behind the distant hills and the shadows to lengthen.

'We must turn our faces homeward,' Lord Brecon said, and Caroline sighed.

'Must we go back?' she asked, and he nodded.

'Supposing we ran away together like Harriet and Thomas Stratton?' she asked. 'Supposing we were lost to all who knew us, to all we once knew, would not that be indeed heaven?'

'Heaven indeed,' Lord Brecon answered; 'but, Caroline, as you are well aware, it is impossible.'

Caroline sighed and knew, though he had not said it in so many words, that wherever they went, however much they cast off the responsibilities of their position, the thought of Cassy must still accompany them.

It was nearly twilight when they reached the Castle. Caroline was tired, but happy with a deep contentment which seemed to make everything, even the darkness of the towers, less fearful.

It seemed as if the golden radiance of the day had seeped into her bones, so that she could not for the moment return to the fears and tremulations which she knew were waiting for her.

She mounted the steps on the front door and looked at the horses as they were being led away to the stables. Then impulsively she put out her hand and slipped it into Lord Brecon's.

'We will have dinner together,' she said in a very small voice. 'Our day is not yet ended.'

'Shall we dine alone in your boudoir?' he inquired.

Caroline's eyes were suddenly bright.

'Could we?' she breathed.

'We can do anything we wish—for today,' he answered.

'Then let us dine alone together, my lord,' Caroline murmured, and she went through the hall and up the stairs swiftly, as if she were half afraid that something in the Castle might awaken her from this dream of happiness and force her to look again on hideous realities.

Maria was waiting for her in her bedchamber.

'Oh, m'lady, such a stir! No sooner had your ladyship left the house than the Reverend Gentleman arrived demanding his lordship. Mrs. Miller spoke with him in the hall and I was able to hear all that passed between them.'

'What did the Vicar say, Maria?' Caroline asked.

'He was in a terrible pucker, m'lady, having found Mr. Stratton's letter to Miss Wantage.'

'How like Harriet to leave such incriminating evidence lying around!' Caroline exclaimed.

'Just what I thought myself, m'lady,' Maria agreed. ' "My daughter is ruined," the Reverend Gentleman shouted, "and I hold his lordship directly responsible for the dastardly behaviour of this rapscallion he calls a friend." "Indeed, sir," Mrs. Miller replied. "If Mr. Stratton has gone off with your daughter, 'tis not his lordship who is at fault, but her ladyship. For having led Mr. Stratton on to declare himself her slave—as I heard with my very own ears—she has obviously cast him from her and in a fit of despondency or pique he has eloped with Miss Wantage." "Gad, Ma'am!" cried the Reverend Gentleman. "Do you infer that he has not even a tenderness for my daughter? This is beyond all bearing. I will to horse and, having caught them, will flog this blackguard until he screams for mercy. As for my daughter—she too shall suffer for this!" With that, m'lady, he pulls on his hat and stumps from the house, without even a good-morrow to Mrs. Miller.'

Caroline clapped her hands.

'Enter the Dragon! Now, Sir Thomas, you must prove yourself. Oh, Maria, nothing could be better, for with the barest minimum of good fortune they should be comfortably married before the Vicar catches up on them.'

'Indeed, m'lady, I hope so, for otherwise I swear Miss Wantage will die of fright.'

'I am not alarmed,' Caroline smiled. 'They have a long start and Mr. Stratton can afford the best horses at the posting inns.'

Thinking of Harriet and wrapped in the wonderment of her own happiness, it was only as Caroline was undressing and Maria was preparing a bath for her that she remembered Mrs. Miller's ominous words of last night and the fact that Mr. Warlingham had left the Castle. Instantly the sense of danger sharpened her wits and she gave a little exclamation.

'What is the matter, m'lady?' Maria asked.

'I have but this moment thought of something,' she said. 'Maria, will you do something for me, for it is of the utmost urgency?'

'I will do anything you ask of me, m'lady; you know that by this time,' Maria replied.

'Then listen,' Caroline said pausing for a moment with only her shift around her, one foot outstretched to test the temperature of her bath water. 'I want you, immediately you have dressed me, to go to a caravan which you will find a little way down the road after you turn out of the main gates of the drive.'

'I know it, m'lady,' Maria exclaimed, 'for is it not a pretty vehicle painted in red and yellow?'

'Yes, that is it,' Caroline said. 'When you reach it, Maria, ask to speak to Gideon. He will be there for a certainty; tell him that I sent you and beg that he will keep a special watch around the Castle tonight and all nights from now onwards.'

'A special watch?' Maria questioned.

'He will, I think, understand,' Caroline said. 'Tell him I fear that Jason Faken and his friends are plotting mischief.'

'I will tell him that, m'lady.'

'Go quickly, Maria,' Caroline said, 'for I have a conviction that danger to his lordship grows nearer hour by hour.'

'Oh, m'lady, you don't think that his enemies, whoever they may be, would kill him?'

'No, I do not fear that,' Caroline said. 'If it were so, it would be easier. What they will do, Maria, is something more subtle, something infinitely more difficult to circumvent. Promise me you will not delay. I shall not feel happy until you have visited the caravan and told Gideon what I require of him.'

'I will do as your ladyship wishes immediately you are dressed,' Maria said simply; and satisfied, Caroline let herself drift away once again into an enveloping haze of happiness.

Dinner alone with Vane was a pleasure such as she had never experienced before. The little boudoir which opened off her bedchamber was a small informal room decorated in the Italian style. Caroline had found no reason to use it and it might have seemed cheerless had not Lord Brecon in the space of time which it took her to bathe and robe herself had it transformed with bowls and garlands of flowers so that it was a veritable bower of beauty.

Caroline had chosen for this evening a soft robe made of a semi-transparent material which in defiance of the new fashion trailed behind her in a little train. Ribbons of blue velvet cupped her breasts and there was a blue velvet ribbon tied among her curls. The very simplicity of her gown enhanced her natural beauty and as she entered the boudoir to find Lord Brecon waiting for her, she knew by the look in his eyes that she was even lovelier than he had anticipated.

'We will have no servants in the room tonight,' he said, 'for I am your servant and would wait upon you.'

They lingered a long time over dinner, though Caroline had no idea of what they ate. She was only conscious that Vane was opposite her. His hands touched hers as he brought the dishes to her side, and every now and then he could control himself no longer and must lift her face to his so that he might kiss her lips. He toasted her with a glass of sparkling champagne.

'To Caroline,' he said softly, 'my most perfect love.'

Caroline raised her glass in response.

'To Vane,' she said, 'the man I shall love for all eternity.'

It was as if for a moment a shadow passed across his face, then he rose and drew her to a sofa beside the fire. Caroline sat down, laid her head against a cushion and looked up at him.

'Was there ever a man like you, Vane?' she asked. 'That very first moment when I saw you in the wood, bemused and distressed though I was, I thought you were the most handsome man I had ever seen.'

'Would you make me conceited?'

'Yes, indeed,' Caroline answered, 'for I vow that I love conceited men, they are invariably masterful.'

'And so you wish to be mastered,' he said softly.

'It would have to be a strong man to do so,' Caroline answered, looking at him from under her long eyelashes.

'Are you suggesting that I am not strong enough?' he enquired, and then suddenly with a swift movement he pulled her to her feet and into his arms.

'I would like to be your master, little Caroline,' he said, 'for methinks at times you are spoilt with too much admiration and too many men bow slavishly to your wishes. I would make you obey me, I would love you, but at the same time you would never forget to whom you belonged, to whom you owed your allegiance.'

'You think that might be difficult?' Caroline asked teasingly.

'I think you have never been conquered,' he answered.

239

'You are like a young horse, wild and beautiful, which has never been broken to the bridle. I would conquer you, Caroline, not by fear but by love, and yet you would know my strength.'

Caroline drew a deep breath for his words had excited her, then she felt herself crushed against him. She knew that he had not boasted lightly of his strength. His lips were fiercely possessive, she felt his hands against her body and knew that it would be indeed impossible to withstand his demands of her.

And yet he had himself under control, though there were moments as the evening passed when their passion seemed to rise like a flame ready to consume them utterly. Yet always at the last moment, when Caroline felt that Vane's will must break beneath the strain, there was that new tenderness and gentleness about him which made her feel that he regarded her not only as a woman, and utterly desirable, but also as something sacred, something for which he had a complete and utter reverence.

There came a moment when Caroline knew that their golden day had ended and they must retire in loneliness to their separate bedchambers. They must say good-bye and spend the night wondering miserably what the morrow must bring.

She had decided earlier that she would make no demands of Vane this evening but would keep strictly to his suggestion that this should be a day apart, a day stolen from eternity. One word out of place and they would start their wrangling with all its attendant bitterness, and Caroline was determined that such things should wait for the morrow. Time enough then to argue, to tell Vane that he should not be rid of her. Tonight they would part—if part they must—in peace.

It was very late and the candles were burning low in their sockets when at last they tore themselves away from one another. With the memory of Vane's lips murmuring against hers, the sound of his voice in her ears, the feeling of his arms around her, of his hands touching her body, Caroline found herself standing alone in the Great State Bedroom and knew that he had gone from her.

For a long, long time she stood in the centre of the room, burning still with an ecstasy, quivering with the thrill of his presence, knowing that the heaviness of her eyelids was not from tiredness, but from a desire that had not been requited.

At length she moved across the room and after snuffing out the candles sat down on the window-seat. Far away in the silence of the sleeping house she heard a clock strike. It was three o'clock. She did not ring for Maria, for she wanted above all things to be alone to savour these moments, to recall the happiness of the day, to let no other voice or presence banish the feeling that Vane was still with her.

She loved him; her love seemed to well up within her so that she tingled all over; and she longed to throw out her arms in her yearning for him and to recall his name. She laid her face against the cold stone of the window-frame. The moon was high in the sky, its silver light seeming cold and ghostlike compared with her memories of the warm sun and of the day that was gone for ever.

Caroline closed her eyes, trying to recapture those hours among the pine trees, trying to remember what they had said to each other.

'Is this the only memory I shall have when I am old?' she asked herself in a sudden passion. 'Will there be nothing in my life save one isolated, perfect day to fill the years?'

It was a terrifying thought, and Caroline raised herself, feeling suddenly chilled and ready for bed. Her coldness made her realise that she must have sat for some time. She was just turning into the darkness of the room when something arrested her attention.

There was a movement in the garden. She was sure that something had moved by the darkness of the trees just where they bordered the lawn. She looked again. Yes, she had not been mistaken. Someone was there! Caroline, watching that shadow, not certain whether it was man or beast, suddenly felt her heart begin to beat quickly. Was this what she had been waiting for? Was this the danger to Vane which she had anticipated for so long?

Someone was moving towards the house; then she saw that it was not one person but two. And one shadow figure, dark because not for one moment did it step into the light of the moon, was grotesque and distorted. Caroline bent forward, straining her eyes, until where the trees ended, the persons, whoever they might be, came to a stop.

There was a sound, a click and a very slight squeak, but Caroline heard it. It came from below; and now, kneeling on the window-seat, she craned her head forward, wondering what she could have heard.

Some dozen feet below her a window was being opened. As she watched it being pushed by some invisible hand, she remembered that the room below was the Library. The State Bedroom in which she slept and the Library had been added to the house at a fairly recent date. The structure jutted out a little awkwardly from the rest of the building, and Caroline saw that the persons who had been lurking in the trees were crossing the lawn swiftly to where the shadow of the house would afford them shelter from the moon.

They had only a short distance to travel, but Caroline saw them clearly, and she kept very still for fear that by some slight movement she would attract their attention.

The first figure was Gervase Warlingham. There was no mistaking his height and his broad shoulders; he was easily recognisable, although he wore a hat pulled down over his forehead. He was followed by another man and Caroline thought at first that he carried a sack upon his shoulder. It was this which had made him seem grotesque in the shadows; but as they drew nearer, she saw that it was not a sack the man carried over his shoulder but a body.

They reached the shaodw of the house and moving quickly against the wall, came to the front where the open window awaited them.

It was difficult for Caroline to bend very far out of her own casement for fear she might attract attention; but she was able to see that Mr. Warlingham climbed in at the window, that the body the other man carried over his shoulder was handed in after him, and then Gervase Warlingham climbed out again and the window closed behind him. There was a click as it was latched and with incredible swiftness the two men, keeping as much as they could to the shadow, hurried round the house and across the lawn to disappear into the darkness of the trees.

Caroline realised that she must have been holding her breath for a long time, for she felt it now come gaspingly between her lips. She stood up and as a sudden thought struck her, moved swiftly across the room. Caroline's bedchamber, like the library below, was connected with the earlier structure by a narrow passage leading from the main corridor. At the end of the passage was a high tallboy. Moving in the dark, Caroline stood sheltered by the tallboy but in a position from which she could see the top of the main staircase and anyone ascending or descending it.

She had hardly been in hiding more than a few seconds when she heard the rustle of someone coming upstairs. The landing was lit only by two guttering candles, but it was light enough for Caroline to see whom she had expected to see. Hester Miller!

The woman was moving on tiptoe and there was something almost snakelike in the way she crept stealthily along, her shoulders hunched as if by being half bowed she was more likely to escape detection. She reached the head of the stairs, then turned and hurried down the corridor which led to her room.

Caroline waited for some minutes; then at length, when she was certain there was no chance of Mrs. Miller returning, she came from her hiding-place. Quickly she descended the stairs. Only when she reached the Great Hall did she realise that she was trembling and that her heart was thumping so noisily against her breast that it was hard for her to breathe.

She did not pause until she found herself at the Library door. Then only did fear make her hesitant and she knew that her hand was shaking as she turned the handle. Very slowly she opened the door.

Though otherwise the room was in darkness the fire was still burning and it was easy to see in the light of the flickering flames. Caroline had always hated this room and now it seemed to her there was a definite sense of lurking evil within it, so that it was with an effort she forced herself to cross the threshold.

Already her mind had anticipated what she would find, but what she saw was more horrifying than anything she had visualised. Lying by Lord Brecon's desk was the body of a boy. As Caroline drew nearer to him, she recognised him instantly.

It was Gervase Warlingham's sharp-faced tiger who had struck the horse and whom Vane had threatened to thrash earlier in the day. He was lying face downwards on the floor. He wore no coat and his shirt, torn in tatters from his back, was soaked in blood. The flesh was broken and bleeding and criss-crossed with a hundred weals. Involuntarily Caroline gave a little cry; and then she saw lying on the floor beside the boy a riding-whip. There was

243

no mistaking it. It was the one Vane always carried and it was red with blood.

But that was not all. Scattered round the boy, one lying within the grasp of his outstretched hand, were four other dead bodies.

They lay there with their little feet bent, their wings broken; and the cage where the budgerigars had fluttered and chirped stood open and empty.

14

For several moments Caroline could not move. She felt as if she were paralysed and could only stand there staring; her very heart appeared to have ceased beating.

Suddenly she was free from her own terrible inertia. She turned and fled from the room, running as swiftly as her feet and the hampering folds of her robe would let her. She shut the Library door behind her and sped down the passage. Only as she reached the staircase and began to climb it, at first swiftly and then more slowly, did her brain once again take control over her scattered senses, and by the time she reached the landing she was breathing more normally and the blood was coming back into her white cheeks.

Sternly she told herself that this was no moment for feminine vapours. She had expected something drastic to happen. Now that it had occurred, she had got to find within herself the strength to meet it. Only for a second did she feel faint and sick as she thought of that still body with the bloodstained scars across its back and of the birds, which had fluttered so prettily but a few hours earlier, lying stiff and lifeless on the carpet.

Gripping her fingers together, digging her nails into the soft palms of her hands in a tremendous effort of self-control, Caroline forced herself to think and to think clearly. Swiftly she walked down the passage to Vane's room. When she reached the door, she paused, then knocked softly, half afraid that someone rather than Vane might hear the sound.

There was no answer and Caroline, not wishing to knock again, turned the handle and walked in. The candles were lit on the bureau at which Vane was sitting at the far end of the room. Caroline did not speak, but crossed the room to his side. As she drew nearer, she saw that he was asleep in the high-backed writing chair. He had taken off his coat, but he still wore his oyster-tinted waistcoat over his frilled and starched shirt. In front of him was an unfinished letter, but the quill had fallen from his hand to the floor.

Caroline thought that he must have sat back to think what else to write and had fallen asleep from sheer exhaustion. The strain and tension of the last two days had taken their toll even of his great strength. For a moment she did not wake him, but stood looking at his face in the light of the candles.

He looked so young, so very young, and it was perhaps for the first time that she had even seen an expression of untroubled peace on his face. The corners of his mouth were curved as if he were about to smile and there was something child-like and vulnerable in his closed eyes and the way his head was turned against the soft velvet of the chair.

Caroline had an overwhelming impulse to put her arms round him and hold him close, to draw his head to her bosom and to protect him. She knew in that moment her first awakening to maternity, the first overwhelming flood of tenderness which motherhood brings eventually to every woman. Then sternly she set her feelings aside and remembered only that every minute was of extreme urgency.

'Vane!' she called softly, and again, 'Vane!'

He stirred and his eyes opened, looking up into hers.

'Caroline, my sweet darling,' he murmured in a soft voice as if he had expected her to be there and she was but part of his dream. Then he was wide awake. 'What has happened?' he asked. 'Why are you here?'

Caroline put out her hands and slipped them into his.

'Listen, Vane,' she said, and in a low voice which only trembled slightly she told him what lay below.

When she had finished speaking, he got to his feet.

'I will go and see,' he said. 'Stay here.'

'Do not touch him,' Caroline said. 'And promise me that before you take any action you will come back to me. I have an idea of what we must do; but hurry, Vane, and see for yourself, for there is no time to be lost.'

He obeyed her and she stood at the open door of his bed-chamber watching him disappear down the Grand Staircase and waiting, her hand to her heart, until he returned. As he came back into the room only a few minutes later, it seemed to Caroline as if he had grown immeasurably older. The expression on his face was dark and there was something else too, an air of despondency about him as if he accepted the inevitable and had ceased to fight.

'It was as you said,' he remarked heavily, and without apology threw himself down into one of the armchairs in front of the dying fire.

'What shall we do?' Caroline asked, her voice hardly above a whisper.

'Nothing,' he replied. 'If, as you say, Hester Miller is involved in this, she will doubtless wait until the housemaids going into the Library to pull the curtains discover the corpse. They will then rush screaming to Mrs. Miller who, shocked and astonished, will send for the village constable.'

'Yes, yes, I collect all that,' Caroline said impatiently, 'but what steps shall we take to circumvent it?'

'Steps? What steps can we take?' Lord Brecon asked. 'There is no possible place where we can hide the body so that it will not be found. You can be sure that Gervase will see there is a hue and cry after the boy. It is a clever plot. You were right, Caroline, about Gervase, if that is any satisfaction to you.'

Caroline put her hands to her forehead.

'I have it,' she said. 'Uncle Francis is at Knole. You told me so yourself yesterday. I will send for him.'

'He will doubtless come anyway in due course in order to arrest me,' Lord Brecon said with a twist of his lips.

'We must avoid that above all things, at any rate until we have some evidence that you were not involved in this crime. Actually you must have been with me at the time the wretched boy was murdered.'

'As my wife,' Lord Brecon interrupted, 'any evidence you give on my behalf would be more or less discredited.'

'Yes, yes, I know that,' Caroline said, 'but there may be others to speak for you.'

'And who may they be?'

'I sent a message this very eve to a friend of mine,' Caroline said, 'but, Vane, there is no time to tell you who it was. You must get away from here at once.'

'Run away? Why should I?'

There was scorn in Lord Brecon's voice; and looking into his eyes, Caroline suddenly gave an exclamation, then knelt beside his chair and put her arms around him.

'Listen, Vane, my darling,' she said. 'You have got to trust me in this if you have trusted me in nothing before. I have a feeling deep within myself that we shall find a way out of this sorry coil, that we shall clear your name and

247

free you from all future danger; but I cannot convince you in words because conviction lies only within my heart and comes of my belief in the mercy of God. Trust me, darling, because I love you, and do what I wish. Please, Vane.'

'And what do you desire me to do?' Lord Brecon asked, and now his voice was less bitter and it seemed to Caroline as if the hardness in his eyes had lightened.

'I want you to take the swiftest horse in your stable and go at once to Mandrake,' Caroline said. 'We will send a groom at the same time to Uncle Francis and ask him to come here with all possible speed. There is still justice in England, Vane, and I do not believe that they will hang an innocent man.'

'You think that by running away I shall prove my innocence?' Lord Brecon questioned.

'It is not a question of running away,' Caroline retorted, 'for I shall tell Uncle Francis where you are. It is just that I do not wish us to play our parts exactly as Gervase and Mrs. Miller must have planned them. They know you are here, and as you have said yourself, they will be ready in the morning, when the body is discovered, to send for the constable. Let us disconcert them in the only way we can. If you are missing—or at least, if you prefer it, away from the Castle—it gives us time to think, to make enquiries, to find out if my friend, the one to whom I sent a message this evening, has a different tale to tell from the one which has been prepared by Gervase and his gang of cut-throats.'

Lord Brecon frowned.

'I see your point, Caroline; but no gentleman worthy of the name could leave his wife to face the sordid and unpleasant circumstances of a crime such as this.'

Caroline made a sound that was almost a laugh, and yet it was perilously near to tears.

'Oh, Vane, have we got to worry about conventions at a moment like this? My dear, my very dear, we have been unconventional since the moment we first met! It does not matter to me whether you behave like a gentleman or not, so long as you remember that you are the man I love.'

'Do you indeed love me still?' Lord Brecon asked. 'I have brought you nothing but unhappiness and horror since the first moment I came into your life.'

Caroline drew a deep breath.

'Shall I tell you what I was thinking just a few seconds ago while you were downstairs?'

'Yes, tell me.'

248

'I was thinking that if you rid yourself of me as you have threatened to do, then I shall no longer remain alive, for without you, Vane, life means nothing.'

In answer he pulled her close to him and put his cheek against hers.

'Oh, Caroline,' he said, 'I am not worthy of you.'

'There is something else I would say,' Caroline went on. 'It is this, Vane, that if things go wrong and you are indeed convicted of this dreadful crime which you and I know you have never committed, then we will cross together to the continent. It would not be difficult if you are at Mandrake. In the past countless boats have crossed the Channel from there in secret. Why should you die to please Gervase? And why should I cease to have any desire for life because of the evil machinations of a murderer? We will live together in exile, and for me it would be no hardship so long as I could be with you.'

For a moment Lord Brecon could not speak, and then she saw there were tears in his eyes. Very tenderly he held her close and then at last he said:

'You make me ashamed, Caroline. I can only say that no man could be worthy of such a love or of a woman such as you.'

He got to his feet and drew her from the kneeling position at his side. Very tenderly he put his arms around her and held her close against his breast. He did not kiss her, but his eyes looked over her head as if he were seeing a vision of the future, as if he were considering whether the gates of Paradise would ever open for them both.

It was Caroline who moved first.

'We have so little time, Vane,' she said. 'You must be gone before the housemaids rise.'

'I cannot do it, Caroline,' he said.

'But you must, Vane, you must,' she replied almost angrily. 'You said you loved me and you know that I love you. Trust me in this one thing, please.'

'And where shall I go?' he asked. 'I cannot move about the country chased by the military—a fugitive who will not face up to justice.'

'No, of course not,' Caroline said; 'as if I should ask such a thing of you. All I beg is that you go at once to Mandrake and when you get there, ask for Newman, my grandfather's valet. He is an old man, but he knows all the secret parts of the Castle. He could hide a hundred fugitives if need be without anyone being the wiser.'

'And what then?'

'I will bring you word as swiftly as possible,' Caroline answered. 'There are only two alternatives, either your name is cleared or else we leave together for the Continent.'

'Caroline, what can I say?' Lord Brecon asked.

He looked for a moment into her eyes and then suddenly he dropped on one knee and raised the hem of her gown to his lips.

'I will do as you want,' he said, 'not because I think you are right, dear love, but because I know you to be the bravest and the most wonderful woman in the whole of the world.'

As he rose, Caroline clasped her arms round his neck. For a long moment they stood there, conscious that they were closer in their understanding of each other than they had ever been before. Then Caroline released herself and and going to the mantelshelf pulled the bell-rope which hung beside it.

'Can you trust your valet?' she asked.

Lord Brecon considered.

'He has not been with me very long. It would be better to instruct him to fetch Bateson, who was here before I was born.'

If when the valet came to the door he was surprised to find his lordship and her ladyship together at such an hour, he gave no sign of it.

'Tell Bateson I require his presence here,' Lord Brecon said, 'and then you can go to bed. I shall not require you further tonight.'

'Thank you, m'lord.'

The valet withdrew quietly and a few minutes later Bateson appeared. Caroline thought that he must have dressed hurriedly, but there was no sign of it as, having knocked quietly at the door, he entered and waited in attentive silence for his lordship's commands.

'Come in, Bateson, and shut the door,' Lord Brecon said.

The butler did as he was told, and then as he crossed the room Lord Brecon said:

'Bateson, I am in trouble.'

The old man drew a deep breath.

'What sort of trouble, m'lord?'

'The worst possible,' Lord Brecon said. 'Bateson, you

250

were here with my father. Tonight someone has placed the corpse of a boy who has been flogged to death in the library. My riding-crop is beside it.'

The butler's face was suddenly convulsed.

'Oh, Master Vane!' he gasped. 'How could that be?'

'It is question I myself have asked,' Lord Brecon replied, 'and so far we have no explanation, save that her ladyship on looking from her casement saw two men carrying the body to the library window which was opened by some-one within the house.'

'Then surely, m'lord, they cannot accuse you?' Bateson asked.

'It would be difficult to prove it was not me, Bateson, for besides reviving the stories which circulated at the time of my father's death, you and a number of other people heard me threaten that same boy this morning when he struck Mr. Warlingham's horse.'

'Oh, m'lord, m'lord,' the butler said.

Lord Brecon looked at him and then said quietly:

'Bateson, I did not murder the boy. Do you believe me?'

It seemed to Caroline there was a sudden light in the old man's eyes.

'I believe you, Master Vane. I have never known you anything but a truthful lad, but there's others that won't believe you, as well your lordship knows.'

'That is the truth,' Lord Brecon said, 'and that is why, Bateson, her ladyship has persuaded me to go away tonight while enquiries are being made. I think it is wrong to leave; I believe I should stay here, but her ladyship is insistent.'

'I'm sure her ladyship is right, m'lord. If we are to find out more about this sorry affair, 'tis better that your lordship were not here.'

'But we must hurry,' Caroline said in a sudden fever of impatience. 'His lordship requires a horse, Bateson, the fastest in the stables, and I want a groom to leave imme-diately for Knole with a message for my Lord Milborne. Will you see to it, for we know we can trust you?'

'You can trust me, m'lady,' Bateson said, 'and there's two of them that you can trust in the stables, for I'll vouch for them. You had best change, m'lord. I won't be more than five or ten minutes getting your horse round.'

He turned towards the door and as he reached it, he looked back, his old face working, his eyes and mouth striv-ing against the tears that seemed about to shake him.

'We'll save you, Master Vane—never fear.'

The door closed behind him and Caroline looked at Lord Brecon.

'He loves you too, Vane.'

Lord Brecon did not answer, but she realised that he was deeply moved by the old man's affection.

'While you change, I will go to my room and write a letter for Newman and one to Uncle Francis. Hurry, Vane.'

In answer he took her hand and raised it to his lips. It was no conventional kiss he laid on her fingers. For a moment she quivered at the touch of his mouth, ready to throw herself into his arms, but with an effort she restrained herself and turned away lest the weakness of her love should delay him.

She wrote the letters and, as she was sanding the one to Lord Milborne, she heard the door of her bedchamber open and saw that Vane stood in the doorway. He had changed into riding clothes. His coat was of steel-grey whipcord, his polished Hessian boots gleamed in the firelight, and it seemed to her suddenly horrible that he should look so elegant and immaculate when he must slip from his own house as if he were indeed the criminal his cousin would make him out to be.

But there was no time for such fancies. Caroline rose from the bureau and crossing the room gave him the letter to Newman which he put inside his coat pocket.

'Speak with no one else at Mandrake if you can help it,' she said. 'The less curiosity you arouse the better. It would be wisest to ride not to the front door but into the stable yard.'

'I understand,' he said and looked deep into her eyes.

'God go with you, Vane, my love,' she said, and her voice broke on the words.

In answer he drew her into his arms, his mouth was on hers for a long, long moment, and then in silence they descended the stairs side by side. It was very dark in the Great Hall save for a single candle burning beside the door. It had been newly lit and Caroline wondered at it until with a start of relief she saw Bateson come from the shadows where he must have been waiting.

'I can hear the horses coming round this instant, m'lord,' he said; and sure enough as he opened the door there was the sudden ring of hoofs on the gravel.

Caroline looked out and saw the horses being brought from the stables. One was ridden by a groom, the other, a magnificent black stallion, was pulling the stable lad who led him almost off his feet, prancing and rearing as if in the very agony of desire to be away.

The sky was growing light and in a very short while now the sun would be up. It was just light enough to see one another's faces. Lord Brecon turned and looked at Caroline. For a moment they looked into each other's eyes, conscious of all the things that were left unsaid, of all the love that might have been expressed, and of an agony at the thought of being apart which was beyond expression.

Then without touching her, without another word, Lord Brecon went down the steps and mounted the black stallion. It reared up with him and then, as if it knew that it had met its master, seemed suddenly docile.

Lord Brecon swept off his hat and turning the horse's head, rode away down the drive. He was almost instantly lost to sight in the shadow of the oaks.

Caroline remembered that she held the letter to Lord Milborne. She gave it into the keeping of the groom.

'Ride as swiftly as you can,' she said. 'I collect that Knole is not far from here?'

' 'Tis but four miles across the fields, m'lady.'

'Very well, then, it should not take you long. When you arrive, demand that my letter be taken immediately to the Chief Justice. Say that it is of the utmost import and let none gainsay you.'

'Very good, m'lady.'

The groom touched his forelock and turned his horse towards the gate which led into the park. Caroline stood watching him out of sight.

'Come in, m'lady,' Bateson whispered, and she turned to look at him in a startled way.

'They have gone, Bateson,' she said in a dazed manner.

'Yes, m'lady, and now we can but wait until the morning.'

'I will go to my room. When the household ask for his lordship, you had best say that he was called away on an urgent matter. It does not signify what you tell them, for when Lord Milborne arrives, he will learn the truth from me.'

'Very good, m'lady,' Bateson said. 'And the body in the library? You would not have me move it?'

'No, no, on no account, and forbid everybody else to touch it. I would have the Chief Justice see it just as it is.'

'Very good, m'lady,' Bateson repeated again; and then

with an utter weariness which seemed to drag her down as if her body were loaded with lead weights, Caroline climbed the stairs.

She was shivering when she reached her own bed-chamber and without troubling to undress she crept beneath the bedclothes for warmth. Sleep was, she believed, impossible, yet later it seemed as if Vane's arms were round her and his lips were on hers, so she must have been dreaming. But mostly as the hours crept by she thought of what lay below her, of Gervase Warlingham and Mrs. Miller, of their plots and schemes and how, somehow, by some miracle she would confront them with the proof of their own evil.

As soon as it was seven o'clock, Caroline rang the bell for Maria. When she answered it, Caroline knew immediately from the expression on her face and the unusual pallor of her cheeks that the horror in the library had been discovered.

For a moment Maria seemed inclined to keep the news from her; but when Caroline pressed her as to what was the matter, she related what one of the housemaids had discovered and what a turmoil there was below stairs.

'The girl who found the poor lad is still having hysterics, m'lady, screaming, laughing and crying she is, and there's nothing they can do with her. Mrs. Timmins swooned dead away and it took five minutes to revive her! Your ladyship has never seen such a to-do. Only Mr. Bateson seems calm among them all, and he says nothing can be done until your ladyship has been called, for his lordship is away.'

'His lordship had to leave the house on important business,' Caroline said.

'That's what Mr. Bateson said, m'lady, and of course I said nothing; but oh, m'lady, what do we do now?'

Mentally Caroline shook herself.

"There's a great deal to be done, Maria,' she said. 'Dress me with all possible haste and as soon as I am dressed, run across the fields as fast as your legs can carry you and ask at the caravan if they saw ought last night.'

'Oh, m'lady, let us pray they did,' Maria said, 'for otherwise we are indeed undone!'

'You are quite certain they understood your message?' Caroline asked.

"There can be no mistake on it,' Maria replied. 'I spoke with the boy Gideon and also with Mr. Hackett, his father. A pleasantly spoken man he is, to be sure—and they both promised that they would keep watch to the very best of their ability.'

Caroline sighed.

'We shall know nothing until you get there, Maria. Hurry now, and bring me my clothes.'

It did not take Caroline long to dress and she forced herself to sip her chocolate while Maria did her hair, knowing that it was essential for her to keep calm and not to get flustered, however infectious the rising hysteria around her might prove.

She had just finished dressing when there came a loud knock at the door. Maria crossed the room, but before she reached the door it opened and Mrs. Miller stood there. When she saw that Caroline was already dressed, her eyes widened in surprise.

'I had not thought you would have been called, Ma'am,' she remarked, 'for I have come to bring you news of a very terrible nature.'

'I know already that which you have come to tell me,' Caroline said coldly. 'You will oblige me, Mrs. Miller, by going at once to your room and staying there. If, when the Chief Justice arrives, his lordship wishes to speak with you, a message will be brought to you.'

'The Chief Justice?' she questioned.

'Yes, my Lord Milborne. I have asked his lordship to come here as swiftly as possible,' Caroline answered; 'and now, Mrs. Miller, kindly obey my command.'

The woman was too taken aback for the moment to know what to say. She went from the room and Maria closed the door behind her. She would have spoken, but Caroline said quickly:

'Go now at once to the caravan, Maria. Tell Bateson to let me know immediately his lordship arrives. I wish to speak with him before anyone else.'

'I understand, m'lady,' Maria answered.

Though she had sent such an instruction, Caroline found it impossible to wait in her bedchamber. She went first to the top of the stairs, then to the centre of the hall, and finally, as her impatience mounted, she waited on the doorstep itself, her eyes searching the long drive for the first sight of Lord Milborne's blue and silver coach. She had not long to wait.

It was just eight o'clock when she had her first sight of the horses and postillions and a few minutes later the coach drew up with a flourish. A footman sprang down

255

to open the door and as Lord Milborne stepped out Caroline ran down the steps, her arms outstretched.

'Oh, Uncle Francis, thank God you have come,' she cried. 'Never have I been so glad to see anyone.'

'I came as speedily as I could, my dear,' he said. 'Are you indeed in such serious trouble, Caroline? Your letter perturbed me.'

'Nothing could be more serious, Uncle Francis,' Caroline said. 'Come into the house; I must speak with you where no one can overhear us.'

She took him into the drawing-room and forgetful of everything save her own urgency began to pour out the story, first of what had occurred the night before; then beginning at the very beginning, she told of her meeting with Vane, of her trick to enter the Castle and of her awakening to love.

It was Bateson who remembered that his lordship would require breakfast, and long before Caroline had reached the end of her tale he came into the room bringing trays of food and drink, setting them on a table in front of the window.

Caroline was impatient at being arrested in the middle of her story, but Lord Milborne, looking at her pale cheeks and the dark lines under her eyes, said:

'I insist, child, that you join me at breakfast. I know that what you have to tell me is of the greatest import, but if you fade away from lack of nourishment, no one will benefit.'

'Yes, Uncle Francis,' Caroline said obediently, but at the same time she got to her feet and moved about restlessly until at last Bateson and the footmen withdrew and they were alone again.

Lord Milborne sat himself at the table and poured out a cup of coffee.

'Continue, Caroline,' he said quietly. 'You had reached the point in your narrative where you had married this young man you had known for but a few weeks.'

'Oh, Uncle Francis,' Caroline said, 'it sounds terrible when told so briefly, but I love him. I loved him from the first moment we met. Cannot you understand that love is sometimes like that? Not a thing that grows slowly and leisurely, but something which is already there, so strong, so overwhelming that it seems as if it must have existed since the beginning of time.'

'Go on, Caroline,' Lord Milborne said. 'I am not as unsympathetic as I may seem.'

'And so we were wed,' Caroline said, 'but . . . but Vane did not take me for his wife.'

She paused for a moment, for the memory of that night could still pain her; then she went on to tell of how Lord Brecon had shown her the secret of the Castle. She had no compunction about speaking of this to Lord Milborne, for for she felt that without revealing what Vane had kept secret for so long she could never make him understand how ghastly and terrible was the suggestion that he might be a murderer like his father.

As she repeated to Lord Milborne what Vane had told her of his father's death, he gave an exclamation.

'Of course!' he said; 'I recall it now. There was a deal of whispered gossip at the time. I was trying to collect what I knew of his father when I met your husband, Caroline, at the enquiry into the murder of Rosenberg, but it escaped me! Now, of course, it all comes back! Yes, there was definitely a mystery regarding the death of the late Lord Brecon and the deaths which preceded his.'

Swiftly Caroline's tale drew to a close. She told of how Gervase Warlingham had tried to blackmail her, of her suspicions that Mrs. Miller was in league with him, of the conversation she had overheard that night near the Temple, of the tiger's cruelty to the horse and her idea that Gervase Warlingham had adjusted his plotting to make good use of Vane's anger, and then finally what she had seen the night before from her bedroom window.

'It was Gervase Warlingham, for I saw him quite clearly in the moonlight,' Caroline continued. 'I could not be mistaken on it even though his hat was pulled low over his eyes. He was wearing a green coat and I recall it as being the same green coat that he wore when I saw him first at *The Dog and Duck*. You do believe me, don't you, Uncle Francis?'

She looked at Lord Milborne anxiously.

'I believe you, Caroline,' he replied. 'I believe every word you have told me, because I am convinced that you are speaking the truth. But, my dear, it is not going to be an easy thing to prove that your husband is innocent.'

'No, Uncle Francis, but you will help us, won't you? Please promise that you will.'

'Do I really need to make that promise?' Lord Milborne asked, and Caroline shook her head.

'I knew I could rely on you. We must save Vane, for I love him so.'

'And if we cannot?' Lord Milborne asked.

Caroline put up her head proudly, and said:

'Then I will escape with him into exile. It would not be exile for me if Vane and I were together.'

Lord Milborne smiled and it seemed to Caroline there was something very wistful in his eyes.

'Once I loved like that,' he said quietly. 'It is a long time ago now, but I have not quite forgotten what one feels. Finish your breakfast, Caroline, for you will need all your strength, my dear.'

Although she felt every mouthful would choke her, Caroline tried to do as she was told. She was sipping her coffee when the door opened and Bateson came into the room.

'Mr. Gervase Warlingham is here, m'lady.'

Lord Milborne raised his eyebrows.

'Mr. Warlingham? I thought he had left the Castle.'

'Yes, m'lord, but he is here with the constable and two Bow Street Runners.'

'Indeed!'

'They have asked to speak with your lordship at your convenience.'

'Ask them to wait in the hall,' Lord Milborne said; then he looked at Caroline.

'Bow Street Runners?' he questioned.

'Oh, Uncle Francis, he will not have had time to bring them from London. What can their business be?'

'Here is another mystery,' Lord Milborne said; 'and now, Caroline, if you have finished, I suggest we go into the hall and start an enquiry into this strange state of affairs, but first I will pay a visit to the Library.'

He went from the drawing-room and ignoring the little group of people standing at the far end of the hall, turned to the right and went down the passage which led to the Library. Caroline went with him, but when he entered the room she waited outside. When he joined her again, she saw that his face was grim.

'What did Brecon do with his whip when he came in from riding yesterday afternoon?' he asked.

'He gave it to Bateson with his hat and gloves,' Caroline answered; 'but, Uncle Francis, it is kept hanging in the cloakroom beside the front door. It would be easy for anyone to take it—especially someone living in the house.'

Lord Milborne nodded, then led the way back to the hall. With great dignity he took a seat in a high-backed chair which Bateson had set for him with an oak table in front of it. It was conveniently placed so that while he had his back to the windows, the light was full on the faces of those to whom he would speak.

Gervase Warlingham was leaning negligently against a tapestry-covered chair. Two men were standing beside him and Caroline recognised them instantly as Bow Street Runners for they wore the bright red waistcoats which had gained them the name of "red-breasts". They were both thin and wiry, with that look of quiet strength which seemed characteristic of all the Runners.

Near them and obviously uncomfortable and ill at ease, was the red-faced village constable, mopping the sweat from his brow, and beside him stood the groom, Jackson. There were several footmen on duty by the front door and Bateson, very much on his dignity and behaving as though nothing untoward was occurring, hovered in the background. Caroline wondered anxiously if Maria had returned from the caravan and it was with a throb of relief that she saw, coming from the passage which led from the back quarters of the house, one of the footmen followed by Gideon and another man whom she had never seen but who she knew from his likeness to his son must be Mr. Hackett.

They were looking a trifle overawed at the grand surroundings in which they found themselves; but when Gideon saw Caroline, he grinned at her and there was something in his cheerful face and in the brightness of his eyes which gave her a sudden hope.

'Who are these people?' Lord Milborne asked.

'They wish to see her ladyship, m'lord,' the footman answered.

'They are friends of mine from the circus, Uncle Francis,' Caroline said quickly. 'You will collect that I told you of them.'

Lord Milborne nodded and then he looked across the room at Gervase Warlingham.

'You wish to speak with me, Mr. Warlingham? Is it concerning the body which was found in this house this morning?'

Slowly and yet with a kind of wordless insolence Gervase Warlingham drew himself up.

'It is, my lord.'

'And how did you know of it?' Lord Milborne asked.

'I am not surprised that your lordship asks me that question,' Mr. Warlingham answered in slow and level tones, 'as I had left the Castle. As it happens, however, I spent the night with an acquaintance of mine in the village—a Mr. Faken. I had made my plans to depart for London this morning when I was awakened at an extremely early hour by these Bow Street Runners, who wished to see me on a private and personal matter. I was speaking with them when my groom, Jackson—whom you see here—came hurrying to tell me that the tiger I had dismissed yesterday at my cousin's insistence because he had been rough to one of the horses was not only missing, but that his voice had been heard screaming for help from the Castle in the early hours of the morning.'

'Who heard it?' Lord Milborne asked.

'My fellow, Jackson, here,' Mr. Warlingham replied.

'Indeed,' Lord Milborne said, 'and what was he doing lurking round the Castle in the early hours of the morning?'

'One of my horses was taken ill and he came to borrow a horse-rug from my cousin's stables. The quickest way from Mr. Faken's house to the stables is through the park and the gardens, and Jackson, who has stayed here on various occasions, knew the way. As he drew nearer to the Castle, thinking naturally to disturb no one at such an hour, he heard the boy yelling for help, but did not dare to go to his rescue.'

'Why not?' Lord Milborne asked.

'Your lordship will understand that it was awkward for the fellow, especially as he realised that the boy's voice came from the Library.'

'He knew that, did he?' Lord Milborne asked.

'Yes, he is well acquainted with the place. He did not know what to do, but after a while the cries ceased and he thought that all was well. Nevertheless, when the boy did not turn up this morning—for although I had dismissed him, I had promised to take him back to London, as it was from there I engaged him—Jackson got worried and came to me with the story of what he had heard.'

'And you deemed it of importance?' Lord Milborne asked.

'Naturally, the boy was my responsibility even though on my cousin's insistence I had dismissed him.'

'So you persuaded the Runners,' Lord Milborne said, 'to set aside the business for which they had come from London, and instead to escort you here to make enquiries into what might prove of infinitely more important matter and one which deeply concerned you personally?'

'If your lordship desires to put it that way,' Mr. Warlingham said, 'I agree—but of course I had no idea then that murder was involved.'

'And when did you hear that such a thing was possible?' Lord Milborne asked.

'Jackson went ahead to ask the servants if ought had been seen of the boy. They told him that the body had been discovered in my cousin's Library.'

'I see! And this, of course, was grave news for you.'

'Very grave,' Mr. Warlingham answered. 'I cannot believe such a thing of my cousin, and yet unfortunately only yesterday I heard him threaten the lad, as did Jackson, his own grooms and of course—her ladyship.'

He looked across the room at Caroline who felt herself shiver at the venom that she saw in his eyes. But she held herself proudly, hoping that nothing of what she was feeling showed in her face.

'I have been told what Lord Brecon said,' Lord Milborne answered.

'My man will repeat it if necessary,' Mr. Warlingham replied. 'It was, of course, a crazed action on the part of the boy to take vengeance on my cousin for his dismissal by killing his pet birds; yet I cannot but think, my lord, that the punishment was somewhat in excess of the crime! Incidentally, where is my cousin, or is it presumptuous to ask such a question?'

'At this stage of the proceedings you will leave the questions to me, Mr. Warlingham,' Lord Milborne said, and turning to the Runners he asked: 'Is this gentleman's explanation of why you are here correct?'

The older of the men stepped forward.

'Yes, m'lord. We came in search of Mr. Warlingham, holding a warrant for his arrest for a debt of two thousand guineas.'

Caroline gave a little start. She remembered that this was the sum for which Gervase Warlingham had tried to blackmail her. He had evidently been in urgent need of it.

'But before you took him to London he persuaded you to visit the Castle because his tiger was missing and the groom told a sinister story of hearing the boy cry out for help?'

'That is right, m'lord.'

261

'Thank you.'

Lord Milborne looked towards Gideon.

'Who are you, boy?' he asked.

'I be Gideon Hackett, if it please yer lordship, and this be me father.'

The older man touched his forelock respectfully.

'Have you anything of interest to tell us?' Lord Milborne enquired of Gideon.

'Yus, m'lady, us gets a message from th' lady yester eve to keep our daylights skinned as her feared somethin' might be a-stirrin' in th' next night or two. Me father and Oi does as the lady asks. Us were walking through th' wood near the house when us hears a scream. Us hurries on and lays low and us sees the gentry swell there'— Gideon pointed to Mr. Warlingham—'and th' other cove'—Gideon motioned his thumb towards Jackson—'a-grappling with a boy. He b'aint but a strip of a lad, but he was millin' like a tough 'un, strugglin' and kickin' and yellin' fit to burst.

'Us waits in th' bushes. Us didn't tumble to it then as to what the well-breeched swell was after; but all of a sudden like Oi be bubbled if the leery cove doesn't up and gives th' boy a custy blow on the back of his head and knock him for six. He falls like a stone and as soon as he's down the swell kneels beside him and puts his hands round his throat. Us keeps our glims on him; 'twas dark to be sure, but me old man and Oi thinks he must have throttled the boy for he never squeaks again. Then th' swell gets up, lifts his whip and fair wallops the body. Oi ain't never seed anyun flog a corpse afore and it fair turns me belly over! Then th' other cove says, 'That's done it, sir,' and the gentry swell stops. Seems to Oi he were not far from enjoying it, for there was a grin on his phys right enough. The big cove lifts the boy—dead as a kipper he looks—on his shoulder and they starts walkin' away towards the Castle. That's what Oi seed, Guv'nor, and 'tis Gawd's truth Oi be tellin' yer.'

There was a tense silence as Gideon's voice died away. Everyone was staring at him. Caroline's hands clutched the arms of the chair. Then the silence was broken by Mr. Warlingham.

'Gammon!' he exclaimed. 'A pretty story and the boy has been well coached in his lies, but your lordship is not likely to believe the fairy tales of gipsies and poachers. Doubtless her ladyship, with her well-known powers of imagination, has invented this smoky yarn, but she should get more reliable witnesses if she would have them credited.'

Lord Milborne glanced at him and then spoke to Mr. Hackett.

'Have you anything to add to your son's testimony?' he asked.

'Only this, m'lord.'

The older man came across the floor. He limped a little and walked stiffly as if his wounds from the tiger still pained him. But he had an honest face and Caroline felt that Lord Milborne must believe him trustworthy. As he reached his lordship, he opened his hand and on the palm of it was a small object.

'What is it?' Lord Milborne asked.

' 'Tis a button, m'lord, which th' boy in his struggles tore from th' gentleman's coat. It fell from his hand among th' fallen leaves in th' wood. Us found it after they was gone.'

Caroline gave a little gasp. Lord Milborne put out his hand and took the button from the man's hand. As he held it, it was easy to see that attached to it there was a piece of material, and it was of olive-green superfine cloth, such as might be used in the making of a very elegant coat.

Lord Milborne turned the button over in his hand; then he raised his quizzing-glass.

'A monogram!' he said quietly, and Caroline bending forward saw that the button was in gold with a pattern of diamonds set in the centre of it.

There was a hush in the hall. Then Lord Milborne said clearly:

'I read this as the entwined initials "G.W." Have you anything to say, Mr. Warlingham?'

Gervase Warlingham's face whitened, and he licked his lips; but even as he was about to speak, there was a sound of the front door being opened by one of the footmen and a man came clumping into the hall. Everyone turned and Caroline saw that it was Jason Faken.

He was looking more disreputable and unpleasant than usual, and as he came into view, Caroline saw that he was dragging by the arm a middle-aged woman whose face for the moment seemed vaguely familiar. She was dressed in neat, clean garments with a shawl round her shoulders and a black bonnet on her head. Her hands were trembling and her eyes seemed wild with fear.

Jason Faken brought her into the hall and then, letting

loose her arm, he walked straight to where Mr. Warlingham was standing. He went very close to him and
said something in a low voice which was not audible, but
Mr. Warlingham's reply was clear to all.

'Why the devil didn't you find it out sooner, you curst
fool?' he asked furiously. Then looking across at Lord Milborne, he said with a sneer on his lips: 'If there is to be a
trial, my lord, which I gather from your lordship's attitude
seems likely, then I demand to be tried by—my peers.'

15

For a moment there was only an astonished silence, and then Lord Milborne asked quietly:

'Will you give a reason for your request, sir?'

Mr. Warlingham drew himself up.

'My reason, my lord, is that I am in truth the rightful Lord Brecon. The man who has hitherto styled himself as such, who has lived here in this Castle and made himself master of the estate, is, as I have proof, nothing more or less than an imposter.'

Caroline gave a little inarticulate sound and would have spoken had not Lord Milborne glanced in her direction, and she knew that he wished her to remain silent.

'Have you your proof here, Mr. Warlingham?' Lord Milborne asked slowly and calmly seeming by his unsurprised dignity to deprive the situation of much of its dramatic quality.

In answer Gervase Warlingham nodded to Jason Faken. The hunchback crossed the hall and, seizing the arm of the woman in the black bonnet, he dragged her forward.

'This woman can supply the proof, m'lord,' he said in a loud, harsh voice.

'One minute,' Lord Milborne said. 'What is your name?'

'Jason Faken.'

'And your profession?'

The hunchback seemed to hesitate, then sullenly he replied:

'Lawyer.'

'In practice?'

Again there was a moment's pause before the reply:

'Formerly in the employment of Rosenberg, Sparrow and Cohen.'

Caroline gave a little gasp. The pieces of the puzzle were falling into place. Now she could see very clearly where Gervase Warlingham had obtained the information that Sir

265

Montagu was blackmailing his cousin. It was Jason Faken who had been the link between Melissa's indiscretion and the murder by the ruined cottage. And Gervase Warlingham, supplied with the knowledge by a dismissed servant of the firm had acted without Rosenberg or Sir Montagu having any idea that he was concerned in their affairs.

It had been just one more weapon to assist him in his plot for ridding himself of his cousin. Caroline thought that somehow Gervase Warlingham must have learnt how the late Lord Brecon had died, and he believed that, if Vane could be accused of murder, it would be comparatively easy to prove that his criminal tendencies were hereditary. Yet this assertion that Vane was an imposter was obviously something new.

Suddenly Caroline remembered Mr. Warlingham coming into the hall when Vane was showing her the pictures of his ancestors. He had observed then that Vane, being blond, was unlike the majority of his forbears. Dorcas with surprising presumption had joined in the conversation! Had she unwittingly given Gervase Warlingham a clue to some strange secret of which even Vane was ignorant? Caroline felt her heart begin to throb with an almost overwhelming excitement.

'Very well, Mr. Faken,' Lord Milborne said, 'you may now continue.'

'I have here beside me,' the hunchback said, 'Mrs. Jenks, who will give your lordship irrefutable proof of my client's statement that he is indeed the rightful and lawful Lord Brecon.'

He gave the woman's arm a shake as he spoke. She gave a little whimper of fear, at which he turned to her and put his ugly, evil face near to hers.

'Speak up! Tell his lordship what you know.'

The woman began to sob as Jason Faken shook her arm again; then suddenly there was an interruption.

'Stop!' a voice said.

Everyone turned and looked towards the top of the stairs whence the voice had come and Caroline saw that Dorcas stood there, her gaunt face almost awe-inspiring in its severity and anger.

The woman in the black bonnet covered her face with her hands. Dorcas came swiftly down the stairs and, crossing the hall, stood beside her.

'Martha Jenks!' she said furiously. 'Have you taken leave of your senses? Do you dare to break your most solemn oath to speak on things that you have vowed should never cross your lips?'

The woman gave a loud sob and taking her hands from her face clasped them together.

' 'Tis no use, Dorcas,' she wailed. 'I had to come . . . they made me. They caught my Tom with . . . a hare in his hand . . . and a net in his pocket. 'Tis transportation for him . . . unless I does as the gentleman commands.'

'Then let him be transported,' Dorcas said, and there was a world of scorn in her voice. 'Better that than that my own sister should turn traitor.'

Mrs. Jenks wrung her hands together.

' 'Tis all very well for you to talk, Dorcas . . . but Tom is my son . . . 'tis more than flesh and blood could stand . . . to see him sent away . . . for what was naught but a boyish prank.'

Dorcas would have spoken again, but Lord Milborne interrupted. 'Silence for a moment,' he said clearly, looking at Dorcas. 'What is your name?'

Caroline thought that Dorcas would not answer, for in her anger she seemed oblivious of everything save her sister who was sobbing now almost uncontrollably. But the habit of a lifetime in service asserted itself. She curtsied as she answered.

'I'm known as Dorcas, m'lord, and I'm personal maid to the Dowager Lady Brecon.'

'It is obvious, Dorcas,' Lord Milborne said, 'that you know things that have been kept secret for some time, but which now must be revealed. We are concerned at the moment with the saving or destroying of two men's lives. One is his lordship, Lord Brecon, and the other is his cousin, Mr. Gervase Warlingham. Furthermore, apart from a charge of murder which will be laid against one of these gentlemen, Mr. Warlingham asserts that he is the rightful owner of the title, of this Castle and its estates. His proof, so he says, rests with this woman whom you have called your sister. But it appears to me that she is in no fit state to tell her story clearly. Would it not be better, as obviously you know it full well, for you to relate what you know, Dorcas? It is too late now to hide anything, for all is bound to be revealed sooner or later.'

Dorcas stared at Lord Milborne all the time he was

speaking, yet the expression on her face was difficult to read. Only when he had finished did she turn once again to her sister standing beside her and ask in a low voice:

'How much have you told, Martha?'

'Ev . . . everything,' came the answer; and now the woman in her agony seemed about to collapse on to the floor, so that both Dorcas and Jason Faken put out their hands to support her.

'Take her to a chair,' Lord Milborne commanded; and when they had done so, the woman bent her head almost to her knees and continued to cry, but quietly.

'Now, Dorcas,' Lord Milborne said.

'Yes, let us hear the unvarnished truth,' Mr. Warlingham sneered.

Dorcas looked across the hall at him.

'I'll tell the truth, sir,' she said, and her tone was ominous, 'but poor comfort will it bring you now.'

She turned to Lord Milborne.

'In speaking, m'lord, I must reveal not my own secrets but those of my mistress. Is that in order?'

'I am afraid so, Dorcas,' Lord Milborne replied, 'for I take it these secrets concern your mistress's son.'

'Yes, m'lord.'

'Then speak.'

Dorcas' voice was steady, but Caroline saw that the knuckles of her fingers linked together over her apron were white.

'I have been personal maid to my mistress,' Dorcas began, 'since she was a girl. Her home was in the North and in those early days my own home was not far distant. My father was a fisherman. Soon after my mistress grew up, she was indisposed after the severity of the north country winter and it was suggested by the family physician that she should travel south. After some discussion it was decided that she should visit my parents who had recently moved to a small fishing village near Plymouth.

'We journeyed there, my mistress and I; and after a few weeks in the milder air there was a vast improvement in her health. She began to enjoy herself and used to go sailing with my father and take walks over the countryside. It was in such a way that she became acquainted with a gentleman——'

'May we know his name?' Lord Milborne interrupted.

'It was Royde,' Dorcas answered. 'Mr. Royde. My mistress saw him every day and in a short while she confessed to me that she was in love. I was sore afraid at the news, for my mistress's father, Colonel Stewart, a widower, was a hard man and proud. I was sure he would not under any circumstances consider a suitor whom his daughter had met in an unconventional manner. Besides, I knew full well that Mr. Royde was by no means wealthy for all that he was a fine, well-bred gentleman and in other circumstances might have made my mistress very happy.

'I begged my mistress there and then to return to Yorkshire. She refused, and a few days later they came to me, bright-faced with happiness, to say that they were wed. I cried out in horror, but they told me not to distress myself. "We will now go together and tell my father," my mistress said; "I would have been afraid alone, but with my husband beside me I fear naught." It was arranged that we should travel north a week later, and the day before we were due to start Mr. Royde my master—for that was how I thought on him—went into Plymouth to make arrangements for the journey and to draw some money from his bank.

'But the hours passed and he did not return. By nightfall my mistress was frantic with anxiety and we sat up together watching for him with fear and trepidation. In the morning when there was still no sign of him she was distraught; but at last we received news from a ragged boy who related that Mr. Royde had been hurried on board His Majesty's ship *Triumph* which had sailed on the tide that very morning.

'My mistress fell swooning to the floor at the news and I thought she was about to die, but there was worse to follow. A week later we learned that the *Triumph* had been engaged by French men-o'-war in the Channel. The odds against her were overwhelming and only the intervention of other British ships at the last moment had saved her from being captured. As it was, she returned to port with but a handful of her crew who were not dead or wounded, and we learned that among those who had been killed was Mr. Royde.

'For some weeks I thought it would be impossible to save my mistress's life, but finally she recovered a little in health, though her spirits were sadly low. By this time it was imperative that we should return to Yorkshire. Colonel Stewart wrote demanding his daughter's presence and I was hard put to explain what could be delaying her.

'We went back, but it did not appear as if the change of

air had done my mistress much good. She was in no state to tell her father that she had been married; indeed for that matter she would speak of her husband to no one, not even to me. The mere mention of his name brought on such a fit of weeping that was unwise to upset her.

'She took up her life at home listlessly; then a month or so after we had returned we knew for certain what I personally had always feared in my heart—my mistress was with child. She was in an agony of terror lest her father should learn of it. Her fear was not without foundation, for Colonel Stewart would never have forgiven her for having married without his approval, and to learn that there was to be a child of the marriage might have driven him to inflict harsh and cruel punishments upon my poor mistress.

'We kept it a secret until we became afraid that her condition must be noticed. It was then my mistress suggested to her father that, as the winter was coming on, it might be wise to spend the worst months of it in the south. By great good fortune Colonel Stewart wished to pay some visits himself in Scotland and he agreed to his daughter returning to my parents. Accordingly we fled back to Plymouth. My mistress's child was born there. It was a boy and he was christened Vane, which had been Mr. Royde's second name.'

Dorcas' voice ceased for a moment. No one spoke. Everyone was listening to her intently, including Lord Milborne, who was leaning forward in his chair, his chin resting on his hand.

'Our anxiety now,' Dorcas continued; 'was to find someone to care for the child. He was a bonny babe; my mistress adored him and would not hear of him being taken to a Foundling Hospital. My parents were old and ailing, otherwise they would have obliged her, for they had grown to love my mistress, as did all who knew her well. It was then I thought of my sister, Martha, who had married a farmer called Jenks and lived at Cuckhurst. I made the journey to see her; she agreed to foster the child and I returned to Plymouth for my mistress. We came back to Cuckhurst, where we handed the babe over to my sister and my mistress and I stayed at the inn.

'It had been our intention to rest there but a night or two and then return to Yorkshire; but when it came to leaving her son, my mistress could not tear herself away. She loved the babe with a passion which was all the greater because she saw in him the last link with the man she had loved so deeply and unforgettably. Every day I suggested that we should be on our way and every day she put me off with excuses, spending all her time at the farm with Master Vane, nursing him, loving him, and breaking her heart because she must leave him behind and return to her home in the north.

'It was then that she met m'lord Brecon. We were returning from the farm to the village, walking across his lordship's own grounds though we had no idea we were trespassing. M'lord was riding and it was obvious from the first moment that he set eyes on my mistress that he was captivated by her pretty, gentle ways. He insisted that she dine with him at the Castle, and before a few more days had passed his lordship had laid his heart and hand at her feet.

'When she told me of it, she said: "Do you realise what it means, Dorcas? If I wed with Lord Brecon, I can see my son. I shall be near him—my darling, my babe, my little Vane." In the end after some hesitation she accepted his lordship and we planned to travel north to tell the news to Colonel Stewart. But the very morning we were due to leave my mistress received the grave tidings that her father was dead. He had died of a stroke at the house of a friend. Despite her fear of her father my mistress was distressed by his death for she had few other relatives. His lordship was most kindly and when the first sharpness of my mistress's grief passed, he pressed her to marry him at once so that he could better protect and comfort her. They were married here in the Castle Chapel quietly, with but a handful of witnesses.

'Nine months after my mistress was married to his lordship she was brought to bed with another child. It was also a boy, but a very different son indeed from the one that had blessed her first marriage. This was a weakly infant who had a convulsion within two hours of his birth and continued to have them at varying intervals, despite all the care that I could give him. But his lordship was overjoyed at being presented with an heir. He heaped presents on my mistress and no expense or care must be spared where it concerned the well-being of his son.

'Unfortunately my mistress's health gave grave cause for anxiety and the physician suggested that a change of air would do both her and the baby good. We were to go to Bath and his lordship went ahead to arrange that everything should be comfortable on our arrival. My mistress and I were to follow the next day; but even as the coach came round to the door, the poor babe had a convulsion and I thought his last hour had come. However, he breathed again and carrying him in my arms, I joined my mistress in the coach. She had been out but once or twice since her confinement, and now, as I sat down beside her, she whispered: "I have told the coachman to stop at the farm, Dorcas. I must see my little Vane, I could not leave without seeing him. I have informed the servants that you wish to say farewell to your sister."

'It was imprudent, but I had not the heart to argue with her. When we reached the farm, she rushed into the kitchen, snatched her baby from the wooden cradle and held him closely in her arms, covering his tiny face with kisses; it was all I could do not to weep! "Look at him, Dorcas," she cried, "how well he looks! See, he is smiling at me! Oh, Vane, Vane, how must I love you, my precious one!"

'It was then that the poor little creature in my arms gave a croak. I looked down at it, comparing the two children, both of the same mother; and God forgive me, a wicked thought came into my head. I knew as surely as if someone had said the words that the child I held had not long to live. His days were numbered and I knew that no care, no money could keep him tied to this earth. I whispered to my mistress, and I can see now the look she gave me, first of horror and then of a sudden hope and happiness which changed her face before my eyes.

' "Oh, Dorcas!" she said. That was all. We told my sister what we were about to do and she swore by everything she held sacred that she would never reveal it to a living soul. It was but a question of moments to change the baby's shawls. It was impossible for them to change clothes, for Master Vane was more than double the size of his poor little step-brother. When my lady went back to the coach, she walked with a springing step, her eyes were shining and she carried Master Vane in her own arms. She would not trust him to me.

'It was difficult, when we arrived at Bath, to keep his lordship from suspecting anything. We might not have managed it but for the fact that m'lord had affairs to attend to on the estate which compelled his return to the Castle. During that short time we succeeded in keeping him in ignorance; for whenever his lordship wished to see the baby I said he was asleep and must on no account be wakened.

'It was several months before we returned from Bath,

and meanwhile my mistress wrote to his lordship, telling him what miracles the air and change had worked for the baby and how big and strong he was growing.

'My mistress, too, was much better in every way, and even the sadness of learning that her second son had died a week after we left the farm could not dim the joy she knew at holding Mr. Royde's child in her arms.

'That is the story, m'lord, and if my mistress has done wrong, then blame not her but me. As God is my judge, I did what was best at the time for my mistress—because my service was to her, as it is and always will be.'

Dorcas finished speaking and then put her hands to her eyes. She was not crying, but it seemed to Caroline that she rubbed them as if they hurt her. She had been staring at Lord Milborne all the time she spoke, and now he sat back in his chair. After a moment he said very softly:

'Thank you, Dorcas.'

He looked across the hall at Mr. Warlingham.

'I think your case is proven, sir,' he said briefly; 'but I charge you with the murder of the stableboy formerly in your employment with the intention of concealing the crime and plotting to implicate an innocent man. You may reserve your defence.'

He turned to the constable.

'With the assistance of the Runners, Constable, you will escort this gentleman and his man, Jackson, to Maidstone jail, there to await trial in due course.'

The constable, who had been listening to the proceedings with a gaping mouth, pulled himself to attention.

'Very good, m'lord.'

His lordship's glance moved to Gideon and his father.

'You will both be required to give evidence at the trial,' he said. 'You will be instructed in due course where and when to attend the Court of Justice, and you must stay here and not move elsewhere until then. You quite understand that?'

'Aye, m'lord.'

They touched their forelocks and then Lord Milborne rose to his feet.

Caroline rose too and saw to her astonishment that Dorcas was still staring at Lord Milborne. Now, as he turned, the light was on his face. Dorcas' eyes opened wide and then almost inarticulately a question fell from her lips. Caroline did not catch what she said, but Lord Milborne obviously understood, for he nodded his head.

'Yes, Dorcas,' he said.

The woman gave a cry and flung up her hands, but Lord Milbourne turning to Caroline said:

'Take me, my dear, to the Dowager Lady Brecon. I would have speech with her.'

'Come with me, Uncle Francis,' Caroline replied, crossing the hall and leading the way upstairs.

She thought Lord Milborne was about to break gently to Lady Brecon that the secret of years had been revealed and the fact of Vane's real identity was known. But as she moved up the stairs, Caroline could think of one thing and one thing only. Vane was no longer a prisoner of his blood. He was free, free from all the horrors that had tortured and beset him, free from Cassy, free from the terror of madness!

Vane was free! To Caroline the whole world seemed suddenly golden. He might be poor and untitled, but the only thing that mattered was that he was a man rich in all other things. Was not a sane mind in a healthy body worth all the wealth in the world? What did anything matter beside the fact that they could belong to each other really and truly as man and wife, that they could bring forth children without fear and that there was nothing to overshadow and dim their love?

Caroline's heart was singing and her eyes were like stars. She could find no words even to speak to Lord Milborne; but she felt he must know and understand, and that his silence was one of sympathy.

They had turned down the corridor which led to Lady Brecon's room when suddenly they heard steps behind them. To Caroline's astonishment she saw Dorcas running clumsily, yet quickly, her cap and apron blowing, the tears running unchecked down her cheeks. Without a word she passed Caroline and Lord Milborne and without knocking burst into Lady Brecon's room.

Apprehensively, thinking that Dorcas must be suddenly deranged, Caroline hurried after her in time to see her fling herself down beside the bed and cry:

'Oh, m'lady, he is alive! Mr. Royde . . . he is alive! Oh, m'lady, m'lady!'

Caroline saw Lady Brecon sit up suddenly and stretch out her hands towards Dorcas, and even as she did so, she turned to see Lord Milborne standing in the doorway. She stared at him for a long moment. There was silence in the room save for Dorcas' sobs; Lady Brecon went very pale, so pale that Caroline thought she was about to faint.

Lord Milborne moved forward and took her hands in his.

'It is I, Margaret,' he said.

Lady Brecon gave a cry such as Caroline had never heard before in her whole life, a cry of such joy and such wonder that the tears suddenly started in Caroline's eyes and she was conscious through a mist which blinded her that Lord Milborne had raised both Lady Brecon's hands to his lips and was holding them as if he would never let them go.

Then she saw that Lady Brecon was not fainting, that she was smiling and her eyes were very bright. Bewildered and feeling that she was not wanted at this moment, Caroline would have withdrawn from the room, but as she reached the door Lord Milborne looked up and stopped her.

'Do not leave us, Caroline,' he said. 'You have heard so much of the story that you must hear the end. And Dorcas too,' he added kindly, looking at the elderly woman who was wiping her eyes on the corner of her apron.

'Francis, dear Francis,' Lady Brecon asked in a low voice, 'is it really you?'

'Yes, my dearest, it is I. Oh, Margaret, if you only know what I have suffered all these past years when I could not find you. I searched everywhere in Yorkshire. They told me your father had died; but they had no idea where you were living, or whether indeed you were alive.'

'But what happened to you, Francis?' Lady Brecon enquired. 'And what has brought you here now?'

'That is another story, my dear,' he said, glancing at Caroline. 'I wish to tell you that in my own way and in my own good time. Let it suffice for the moment to say that through the strange twists and turns of fate you have been brought back into my life so that I can claim you as my wife and—Vane as my son.'

Lady Brecon gave a little start and Caroline saw that her fingers tightened on Lord Milborne's. Then she said in a very low voice:

'You know then?'

'Yes, dearest—I know.'

'And you forgive me? I did it for the best—for Vane. I believed that you were dead and I could not bear that he should be poor and in want. You are not angry with me?'

Lord Milborne bent and kissed her hand.

'How could I ever be angry with you? All will be righted now—and that I promise you.'

Lady Brecon sighed in relief.

'And Vane will learn that you are his father. That is what I always wished above all things.'

'When I searched for you, I did not know of his existence,' Lord Milborne said; 'I am glad of it now. It was bad enough to lose you, Margaret, without thinking that I had also lost a son.'

'But what happened to you, my dearest?' Lady Brecon enquired again.

'I seem a long time in coming to the point,' Lord Milborne answered with a smile. 'Thank God, Margaret, there is still a deal of our lives left in which we can relate everything to one another! Briefly, this is what happened to me. After I was press-ganged and dragged aboard the *Triumph*, we were, as you rightly heard, fired on by some French ships. We fought gallantly, but they out-numbered us four to one. Dorcas has said that the ship was not finally captured and some other British ships came to the rescue. I knew nothing of that. I was wounded in the head and must have fallen overboard. When I came to myself, I was floating on a raft with another seaman who had rescued me.

'I was badly hurt and I remembered little save an overwhelming thirst and my companion's insistence that I should not roll off the raft. We floated about for two days before we were picked up by some French fisherfolk. They took us ashore on the Brittany coast and treated us most kindly, but I had lost my memory. I had no idea who I was or where I had come from. The local leech patched up the wound in my head, but he could do little else for me.

'I stayed with the fisherfolk as an invalid, being quite useless to them in any way, for over six months. It says a great deal for their kindness of heart that they did not push me into prison or throw me back into the sea. Then by a most fortunate chance I became friendly with a French gentleman who was both a philosopher and a student of literature. We talked together and he soon realised, despite the humble garments I wore, that I wasn't the peasant I seemed. He took me into his own house and sent for a physician from Paris, who pronounced my case to be an interesting one, but in his opinion incurable; my friend then took me to see various other physicians, all of whom found there was nothing they could do for me.

'It is, in my opinion, because, thanks to him, I returned

to a luxurious way of living, because I rested and had interests befitting my station, that gradually my memory returned. First of all I remembered your face, Margaret. It came to me very clearly, but it was a long time before I could recall your name or even the fact that we were wed; then gradually bit by bit it all came back to me. Instantly I was seized with a fever to return home and to find you. It was a feeling of horror that I realised we had now been parted for nearly three years.

'My friend gave me money with which to return to England and arranged for my transport—which was no easy matter, as our countries were still at war. I came back to find that you had disappeared and that your father had died. The old fisherfolk with whom you had lodged near Plymouth were dead also. I was driven nearly frantic by my efforts to trace you, which were, alas, doomed to failure.

'Eighteen months later my entire circumstances changed. My two cousins were killed fighting against Bonaparte, and my uncle, the Earl of Milborne, died. To my astonishment I found myself his heir. From being penniless and of no consequence save to you, my dear, I became a man of wealth and the possessor of an old and honoured title. Can you imagine how much I needed you then?'

'Oh, my poor Francis! If you had only known that I was here, longing for you, aching for you, so bereft without you that after my third child was born I made no effort to take up the threads of life again. I wanted to be alone only with my memories of you. I thought I was doing what was best for Vane. My father left me some money on his death, but not enough for Vane to live in the comfort I wished for him. My only excuse for the manner in which I deceived Lord Brecon was that in believing Vane was his son he was very happy.'

'You shall not reproach yourself, Margaret,' Lord Milborne said; 'we will talk of all this later, but now, my beloved, I have to leave you.'

'Oh no, Francis!'

Lady Brecon's protest was a cry.

'For a very short while, I assure you; but I must accompany Caroline in search of Vane. He is not in the Castle at present and that again involves a story which is too long to relate to you at this moment. Besides, I think you have had enough excitement for today. Will you trust me, Margaret, to return to you with all possible speed? It is of great urgency that Caroline and I should see your son . . . and mine.'

'I will do anything you wish,' Lady Brecon said, 'but oh, my Francis, my very dear, do not tarry.'

'Do you imagine I will? We have so many years of separation to account for,' Lord Milborne replied.

He kissed Lady Brecon's hands again, but she took them from his grasp and held out her arms to him. Caroline turned away so that she should not see the tenderness of the embrace between them.

Lord Milborne came from her ladyship's room with an expression of happiness on his face which made him seem as if the years had dropped from him, and he were a young man again. But he was not too bemused to give the most efficient orders. Maria and Vane's valet were commanded to pack with all possible speed, and a chaise was ordered for them and the luggage, while in a very short time Caroline found herself in Lord Milborne's coach travelling swiftly down the Dover Road. Her hand was clasped in his and it seemed to her that they were both wrapped in a radiant contentment which was beyond all verbal expression.

They made good time and stopped for luncheon at Sale Park, which was near Canterbury. Here the horses were changed while Caroline and Lord Milborne had a quick meal. Never, it seemed to Caroline, had Sale Park looked more beautiful or more welcoming. Its famous gardens were ablaze with colour. The sun shone on the mellow red bricks of the house and on its glistening, opalescent windows. White, fantailed pigeons flew over the terraced lawns, and the swans were mirrored in the silver lake.

There was, however, no time to lose and when they started off again, Caroline said with a sudden anxiety:

'Vane promised me that he would wait for me at Mandrake. You do not suppose, Uncle Francis, that he would go elsewhere in some mistaken idea that he was saving me from unhappiness?'

'Wherever he goes, we will find him,' Lord Milborne said determinedly, and Caroline, looking up at his kind face, nestled a little closer to him.

'Oh, Uncle Francis, it is indeed wonderful that you are my father-in-law. I can hardly believe it possible. In fact, I am pinching myself to be quite certain I am not but dreaming.'

'I cannot imagine anyone I would rather have for my daughter,' Lord Milborne said with a smile.

278

'And to think that one day Sale Park will be ours——'
Caroline began impetuously. 'Oh, Uncle Francis, I did not
mean that . . . it sounds as if I were wishing you to die, but
I did so detest Brecon Castle.'

'Then do not be afraid to say so,' Lord Milborne said.
'Yes, Caroline, one day Sale Park will be Vane's and yours;
and as it has over a hundred bedrooms, you will not, I
hope, disdain to occupy a part of it now, at any rate until
you find a house that pleases you better. You need not be
afraid that Margaret and I will force ourselves upon you.
Indeed, I have reason to think we shall wish to be alone
together as much as you and Vane desire the same.'

'Oh, Uncle Francis, I would love above all things to live
at Sale Park,' Caroline exclaimed.

'What is more,' Lord Milborne continued, 'there is Milborne House in London and a shooting-box in Leicester-
shire, both of which are at the disposal of you young people. There will be many things you will want to do
together, and it will be good for Vane to make some more
respectable friends, indeed I shall insist upon it.'

Caroline laughed.

'They were of a truth a sorry crowd. But, Uncle Francis, you can understand what he felt and how it was
impossible not to be reckless with such a horror menacing
him at all times.'

'I can indeed understand,' Lord Milborne agreed.

Caroline gave a sigh of happiness.

'I feel as if all the cares in the world have fallen from
my shoulders, and Vane will feel the same. Let Gervase
Warlingham enjoy the privilege of being Lord Brecon
while he can, for no one else would wish the title, I swear
'tis curst.'

She gave a sudden exclamation.

'Lud! I have but just thought on it. I have no idea what
is Vane's name, nor mine for that matter.'

'Vane is the Viscount Sherringham,' Lord Milborne
answered, 'and I have the honour to salute your ladyship.'

'It is a name to which I have this instant taken a great
partiality,' Caroline said, then added in a sudden fright.
'But, Uncle Francis, am I still married to Vane?'

'Indeed you are!' Lord Milborne replied smiling at her
fear. 'To be sure the names on the certificate of marriage
will have to be altered, and I will myself see the Bishop
regarding it; but you are Vane's wife both legally and in
the sight of God.'

'How wonderful that sounds!'

Caroline gave a deep sigh of relief and then with her head against Lord Milborne's shoulder she sat in contented silence as the miles sped past.

She gave a sudden cry when, an hour later, they had their first glimpse of the sea.

'We are nearly there, Uncle Francis!' she said. 'Pray heaven that Vane is waiting for us and that he has not done anything foolish.'

She felt her heart beating and it was with an impatience that she could not conceal that she watched for the great roofs of Mandrake. They drove through the park; the coach drew up with a flourish in the courtyard; and the front door was opened by the flunkeys in claret and silver livery. Forgetful of her bonnet which she left on the seat, of her manners, of Lord Milborne and of everything save her desire to see Vane, Caroline jumped out of the coach and ran up the steps to where the old butler whom she had known since childhood was standing.

'Where is Newman?' she asked breathlessly.

'I will send for him if it pleases your ladyship,' the butler replied. 'You will find his lordship and her ladyship in the Silver Drawing-room.'

'Who?' Caroline questioned, and without waiting for an answer she sped across the hall and flung open the door of the drawing-room.

To her astonishment she saw three people at the far end of the room by the fireplace; one was her father, beside him was Vane, while seated on the sofa and looking up at them was her mother, her fair hair haloed by the afternoon sun.

'Papa! Mama!' Caroline exclaimed.

She ran across the room to her husband, her face alight, her hands outstretched.

'Oh, Vane, Vane,' she cried. 'I was so desperately afeared that you would not have waited for me!'

He gave her a quick glance and then to her surprise moved past her to Lord Milborne who had just appeared in the doorway. He walked up to him, his head high, his shoulders squared as if he were on parade.

'I am ready to give myself up, my lord,' he said in a clear voice.

Lord Milborne put out his hand and laid it on his shoulder.

'All is well; there is no need, my boy,' he said, then repeated in a voice that broke suddenly. '. . . My boy.'

It was then that Caroline could restrain herself no longer. She flung herself against Vane, her words falling over themselves as they came from her excited lips.

'All is indeed well, Vane, I can scarce believe it is true! You are not Lord Brecon, you are my Lord Sherringham, and there is no longer any secret. No shadows. No horror. You need never be afraid again. It is Gervase who bears that title and stands also convicted of murder.'

Vane stared at Caroline as if she were crazed. Resolutely Lord Vulcan intervened.

'What is all this?' he asked, 'for I can make neither head nor tail of it. Can you explain, Francis?'

'I can indeed,' Lord Milborne answered, 'and you, Justine and Serena, must congratulate me, for I am today the happiest man in the whole world. I have found both my wife and—my son.'

'Your son?' Lord Vulcan ejaculated.

'Yes, indeed,' Lord Milborne answered, 'and strangely enough, I find him already wed to your daughter, Justin.'

There was an expression of stupefied astonishment on Lord Vulcan's face and on Vane's too, and then Lady Vulcan rose to her feet and coming to Lord Milborne, lifted her lovely face to his.

'I cannot not quite collect what has occurred, Francis, but as our oldest friend and indeed our dearest one, your happiness must make us happy too.'

Lord Milborne bent to kiss her cheek and then suddenly Caroline was in her mother's arms.

'Oh, Mama! Mama!' she said. 'It is all so wonderful. I am so happy! I know not how to begin to tell you what has occurred. But why are you here? I thought that you and Papa were on the Continent.'

'We were indeed,' Lady Vulcan answered in her sweet voice, 'but fortunately we were resting but a mile or so from Calais when Cousin Debby sent a groom to recall us because of your marriage. Oh, Caroline, you naughty child, how could you do such a thing in our absence?'

'But, Mama——' Caroline began in a very small voice.

Lady Vulcan laughed.

'Do not be feared. We are not angry with you, not since we have met your husband, darling, for I vow that your father and I are already delighted with our son-in-law.

281

Despite the grave things he has related to us with most estimable frankness, he is all that we ever wished for you.'

She smiled up at Vane. And Caroline, looking at him too, was aware that somehow her hand had crept into his and he was holding it so tightly that her fingers were crushed bloodless beneath his strength. At last Vane found his voice.

'Is this indeed the truth, sir?' he asked of Lord Milborne, and his voice was low and not entirely steady.

'The absolute truth,' Lord Milborne replied. 'You are my son, born of your mother's marriage with me before she wed with Lord Brecon, thinking I was dead, and you have no relation whatsoever with the Warlingham family and its tainted blood.'

'Thank God!'

The ejaculation seemed to burst from Vane's lips. He looked down into Caroline's eyes and then they forgot everything else save themselves. They did not hear their elders go on talking; they did not see the understanding smiles which passed between Lord and Lady Vulcan and Lord Milborne; they did not notice when the Marchioness, her arm through each of the older men's drew them tactfully through the open window on to the sunlit terrace outside.

Hand in hand, still looking into each other's face, they stood there.

Suddenly Vane sighed deeply as if all the pent-up miseries of the past years were squeezed from his heart. Slowly he released Caroline's hand and the grim lines of strain and tension disappeared from his face as if they had been wiped away by an invisible hand.

He stood looking at her lovely face, at the firm little chin of the girl whose courage and resolve had led him triumphantly through horrors and desolations which would have frightened most of her sex almost unto death. He looked at the beautiful sensitive mouth with its rosy lips; and last of all he looked into her eyes which were soft with love and shining with that unquenchable spirit which he knew full well would guide him all through his life.

And in that moment Caroline understood the change in him. Never again would she take the initiative, never again would she be able to impel and goad him into obeying her commands. Her old suzerainty had ended. She might coax, cajole and entice him, but he would be her master.

Then as she thought these things and his scrutiny brought the colour to her cheeks, making her suddenly and unexpectedly shy, Vane smiled—it was the smile of a young and carefree man. He bowed to her and spoke for the first time since they had been alone together, his voice deep and low, yet with a hint of irrepressible laughter in it:

'Your servant, Lady Sherringham.'

The joy in her heart made Caroline feel almost light-headed and her eyes were alight with mischief as she replied:

'Indeed, sir, I doubt if I have the pleasure of your acquaintance.'

'Your ladyship must have a remarkably short memory. I seem to remember a kiss exchanged through the window of a post-chaise, a golden day snatched from eternity among the pines, a dinner alone when we drank nectar.'

Caroline raised her eyebrows.

'Lud, how strange that I, on the contrary, have but a trifling recollection of the Viscount Sherringham.'

'But you would wish to know him better, Ma'am?'

Caroline pursed her lips.

'I declare I am not quite certain. He is a handsome gentleman to be sure, but I have been warned that wolves are oft disguised in sheep's clothing. He might be . . . brutal, if it pleased him.'

'So brutal indeed that once he left your ladyship alone when, with any sensibility, he should have stayed. I recall it well. Your ladyship was in the firelight. At first you wore a robe of white, but later——'

The blood flamed into Caroline's cheeks and she raised her hands in protest.

'Stop! Stop! It is too much. You will excuse me, my lord, I would change my gown and arrange my hair.'

Still blushing, Caroline turned and sped towards the door. She had hardly reached it when Vane said quietly, but in a tone to which she must pay heed:

'Come here!'

She was arrested in full flight, yet she did not turn, but answered with her back towards him.

'I . . . will return . . . later.'

'Come here, Caroline.'

There was no mistaking the authority in his voice, though his eyes still smiled.

'Do you . . . command me?'

'Yes, and you shall obey me.'

'Indeed, and would it be indiscreet to ask why I should do so?'

'Come here and I will tell you.'

At last Caroline turned. She looked across the room at Vane, then she drew in her breath and her lips parted. Very, very slowly she retraced her steps, her eyes on his, her cheeks flushed, the soft laces of her gown fluttering from the tumult within her breast.

She drew nearer, and yet Vane made no movement towards her, but waited until she stood beside him. Then her eyes dropped before the look in his. For a moment, watching her, he did not speak, but at last he asked very gently:

'Are you afraid of me, Caroline?'

She glanced up at him, then as quickly veiled her eyes again with her long lashes.

'Answer me,' he said when she did not reply.

'A . . . little . . . I think,' she whispered.

'Look at me!' he commanded, but she could not for an overwhelming shyness and a sweet trembling of her limbs.

It was then Vane put his arms around her and, when she would have hidden her face against his shoulder, he raised his hand to her chin and turned her face up to his.

'Tomorrow we leave for Paris, you and I, Caroline,' he said softly; then, as her eyes widened, he added: 'We go on our honeymoon. We shall be alone. Will you be afraid of being alone with me, my sweet, wild, unconquered love?'

'Oh, Vane!'

Caroline was quivering now beneath the touch of his hand.

'And even if you are afraid, my darling, it will avail you little, for I would remind you of something.'

Vane's hold tightened. Caroline saw the sudden fire in his eyes, felt the quick beating of his heart, and was conscious of an answering flame rising within herself.

'I would remind you,' Vane repeated, his mouth very near to hers, 'that you are mine, my lovely. Mine now—and for all time—mine and . . . my wife.'